Additional praise for

i n f i d e l

"Brilliant horror with a terrifying contemporary resonance."
— **MIKE CAREY** (*The Girl with All the Gifts, Lucifer*)

"Pulls from the modern tumult to tell a thrilling
genre story the way that only comics can."
— **PASTE MAGAZINE**

"Both as timely as it is genuinely freaky."
— **SCREAM MAGAZINE**

"Horrifically great."
— **KAREN BERGER** (founder of Vertigo, Berger Books)

"Left me an emotional wreck… an uncompromising,
powerful book that demands your complete attention."
— **MULTIVERSITY COMICS**

"This is a must for horror fans or those that like stories with some layers."
— **GRAPHIC POLICY**

"Not just the horror book of the moment, to my mind
INFIDEL will go down as a definitive comic of 2018."
— **JOSHUA DYSART** (*Swamp Thing*)

"These are some of the scariest panels I've seen in a comic."
— **LEO WEEKLY**

"A strong debut… should not be ignored.
— **NEWSARAMA**

IMAGE COMICS, INC.

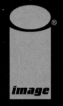

IMAGECOMICS.COM

Robert Kirkman — Chief Operating Officer
Erik Larsen — Chief Financial Officer
Todd McFarlane — President
Marc Silvestri — Chief Executive Officer
Jim Valentino — Vice President
Eric Stephenson — Publisher/Chief Creative Officer
Corey Hart — Director of Sales
Jeff Boison — Director of Publishing Planning & Book Trade Sales
Chris Ross — Director of Digital Sales
Jeff Stang — Director of Specialty Sales
Kat Salazar — Director of PR & Marketing
Drew Gill — Art Director
Heather Doornink — Production Director
Nicole Lapalme — Controller

COLLECTION DESIGN BY **JEFF POWELL**

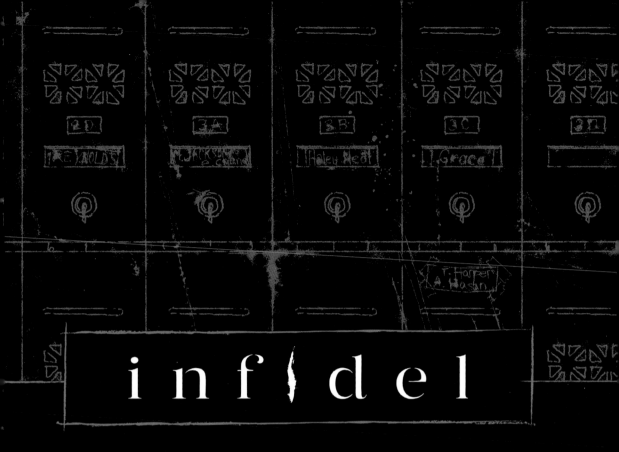

i n f i d e l

Writer
PORNSAK PICHETSHOTE

Artist
AARON CAMPBELL

Colorist & Editor
JOSÉ VILLARRUBIA

Letterer & Designer
JEFF POWELL

Infidel created by
Pornsak Pichetshote & Aaron Campbell

introduction

**"Racism's a cancer that never gets cured.
The best you get is remission."**

– Medina, *Infidel*

AS A LIFELONG HORROR FAN, I've been waiting for this era my whole life: Horror is growing up. For too long, those of us who were black or PoC had to accept being invisible in the horror stories we loved, or else diminished to hurtful and repetitive tropes: magical guides to the white protagonists, first to die to create peril for the "real" characters, or outright sacrifices – useful only for cultural heritage to be exploited for scares.

But in the age of Jordan Peele's *Get Out*, a more inclusive era in horror is emerging, not only making room for inclusive characters all readers can identify with, but using the supernatural to examine the real-life horror facing so many of us: racism, xenophobia, and Islamophobia. Growing up as the daughter of two civil rights activists – and learning daily the physical and emotional costs of discrimination – racism has always been a monster to me. In many ways, racism may be the reason I write, read, and love horror.

INFIDEL introduces characters – and women! – of color in my favorite horror setting, the haunted home, and it's not "horror lite," as window dressing for a

social justice message: *It's actually scary*. Almost uncannily
so. It's no wonder Hollywood snapped it up before
the comic series finished its run. Between the sharp
storytelling and dialogue of Pornsak Pichetshote, whose
characters remind us of our own friends and family, and
the exceptionally imaginative art of Aaron Campbell
(just…WOW), INFIDEL creates the illusion of walking
into the pages.

And if you're a horror fan of any stripe, these pages won't
let you go. Like all good horror, the story and images will
haunt you long after you've finished this book.

And long after you've turned off the lights.

–Tananarive Due
American Book Award winner / author
Author of *The Good House* and *Ghost Summer*

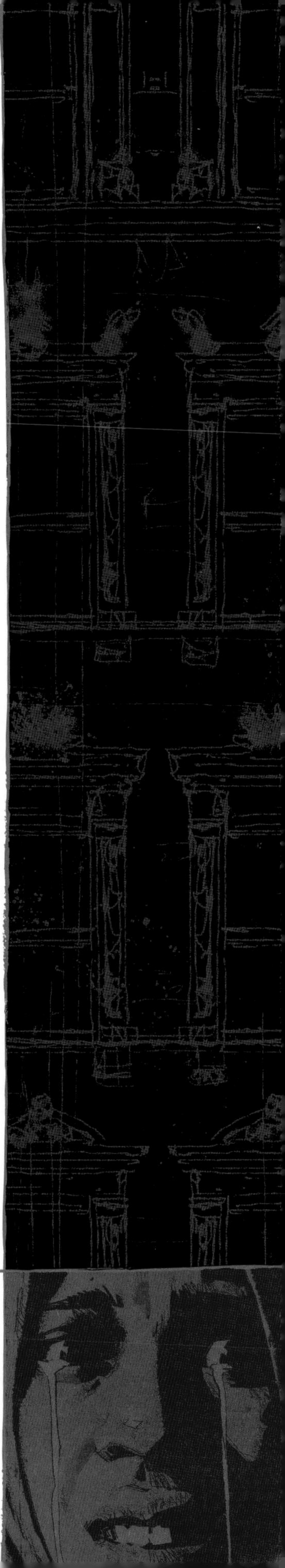

*Tananarive Due is a leading voice in black speculative fiction. She's
written a dozen supernatural suspense novels, including the African
Immortals series that began with* My Soul to Keep. *Due has won an
American Book Award for her supernatural thriller* The Living Blood,
*and she and Steven Barnes won an NAACP Image Award for the
mystery novel* In the Night of the Heat, *also co-authored with Barnes, in
collaboration with actor Blair Underwood. Her latest book is an award-
winning collection of her short stories entitled* Ghost Summer: Stories.

special thanks

Tahanie A. Aboushi
Karen Berger
Mel Caylo
Will Dennis
Sebastian Girner
Tanya Khokar
Jody LeHeup
Jeff Lemire
A. David Lewis
Jason Garret Lewis
Ibrahim Matin
Sophia Parrino
Arasay Pérez
Nolan Rudi
Yuko Shimizu
Shannon Marie Smith
Joon Yoo
The Digital Dungeon Dragons boys

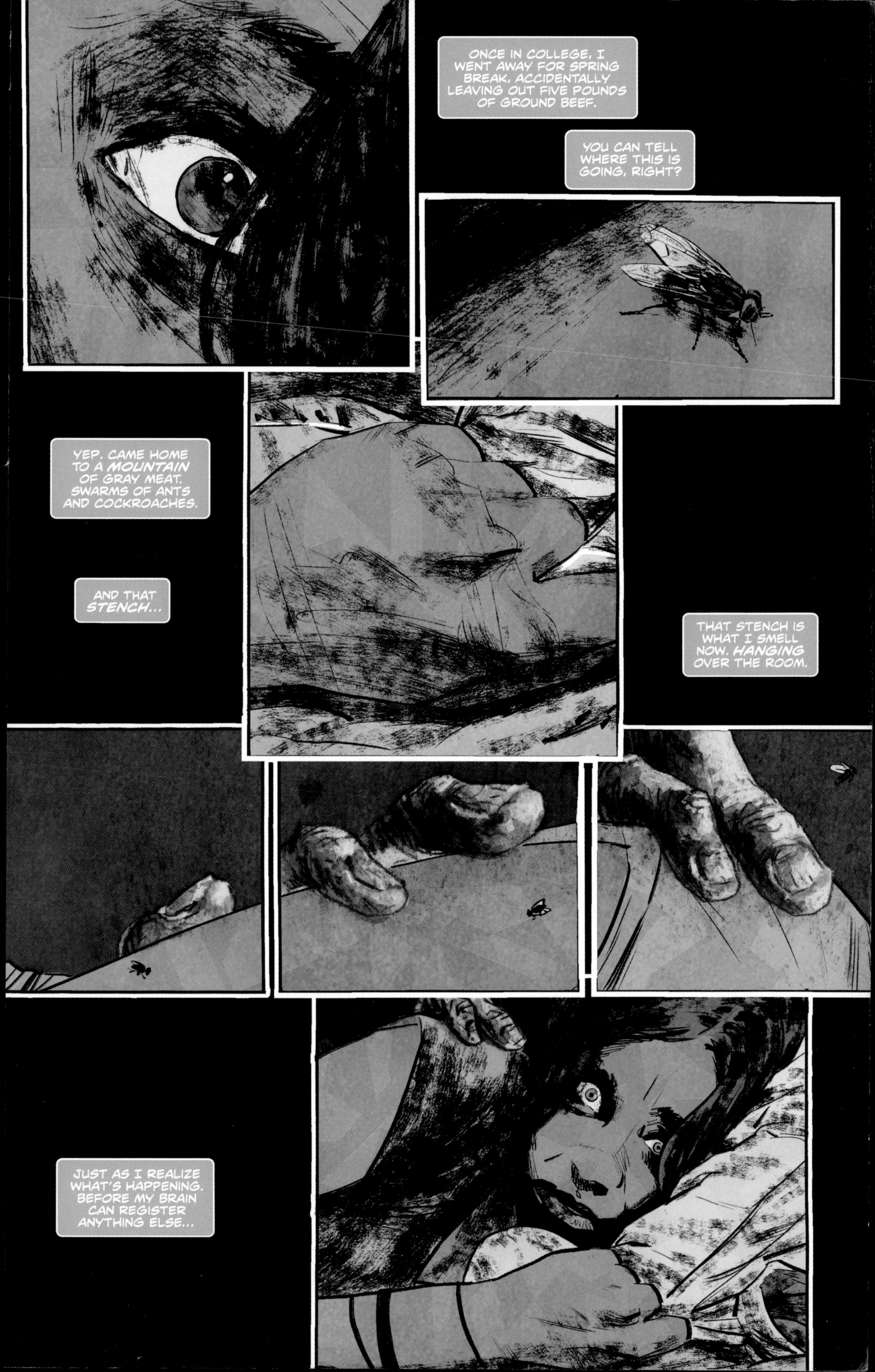
ONCE IN COLLEGE, I WENT AWAY FOR SPRING BREAK, ACCIDENTALLY LEAVING OUT FIVE POUNDS OF GROUND BEEF.
YOU CAN TELL WHERE THIS IS GOING, RIGHT?
YEP. CAME HOME TO A *MOUNTAIN* OF GRAY MEAT. SWARMS OF ANTS AND COCKROACHES.
AND THAT *STENCH...*
THAT STENCH IS WHAT I SMELL NOW. *HANGING* OVER THE ROOM.
JUST AS I REALIZE WHAT'S HAPPENING. BEFORE MY BRAIN CAN REGISTER ANYTHING ELSE...

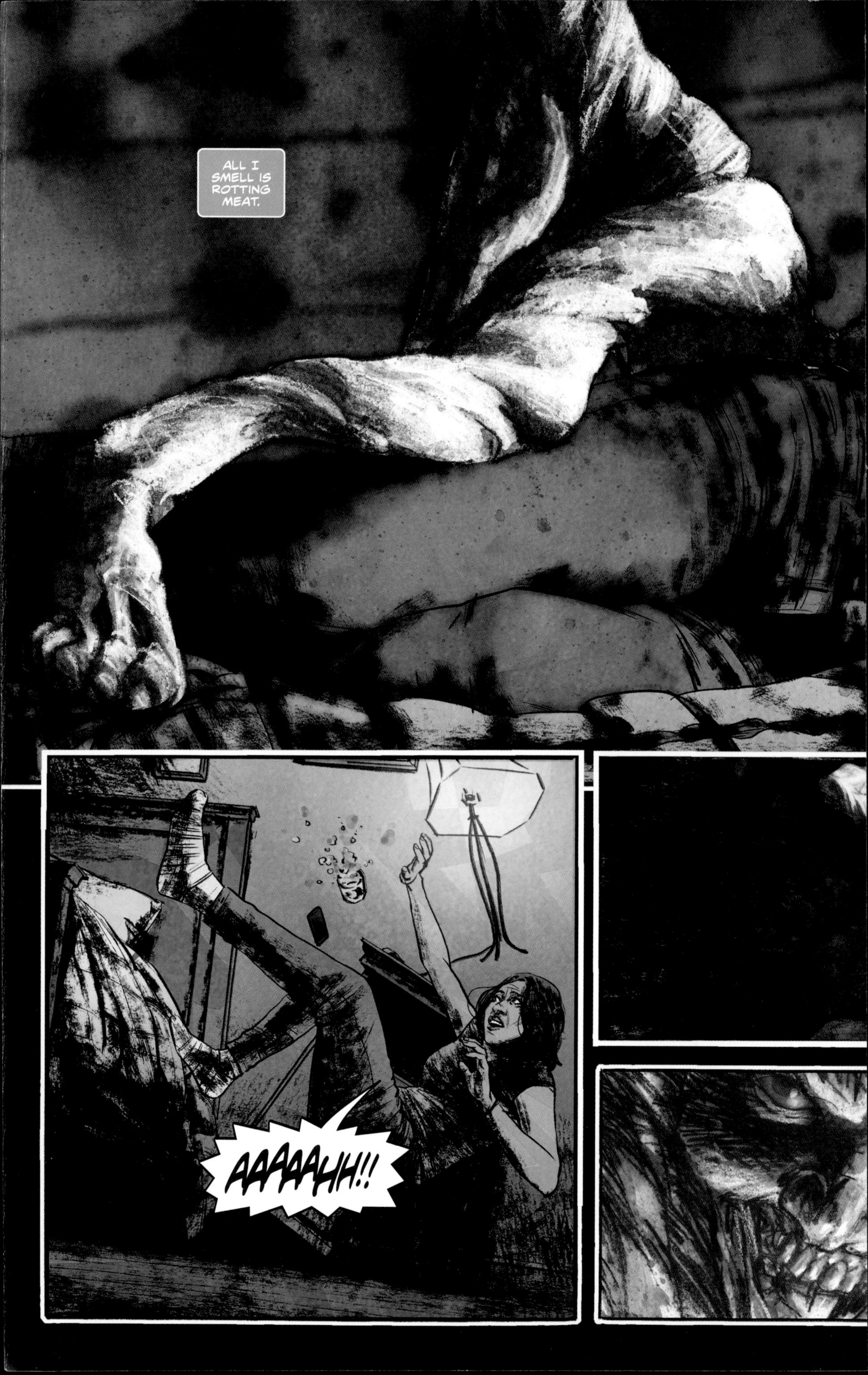
ALL I SMELL IS ROTTING MEAT.
AAAAAHH!!

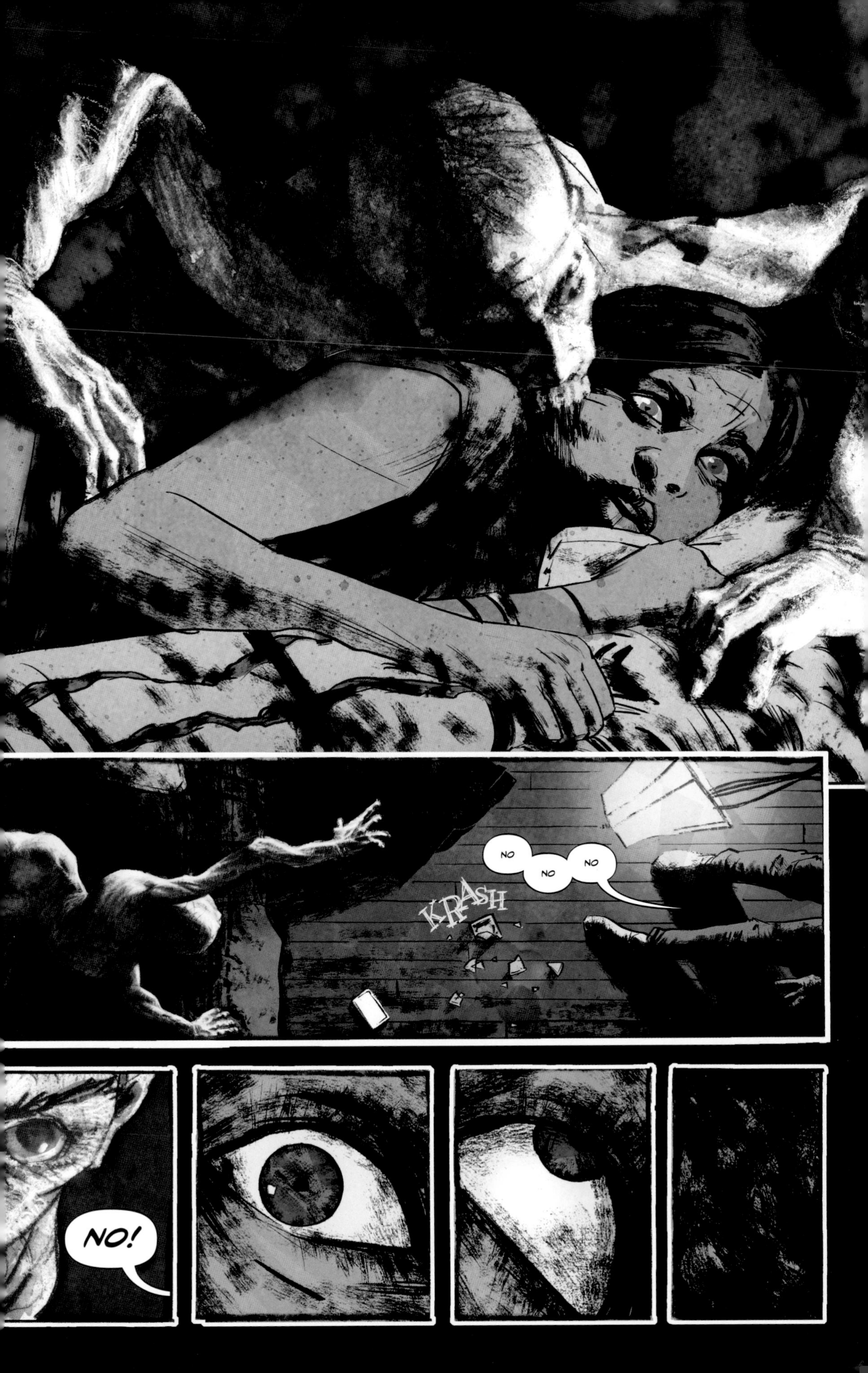
NO
NO
NO
KRASH
NO!

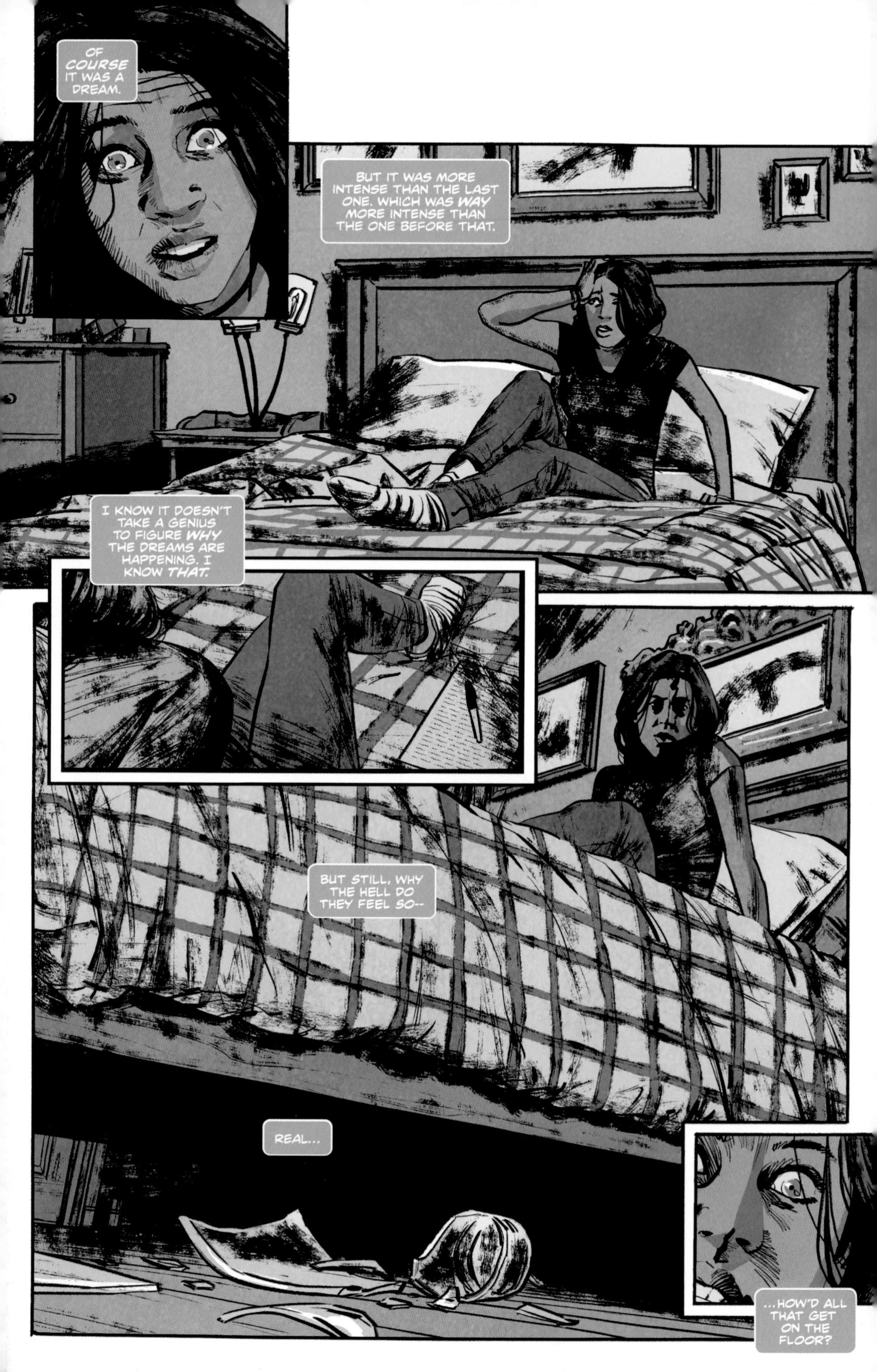
OF COURSE IT WAS A DREAM.
BUT IT WAS MORE INTENSE THAN THE LAST ONE. WHICH WAS WAY MORE INTENSE THAN THE ONE BEFORE THAT.
I KNOW IT DOESN'T TAKE A GENIUS TO FIGURE WHY THE DREAMS ARE HAPPENING. I KNOW THAT.
BUT STILL, WHY THE HELL DO THEY FEEL SO--
REAL...
...HOW'D ALL THAT GET ON THE FLOOR?

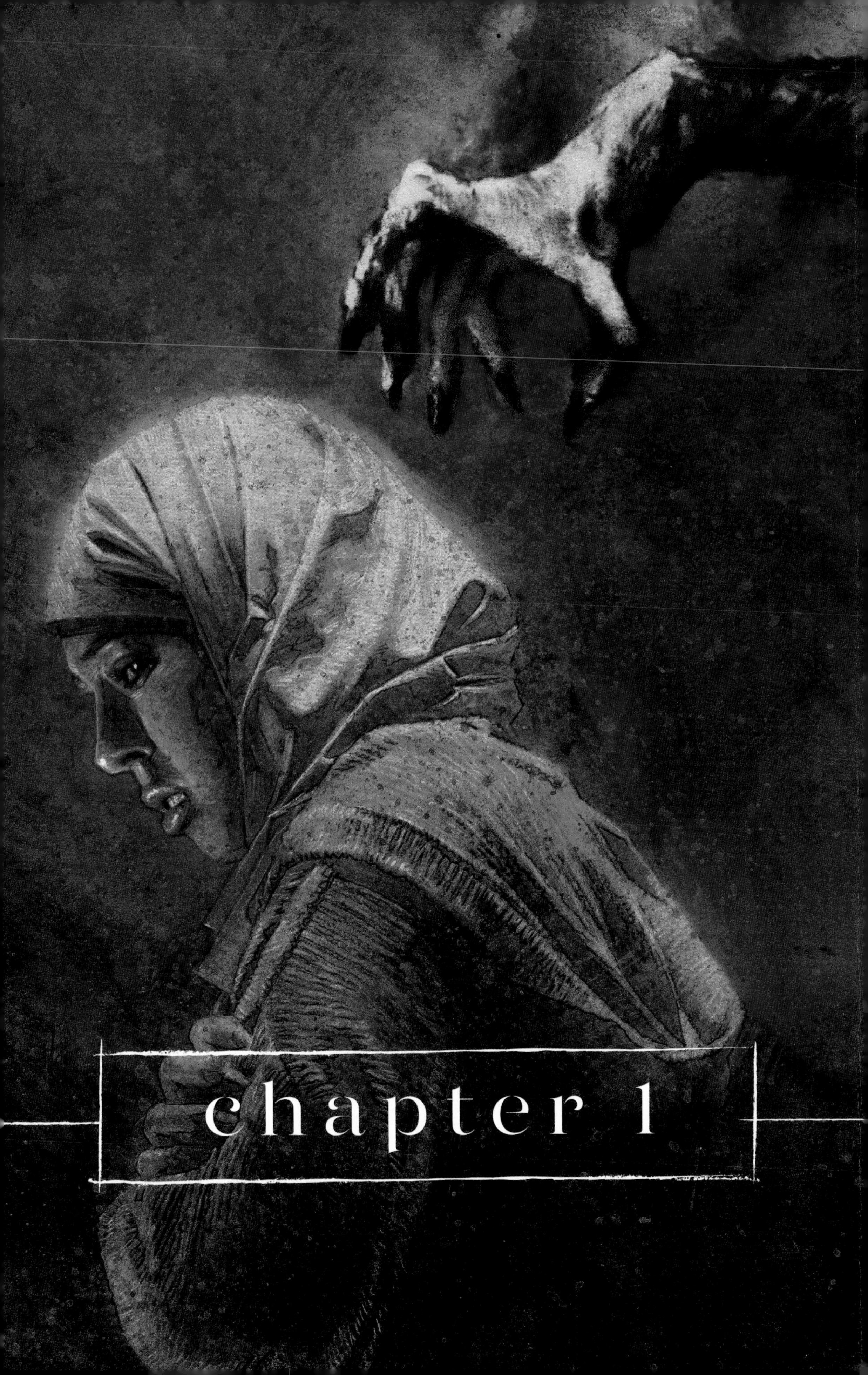
chapter 1

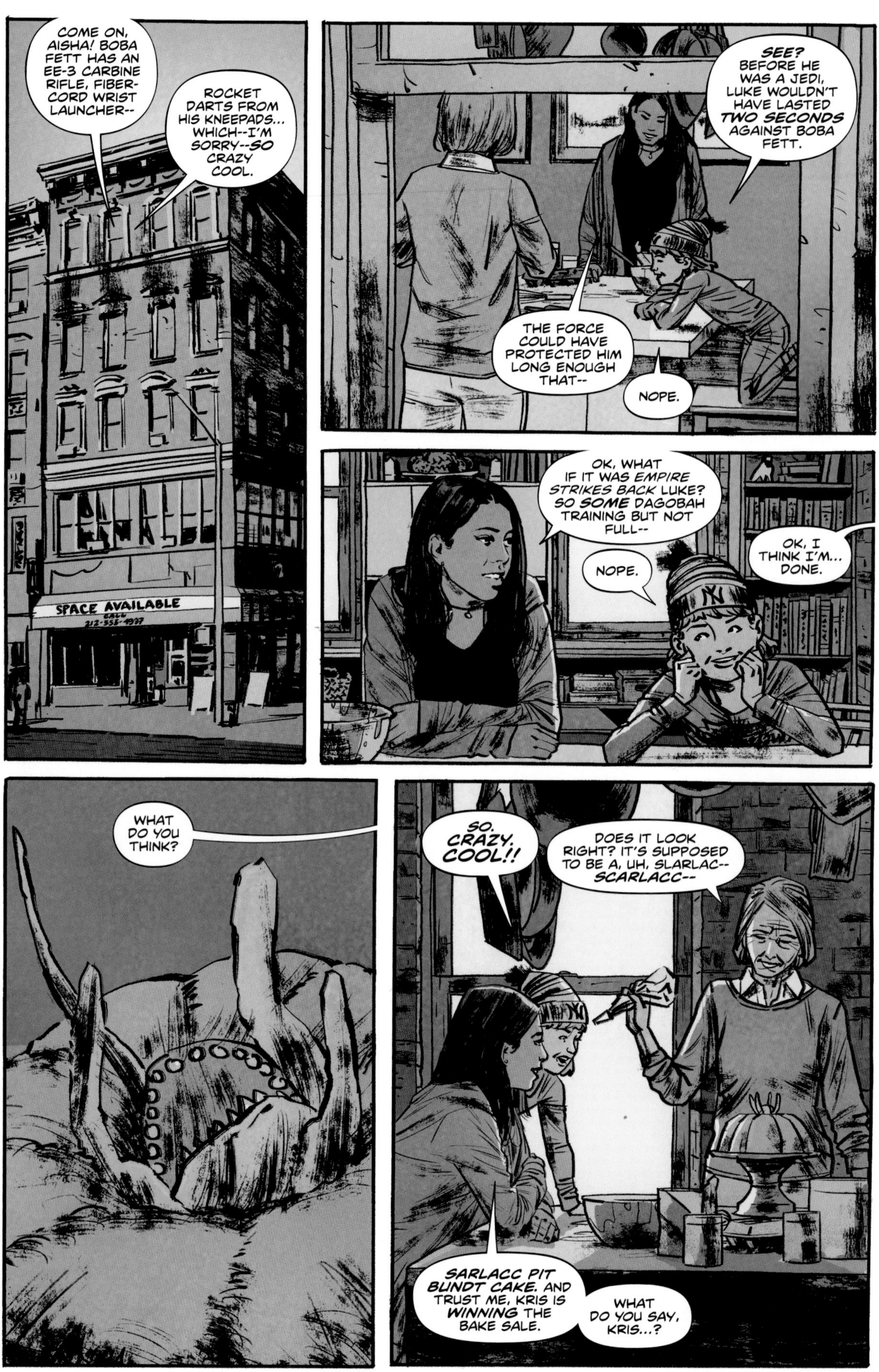
COME ON, AISHA! BOBA FETT HAS AN EE-3 CARBINE RIFLE, FIBER-CORD WRIST LAUNCHER--
ROCKET DARTS FROM HIS KNEEPADS... WHICH--I'M SORRY--SO CRAZY COOL.
SPACE AVAILABLE
SEE? BEFORE HE WAS A JEDI, LUKE WOULDN'T HAVE LASTED TWO SECONDS AGAINST BOBA FETT.
THE FORCE COULD HAVE PROTECTED HIM LONG ENOUGH THAT--
NOPE.
OK, WHAT IF IT WAS EMPIRE STRIKES BACK LUKE? SO SOME DAGOBAH TRAINING BUT NOT FULL--
NOPE.
OK, I THINK I'M... DONE.
WHAT DO YOU THINK?
SO. CRAZY. COOL!!
DOES IT LOOK RIGHT? IT'S SUPPOSED TO BE A, UH, SLARLAC-- SCARLACC--
SARLACC PIT BUNDT CAKE. AND TRUST ME, KRIS IS WINNING THE BAKE SALE.
WHAT DO YOU SAY, KRIS...?

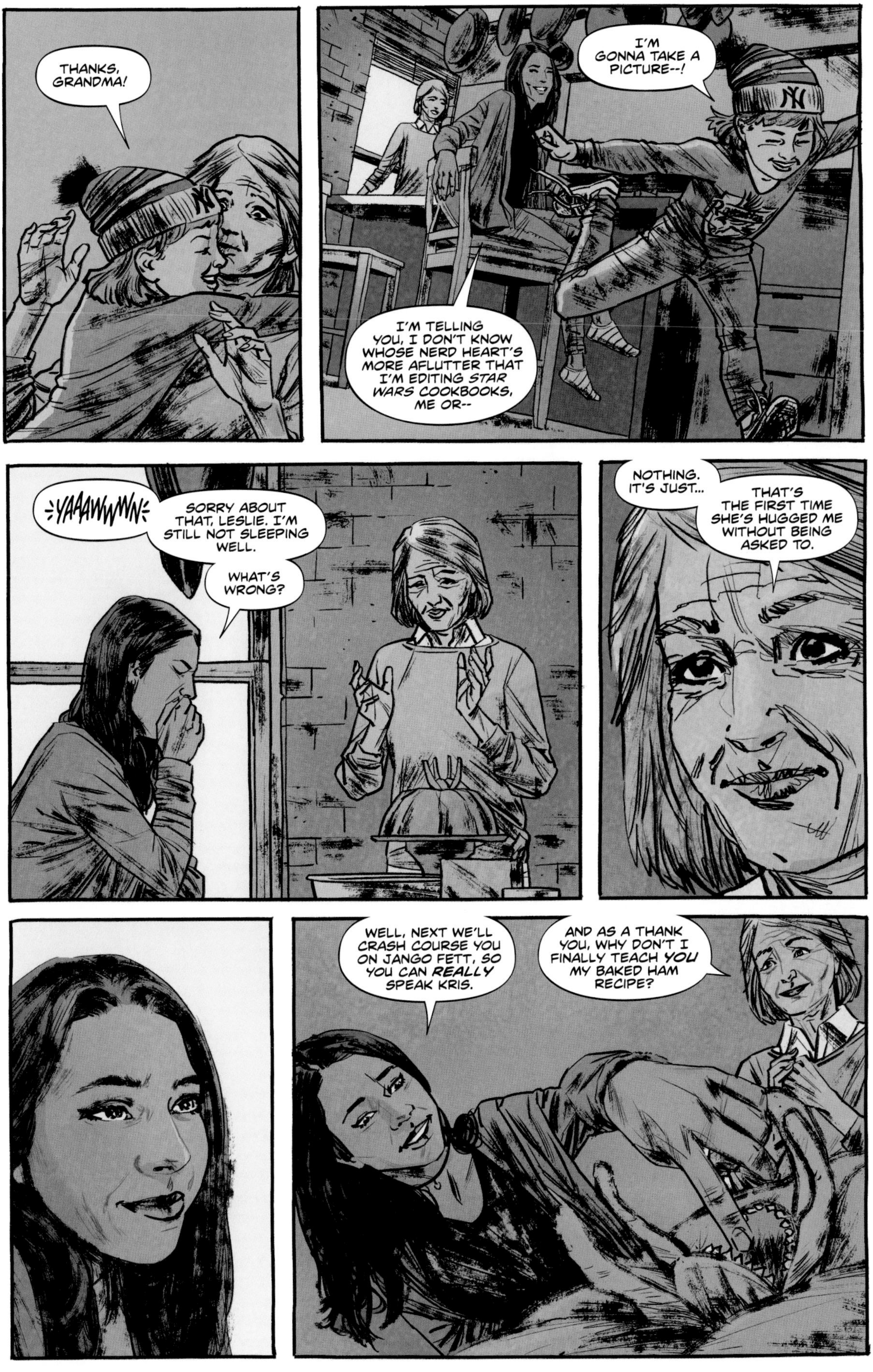
THANKS, GRANDMA!
I'M GONNA TAKE A PICTURE--!
I'M TELLING YOU, I DON'T KNOW WHOSE NERD HEART'S MORE AFLUTTER THAT I'M EDITING STAR WARS COOKBOOKS, ME OR--
YAAAWWWN
SORRY ABOUT THAT, LESLIE. I'M STILL NOT SLEEPING WELL.
WHAT'S WRONG?
NOTHING. IT'S JUST...
THAT'S THE FIRST TIME SHE'S HUGGED ME WITHOUT BEING ASKED TO.
WELL, NEXT WE'LL CRASH COURSE YOU ON JANGO FETT, SO YOU CAN REALLY SPEAK KRIS.
AND AS A THANK YOU, WHY DON'T I FINALLY TEACH YOU MY BAKED HAM RECIPE?

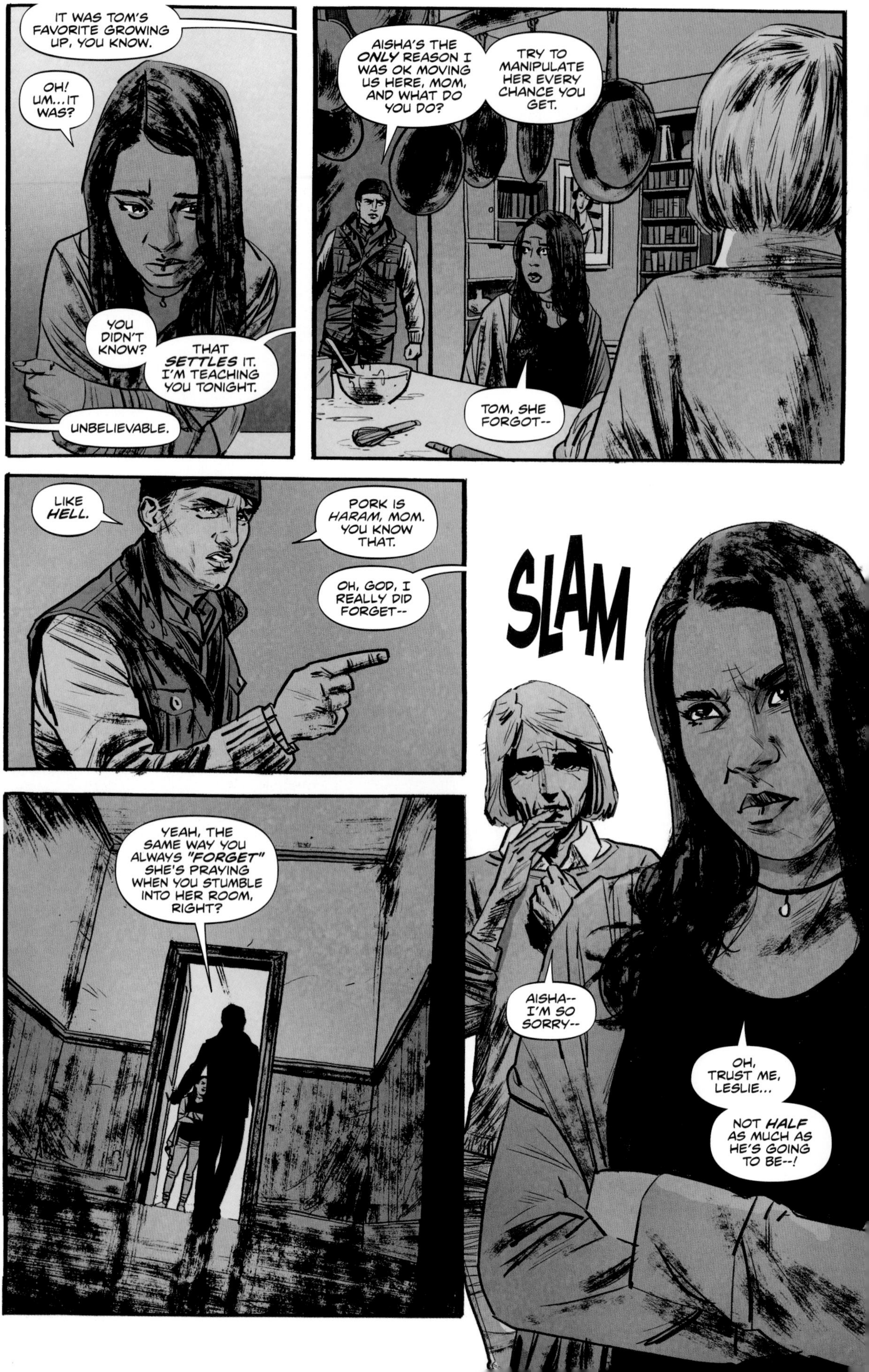
IT WAS TOM'S FAVORITE GROWING UP, YOU KNOW.
OH! UM...IT WAS?
YOU DIDN'T KNOW?
THAT SETTLES IT. I'M TEACHING YOU TONIGHT.
UNBELIEVABLE.
AISHA'S THE ONLY REASON I WAS OK MOVING US HERE, MOM, AND WHAT DO YOU DO?
TRY TO MANIPULATE HER EVERY CHANCE YOU GET.
TOM, SHE FORGOT--
LIKE HELL.
PORK IS HARAM, MOM. YOU KNOW THAT.
OH, GOD, I REALLY DID FORGET--
SLAM
YEAH, THE SAME WAY YOU ALWAYS "FORGET" SHE'S PRAYING WHEN YOU STUMBLE INTO HER ROOM, RIGHT?
AISHA-- I'M SO SORRY--
OH, TRUST ME, LESLIE...
NOT HALF AS MUCH AS HE'S GOING TO BE--!

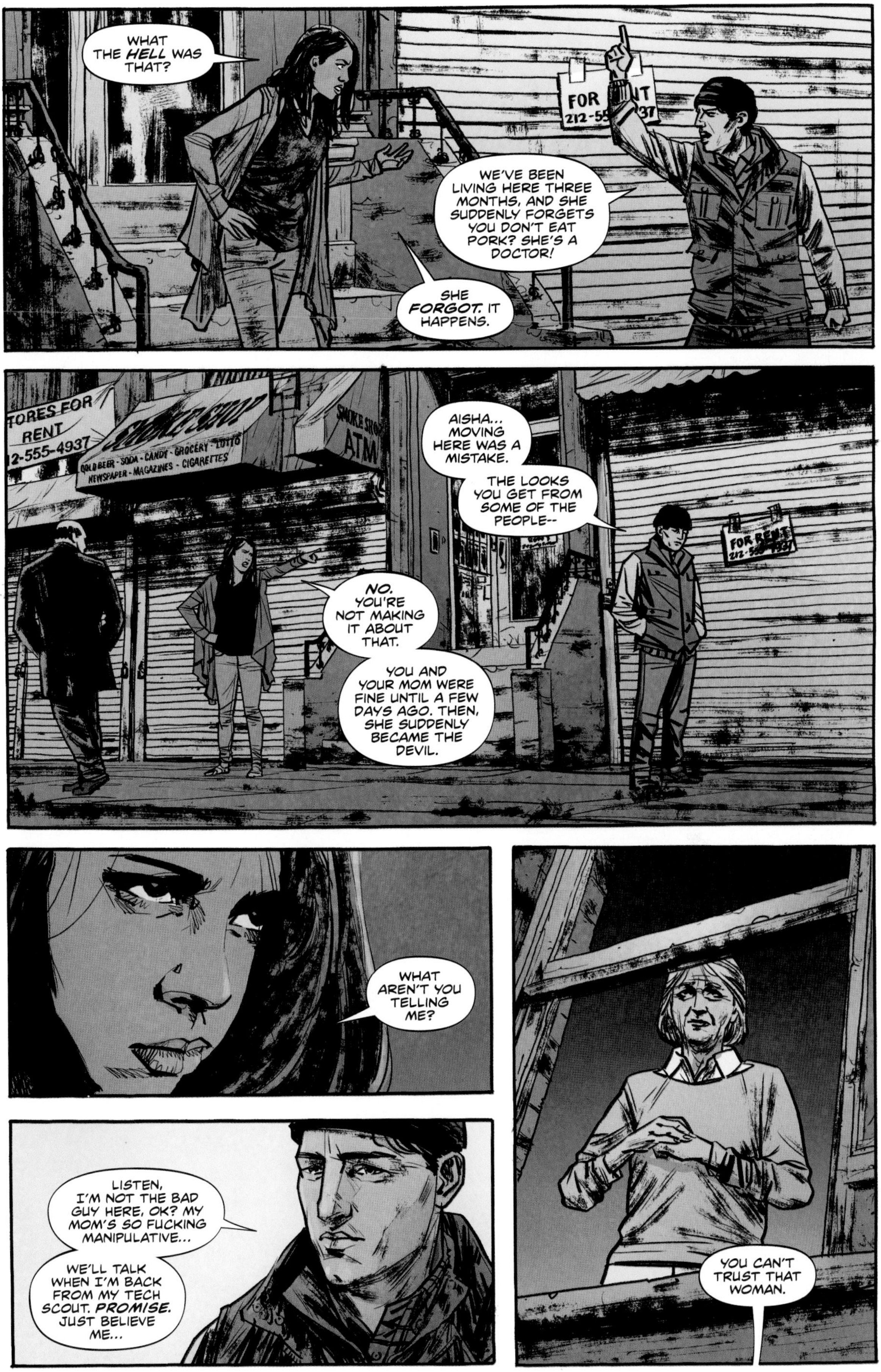
WHAT THE HELL WAS THAT?
FOR RENT 212-555-4937
WE'VE BEEN LIVING HERE THREE MONTHS, AND SHE SUDDENLY FORGETS YOU DON'T EAT PORK? SHE'S A DOCTOR!
SHE FORGOT. IT HAPPENS.
STORES FOR RENT 212-555-4937
COLD BEER - SODA - CANDY - GROCERY - LOTTO
NEWSPAPER - MAGAZINES - CIGARETTES
SMOKE SHOP
ATM
AISHA... MOVING HERE WAS A MISTAKE.
THE LOOKS YOU GET FROM SOME OF THE PEOPLE--
FOR RENT 212-555-4937
NO. YOU'RE NOT MAKING IT ABOUT THAT.
YOU AND YOUR MOM WERE FINE UNTIL A FEW DAYS AGO. THEN, SHE SUDDENLY BECAME THE DEVIL.
WHAT AREN'T YOU TELLING ME?
LISTEN, I'M NOT THE BAD GUY HERE, OK? MY MOM'S SO FUCKING MANIPULATIVE...
WE'LL TALK WHEN I'M BACK FROM MY TECH SCOUT. PROMISE. JUST BELIEVE ME...
YOU CAN'T TRUST THAT WOMAN.

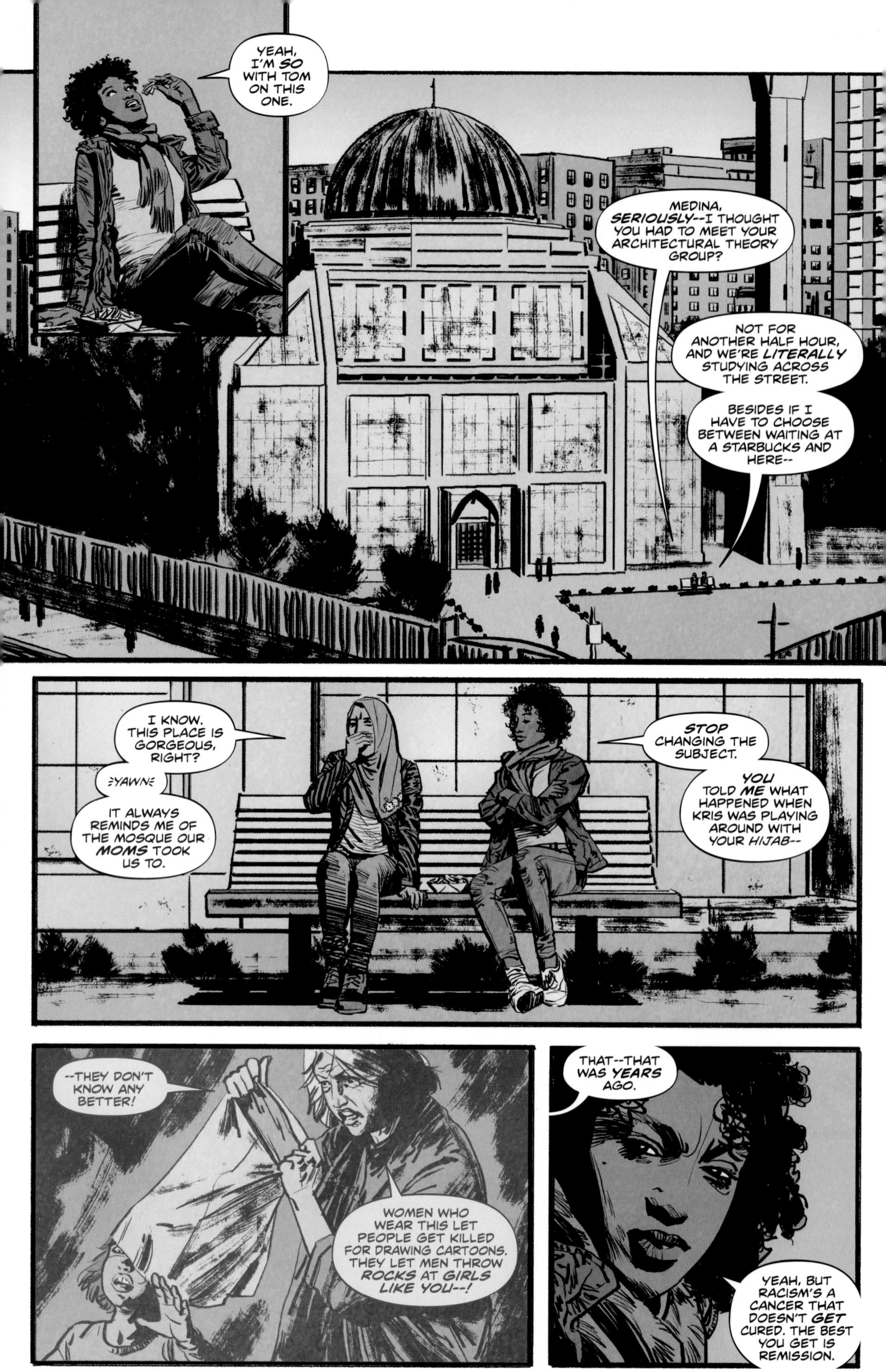
YEAH, I'M SO WITH TOM ON THIS ONE.
MEDINA, SERIOUSLY--I THOUGHT YOU HAD TO MEET YOUR ARCHITECTURAL THEORY GROUP?
NOT FOR ANOTHER HALF HOUR, AND WE'RE LITERALLY STUDYING ACROSS THE STREET.
BESIDES IF I HAVE TO CHOOSE BETWEEN WAITING AT A STARBUCKS AND HERE--
I KNOW. THIS PLACE IS GORGEOUS, RIGHT?
YAWN
IT ALWAYS REMINDS ME OF THE MOSQUE OUR MOMS TOOK US TO.
STOP CHANGING THE SUBJECT.
YOU TOLD ME WHAT HAPPENED WHEN KRIS WAS PLAYING AROUND WITH YOUR HIJAB--
--THEY DON'T KNOW ANY BETTER!
WOMEN WHO WEAR THIS LET PEOPLE GET KILLED FOR DRAWING CARTOONS. THEY LET MEN THROW ROCKS AT GIRLS LIKE YOU--!
THAT--THAT WAS YEARS AGO.
YEAH, BUT RACISM'S A CANCER THAT DOESN'T GET CURED. THE BEST YOU GET IS REMISSION.

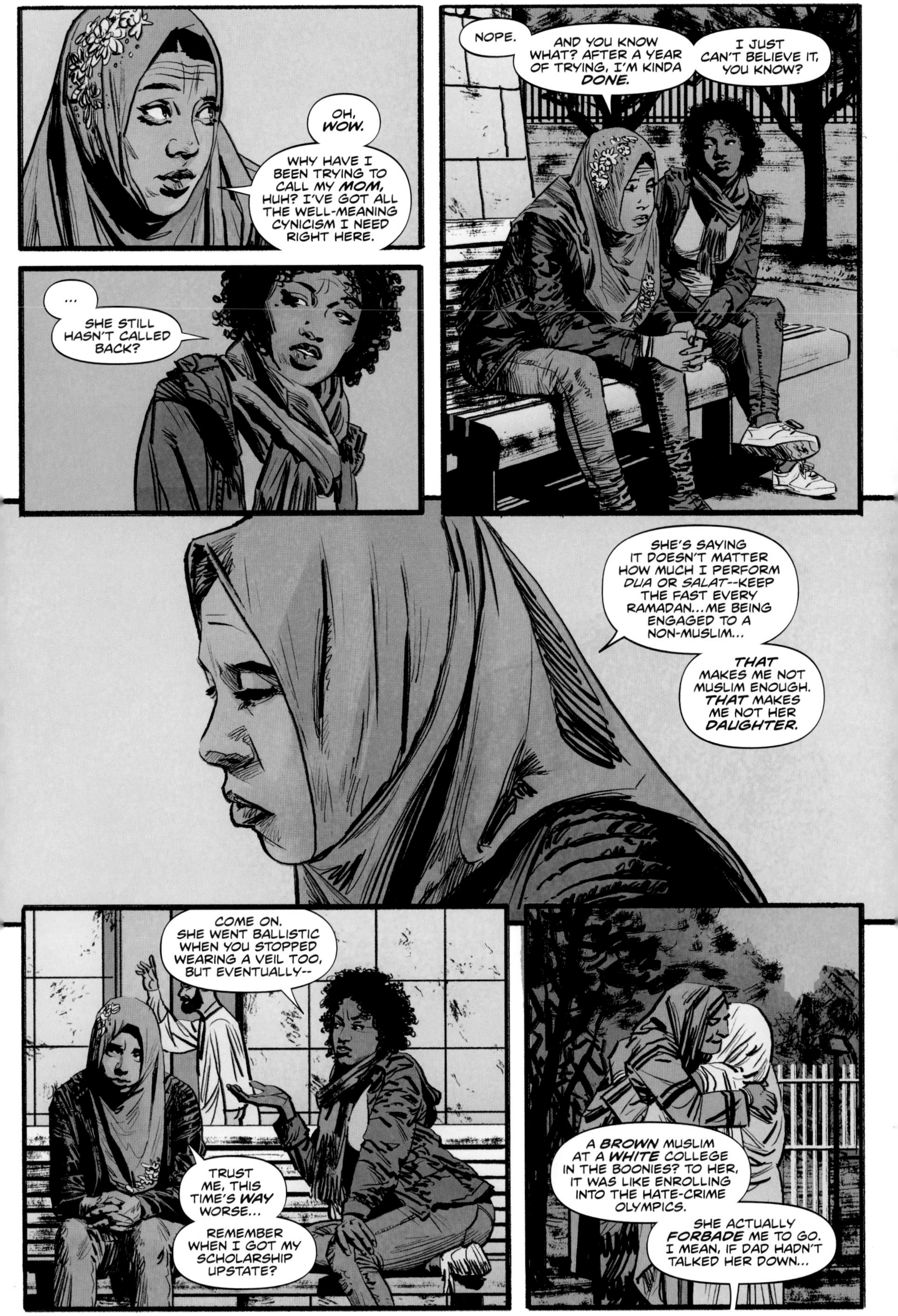
OH, WOW.
WHY HAVE I BEEN TRYING TO CALL MY MOM, HUH? I'VE GOT ALL THE WELL-MEANING CYNICISM I NEED RIGHT HERE.
...
SHE STILL HASN'T CALLED BACK?
NOPE.
AND YOU KNOW WHAT? AFTER A YEAR OF TRYING, I'M KINDA DONE.
I JUST CAN'T BELIEVE IT, YOU KNOW?
SHE'S SAYING IT DOESN'T MATTER HOW MUCH I PERFORM DUA OR SALAT--KEEP THE FAST EVERY RAMADAN...ME BEING ENGAGED TO A NON-MUSLIM...
THAT MAKES ME NOT MUSLIM ENOUGH. THAT MAKES ME NOT HER DAUGHTER.
COME ON. SHE WENT BALLISTIC WHEN YOU STOPPED WEARING A VEIL TOO, BUT EVENTUALLY--
TRUST ME, THIS TIME'S WAY WORSE...
REMEMBER WHEN I GOT MY SCHOLARSHIP UPSTATE?
A BROWN MUSLIM AT A WHITE COLLEGE IN THE BOONIES? TO HER, IT WAS LIKE ENROLLING INTO THE HATE-CRIME OLYMPICS.
SHE ACTUALLY FORBADE ME TO GO. I MEAN, IF DAD HADN'T TALKED HER DOWN...

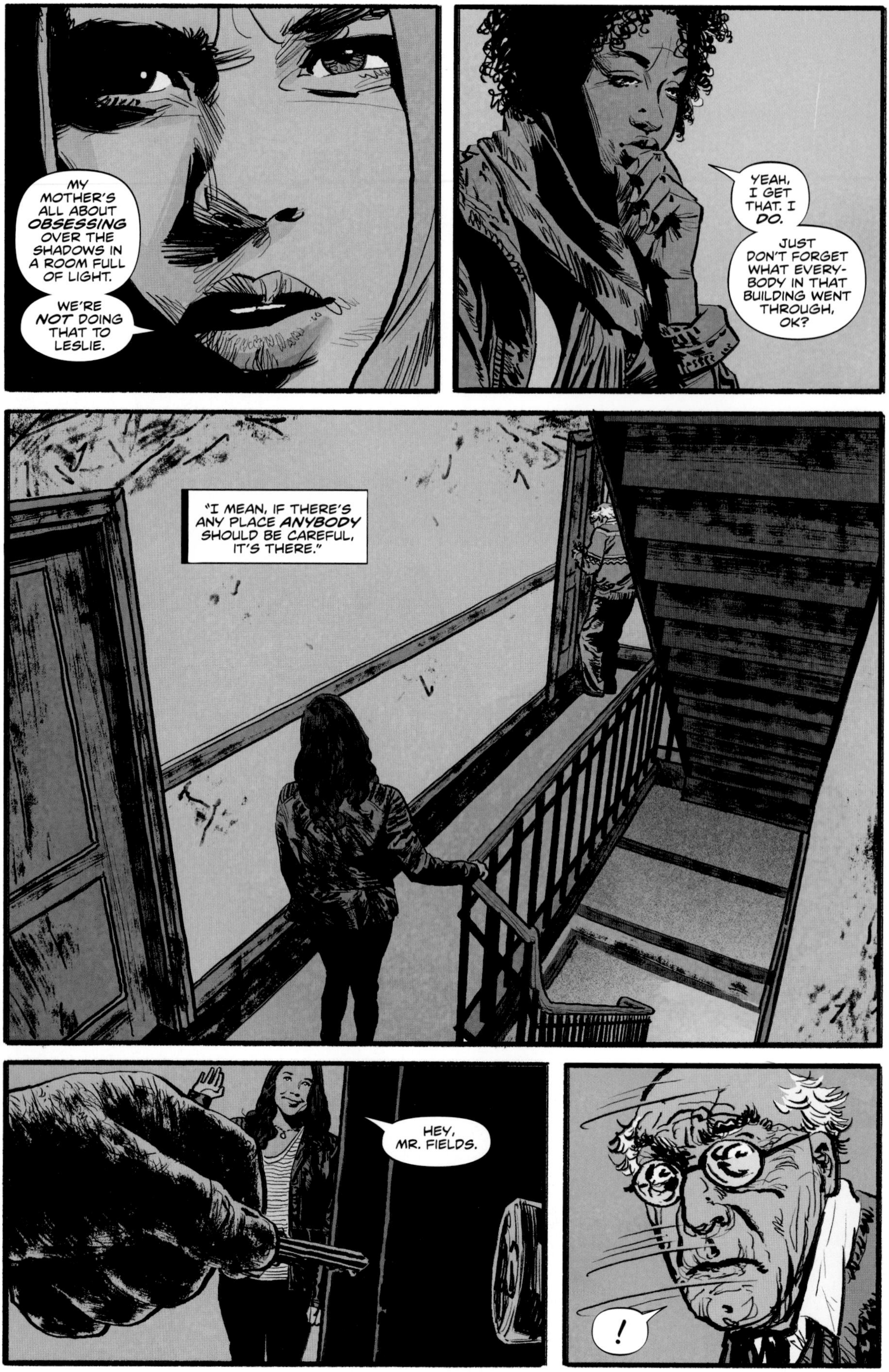
MY MOTHER'S ALL ABOUT OBSESSING OVER THE SHADOWS IN A ROOM FULL OF LIGHT.
WE'RE NOT DOING THAT TO LESLIE.
YEAH, I GET THAT. I DO.
JUST DON'T FORGET WHAT EVERY-BODY IN THAT BUILDING WENT THROUGH, OK?
"I MEAN, IF THERE'S ANY PLACE ANYBODY SHOULD BE CAREFUL, IT'S THERE."
HEY, MR. FIELDS.
!

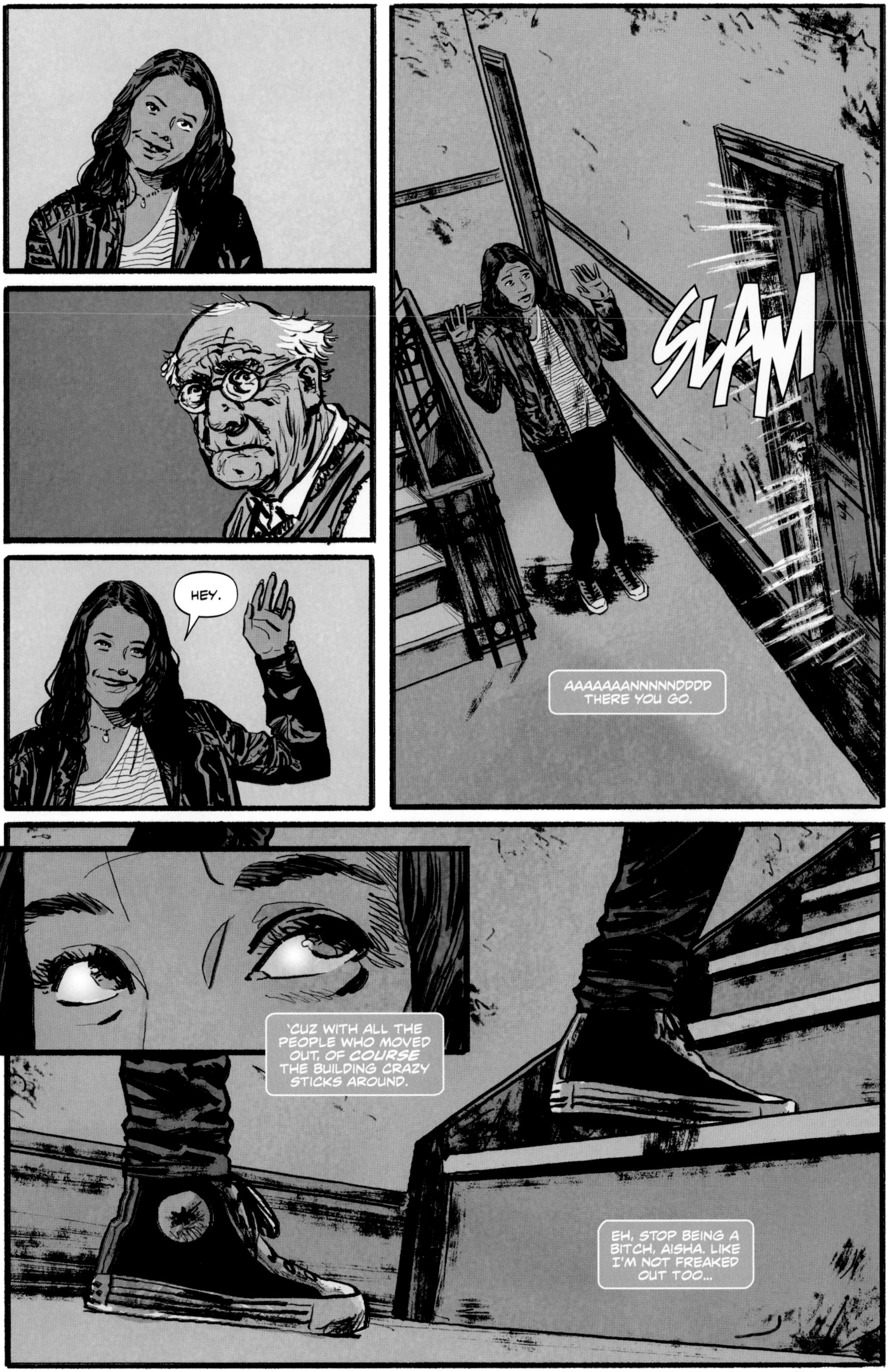
HEY.
SLAM
AAAAAAANNNNNDDDD THERE YOU GO.
'CUZ WITH ALL THE PEOPLE WHO MOVED OUT, OF COURSE THE BUILDING CRAZY STICKS AROUND.
EH, STOP BEING A BITCH, AISHA. LIKE I'M NOT FREAKED OUT TOO...

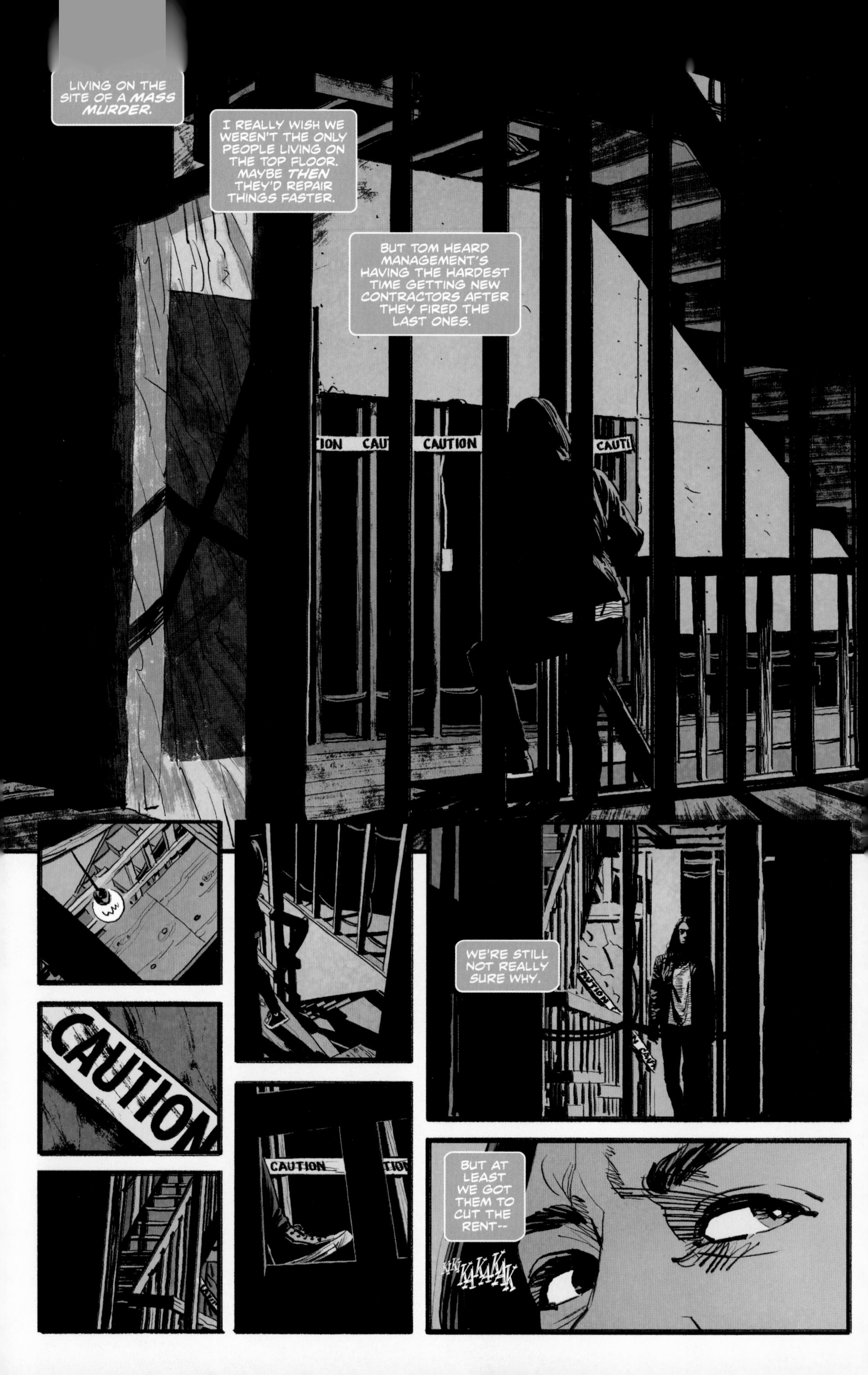
LIVING ON THE SITE OF A MASS MURDER.
I REALLY WISH WE WEREN'T THE ONLY PEOPLE LIVING ON THE TOP FLOOR. MAYBE THEN THEY'D REPAIR THINGS FASTER.
BUT TOM HEARD MANAGEMENT'S HAVING THE HARDEST TIME GETTING NEW CONTRACTORS AFTER THEY FIRED THE LAST ONES.
CAUTION
CAUTION
CAUTION
WE'RE STILL NOT REALLY SURE WHY.
BUT AT LEAST WE GOT THEM TO CUT THE RENT--
KAKAKAK

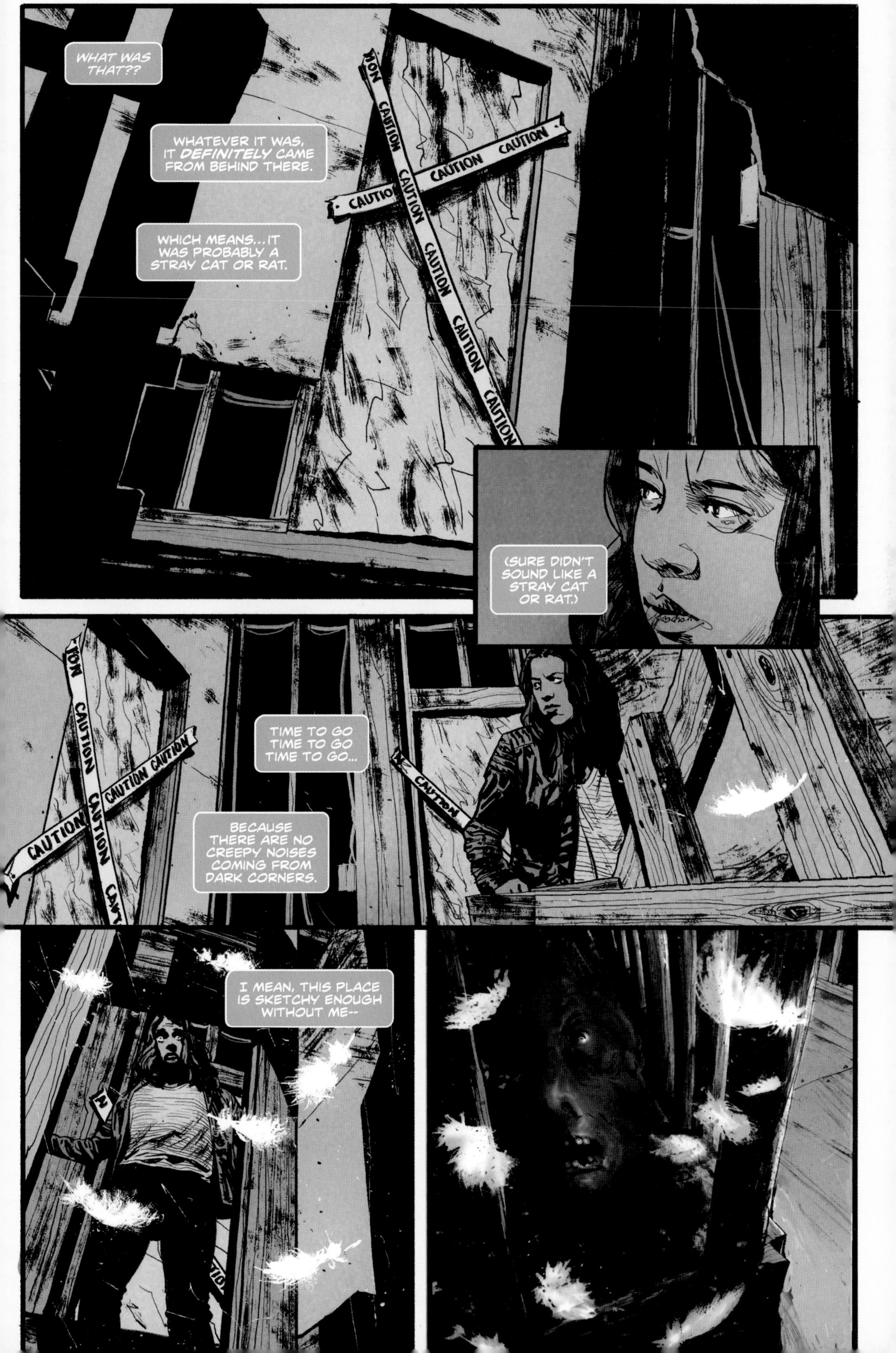
WHAT WAS THAT??
WHATEVER IT WAS, IT DEFINITELY CAME FROM BEHIND THERE.
WHICH MEANS... IT WAS PROBABLY A STRAY CAT OR RAT.
CAUTION
(SURE DIDN'T SOUND LIKE A STRAY CAT OR RAT.)
TIME TO GO TIME TO GO TIME TO GO...
BECAUSE THERE ARE NO CREEPY NOISES COMING FROM DARK CORNERS.
I MEAN, THIS PLACE IS SKETCHY ENOUGH WITHOUT ME--

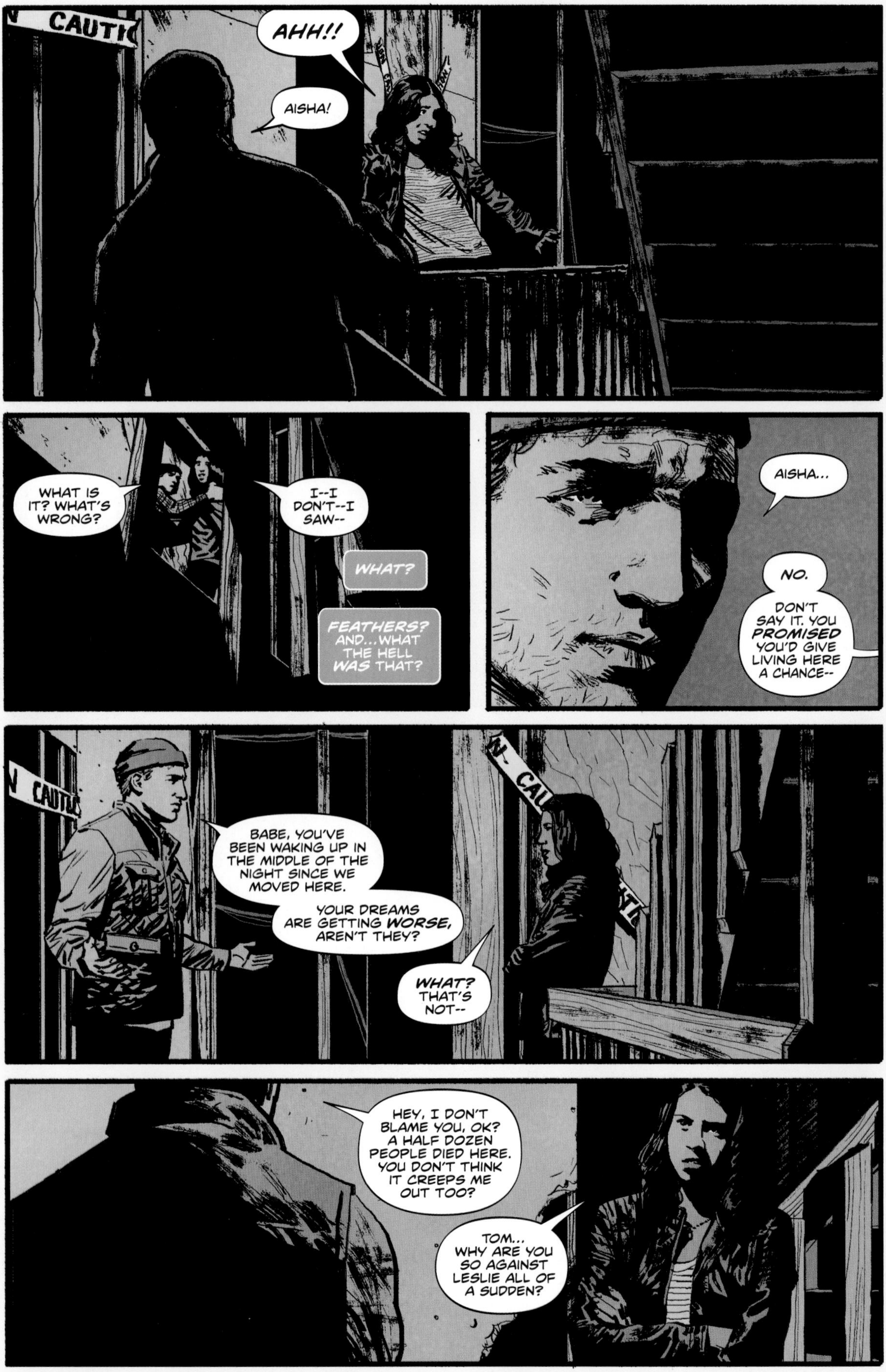
CAUTI
AHH!!
AISHA!
WHAT IS IT? WHAT'S WRONG?
I--I DON'T--I SAW--
WHAT?
FEATHERS? AND...WHAT THE HELL WAS THAT?
AISHA...
NO.
DON'T SAY IT. YOU PROMISED YOU'D GIVE LIVING HERE A CHANCE--
CAUTI
BABE, YOU'VE BEEN WAKING UP IN THE MIDDLE OF THE NIGHT SINCE WE MOVED HERE.
YOUR DREAMS ARE GETTING WORSE, AREN'T THEY?
WHAT? THAT'S NOT--
HEY, I DON'T BLAME YOU, OK? A HALF DOZEN PEOPLE DIED HERE. YOU DON'T THINK IT CREEPS ME OUT TOO?
TOM... WHY ARE YOU SO AGAINST LESLIE ALL OF A SUDDEN?

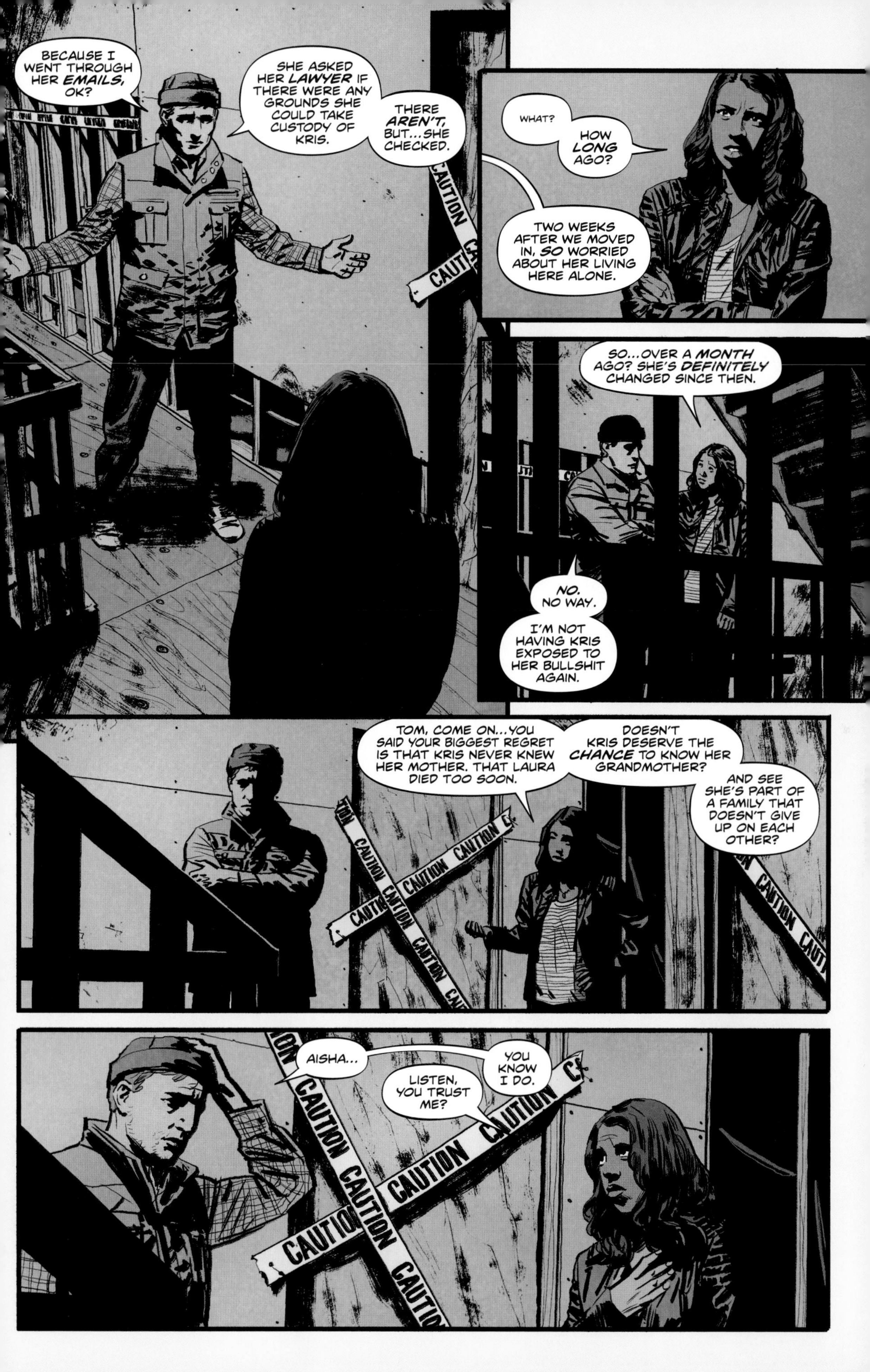

BECAUSE I WENT THROUGH HER EMAILS, OK?
SHE ASKED HER LAWYER IF THERE WERE ANY GROUNDS SHE COULD TAKE CUSTODY OF KRIS.
THERE AREN'T, BUT...SHE CHECKED.
WHAT?
HOW LONG AGO?
TWO WEEKS AFTER WE MOVED IN, SO WORRIED ABOUT HER LIVING HERE ALONE.
SO...OVER A MONTH AGO? SHE'S DEFINITELY CHANGED SINCE THEN.
NO. NO WAY.
I'M NOT HAVING KRIS EXPOSED TO HER BULLSHIT AGAIN.
TOM, COME ON...YOU SAID YOUR BIGGEST REGRET IS THAT KRIS NEVER KNEW HER MOTHER. THAT LAURA DIED TOO SOON.
DOESN'T KRIS DESERVE THE CHANCE TO KNOW HER GRANDMOTHER?
AND SEE SHE'S PART OF A FAMILY THAT DOESN'T GIVE UP ON EACH OTHER?
CAUTION
AISHA...
LISTEN, YOU TRUST ME?
YOU KNOW I DO.
CAUTION

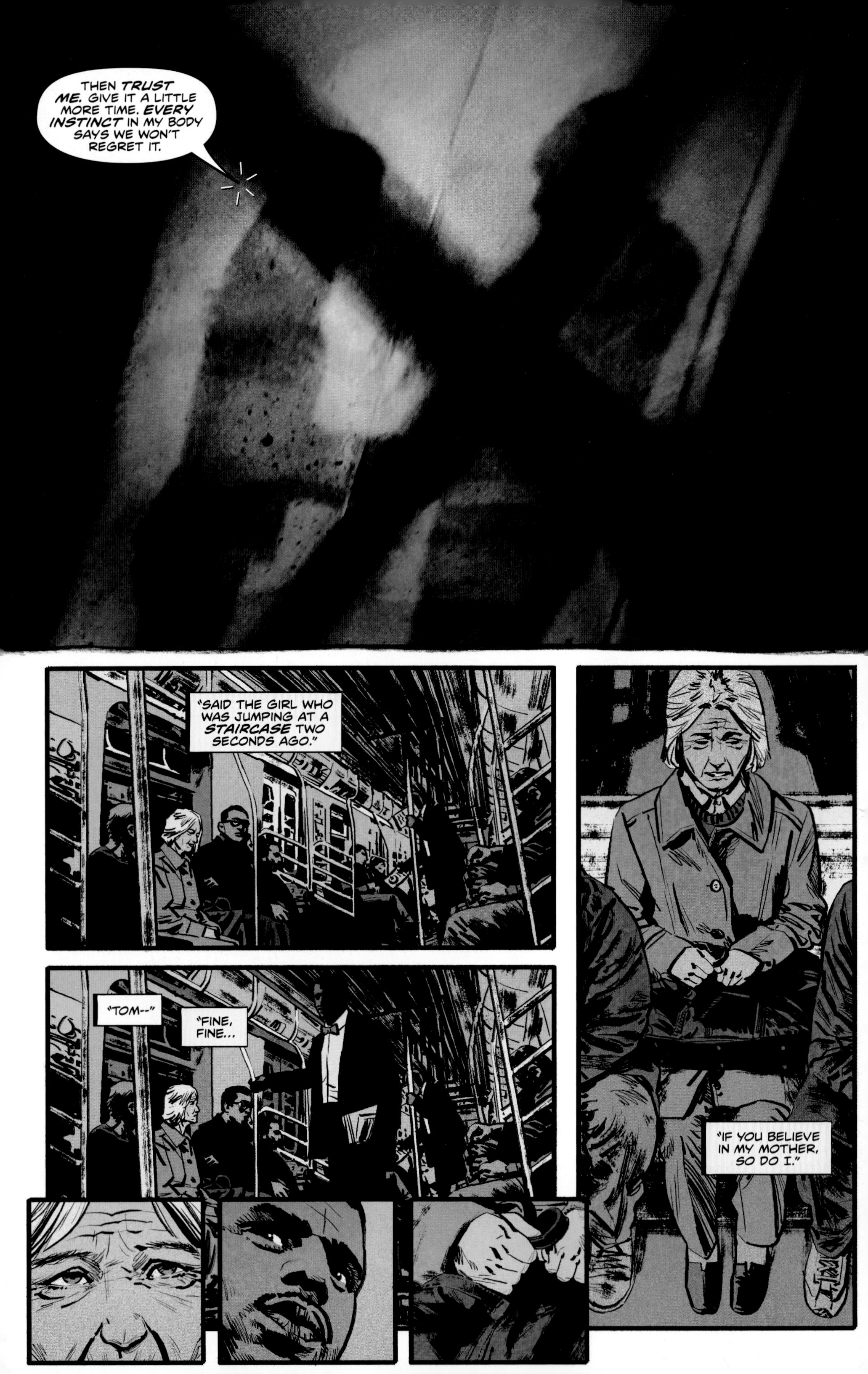

THEN TRUST ME. GIVE IT A LITTLE MORE TIME. EVERY INSTINCT IN MY BODY SAYS WE WON'T REGRET IT.
"SAID THE GIRL WHO WAS JUMPING AT A STAIRCASE TWO SECONDS AGO."
"TOM--"
"FINE, FINE...
"IF YOU BELIEVE IN MY MOTHER, SO DO I."

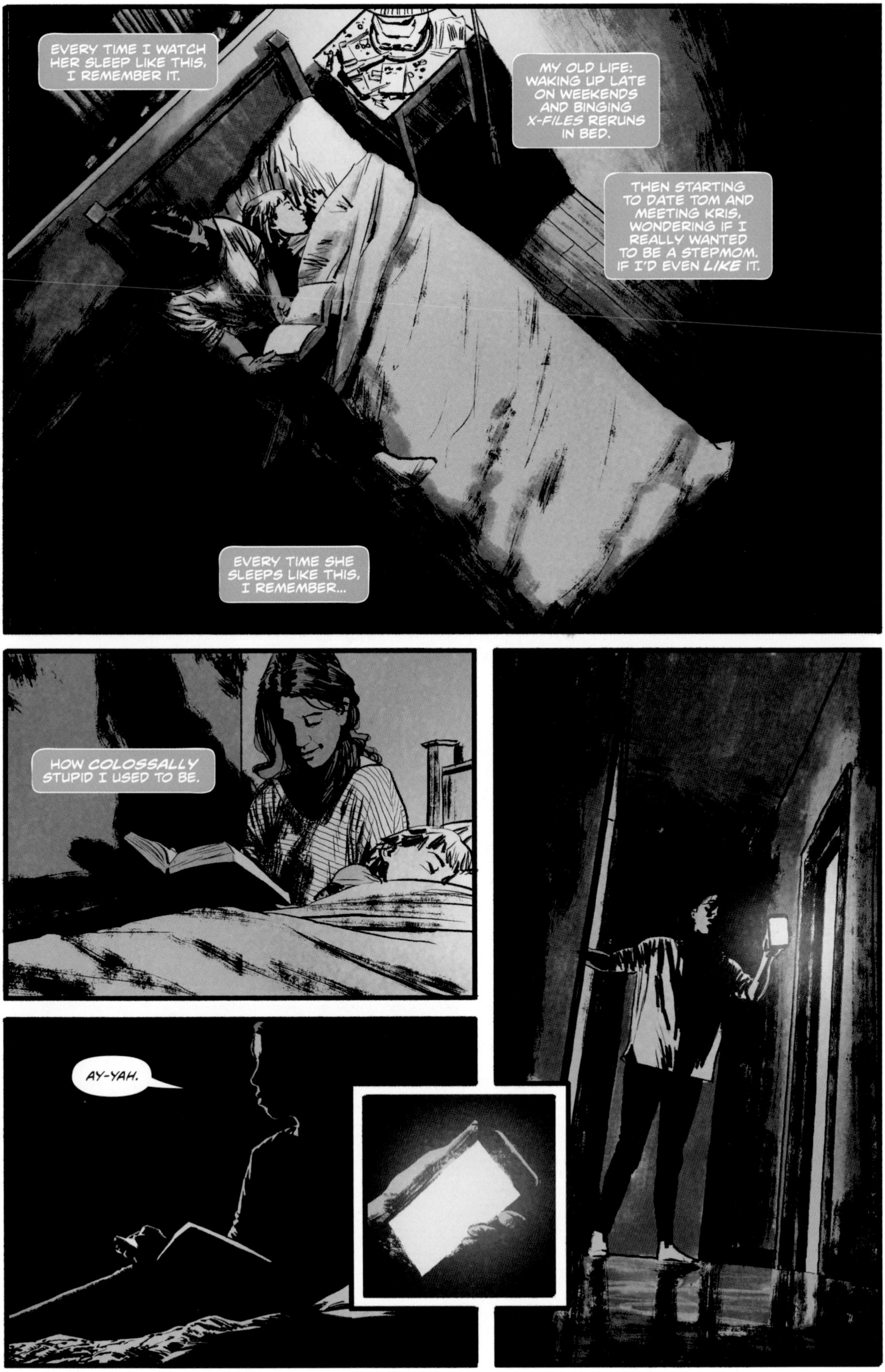
EVERY TIME I WATCH HER SLEEP LIKE THIS, I REMEMBER IT.
MY OLD LIFE: WAKING UP LATE ON WEEKENDS AND BINGING X-FILES RERUNS IN BED.
THEN STARTING TO DATE TOM AND MEETING KRIS, WONDERING IF I REALLY WANTED TO BE A STEPMOM. IF I'D EVEN LIKE IT.
EVERY TIME SHE SLEEPS LIKE THIS, I REMEMBER...
HOW COLOSSALLY STUPID I USED TO BE.
AY-YAH.

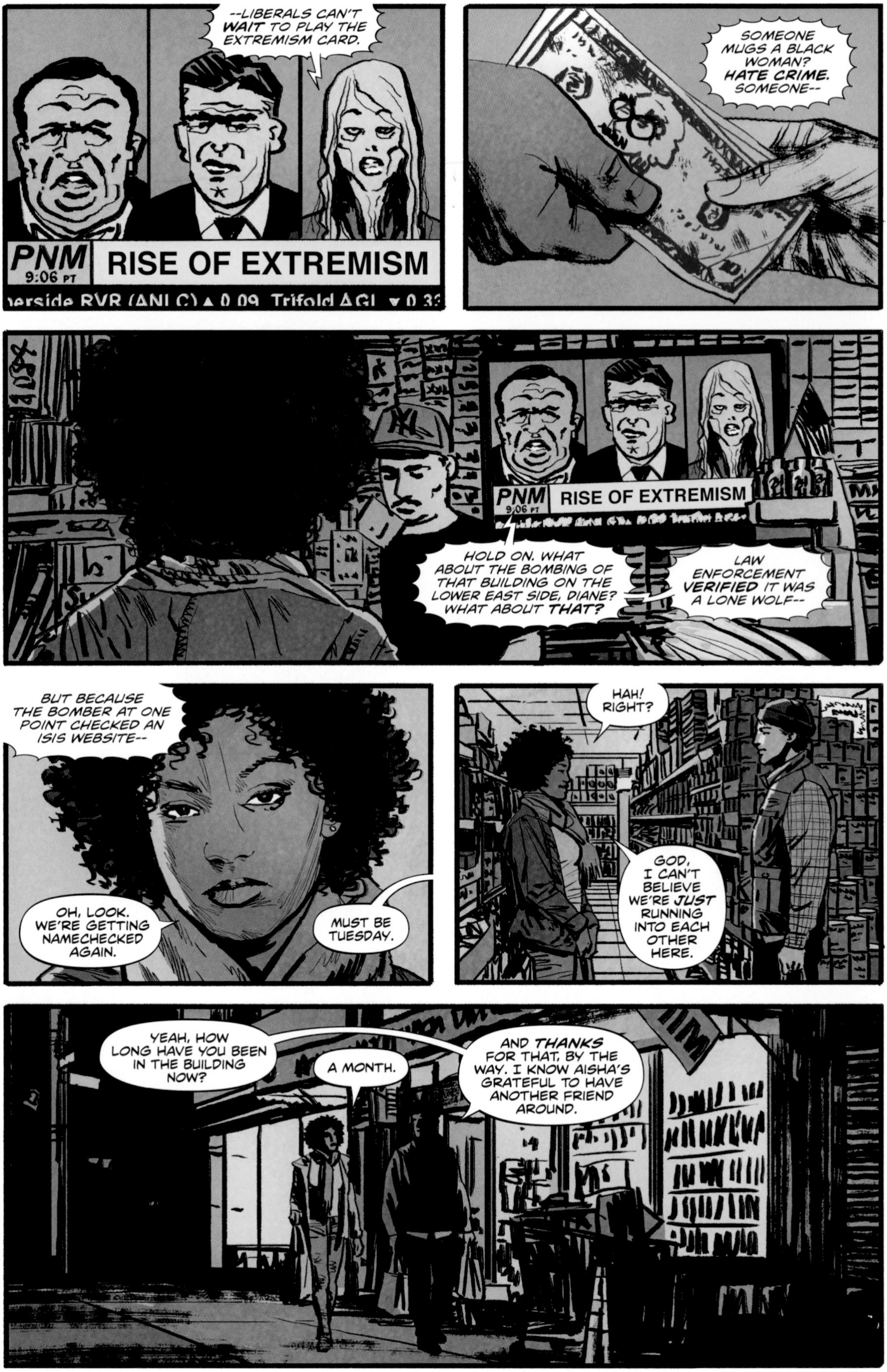
--LIBERALS CAN'T WAIT TO PLAY THE EXTREMISM CARD.
PNM 9:06 PT
RISE OF EXTREMISM
erside RVR (ANLC) ▲ 0.09 Trifold AGI ▼ 0.33
SOMEONE MUGS A BLACK WOMAN? HATE CRIME. SOMEONE--
PNM 9:06 PT
RISE OF EXTREMISM
HOLD ON. WHAT ABOUT THE BOMBING OF THAT BUILDING ON THE LOWER EAST SIDE, DIANE? WHAT ABOUT THAT?
LAW ENFORCEMENT VERIFIED IT WAS A LONE WOLF--
BUT BECAUSE THE BOMBER AT ONE POINT CHECKED AN ISIS WEBSITE--
OH, LOOK. WE'RE GETTING NAMECHECKED AGAIN.
MUST BE TUESDAY.
HAH! RIGHT?
GOD, I CAN'T BELIEVE WE'RE JUST RUNNING INTO EACH OTHER HERE.
YEAH, HOW LONG HAVE YOU BEEN IN THE BUILDING NOW?
A MONTH.
AND THANKS FOR THAT, BY THE WAY. I KNOW AISHA'S GRATEFUL TO HAVE ANOTHER FRIEND AROUND.

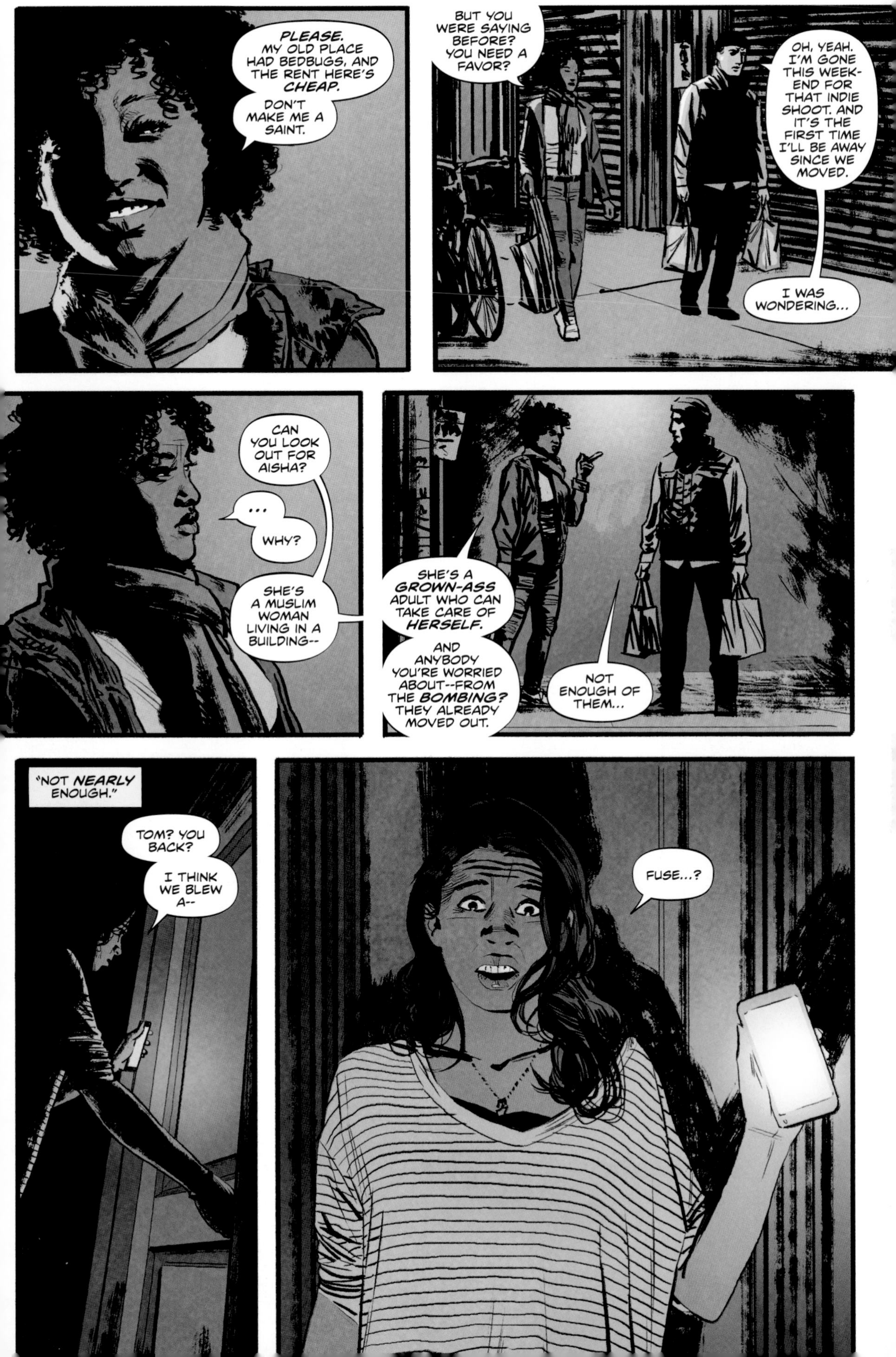
PLEASE. MY OLD PLACE HAD BEDBUGS, AND THE RENT HERE'S CHEAP.
DON'T MAKE ME A SAINT.
BUT YOU WERE SAYING BEFORE? YOU NEED A FAVOR?
OH, YEAH. I'M GONE THIS WEEK-END FOR THAT INDIE SHOOT. AND IT'S THE FIRST TIME I'LL BE AWAY SINCE WE MOVED.
I WAS WONDERING...
CAN YOU LOOK OUT FOR AISHA?
...
WHY?
SHE'S A MUSLIM WOMAN LIVING IN A BUILDING--
SHE'S A GROWN-ASS ADULT WHO CAN TAKE CARE OF HERSELF.
AND ANYBODY YOU'RE WORRIED ABOUT--FROM THE BOMBING? THEY ALREADY MOVED OUT.
NOT ENOUGH OF THEM...
"NOT NEARLY ENOUGH."
TOM? YOU BACK?
I THINK WE BLEW A--
FUSE...?

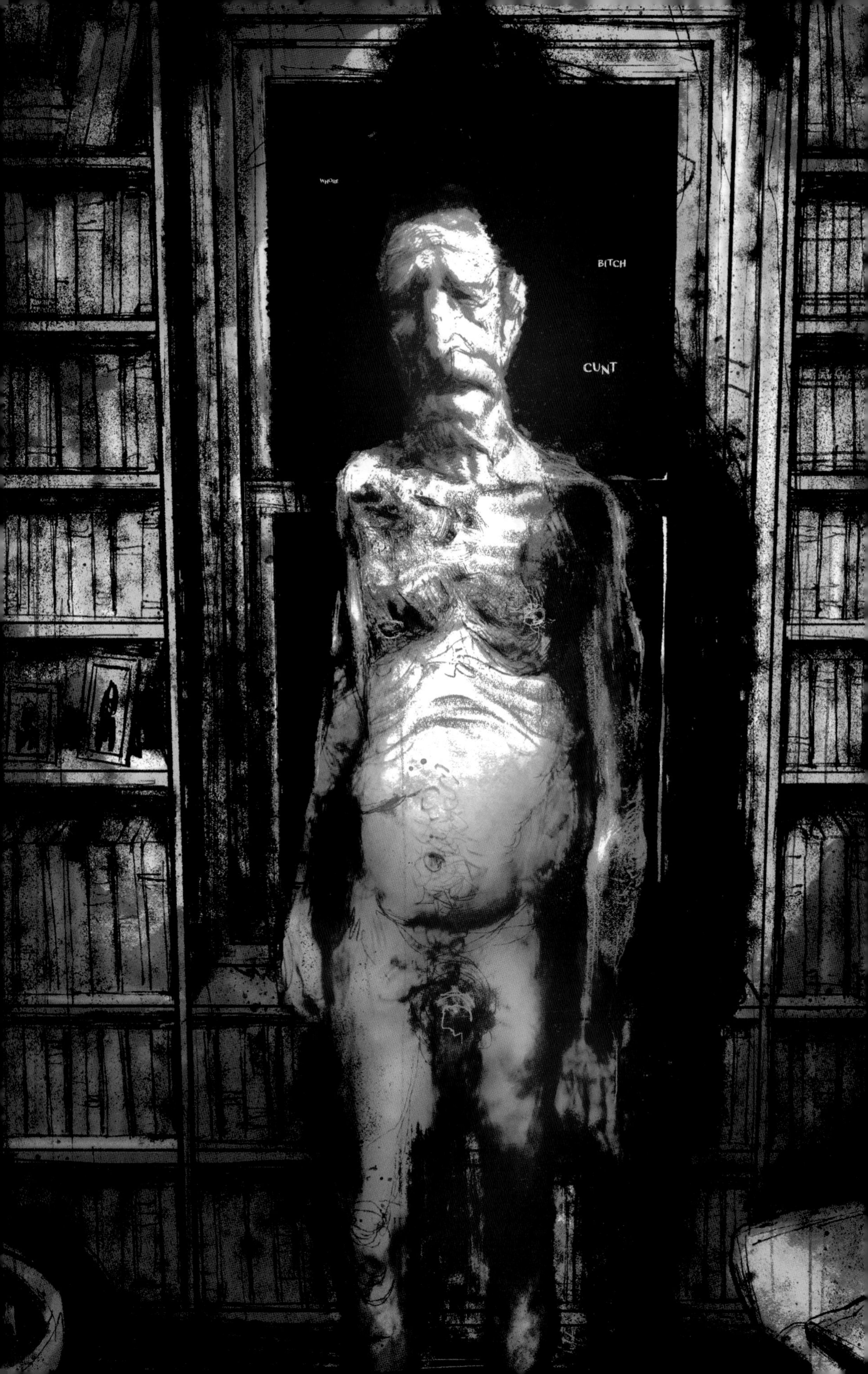
WHORE
BITCH
CUNT

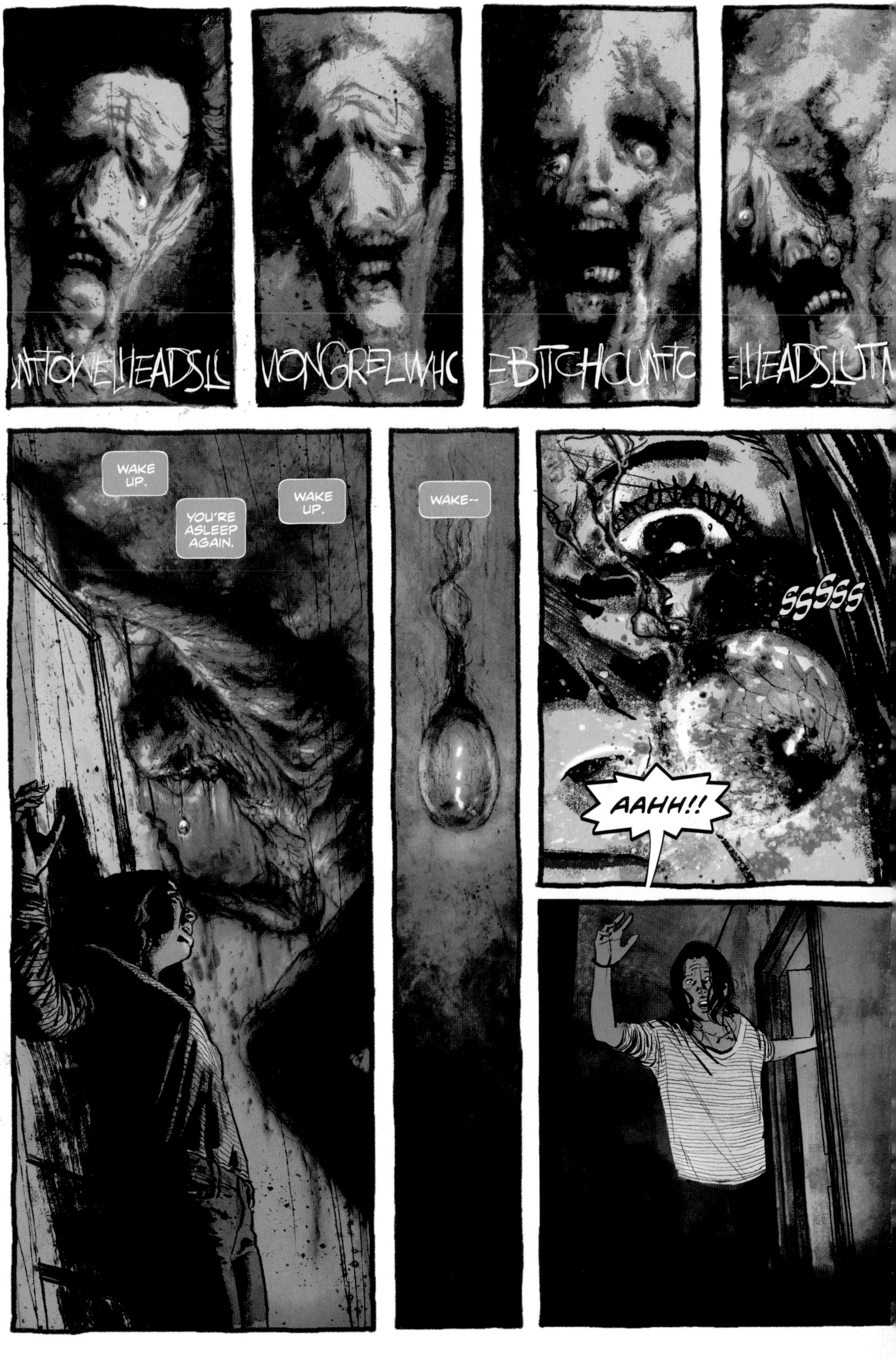
NTTOWELHEADSLU
MONGRELWHO
EBITCHCUNTC
ELHEADSLUTM
WAKE UP.
YOU'RE ASLEEP AGAIN.
WAKE UP.
WAKE--
SSSSS
AAHH!!

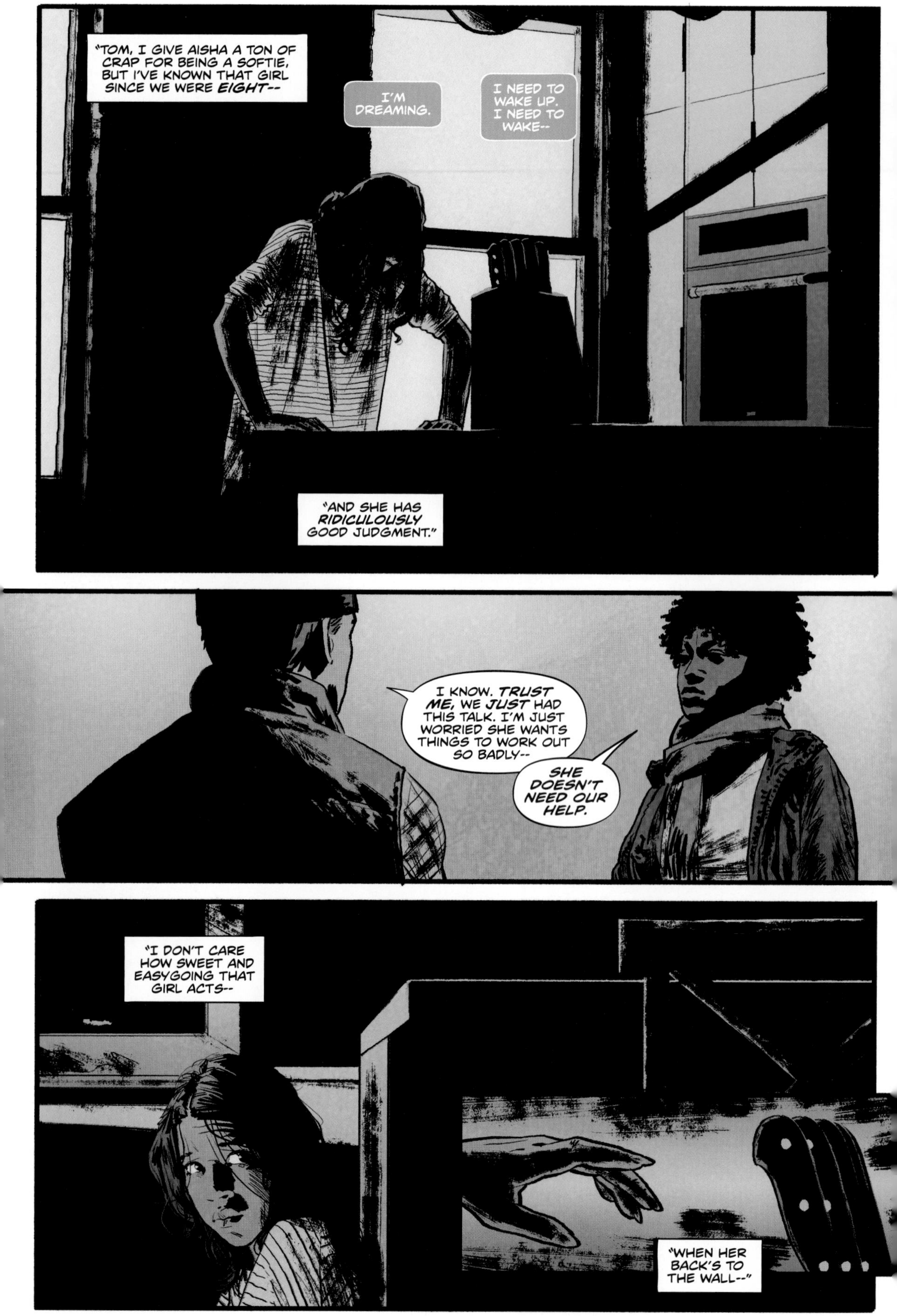
"TOM, I GIVE AISHA A TON OF CRAP FOR BEING A SOFTIE, BUT I'VE KNOWN THAT GIRL SINCE WE WERE EIGHT--
I'M DREAMING.
I NEED TO WAKE UP. I NEED TO WAKE--
"AND SHE HAS RIDICULOUSLY GOOD JUDGMENT."
I KNOW. TRUST ME, WE JUST HAD THIS TALK. I'M JUST WORRIED SHE WANTS THINGS TO WORK OUT SO BADLY--
SHE DOESN'T NEED OUR HELP.
"I DON'T CARE HOW SWEET AND EASYGOING THAT GIRL ACTS--
"WHEN HER BACK'S TO THE WALL--"

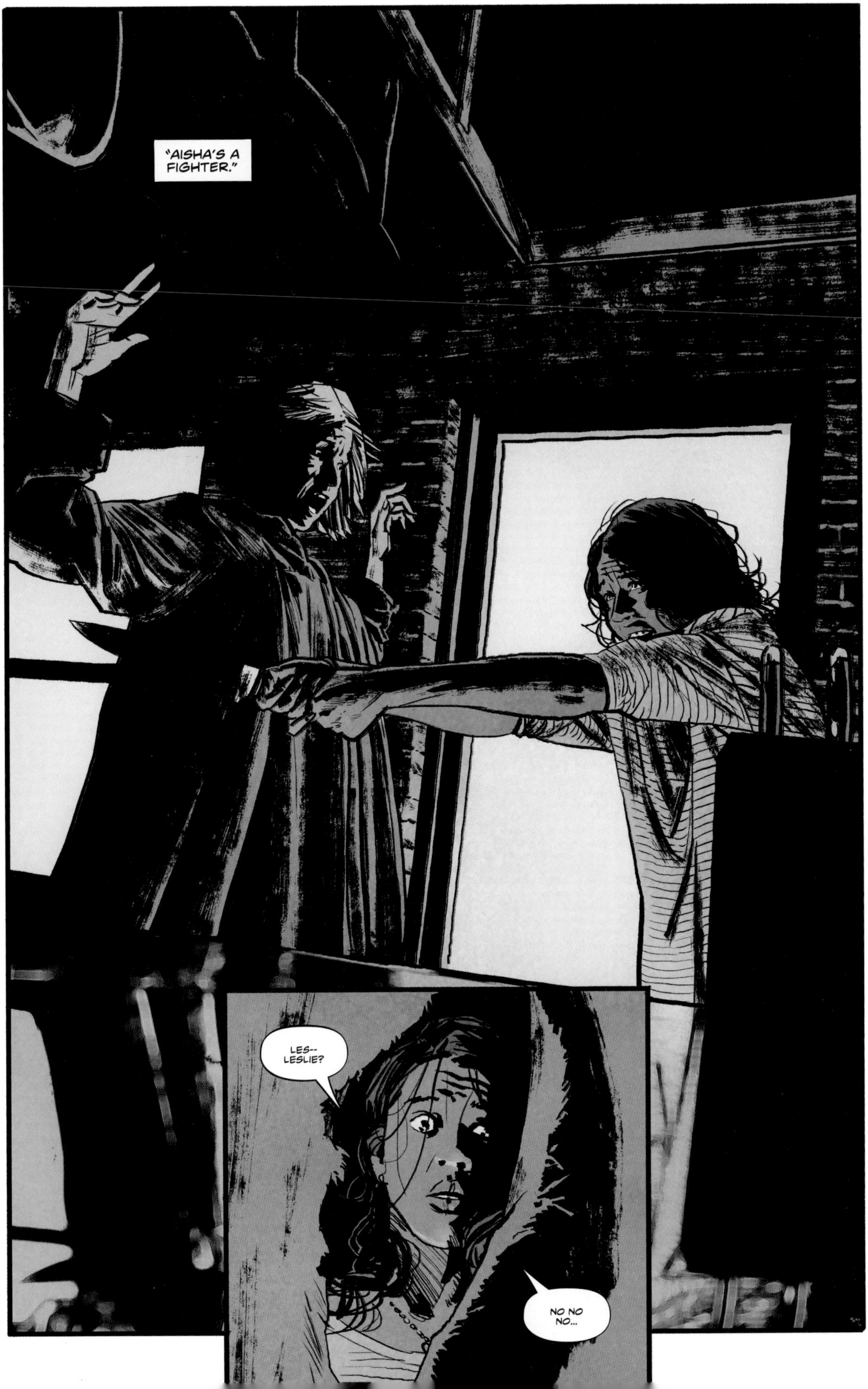
"AISHA'S A FIGHTER."
LES-- LESLIE?
NO NO NO...

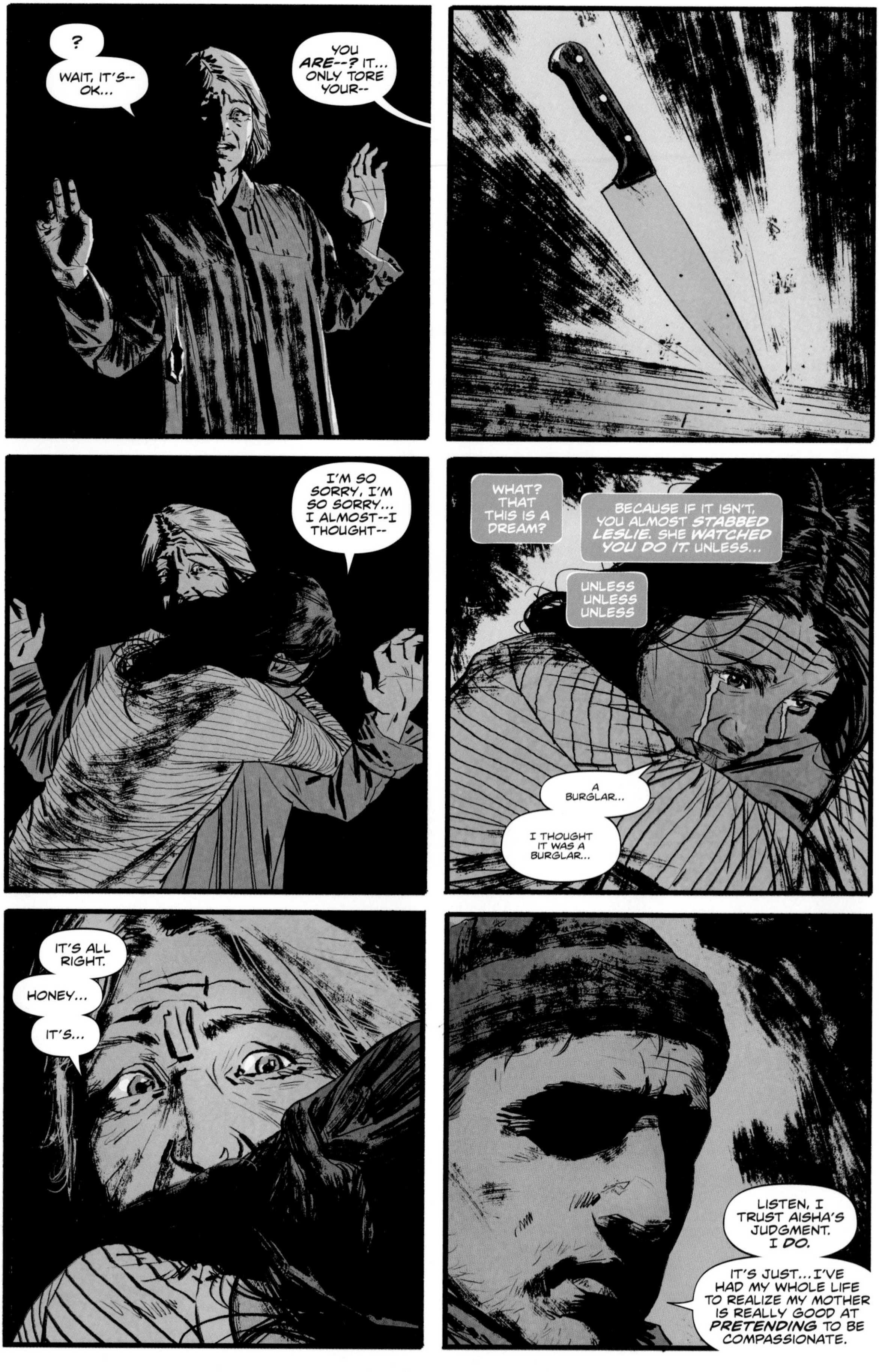
?
WAIT, IT'S--OK...
YOU ARE--? IT... ONLY TORE YOUR--
I'M SO SORRY, I'M SO SORRY... I ALMOST--I THOUGHT--
WHAT? THAT THIS IS A DREAM?
BECAUSE IF IT ISN'T, YOU ALMOST STABBED LESLIE. SHE WATCHED YOU DO IT. UNLESS...
UNLESS UNLESS UNLESS
A BURGLAR...
I THOUGHT IT WAS A BURGLAR...
IT'S ALL RIGHT.
HONEY...
IT'S...
LISTEN, I TRUST AISHA'S JUDGMENT. I DO.
IT'S JUST...I'VE HAD MY WHOLE LIFE TO REALIZE MY MOTHER IS REALLY GOOD AT PRETENDING TO BE COMPASSIONATE.

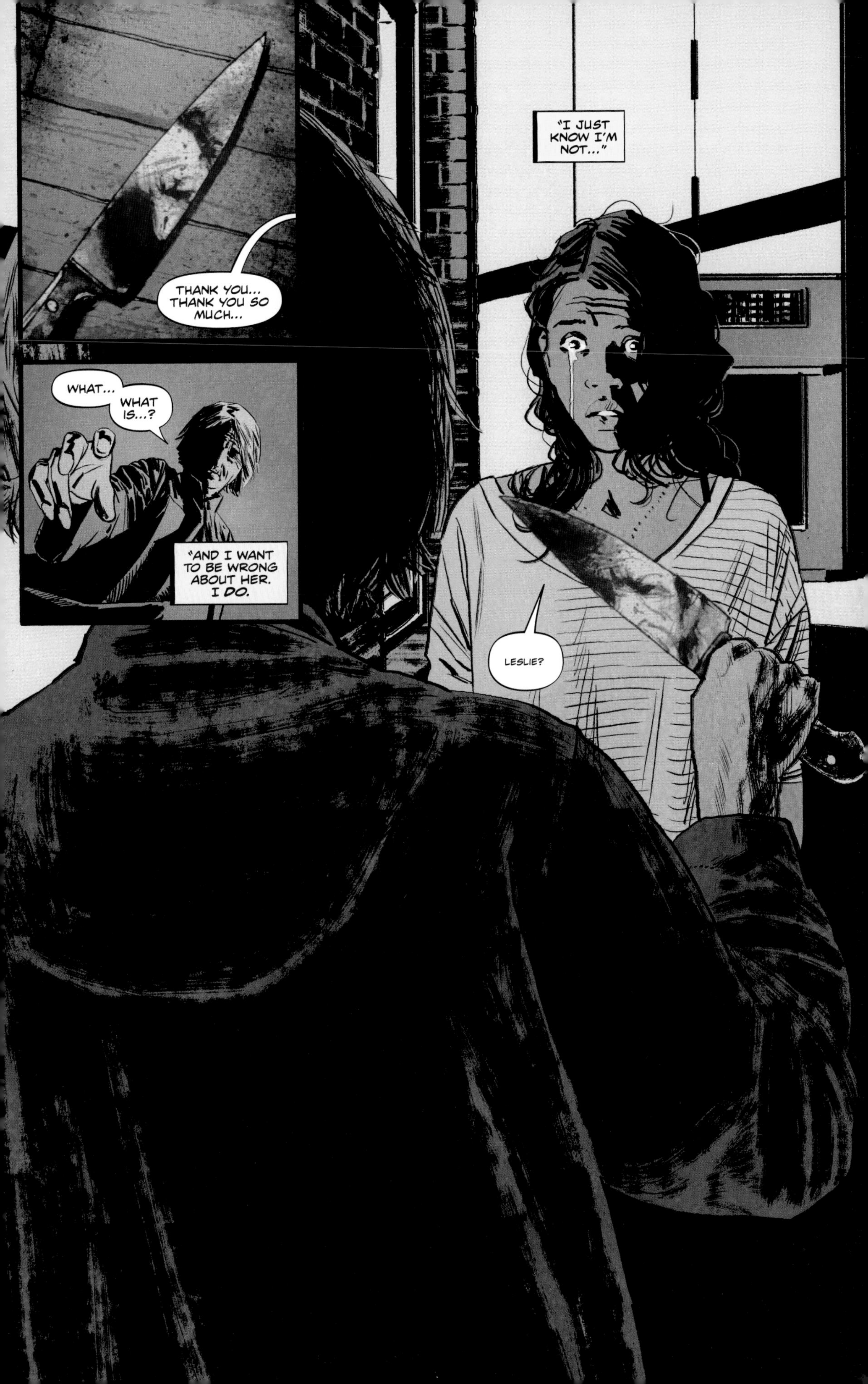
THANK YOU... THANK YOU SO MUCH...
WHAT...
WHAT IS...?
"AND I WANT TO BE WRONG ABOUT HER. I DO.
"I JUST KNOW I'M NOT..."
LESLIE?

chapter 2

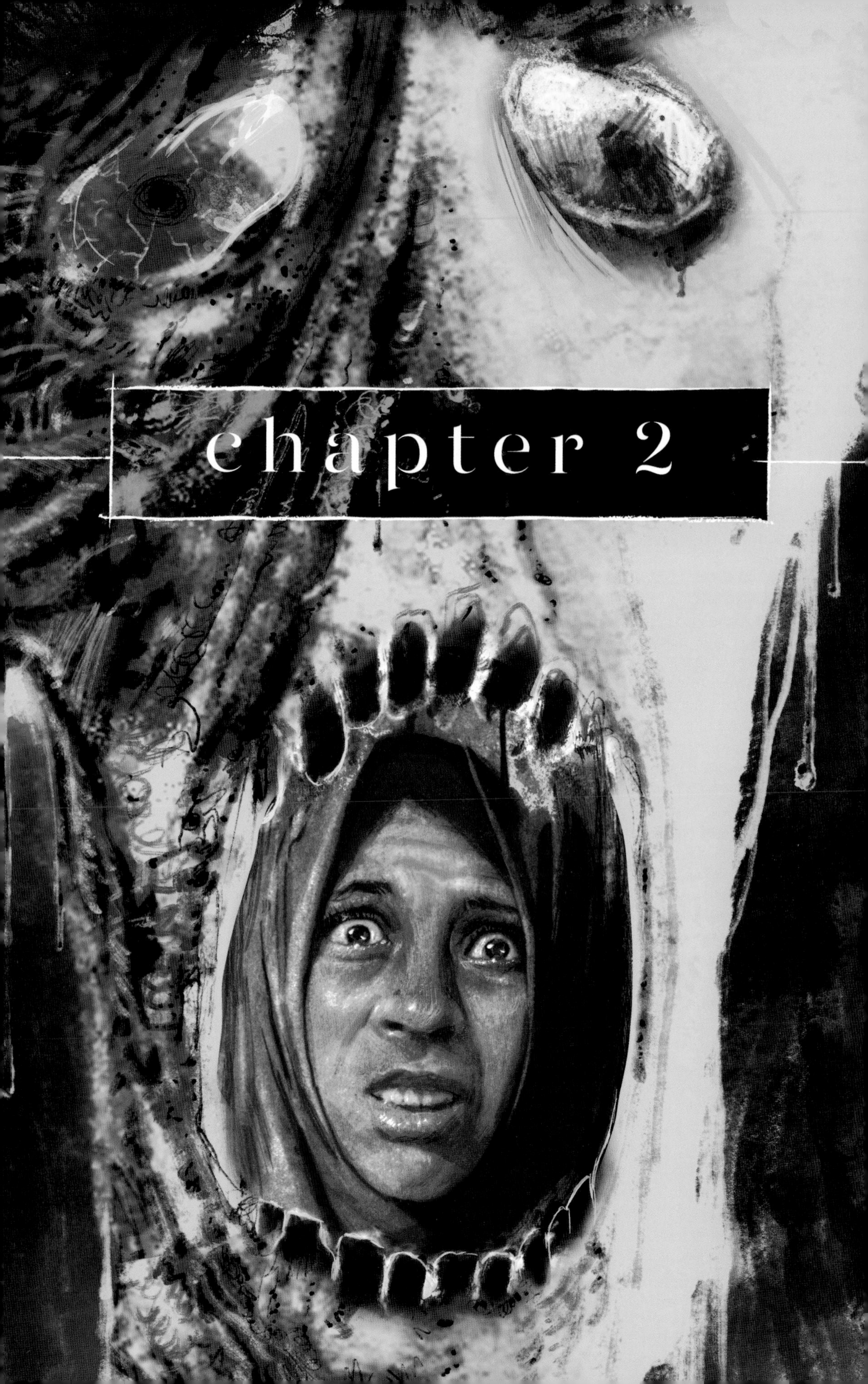

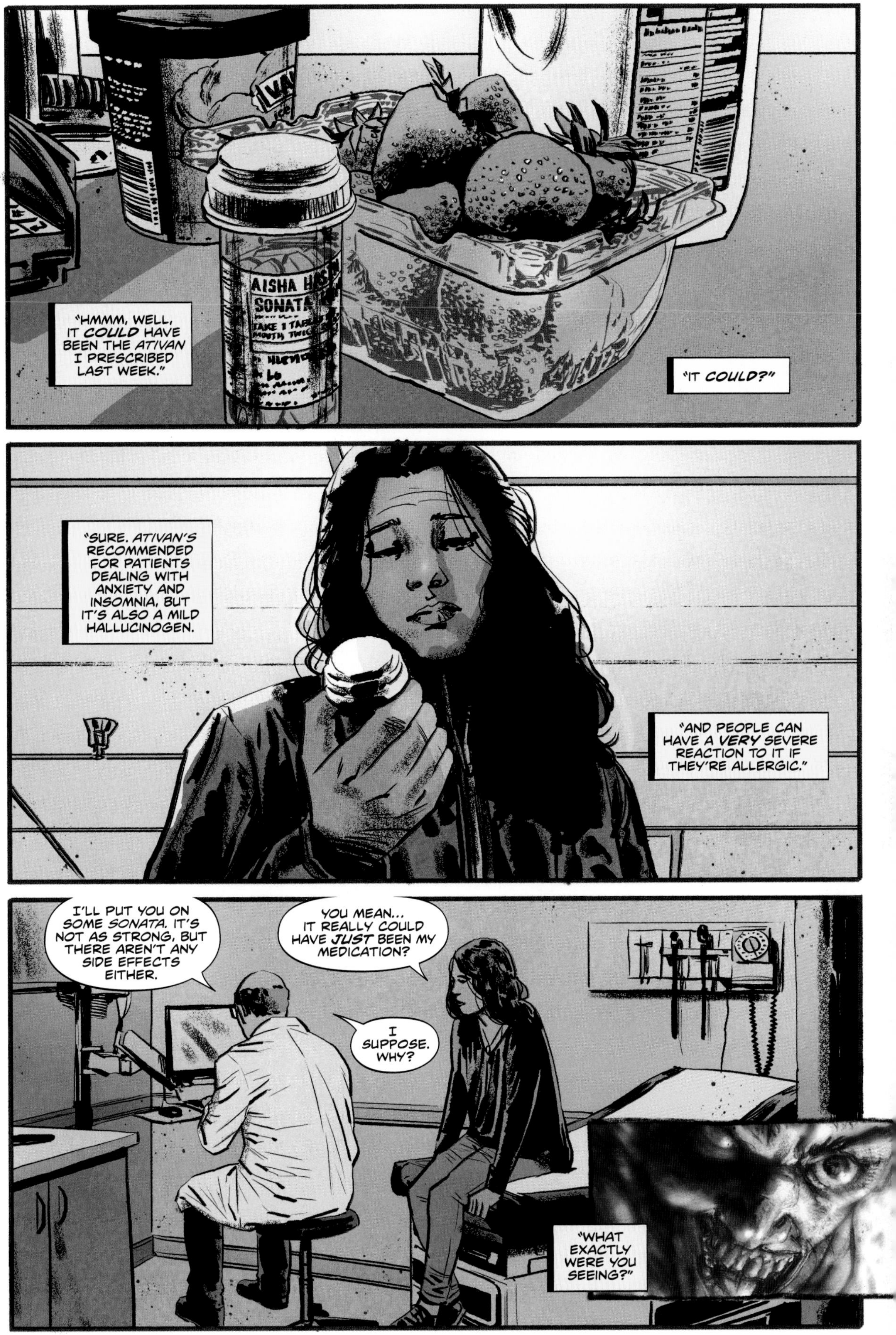
"HMMM, WELL, IT COULD HAVE BEEN THE ATIVAN I PRESCRIBED LAST WEEK."
"IT COULD?"
"SURE. ATIVAN'S RECOMMENDED FOR PATIENTS DEALING WITH ANXIETY AND INSOMNIA, BUT IT'S ALSO A MILD HALLUCINOGEN.
"AND PEOPLE CAN HAVE A VERY SEVERE REACTION TO IT IF THEY'RE ALLERGIC."
I'LL PUT YOU ON SOME SONATA. IT'S NOT AS STRONG, BUT THERE AREN'T ANY SIDE EFFECTS EITHER.
YOU MEAN... IT REALLY COULD HAVE JUST BEEN MY MEDICATION?
I SUPPOSE. WHY?
"WHAT EXACTLY WERE YOU SEEING?"

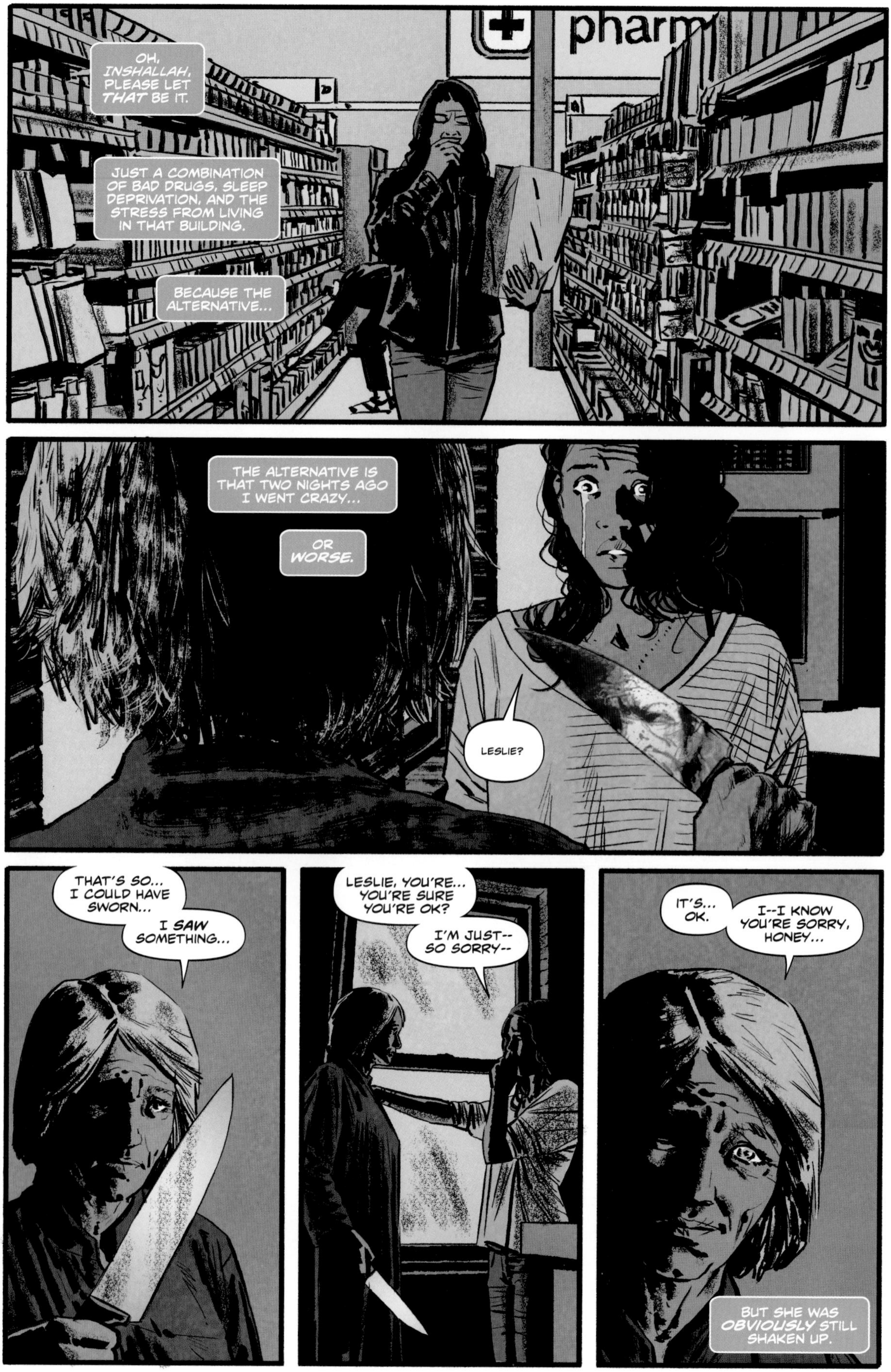

OH, INSHALLAH, PLEASE LET THAT BE IT.
JUST A COMBINATION OF BAD DRUGS, SLEEP DEPRIVATION, AND THE STRESS FROM LIVING IN THAT BUILDING.
BECAUSE THE ALTERNATIVE...
pharm
THE ALTERNATIVE IS THAT TWO NIGHTS AGO I WENT CRAZY...
OR WORSE.
LESLIE?
THAT'S SO... I COULD HAVE SWORN...
I SAW SOMETHING...
LESLIE, YOU'RE... YOU'RE SURE YOU'RE OK?
I'M JUST-- SO SORRY--
IT'S... OK.
I--I KNOW YOU'RE SORRY, HONEY...
BUT SHE WAS OBVIOUSLY STILL SHAKEN UP.

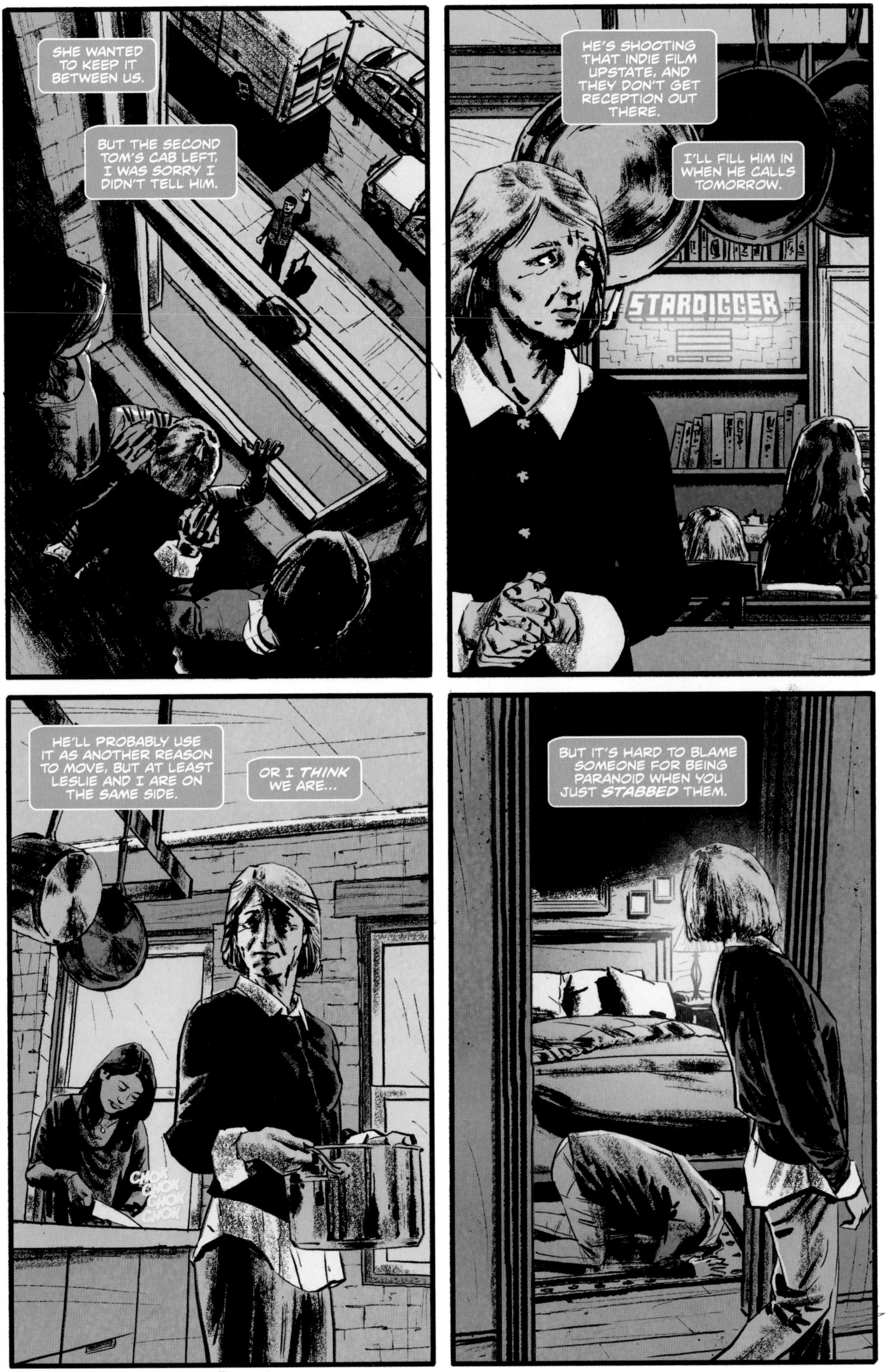
SHE WANTED TO KEEP IT BETWEEN US.
BUT THE SECOND TOM'S CAB LEFT, I WAS SORRY I DIDN'T TELL HIM.
HE'S SHOOTING THAT INDIE FILM UPSTATE, AND THEY DON'T GET RECEPTION OUT THERE.
I'LL FILL HIM IN WHEN HE CALLS TOMORROW.
STARDIGGER
HE'LL PROBABLY USE IT AS ANOTHER REASON TO MOVE, BUT AT LEAST LESLIE AND I ARE ON THE SAME SIDE.
OR I *THINK* WE ARE...
CHOK CHOK CHOK CHOK
BUT IT'S HARD TO BLAME SOMEONE FOR BEING PARANOID WHEN YOU JUST *STABBED* THEM.

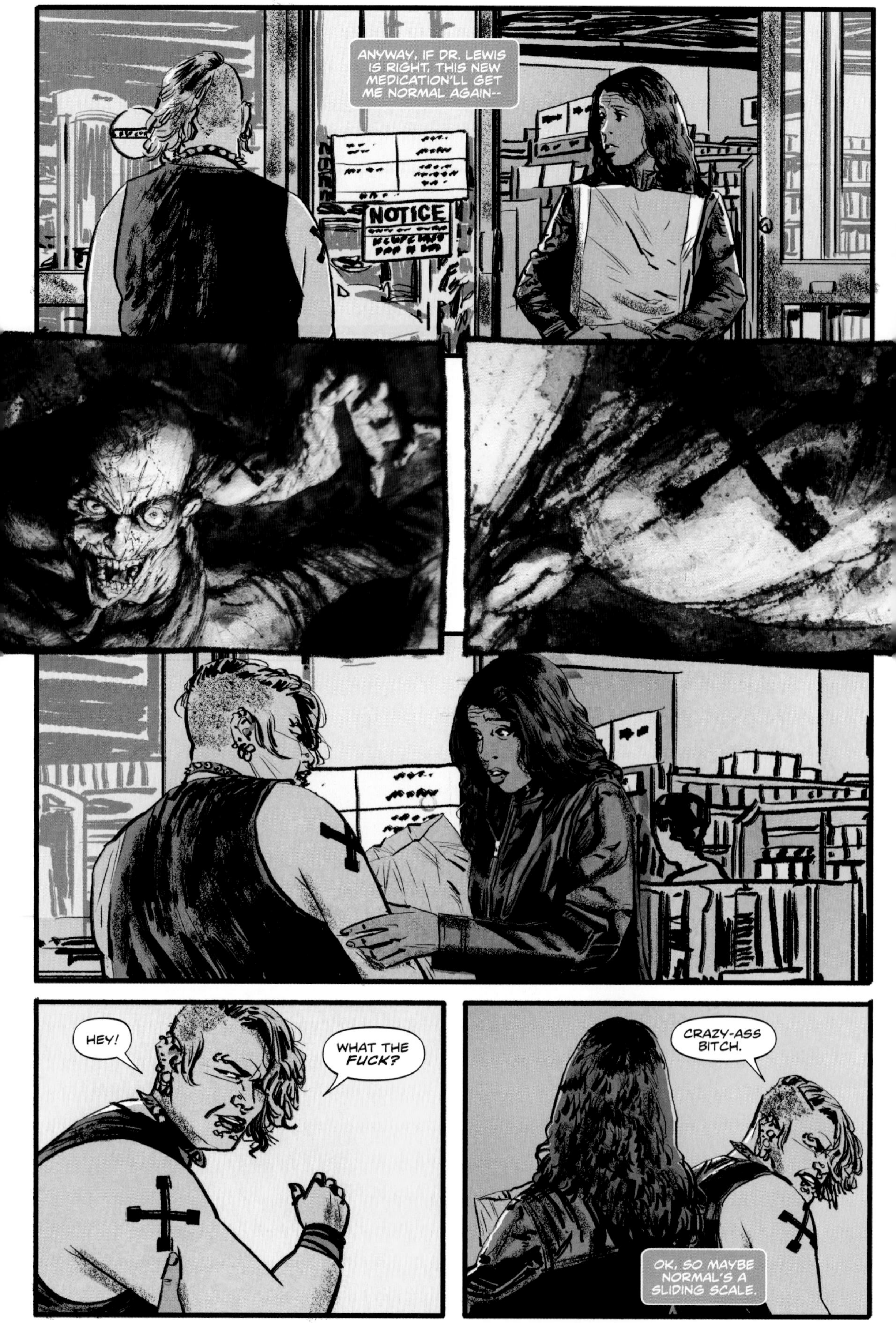
ANYWAY, IF DR. LEWIS IS RIGHT, THIS NEW MEDICATION'LL GET ME NORMAL AGAIN--
NOTICE
HEY!
WHAT THE FUCK?
CRAZY-ASS BITCH.
OK, SO MAYBE NORMAL'S A SLIDING SCALE.

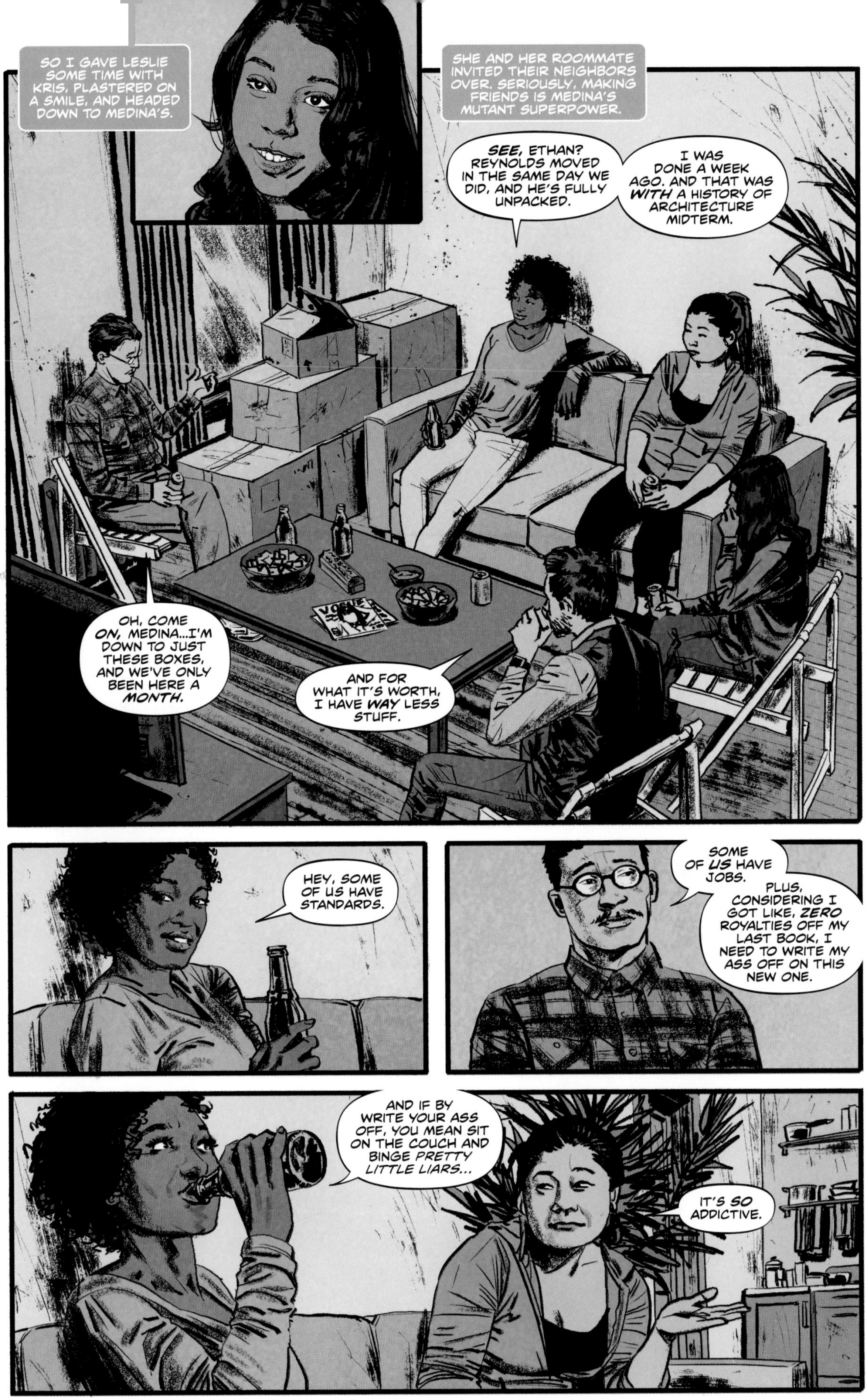
SO I GAVE LESLIE SOME TIME WITH KRIS, PLASTERED ON A SMILE, AND HEADED DOWN TO MEDINA'S.
SHE AND HER ROOMMATE INVITED THEIR NEIGHBORS OVER. SERIOUSLY, MAKING FRIENDS IS MEDINA'S MUTANT SUPERPOWER.
SEE, ETHAN? REYNOLDS MOVED IN THE SAME DAY WE DID, AND HE'S FULLY UNPACKED.
I WAS DONE A WEEK AGO. AND THAT WAS WITH A HISTORY OF ARCHITECTURE MIDTERM.
OH, COME ON, MEDINA...I'M DOWN TO JUST THESE BOXES, AND WE'VE ONLY BEEN HERE A MONTH.
AND FOR WHAT IT'S WORTH, I HAVE WAY LESS STUFF.
HEY, SOME OF US HAVE STANDARDS.
SOME OF US HAVE JOBS.
PLUS, CONSIDERING I GOT LIKE, ZERO ROYALTIES OFF MY LAST BOOK, I NEED TO WRITE MY ASS OFF ON THIS NEW ONE.
AND IF BY WRITE YOUR ASS OFF, YOU MEAN SIT ON THE COUCH AND BINGE PRETTY LITTLE LIARS...
IT'S SO ADDICTIVE.

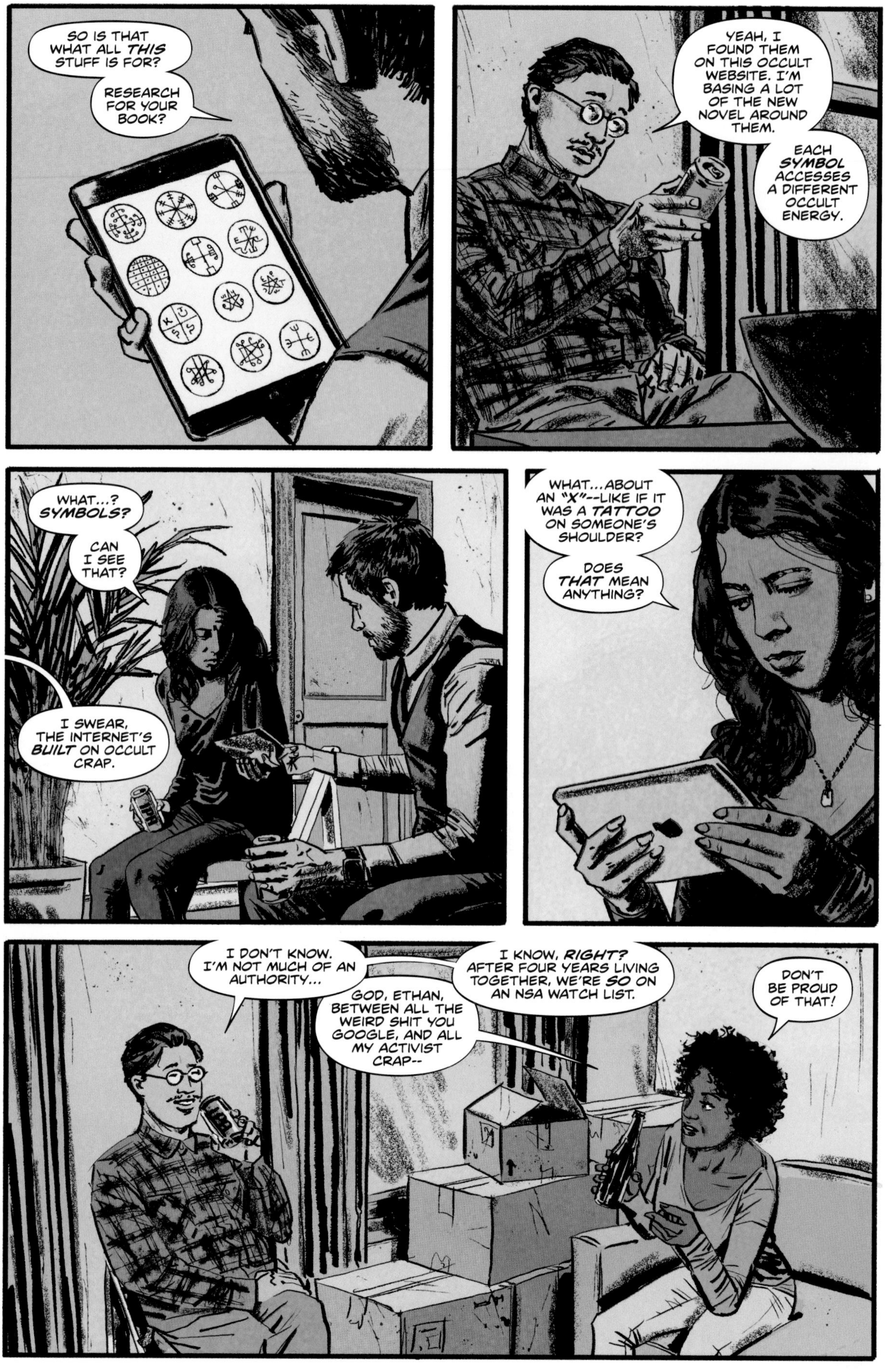
SO IS THAT WHAT ALL THIS STUFF IS FOR?
RESEARCH FOR YOUR BOOK?
YEAH, I FOUND THEM ON THIS OCCULT WEBSITE. I'M BASING A LOT OF THE NEW NOVEL AROUND THEM.
EACH SYMBOL ACCESSES A DIFFERENT OCCULT ENERGY.
WHAT...? SYMBOLS?
CAN I SEE THAT?
I SWEAR, THE INTERNET'S BUILT ON OCCULT CRAP.
WHAT...ABOUT AN "X"--LIKE IF IT WAS A TATTOO ON SOMEONE'S SHOULDER?
DOES THAT MEAN ANYTHING?
I DON'T KNOW. I'M NOT MUCH OF AN AUTHORITY...
GOD, ETHAN, BETWEEN ALL THE WEIRD SHIT YOU GOOGLE, AND ALL MY ACTIVIST CRAP--
I KNOW, RIGHT? AFTER FOUR YEARS LIVING TOGETHER, WE'RE SO ON AN NSA WATCH LIST.
DON'T BE PROUD OF THAT!

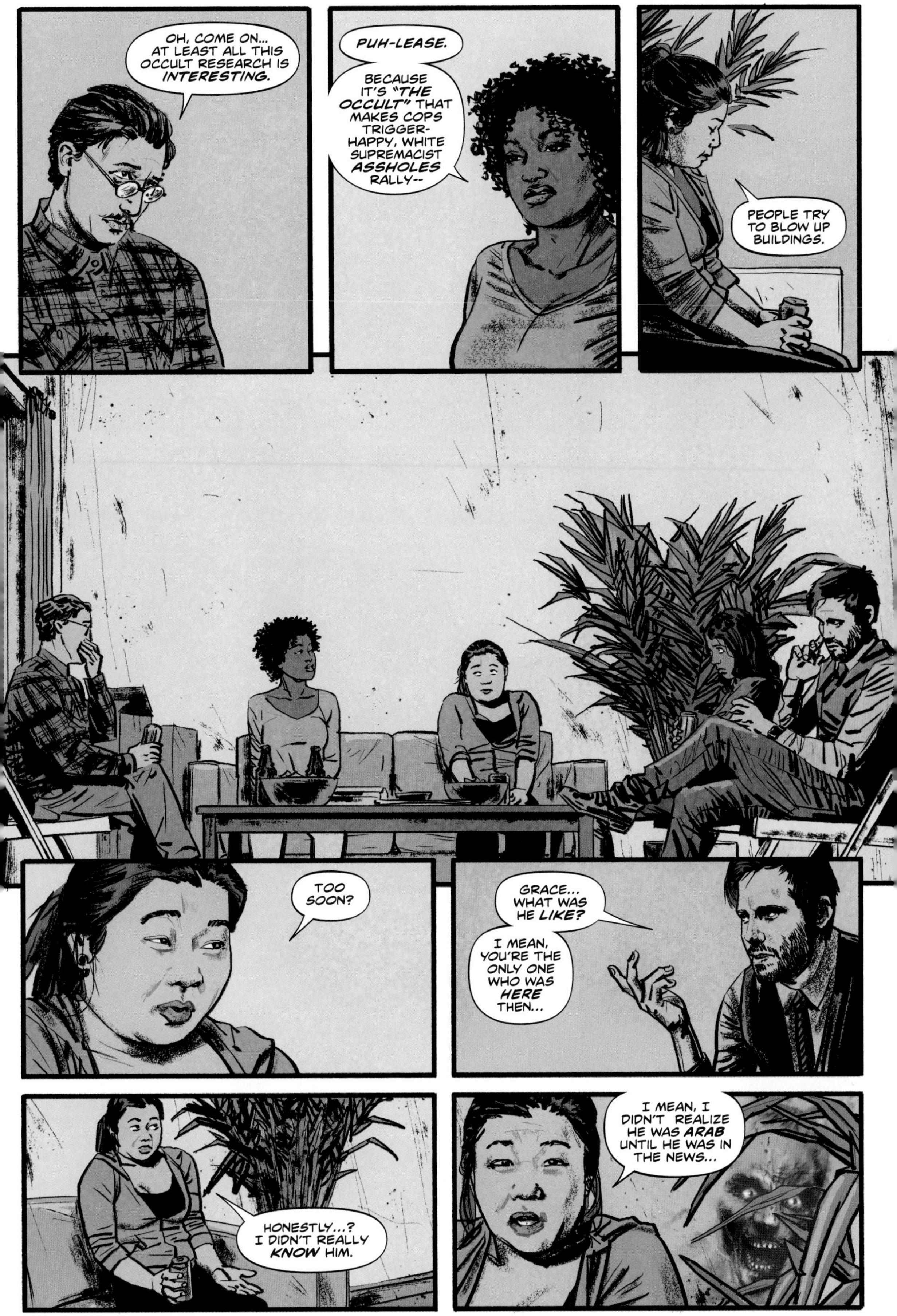
OH, COME ON... AT LEAST ALL THIS OCCULT RESEARCH IS *INTERESTING.*
PUH-LEASE.
BECAUSE IT'S *"THE OCCULT"* THAT MAKES COPS TRIGGER-HAPPY, WHITE SUPREMACIST ***ASSHOLES*** RALLY--
PEOPLE TRY TO BLOW UP BUILDINGS.
TOO SOON?
GRACE... WHAT WAS HE *LIKE?*
I MEAN, YOU'RE THE ONLY ONE WHO WAS *HERE* THEN...
HONESTLY...? I DIDN'T REALLY ***KNOW*** HIM.
I MEAN, I DIDN'T REALIZE HE WAS *ARAB* UNTIL HE WAS IN THE NEWS...

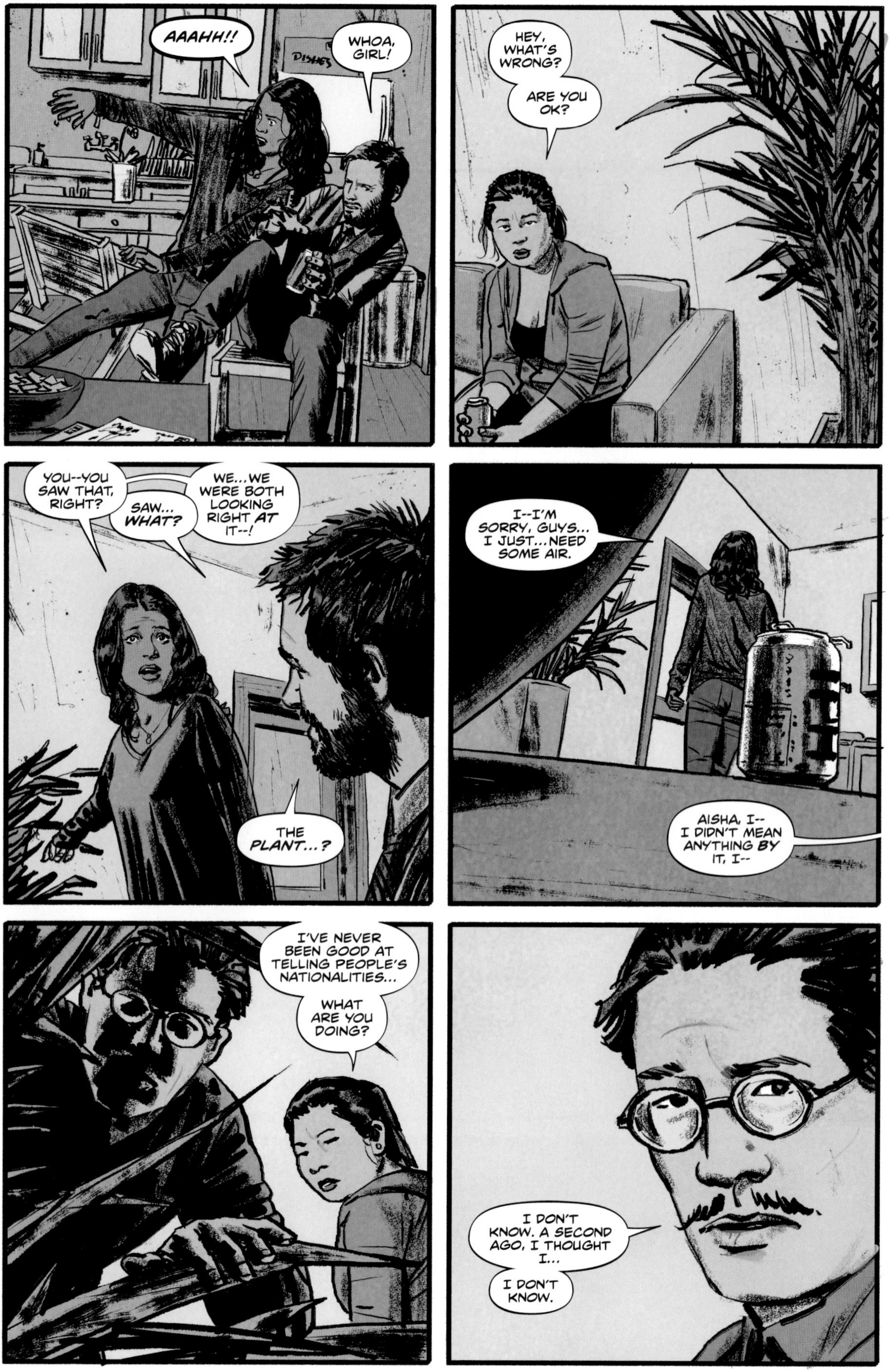
AAAHH!!
WHOA, GIRL!
DISHES
HEY, WHAT'S WRONG?
ARE YOU OK?
YOU--YOU SAW THAT, RIGHT?
SAW... WHAT?
WE...WE WERE BOTH LOOKING RIGHT AT IT--!
THE PLANT...?
I--I'M SORRY, GUYS... I JUST...NEED SOME AIR.
AISHA, I-- I DIDN'T MEAN ANYTHING BY IT, I--
I'VE NEVER BEEN GOOD AT TELLING PEOPLE'S NATIONALITIES...
WHAT ARE YOU DOING?
I DON'T KNOW. A SECOND AGO, I THOUGHT I...
I DON'T KNOW.

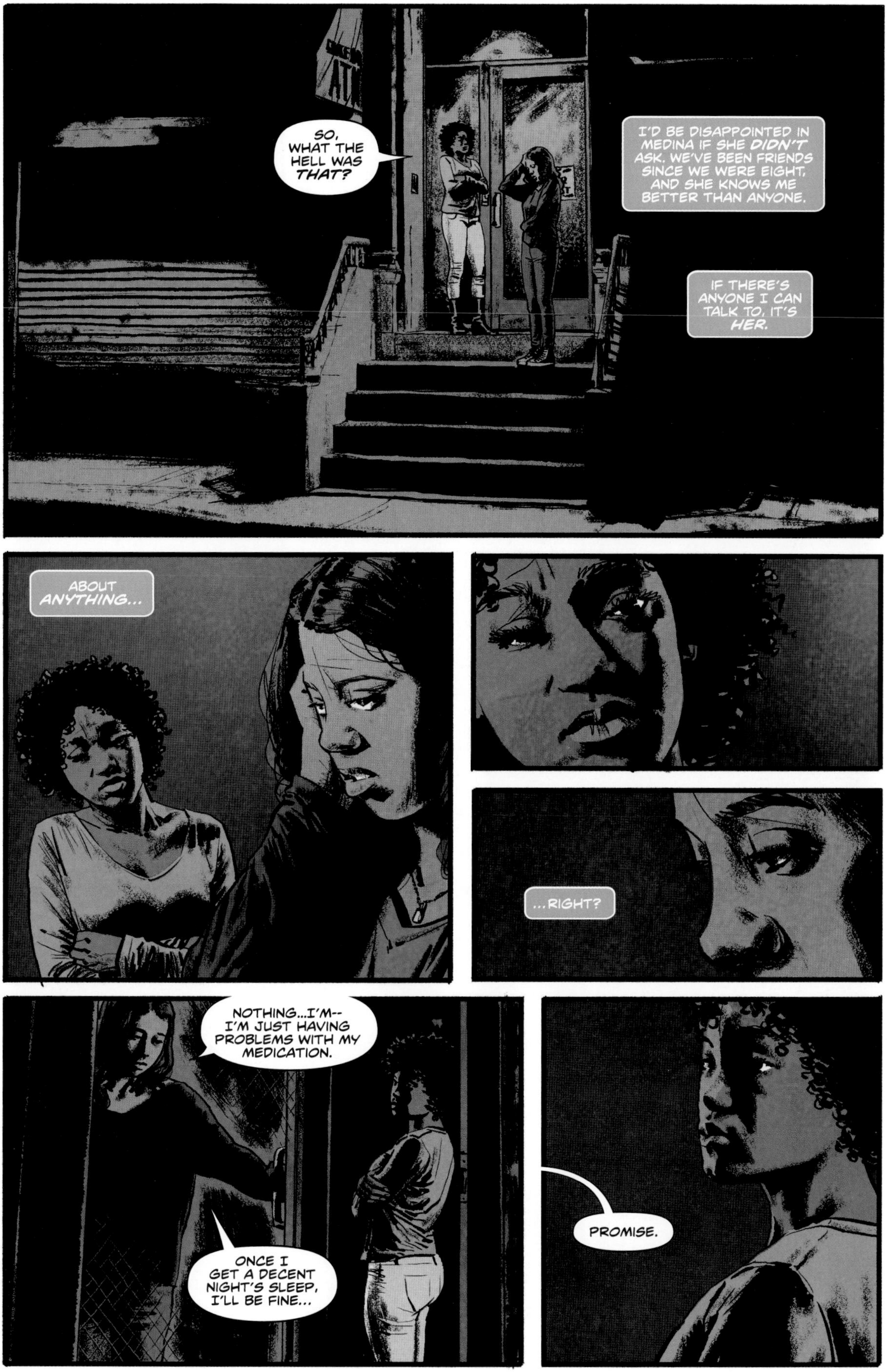
SO, WHAT THE HELL WAS *THAT?*
I'D BE DISAPPOINTED IN MEDINA IF SHE *DIDN'T* ASK. WE'VE BEEN FRIENDS SINCE WE WERE EIGHT, AND SHE KNOWS ME BETTER THAN ANYONE.
IF THERE'S ANYONE I CAN TALK TO, IT'S *HER.*
ABOUT *ANYTHING...*
...RIGHT?
NOTHING...I'M-- I'M JUST HAVING PROBLEMS WITH MY MEDICATION.
ONCE I GET A DECENT NIGHT'S SLEEP, I'LL BE FINE...
PROMISE.

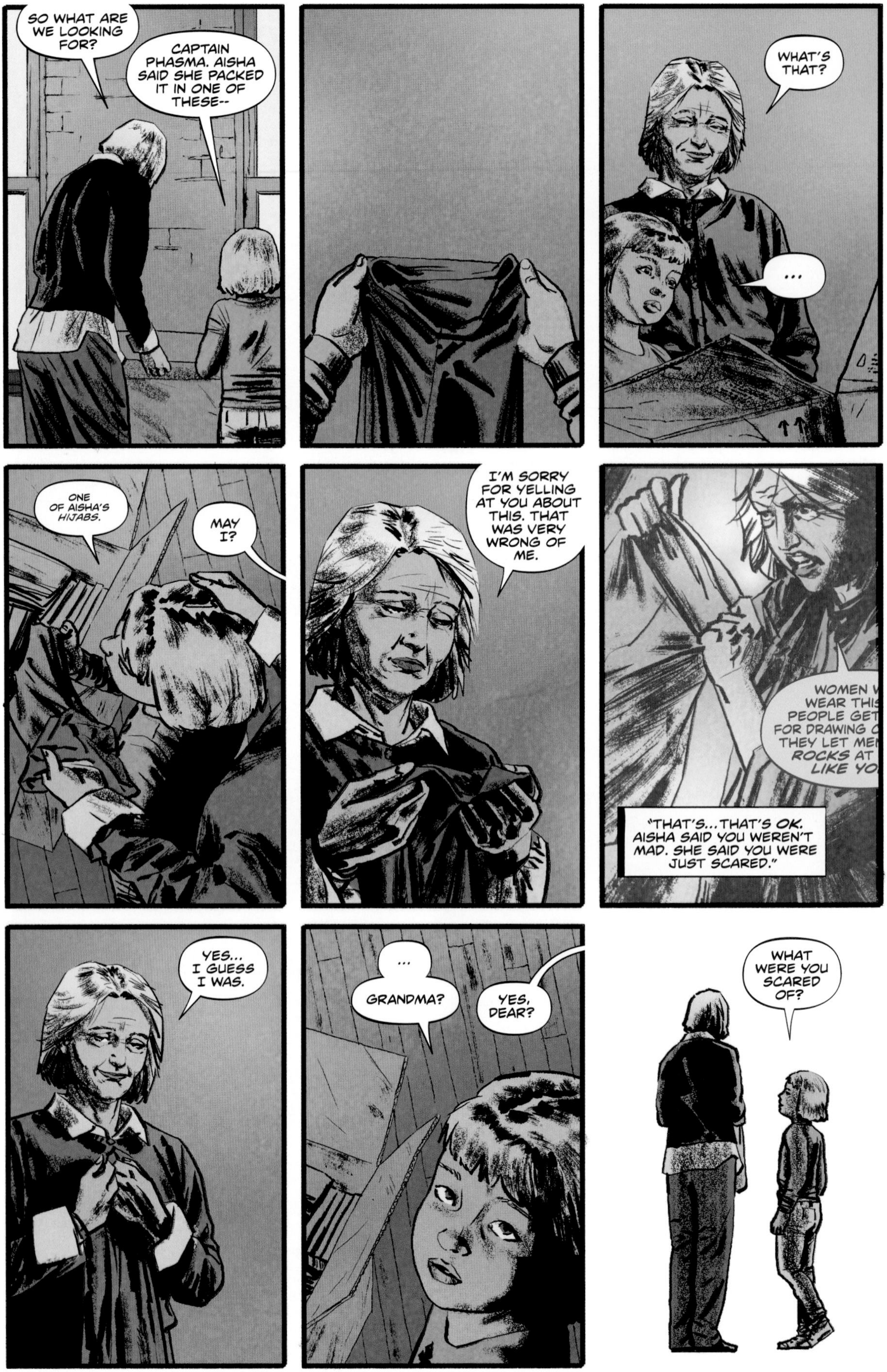
SO WHAT ARE WE LOOKING FOR?
CAPTAIN PHASMA. AISHA SAID SHE PACKED IT IN ONE OF THESE--
WHAT'S THAT?
...
ONE OF AISHA'S HIJABS.
MAY I?
I'M SORRY FOR YELLING AT YOU ABOUT THIS. THAT WAS VERY WRONG OF ME.
"THAT'S...THAT'S OK. AISHA SAID YOU WEREN'T MAD. SHE SAID YOU WERE JUST SCARED."
YES... I GUESS I WAS.
...
GRANDMA?
YES, DEAR?
WHAT WERE YOU SCARED OF?

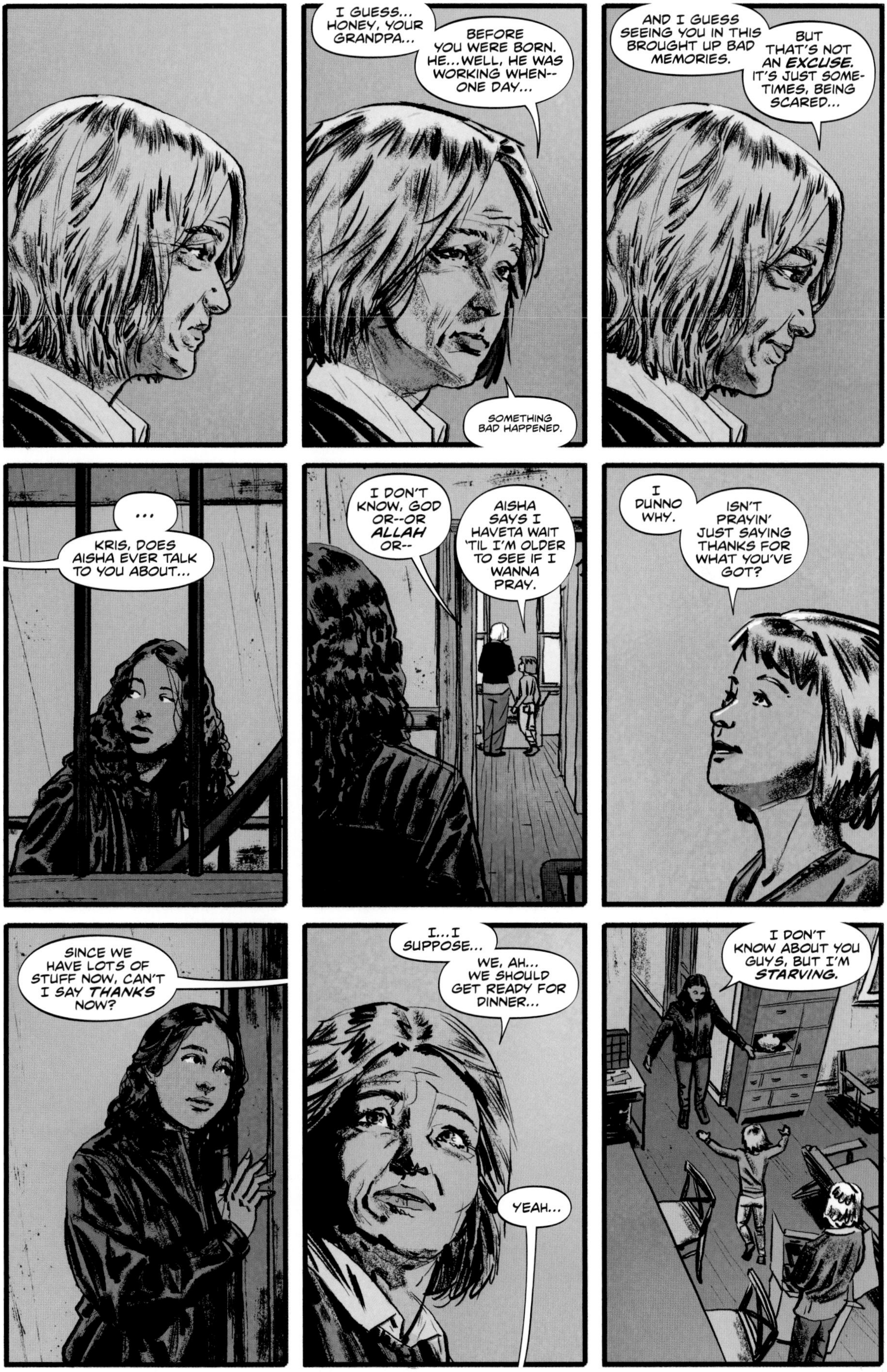
I GUESS... HONEY, YOUR GRANDPA...
BEFORE YOU WERE BORN. HE...WELL, HE WAS WORKING WHEN-- ONE DAY...
SOMETHING BAD HAPPENED.
AND I GUESS SEEING YOU IN THIS BROUGHT UP BAD MEMORIES.
BUT THAT'S NOT AN *EXCUSE.* IT'S JUST SOME-TIMES, BEING SCARED...
...
KRIS, DOES AISHA EVER TALK TO YOU ABOUT...
I DON'T KNOW, GOD OR--OR *ALLAH* OR--
AISHA SAYS I HAVETA WAIT 'TIL I'M OLDER TO SEE IF I WANNA PRAY.
I DUNNO WHY.
ISN'T PRAYIN' JUST SAYING THANKS FOR WHAT YOU'VE GOT?
SINCE WE HAVE LOTS OF STUFF NOW, CAN'T I SAY *THANKS* NOW?
I...I SUPPOSE...
WE, AH... WE SHOULD GET READY FOR DINNER...
YEAH...
I DON'T KNOW ABOUT YOU GUYS, BUT I'M *STARVING.*

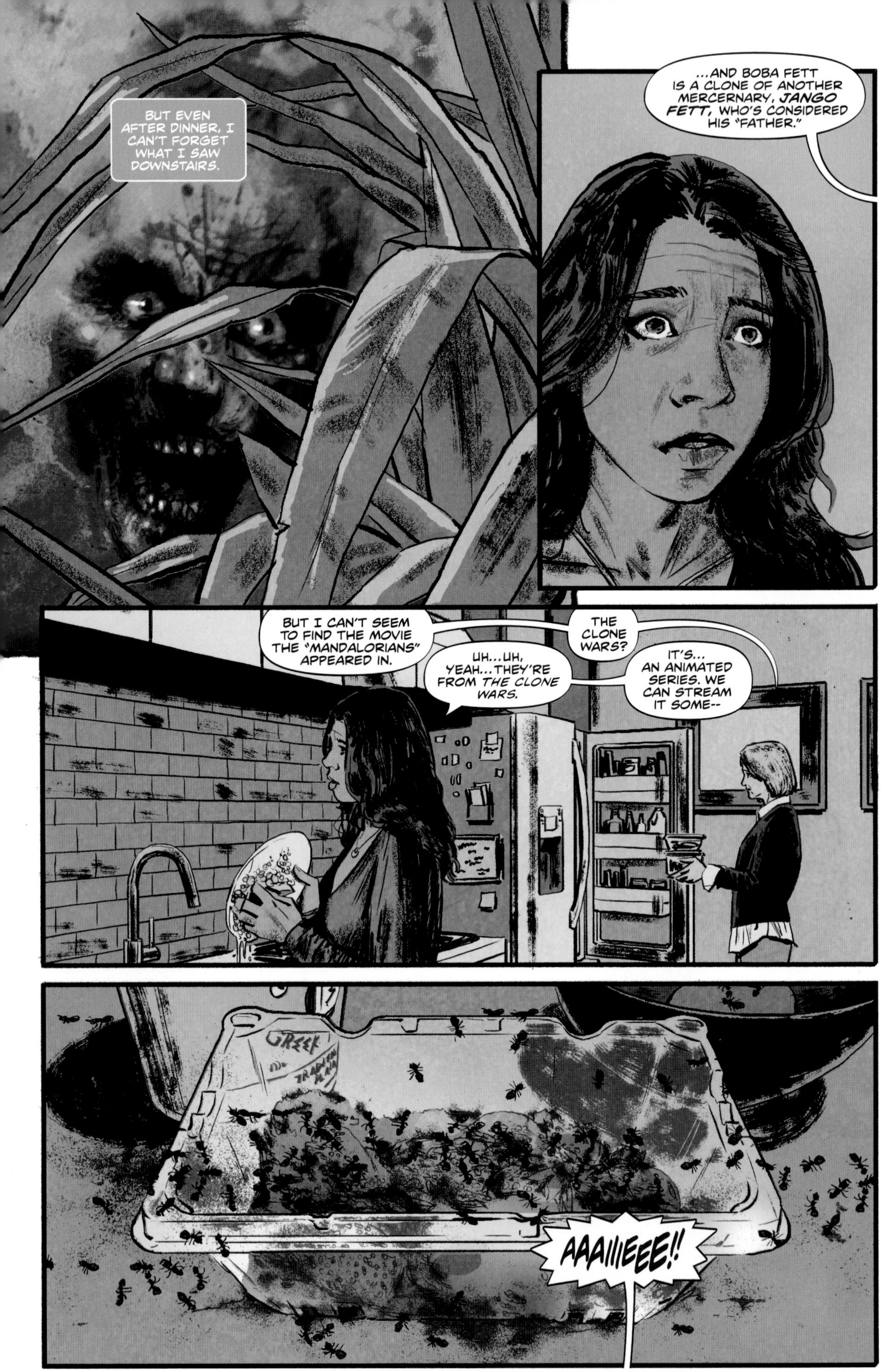
BUT EVEN AFTER DINNER, I CAN'T FORGET WHAT I SAW DOWNSTAIRS.
...AND BOBA FETT IS A CLONE OF ANOTHER MERCENARY, *JANGO FETT*, WHO'S CONSIDERED HIS "FATHER."
BUT I CAN'T SEEM TO FIND THE MOVIE THE "MANDALORIANS" APPEARED IN.
UH...UH, YEAH...THEY'RE FROM *THE CLONE WARS*.
THE CLONE WARS?
IT'S... AN ANIMATED SERIES. WE CAN STREAM IT SOME--
GREEK
AAAIIIEEE!!

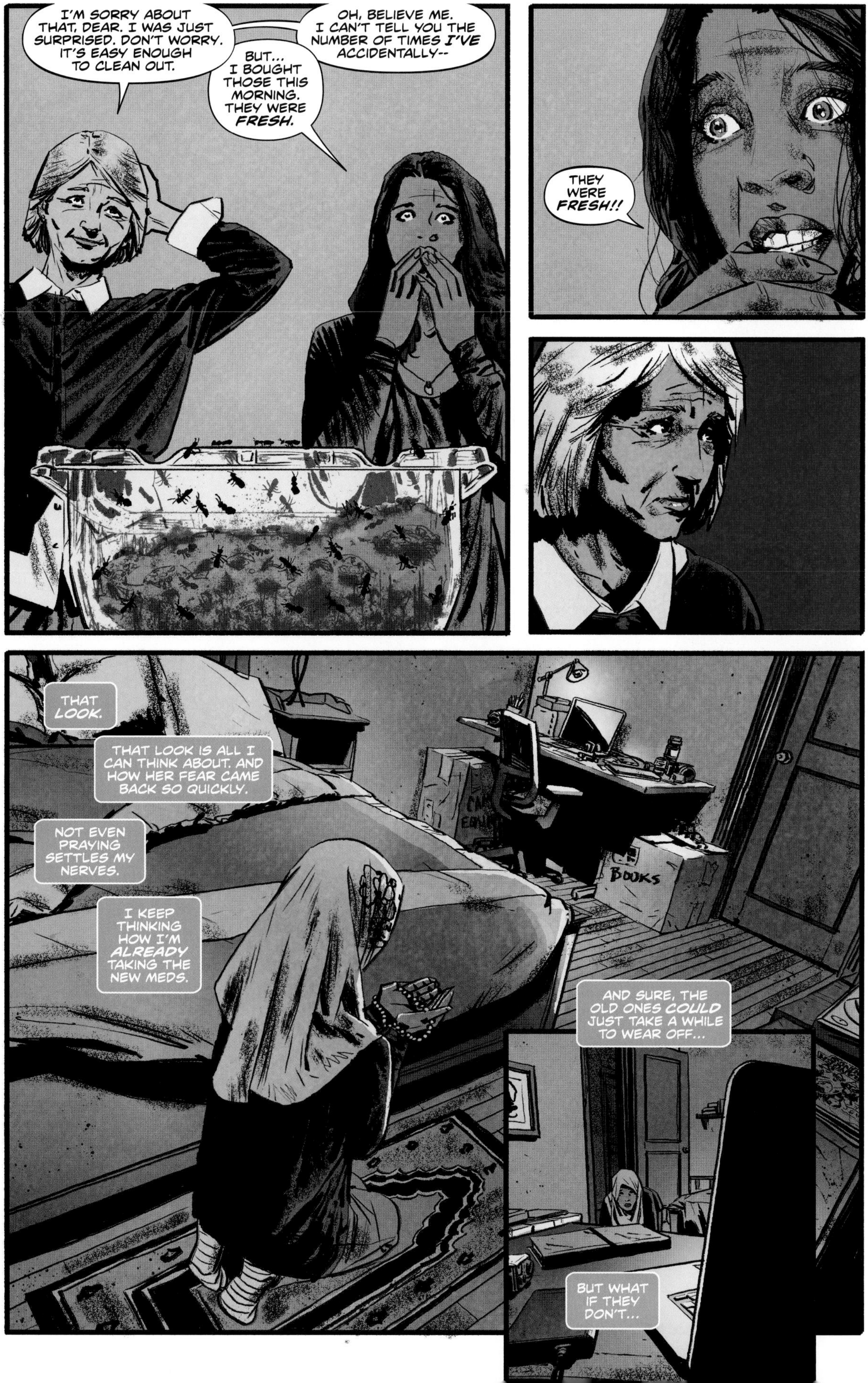
I'M SORRY ABOUT THAT, DEAR. I WAS JUST SURPRISED. DON'T WORRY. IT'S EASY ENOUGH TO CLEAN OUT.
BUT... I BOUGHT THOSE THIS MORNING. THEY WERE FRESH.
OH, BELIEVE ME. I CAN'T TELL YOU THE NUMBER OF TIMES I'VE ACCIDENTALLY--
THEY WERE FRESH!!
THAT LOOK.
THAT LOOK IS ALL I CAN THINK ABOUT. AND HOW HER FEAR CAME BACK SO QUICKLY.
NOT EVEN PRAYING SETTLES MY NERVES.
I KEEP THINKING HOW I'M ALREADY TAKING THE NEW MEDS.
BOOKS
AND SURE, THE OLD ONES COULD JUST TAKE A WHILE TO WEAR OFF...
BUT WHAT IF THEY DON'T...

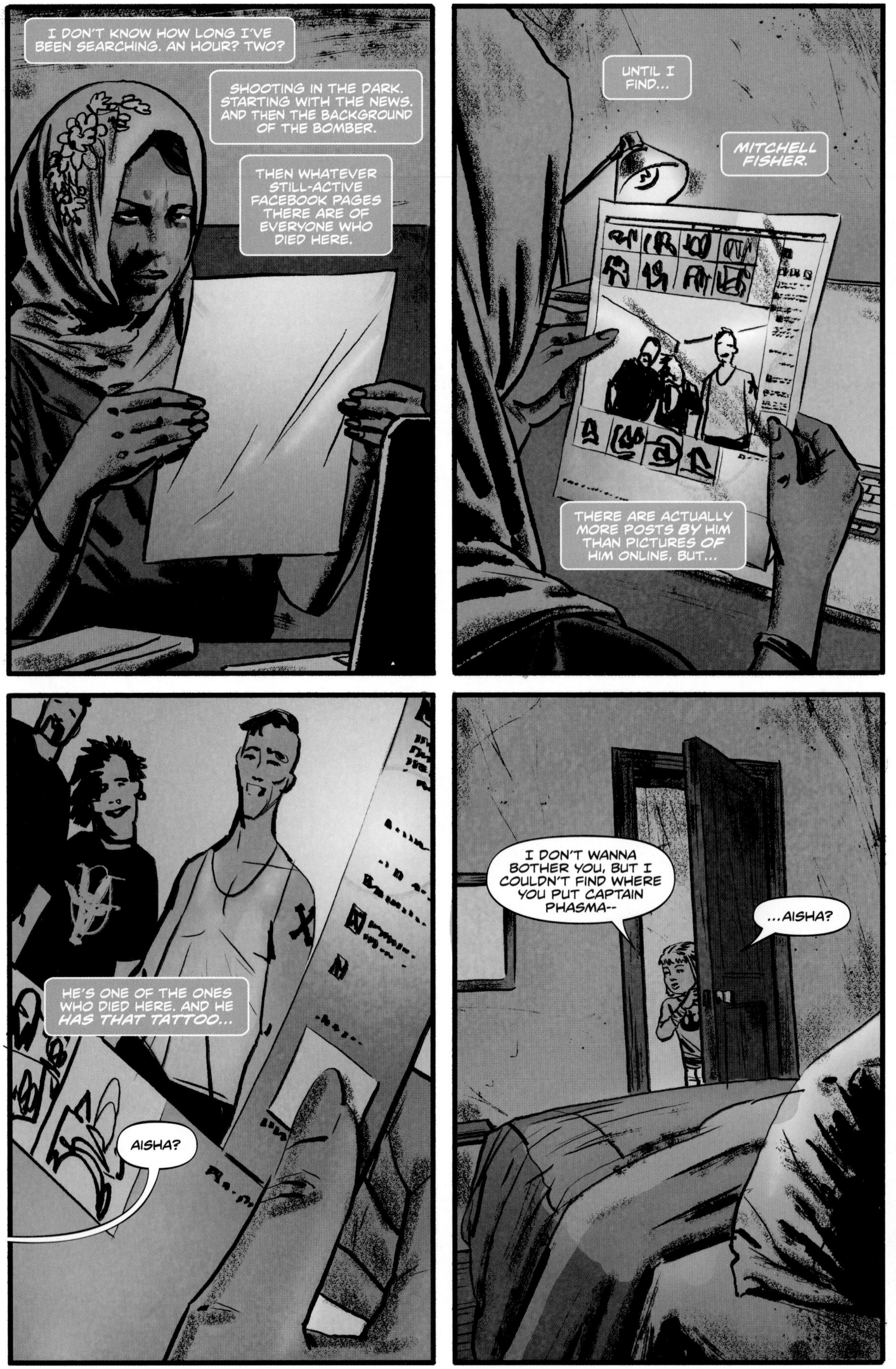
I DON'T KNOW HOW LONG I'VE BEEN SEARCHING. AN HOUR? TWO?
SHOOTING IN THE DARK. STARTING WITH THE NEWS. AND THEN THE BACKGROUND OF THE BOMBER.
THEN WHATEVER STILL-ACTIVE FACEBOOK PAGES THERE ARE OF EVERYONE WHO DIED HERE.
UNTIL I FIND...
MITCHELL FISHER.
THERE ARE ACTUALLY MORE POSTS BY HIM THAN PICTURES OF HIM ONLINE, BUT...
HE'S ONE OF THE ONES WHO DIED HERE. AND HE HAS THAT TATTOO...
AISHA?
I DON'T WANNA BOTHER YOU, BUT I COULDN'T FIND WHERE YOU PUT CAPTAIN PHASMA--
...AISHA?

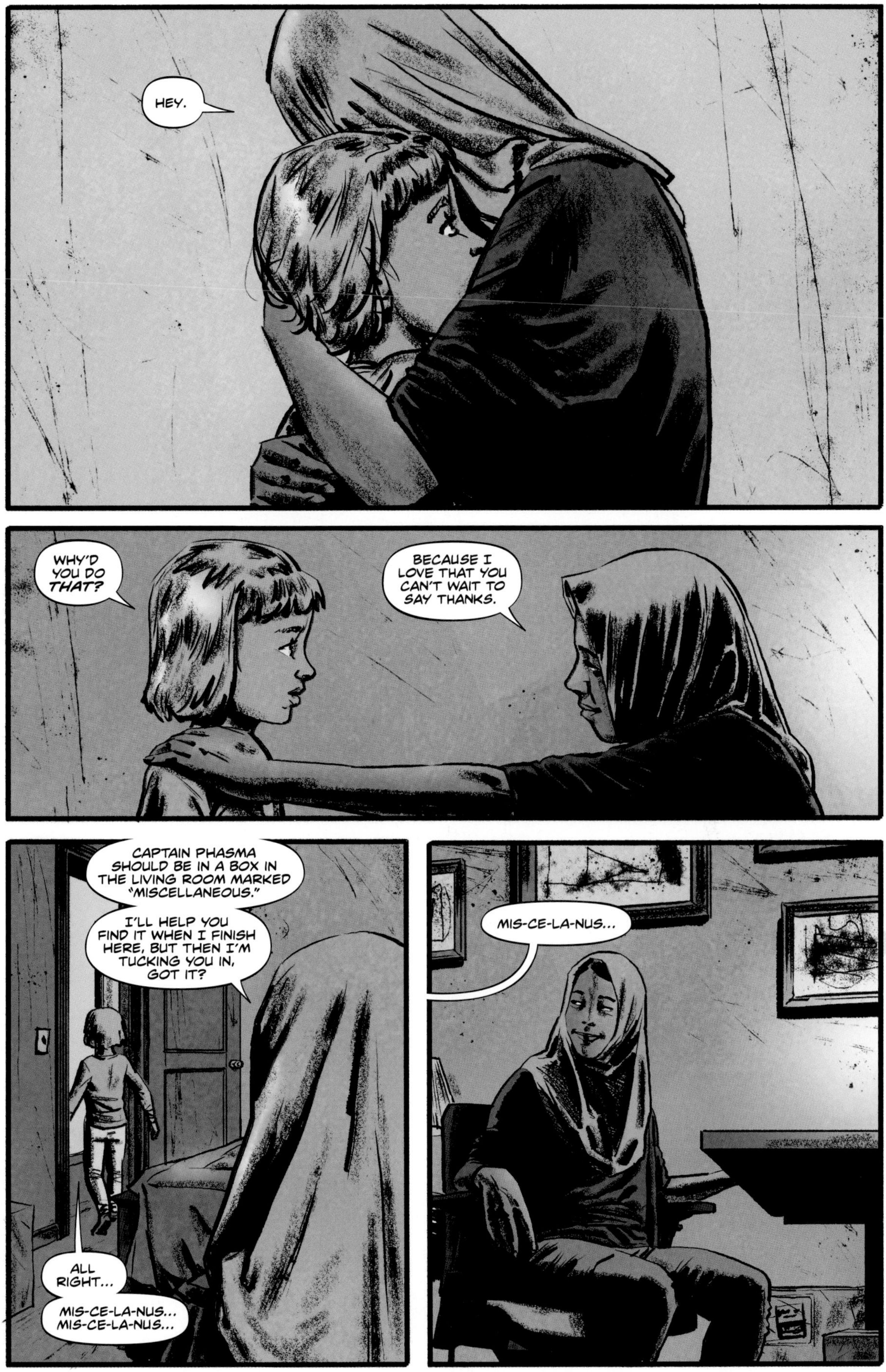
HEY.
WHY'D YOU DO *THAT*?
BECAUSE I LOVE THAT YOU CAN'T WAIT TO SAY THANKS.
CAPTAIN PHASMA SHOULD BE IN A BOX IN THE LIVING ROOM MARKED "MISCELLANEOUS."
I'LL HELP YOU FIND IT WHEN I FINISH HERE, BUT THEN I'M TUCKING YOU IN, GOT IT?
ALL RIGHT...
MIS-CE-LA-NUS... MIS-CE-LA-NUS...
MIS-CE-LA-NUS...

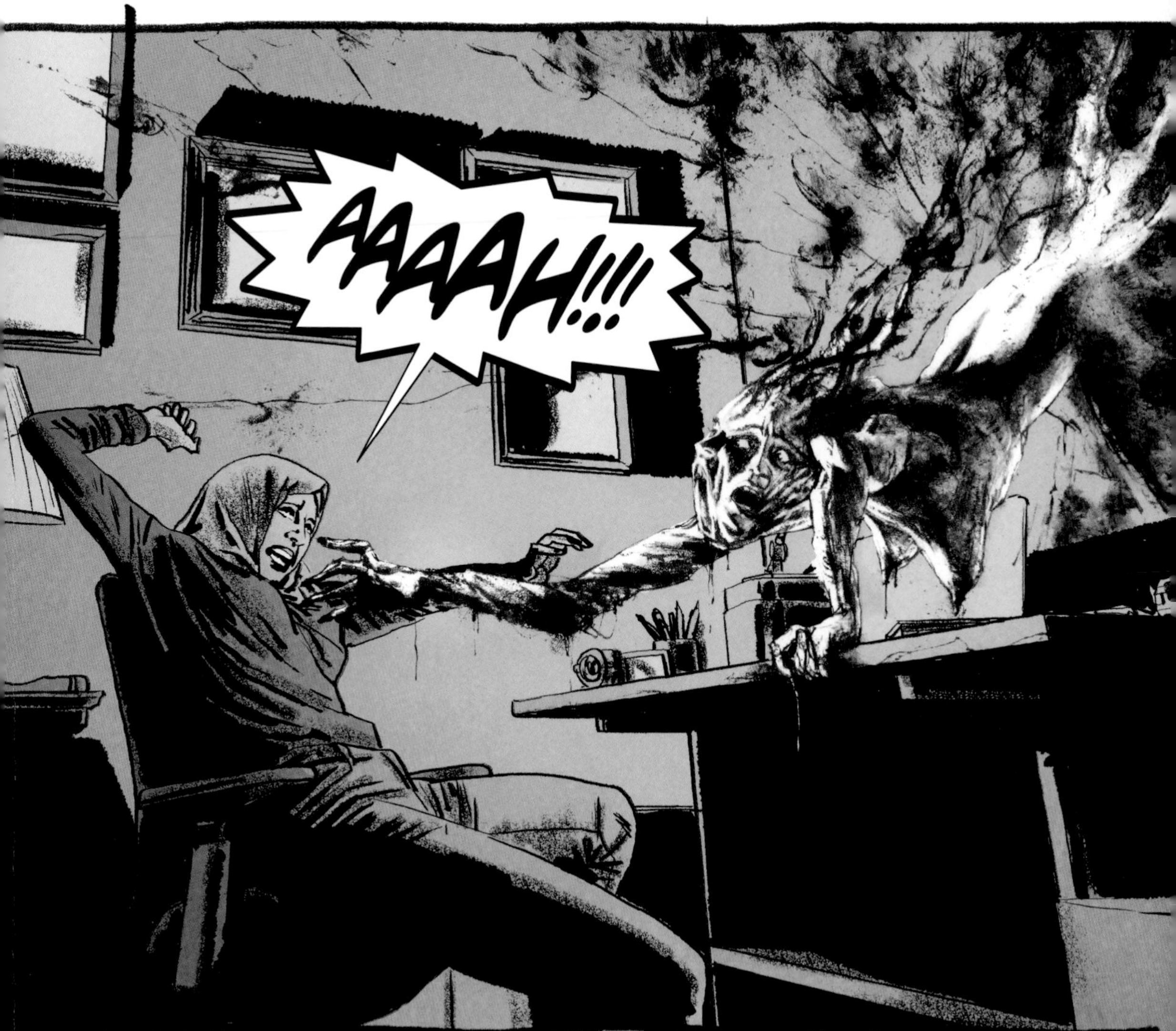
AAAAAH!!!

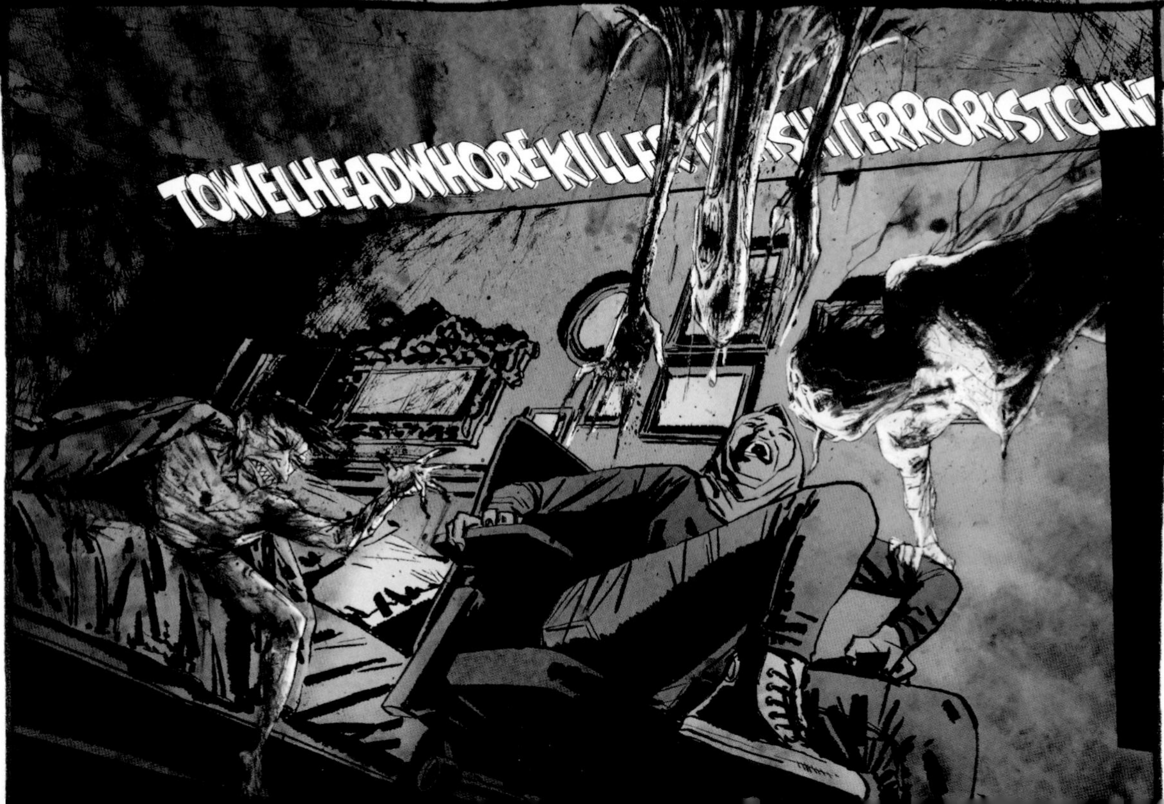
TOWELHEADWHOREKILL
TERRORISTCUNT

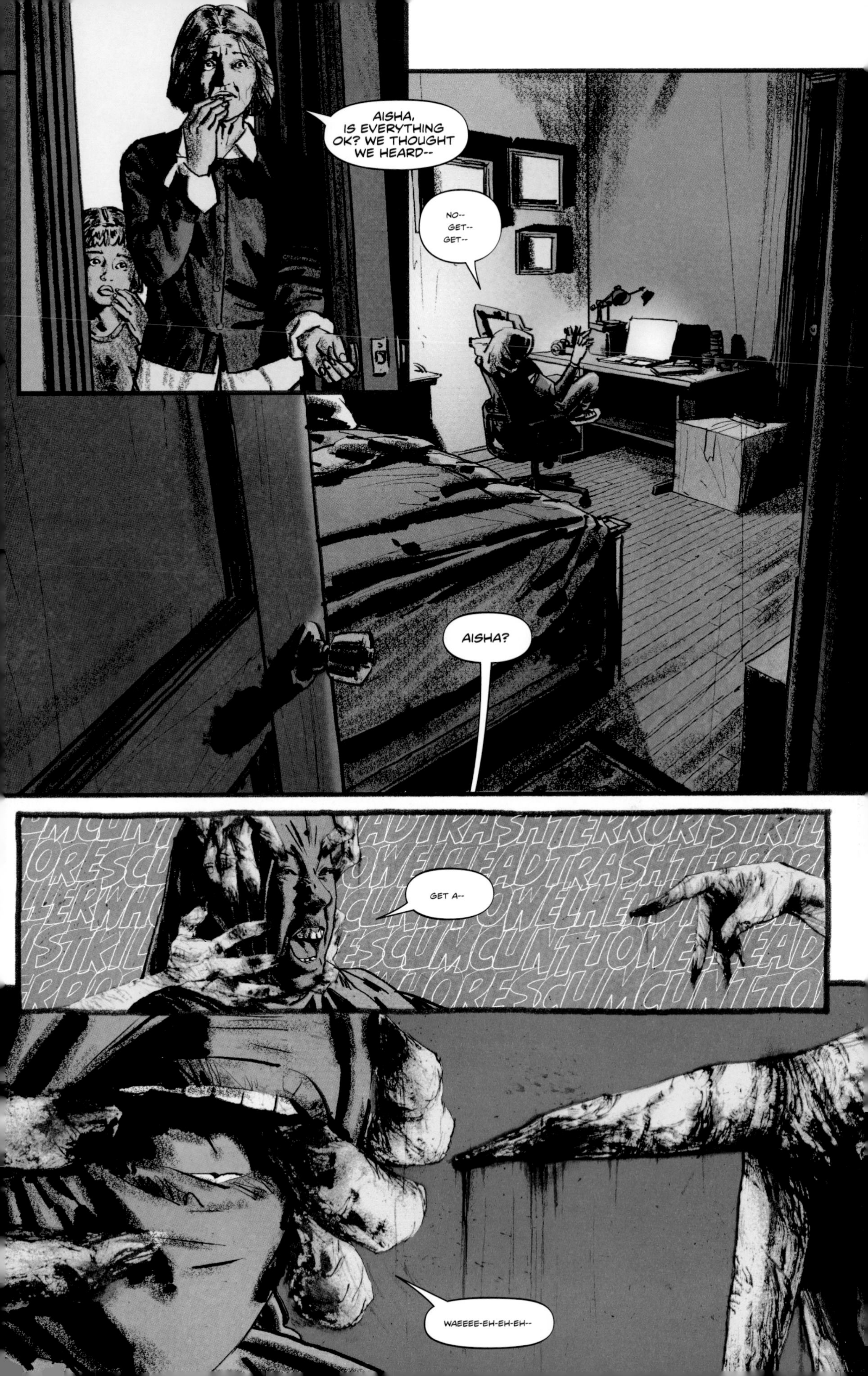
AISHA, IS EVERYTHING OK? WE THOUGHT WE HEARD--
NO-- GET-- GET--
AISHA?
GET A--
WAEEEE-EH-EH-EH--

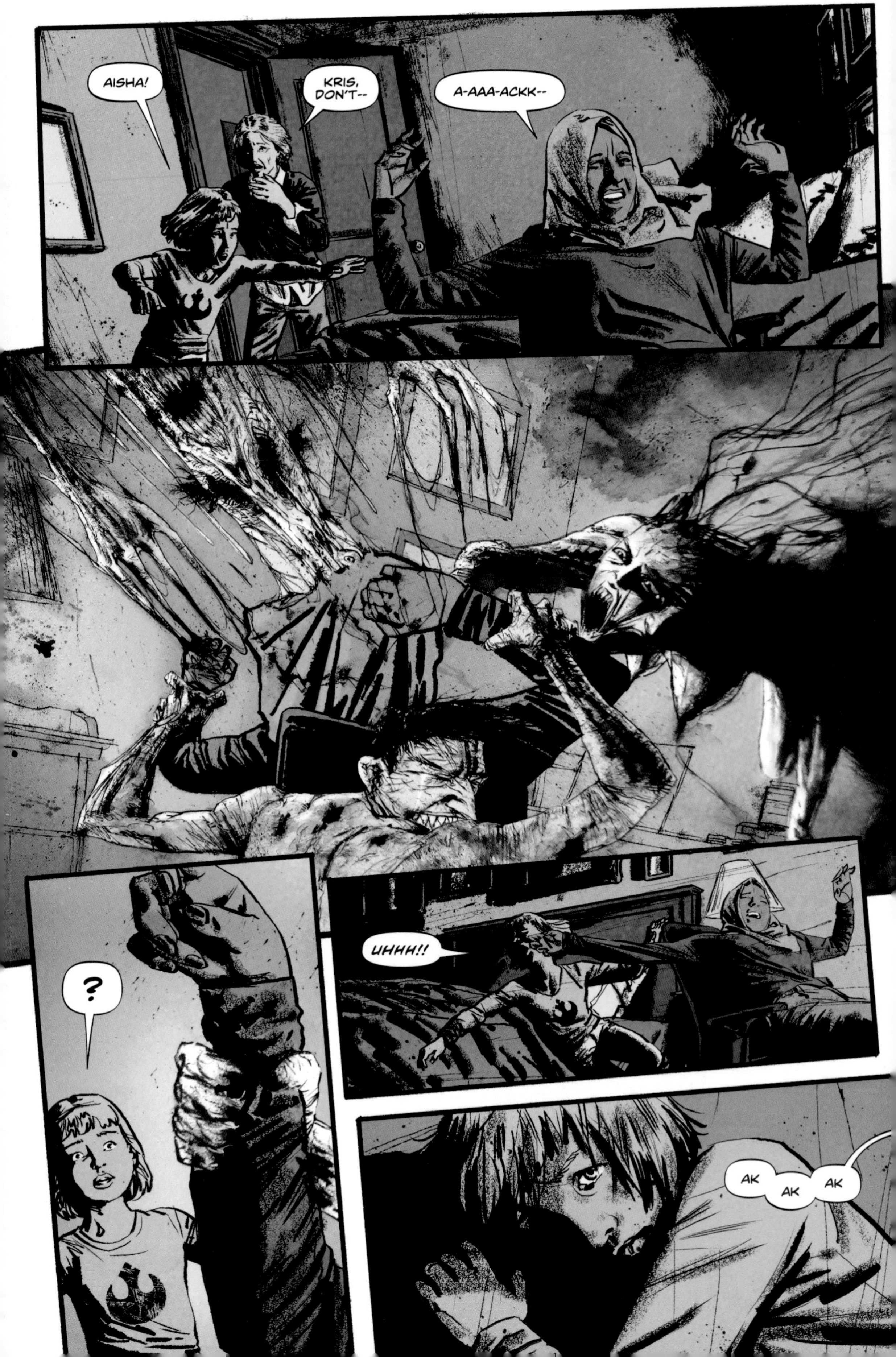
AISHA!
KRIS, DON'T--
A-AAA-ACKK--
?
UHHH!!
AK
AK
AK

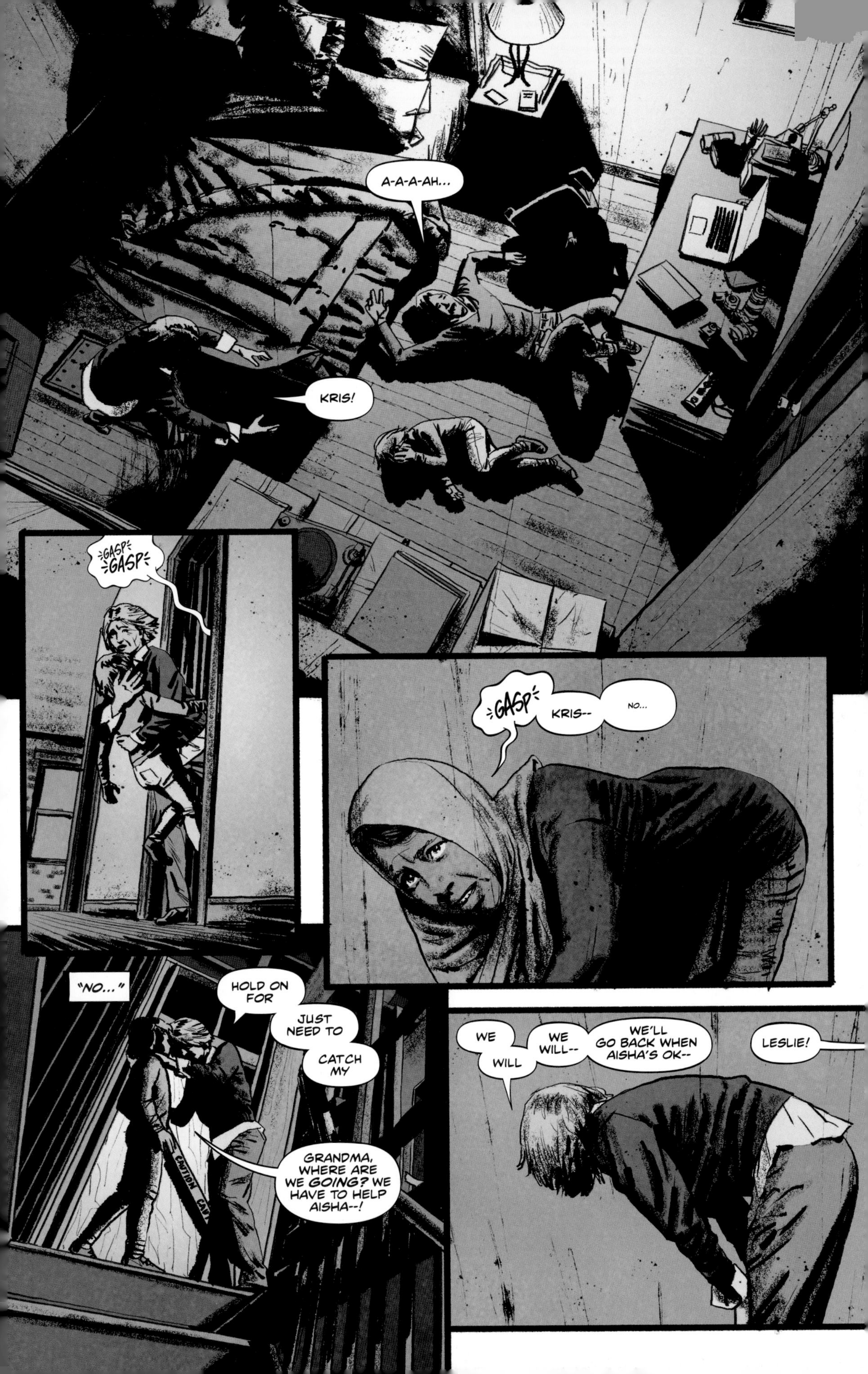
A-A-A-AH...
KRIS!
GASP GASP
GASP
KRIS--
NO...
"NO..."
HOLD ON FOR
JUST NEED TO
CATCH MY
GRANDMA, WHERE ARE WE GOING? WE HAVE TO HELP AISHA--!
WE
WILL
WE WILL--
WE'LL GO BACK WHEN AISHA'S OK--
LESLIE!

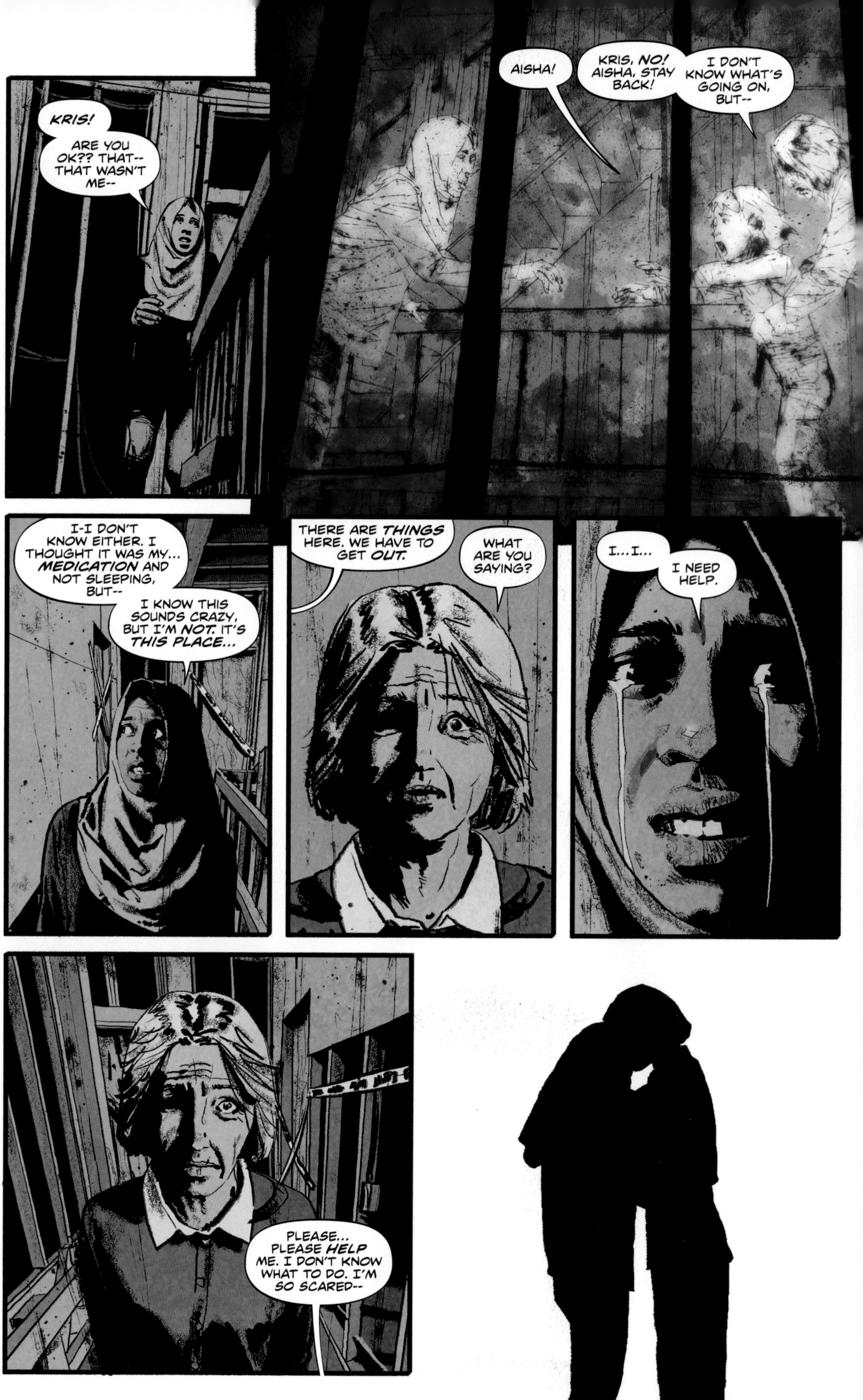
KRIS!
ARE YOU OK?? THAT-- THAT WASN'T ME--
AISHA!
KRIS, NO! AISHA, STAY BACK!
I DON'T KNOW WHAT'S GOING ON, BUT--
I-I DON'T KNOW EITHER. I THOUGHT IT WAS MY... MEDICATION AND NOT SLEEPING, BUT--
I KNOW THIS SOUNDS CRAZY, BUT I'M NOT. IT'S THIS PLACE...
THERE ARE THINGS HERE. WE HAVE TO GET OUT.
WHAT ARE YOU SAYING?
I...I...
I NEED HELP.
PLEASE... PLEASE HELP ME. I DON'T KNOW WHAT TO DO. I'M SO SCARED--

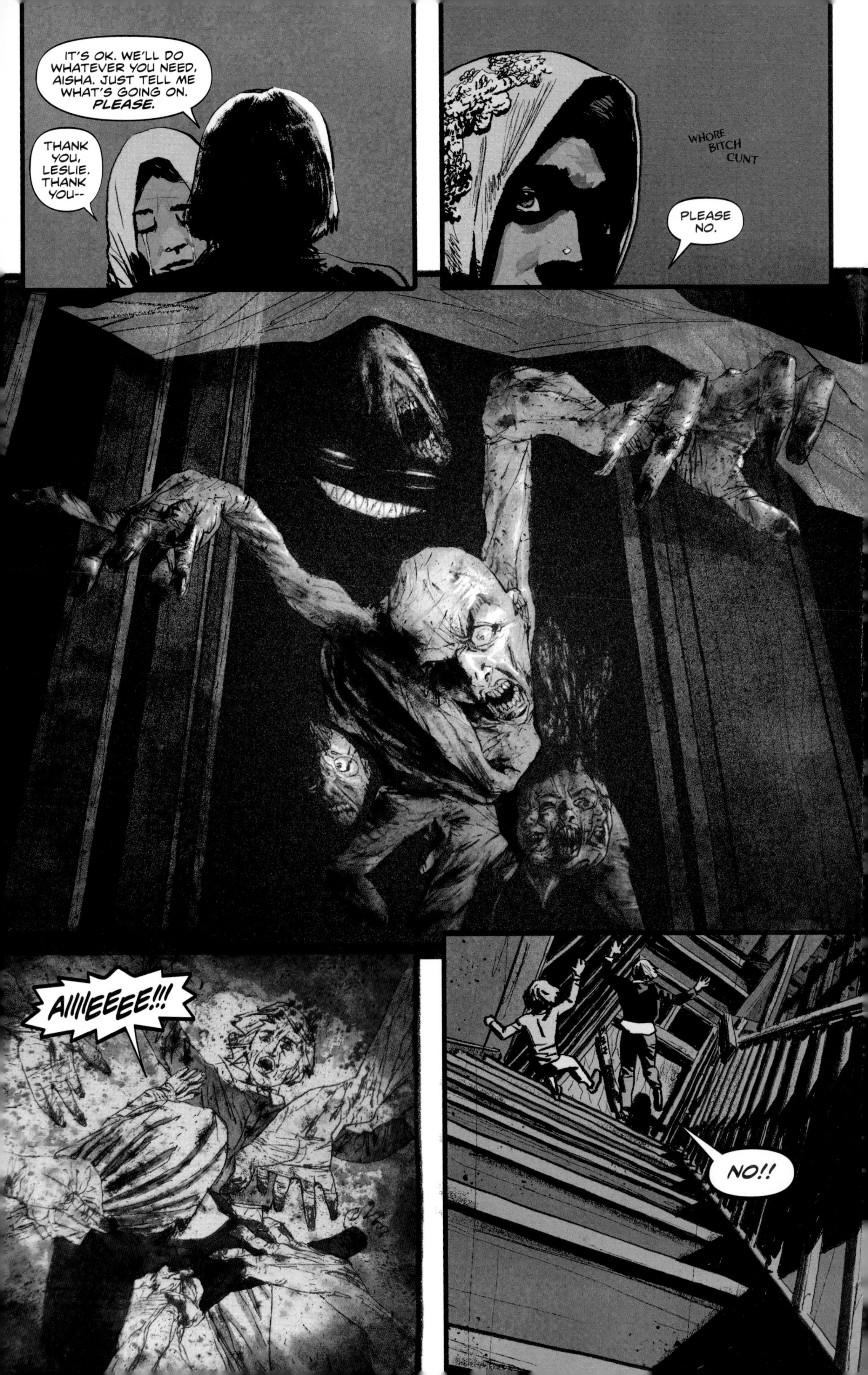
IT'S OK. WE'LL DO WHATEVER YOU NEED, AISHA. JUST TELL ME WHAT'S GOING ON. PLEASE.
THANK YOU, LESLIE. THANK YOU--
WHORE BITCH CUNT
PLEASE NO.
AIIIEEEEE!!!
NO!!

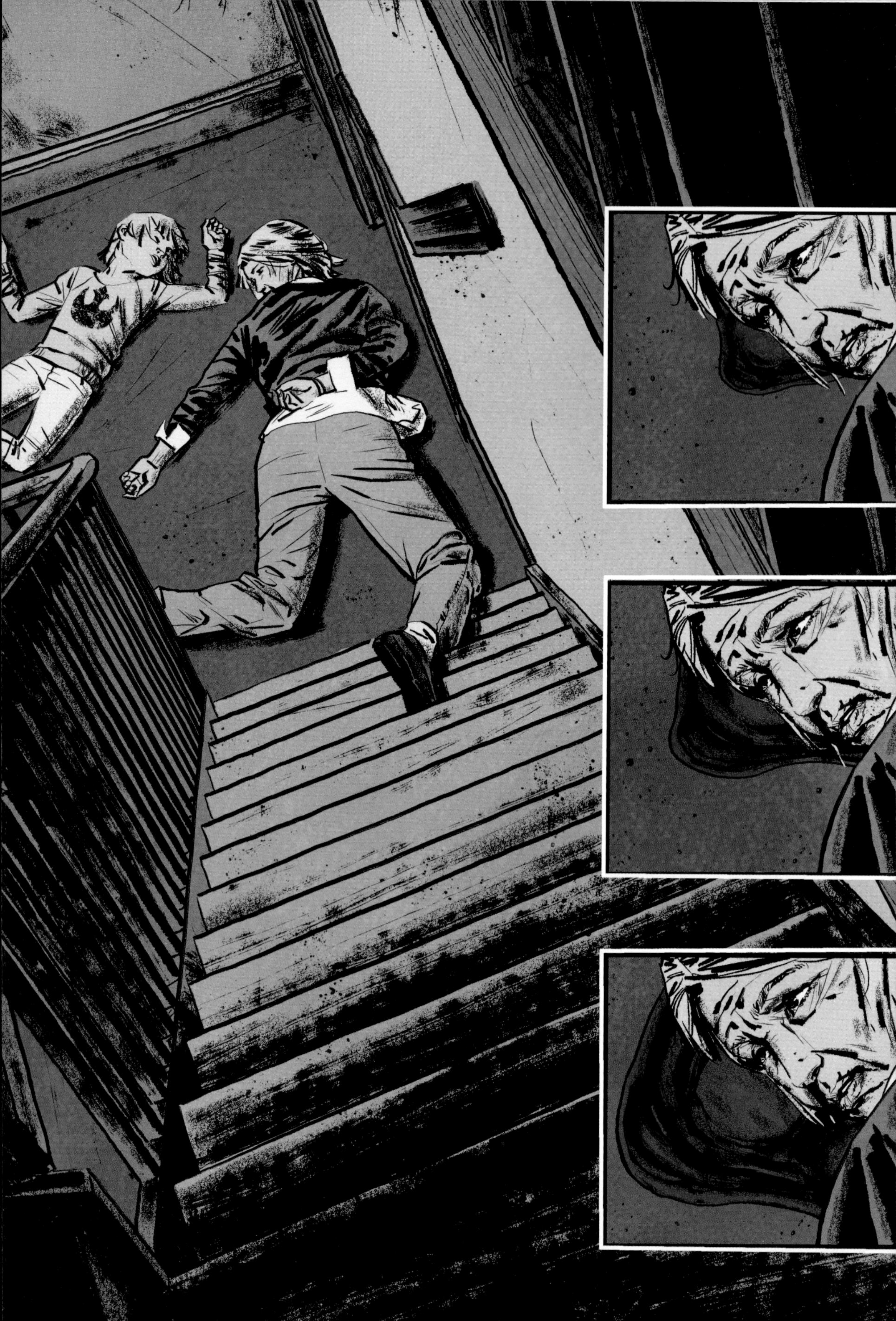

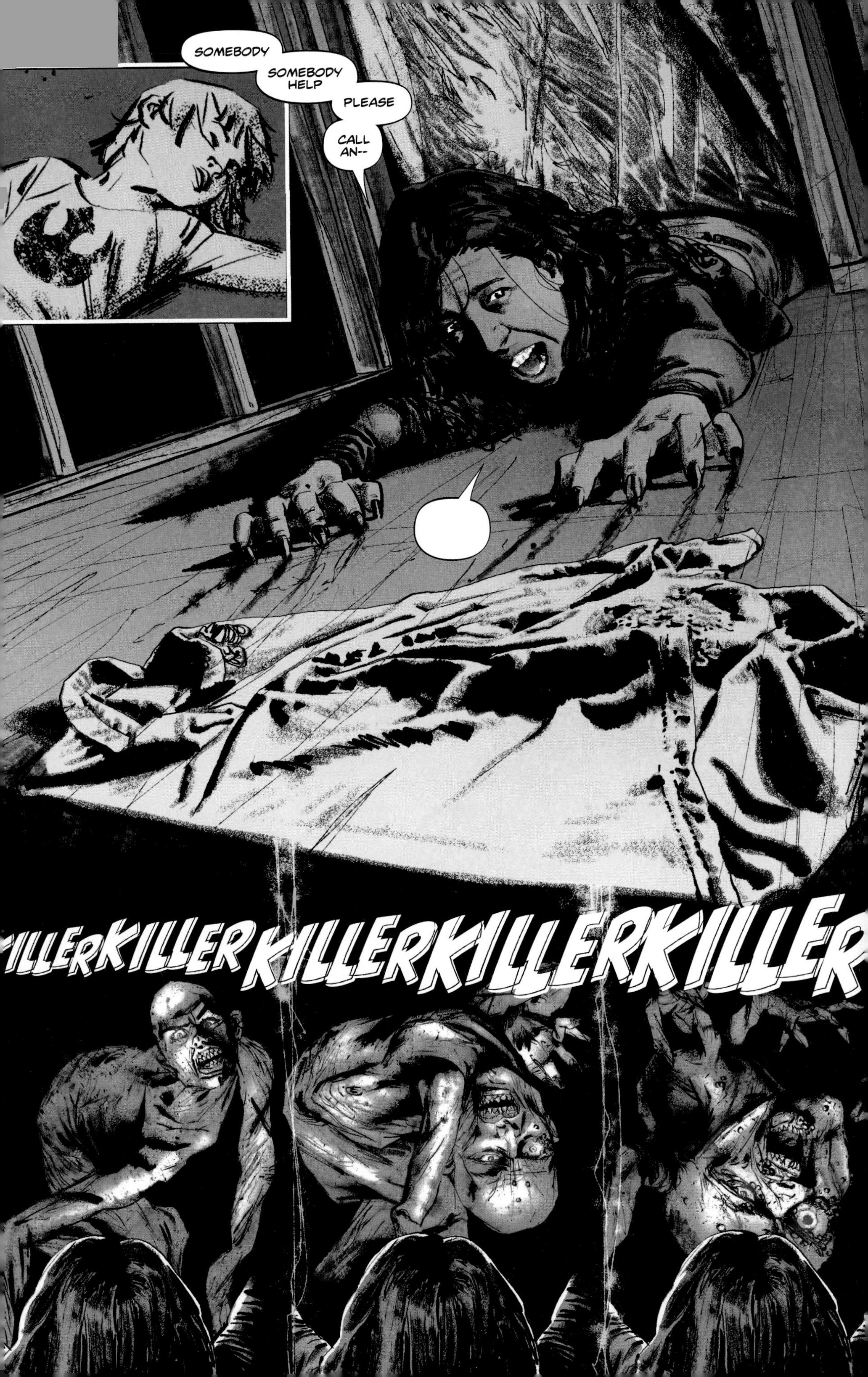
SOMEBODY
SOMEBODY HELP
PLEASE
CALL AN--
ILLERKILLERKILLERKILLERKILLER

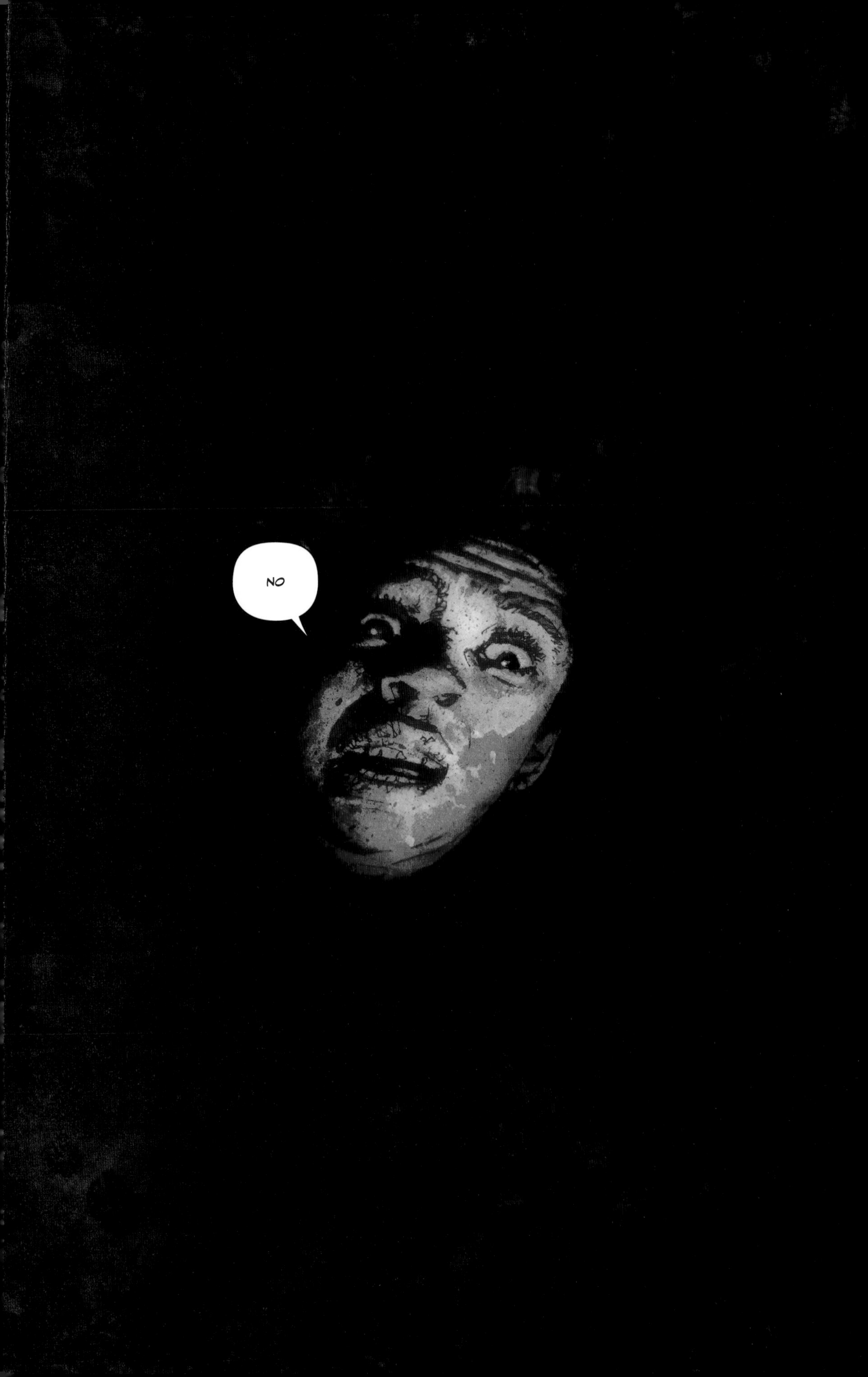
NO

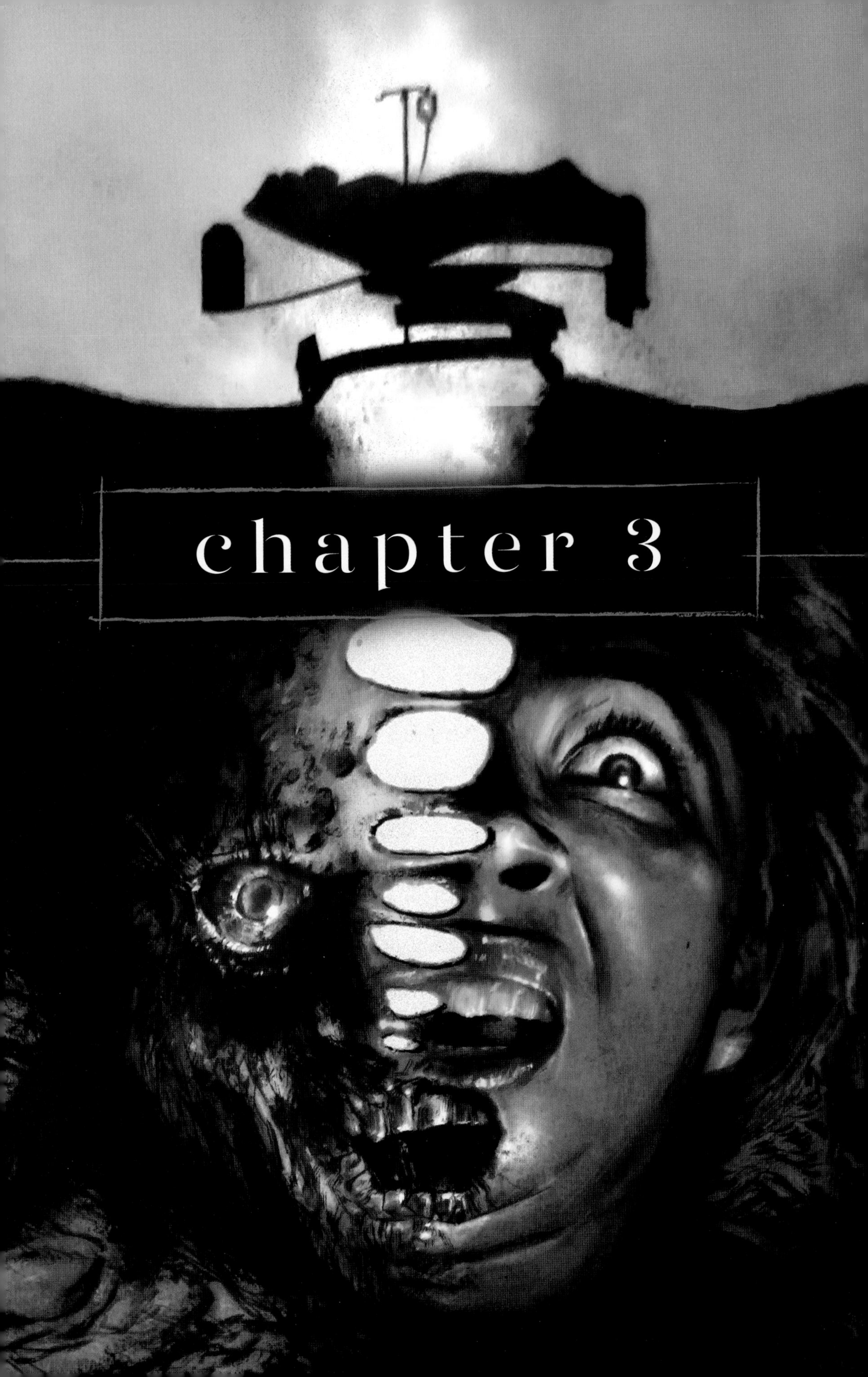
chapter 3

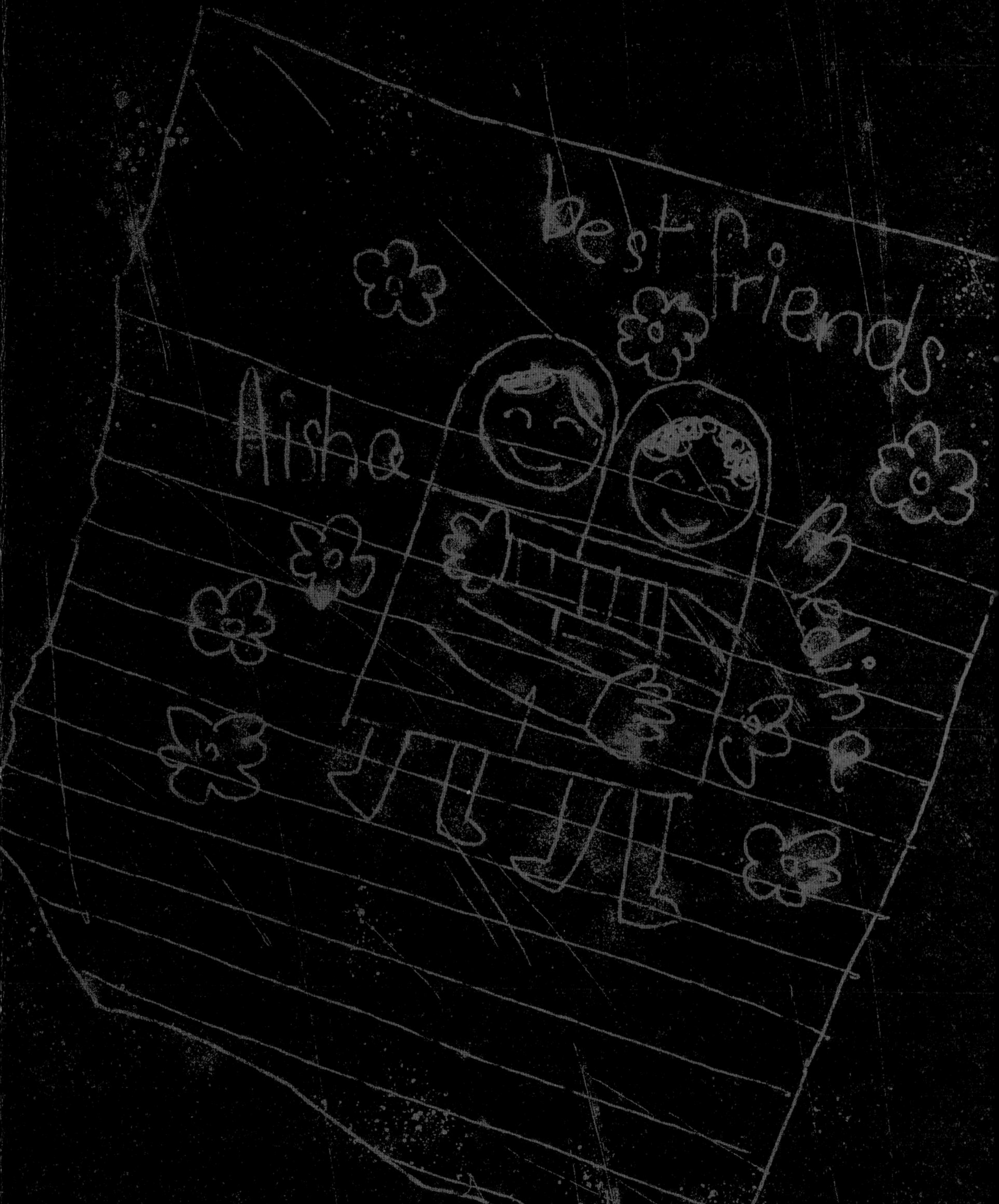
best friends
Aisha

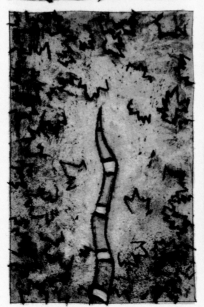

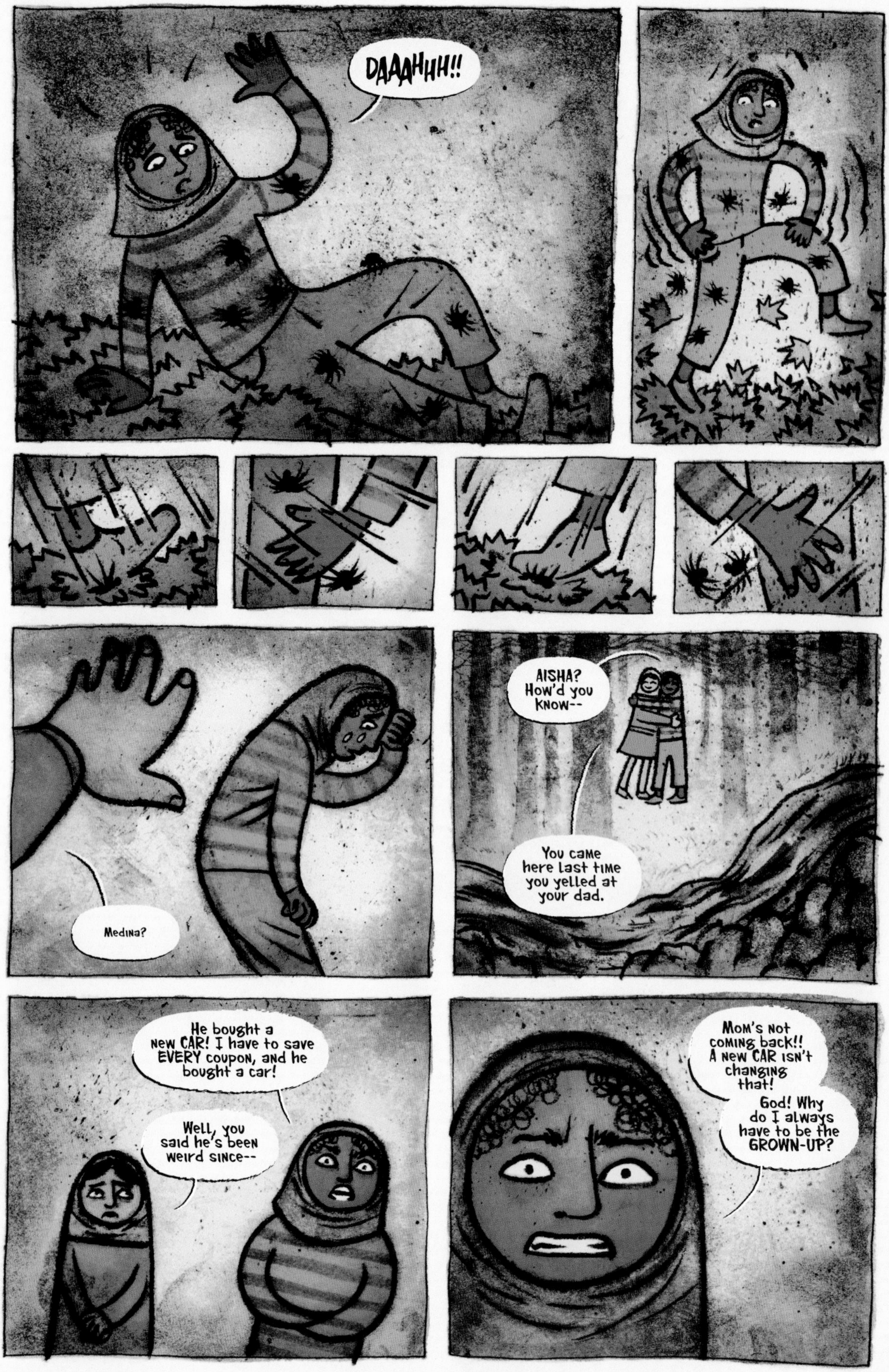
DAAAHHH!!
Medina?
AISHA? How'd you know--
You came here last time you yelled at your dad.
He bought a new CAR! I have to save EVERY coupon, and he bought a car!
Well, you said he's been weird since--
Mom's not coming back!! A new CAR isn't changing that!
God! Why do I always have to be the GROWN-UP?

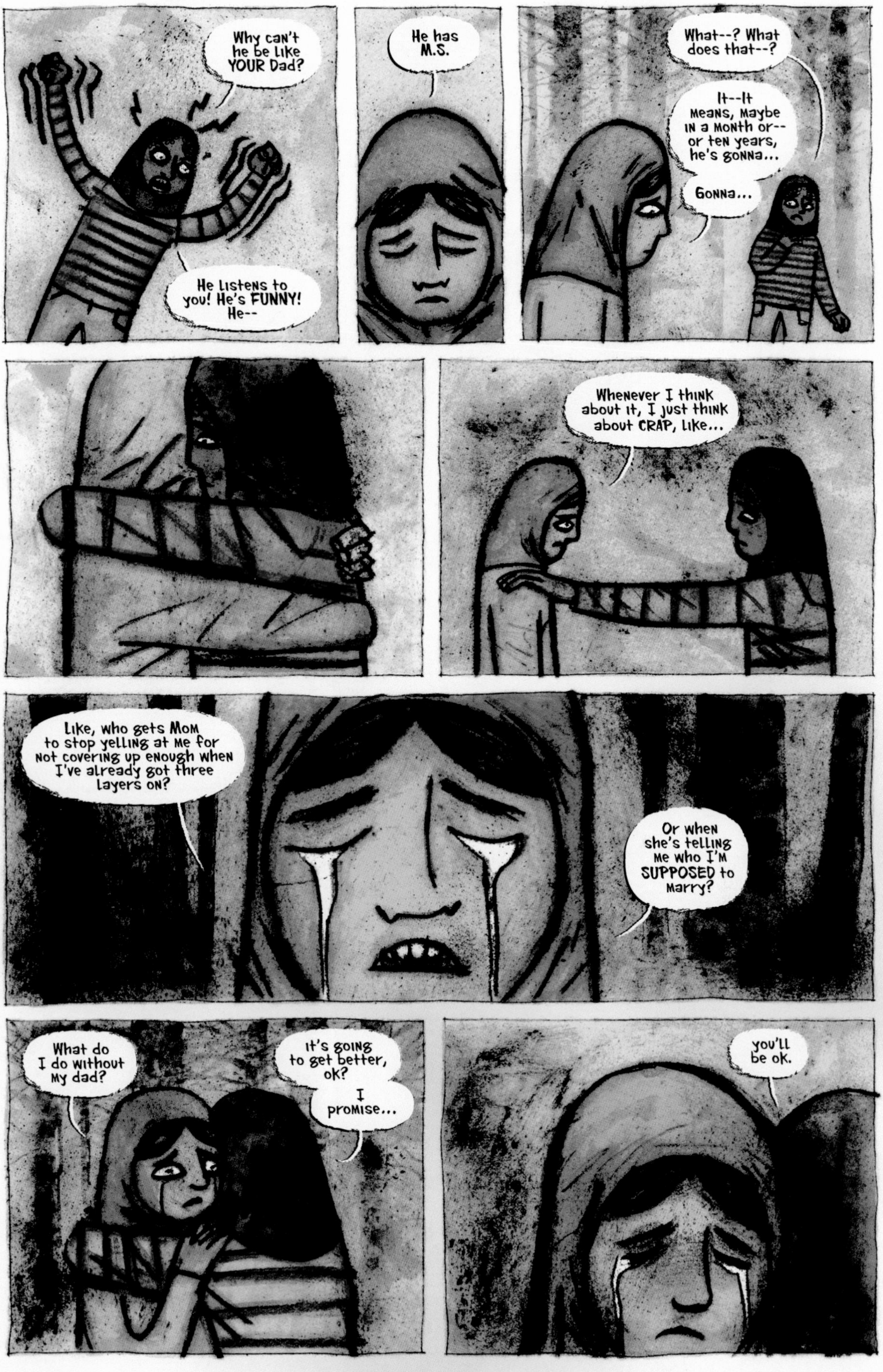
Why can't he be Like YOUR Dad?
He Listens to you! He's FUNNY! He--
He has M.S.
What--? What does that--?
It--It Means, Maybe in a Month or-- or ten years, he's gonna...
Gonna...
Whenever I think about it, I just think about CRAP, Like...
Like, who gets Mom to stop yelling at me for not covering up enough when I've already got three Layers on?
Or when she's telling me who I'M SUPPOSED to marry?
What do I do without my dad?
It's going to get better, ok?
I promise...
you'll be ok.

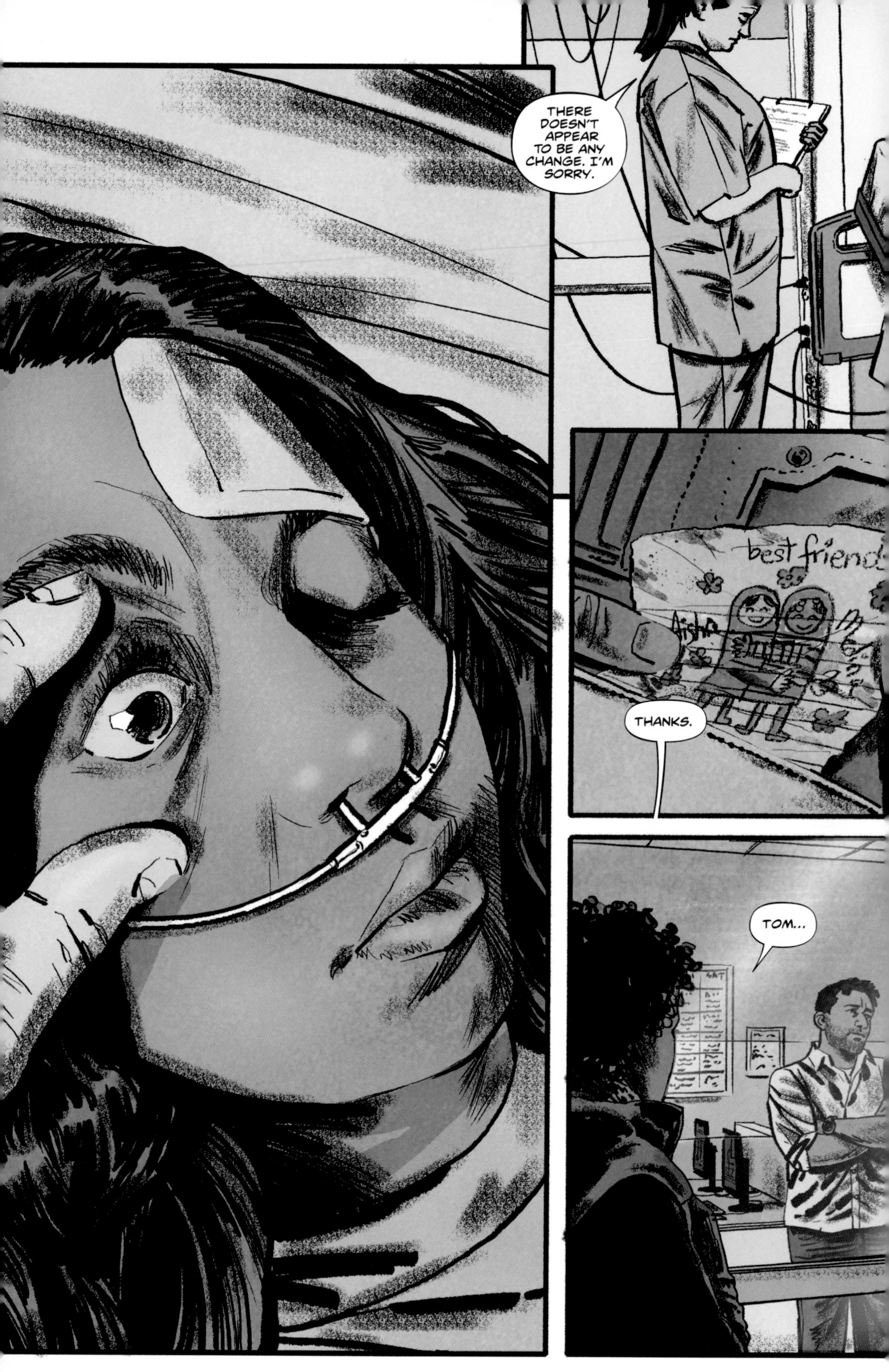
THERE DOESN'T APPEAR TO BE ANY CHANGE. I'M SORRY.
best friends
Aisha
THANKS.
TOM...

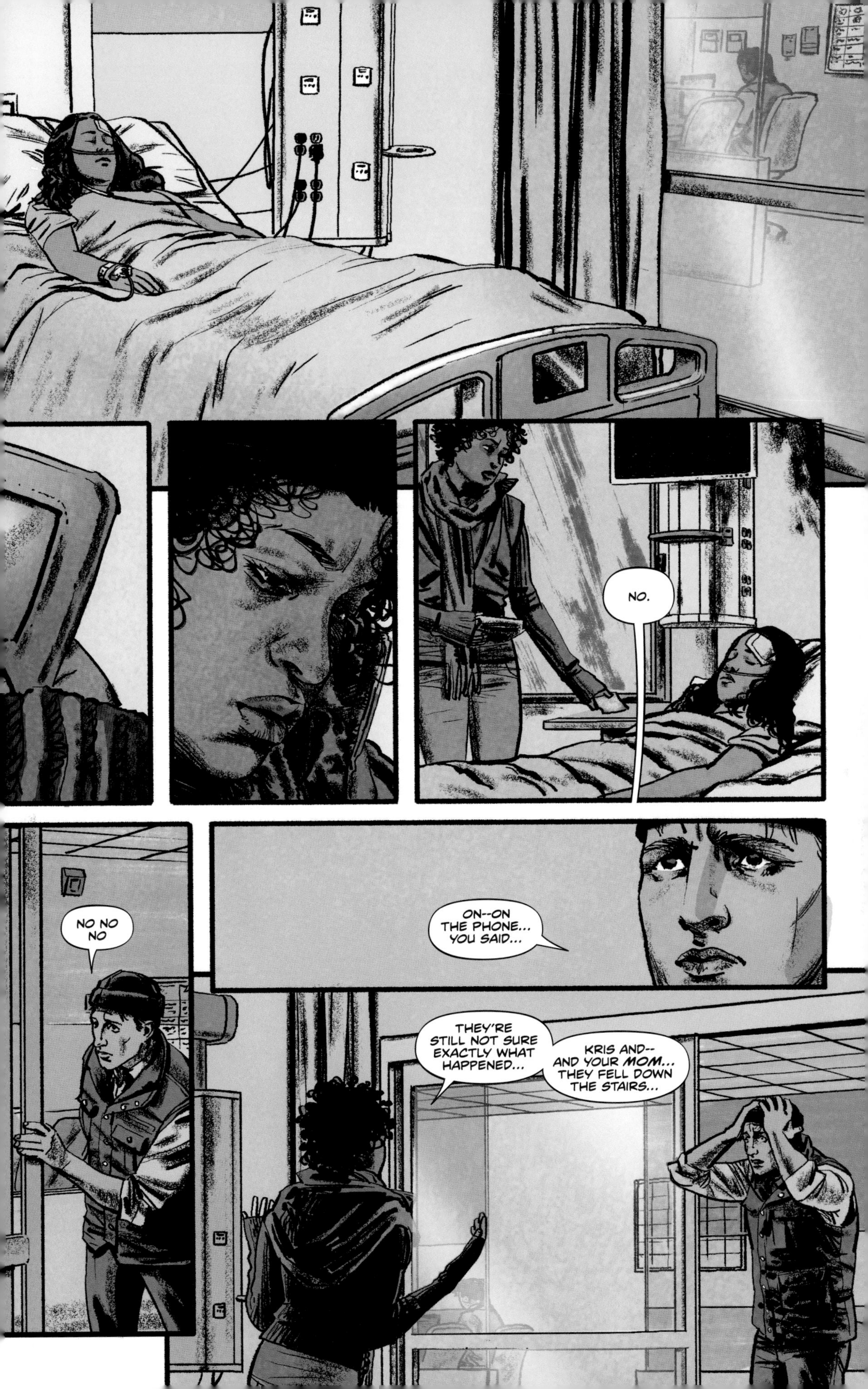
NO.
NO NO NO
ON--ON THE PHONE... YOU SAID...
THEY'RE STILL NOT SURE EXACTLY WHAT HAPPENED...
KRIS AND-- AND YOUR *MOM*... THEY FELL DOWN THE STAIRS...

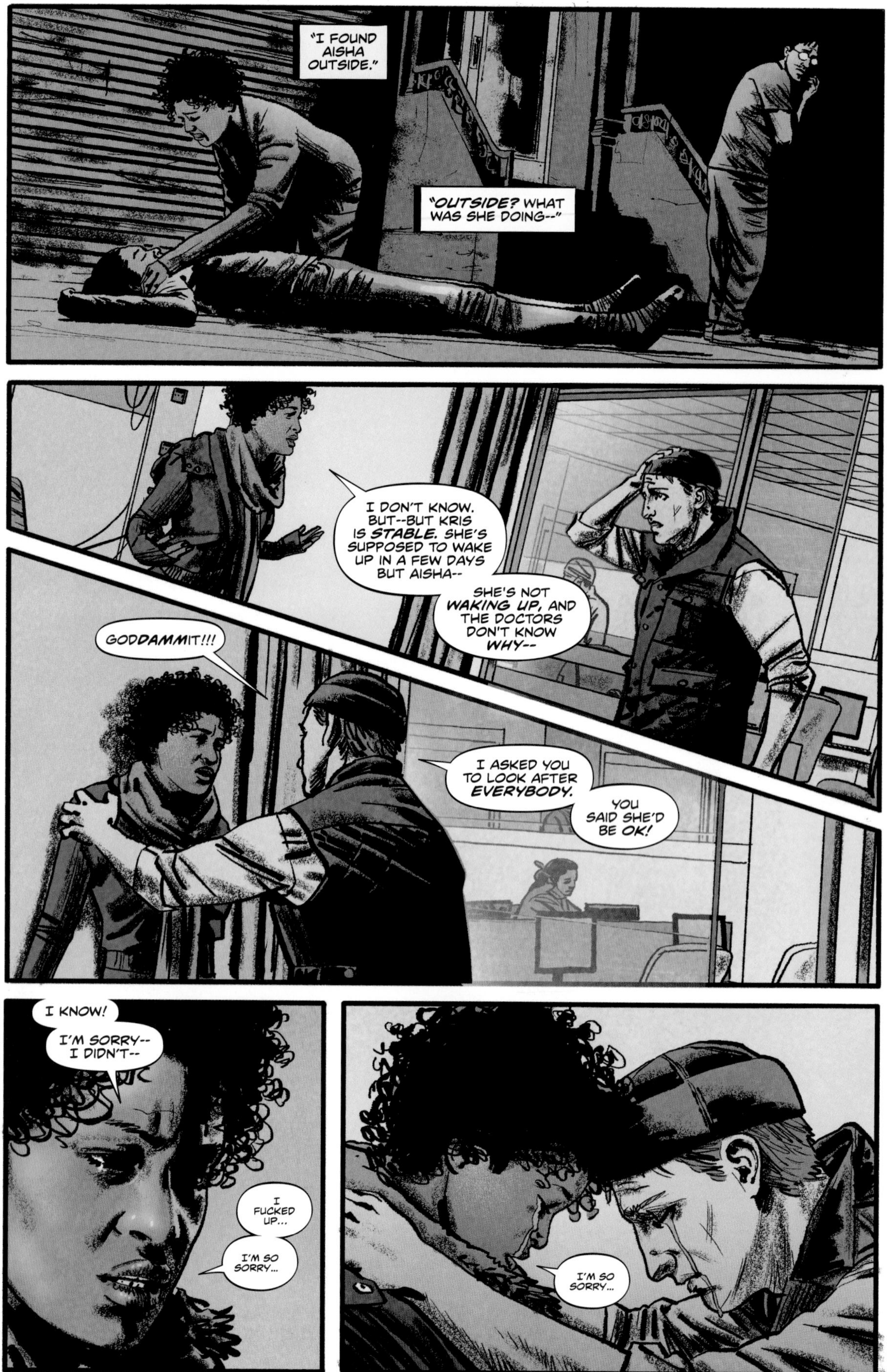
"I FOUND AISHA OUTSIDE."
"OUTSIDE? WHAT WAS SHE DOING--"
I DON'T KNOW. BUT--BUT KRIS IS STABLE. SHE'S SUPPOSED TO WAKE UP IN A FEW DAYS BUT AISHA--
SHE'S NOT WAKING UP, AND THE DOCTORS DON'T KNOW WHY--
GODDAMMIT!!!
I ASKED YOU TO LOOK AFTER EVERYBODY.
YOU SAID SHE'D BE OK!
I KNOW!
I'M SORRY-- I DIDN'T--
I FUCKED UP...
I'M SO SORRY...
I'M SO SORRY...

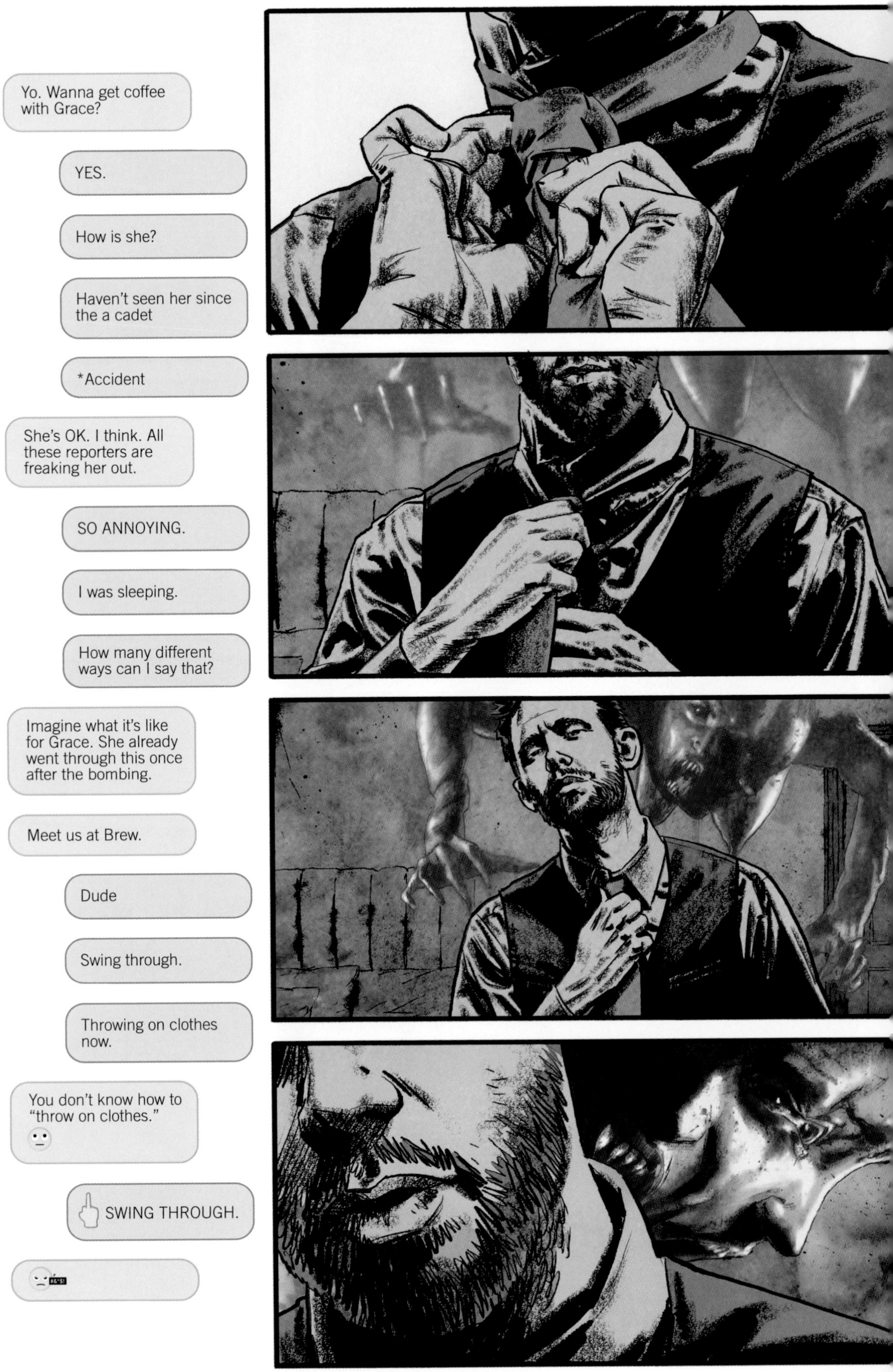
Yo. Wanna get coffee with Grace?
YES.
How is she?
Haven't seen her since the a cadet
*Accident
She's OK. I think. All these reporters are freaking her out.
SO ANNOYING.
I was sleeping.
How many different ways can I say that?
Imagine what it's like for Grace. She already went through this once after the bombing.
Meet us at Brew.
Dude
Swing through.
Throwing on clothes now.
You don't know how to "throw on clothes."
SWING THROUGH.

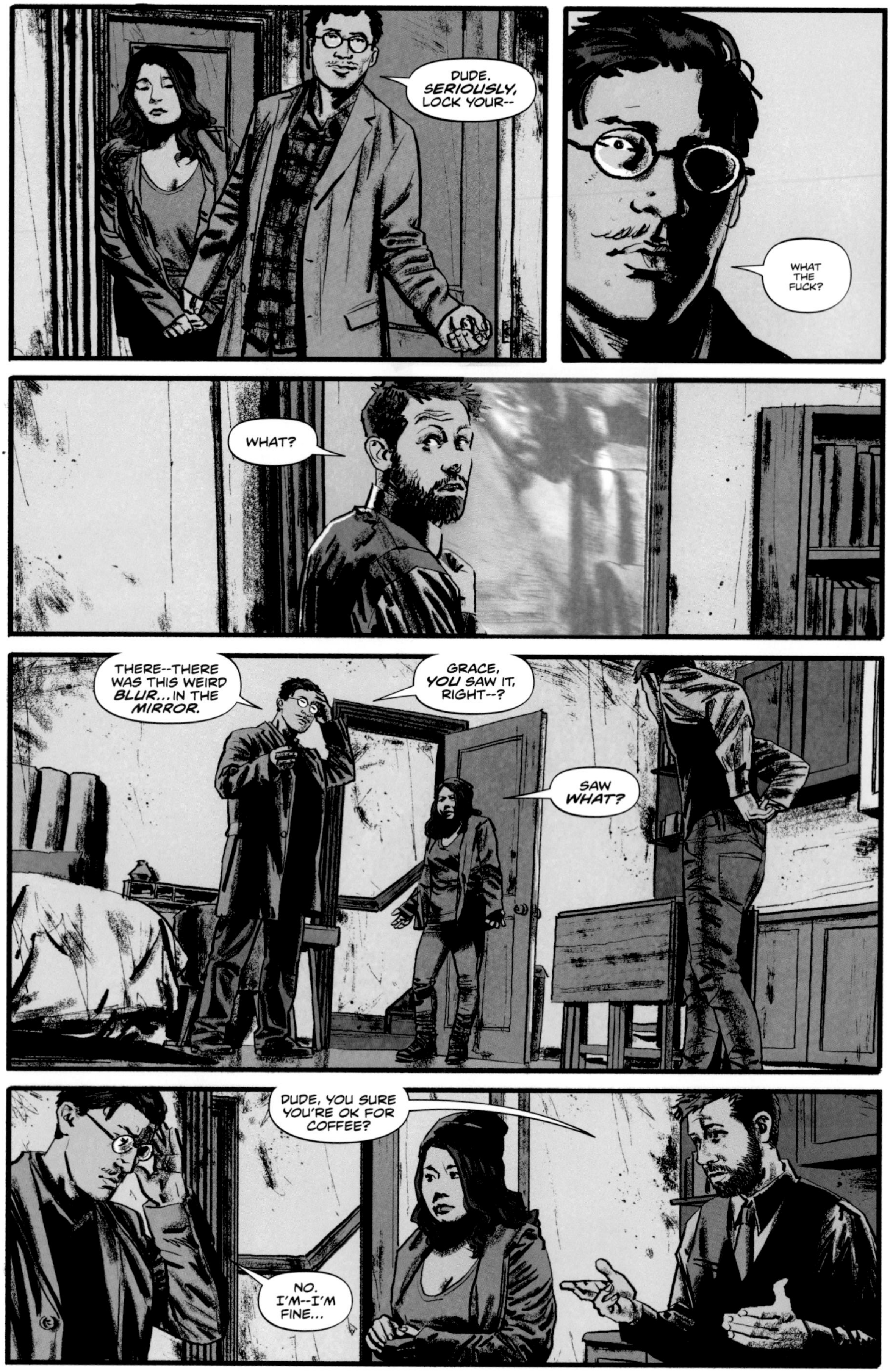
DUDE. SERIOUSLY, LOCK YOUR--
WHAT THE FUCK?
WHAT?
THERE--THERE WAS THIS WEIRD BLUR... IN THE MIRROR.
GRACE, YOU SAW IT, RIGHT--?
SAW WHAT?
DUDE, YOU SURE YOU'RE OK FOR COFFEE?
NO. I'M--I'M FINE...

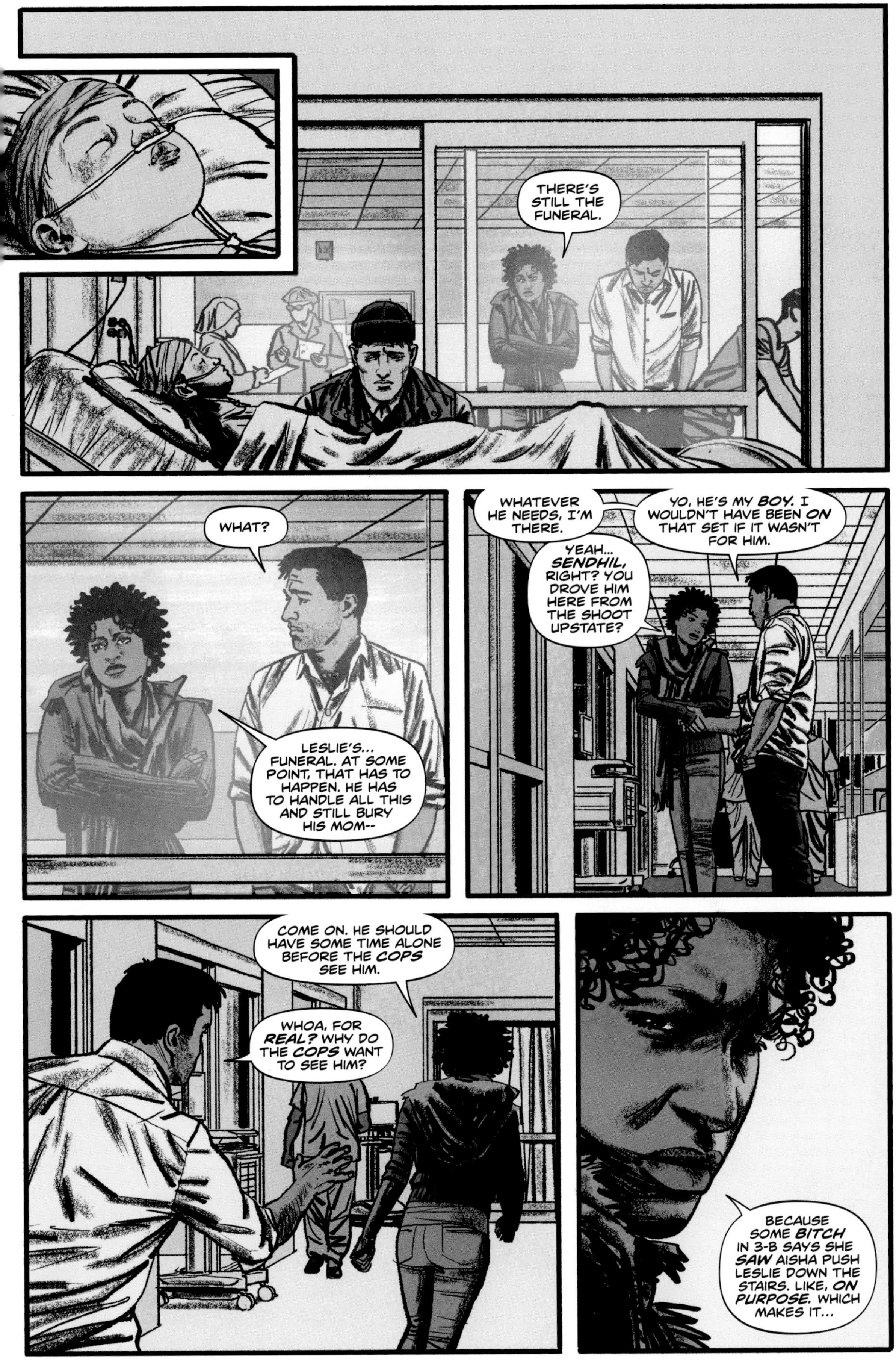
THERE'S STILL THE FUNERAL.
WHAT?
LESLIE'S... FUNERAL. AT SOME POINT, THAT HAS TO HAPPEN. HE HAS TO HANDLE ALL THIS AND STILL BURY HIS MOM--
WHATEVER HE NEEDS, I'M THERE.
YO, HE'S MY BOY. I WOULDN'T HAVE BEEN ON THAT SET IF IT WASN'T FOR HIM.
YEAH... SENDHIL, RIGHT? YOU DROVE HIM HERE FROM THE SHOOT UPSTATE?
COME ON. HE SHOULD HAVE SOME TIME ALONE BEFORE THE COPS SEE HIM.
WHOA, FOR REAL? WHY DO THE COPS WANT TO SEE HIM?
BECAUSE SOME BITCH IN 3-B SAYS SHE SAW AISHA PUSH LESLIE DOWN THE STAIRS. LIKE, ON PURPOSE. WHICH MAKES IT...

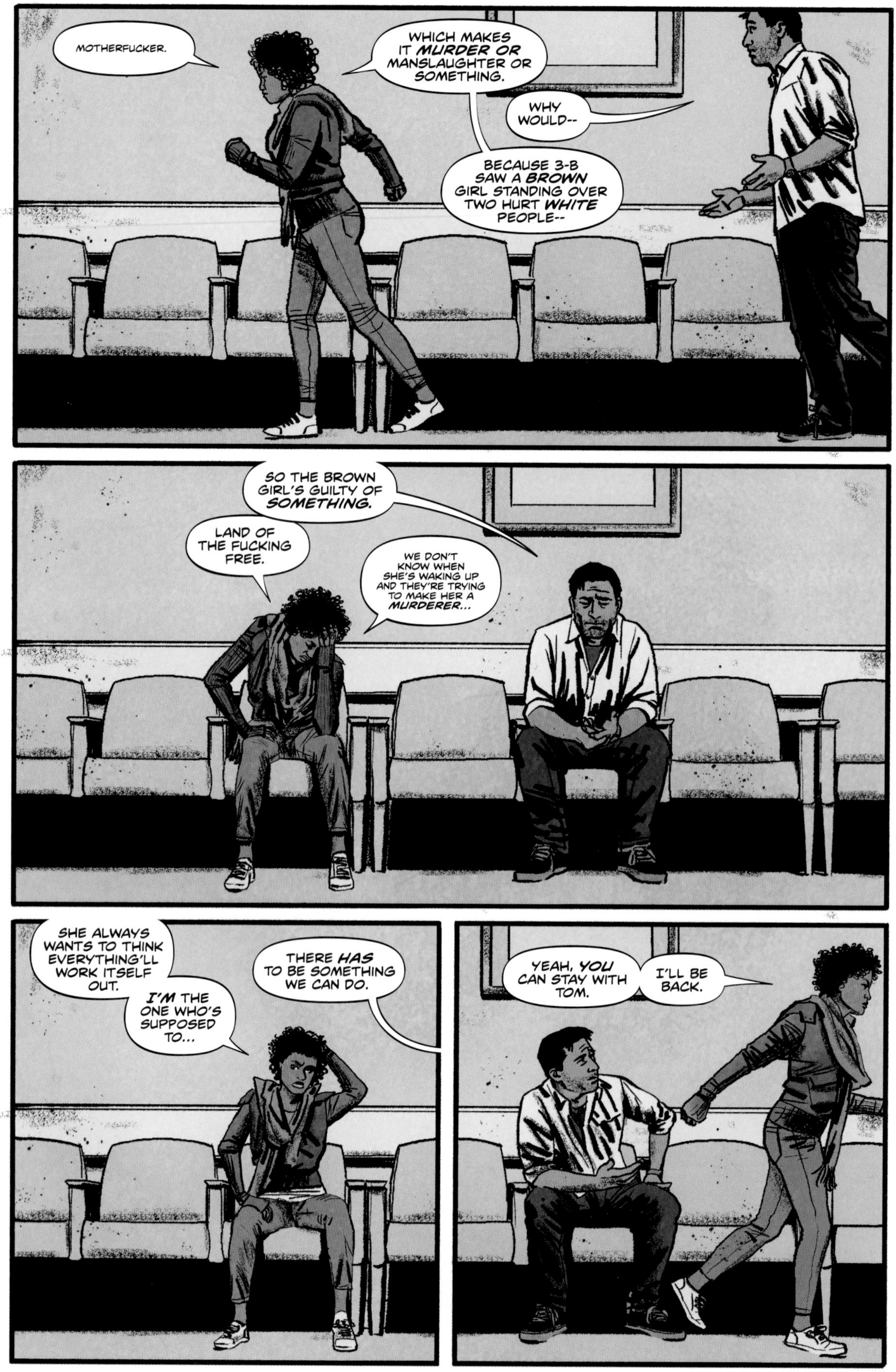
MOTHERFUCKER.
WHICH MAKES IT MURDER OR MANSLAUGHTER OR SOMETHING.
WHY WOULD--
BECAUSE 3-B SAW A BROWN GIRL STANDING OVER TWO HURT WHITE PEOPLE--
SO THE BROWN GIRL'S GUILTY OF SOMETHING.
LAND OF THE FUCKING FREE.
WE DON'T KNOW WHEN SHE'S WAKING UP AND THEY'RE TRYING TO MAKE HER A MURDERER...
SHE ALWAYS WANTS TO THINK EVERYTHING'LL WORK ITSELF OUT.
I'M THE ONE WHO'S SUPPOSED TO...
THERE HAS TO BE SOMETHING WE CAN DO.
YEAH, YOU CAN STAY WITH TOM.
I'LL BE BACK.

"THE GUY IN 4-D KEPT A LOT OF ***BOXES*** OUT IN THE HALL. BUT EVERYONE USED THE COMMON AREAS AS STORAGE, YOU KNOW? I MEAN, I DON'T THINK I ***EVER*** BROUGHT MY BIKE ***INSIDE*** BEFORE THE BOMBS.

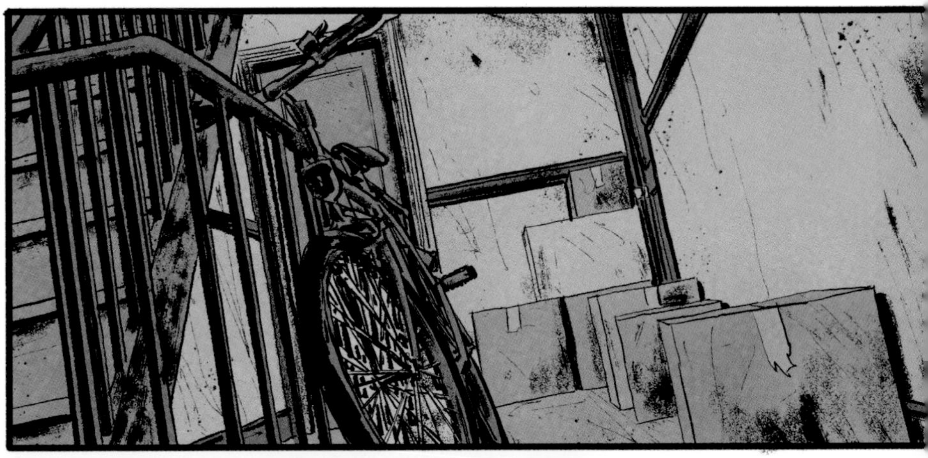

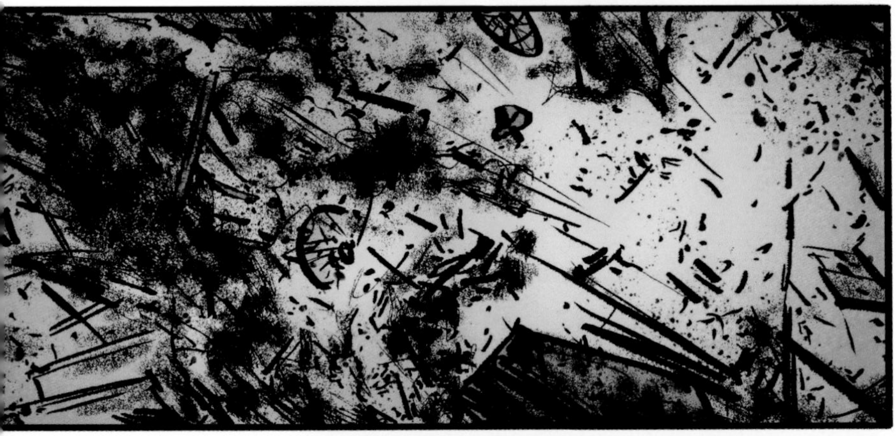

"BUT ***4-D'S*** BOXES WERE FILLED WITH EXPLOSIVES AND NAPALM HE MADE FROM PLANS OFF THE INTERNET--

"THEY WENT OFF IN THE MIDDLE OF THE NIGHT, SETTING OFF ***MORE*** EXPLOSIVES HE KEPT ***INSIDE*** HIS APARTMENT.

"THE ONLY REASON THE BUILDING'S STILL ***AROUND*** IS 'CUZ IT WAS BUILT BEFORE THE WAR. BACK THEN, THEY BUILT BUILDING SKELETONS OUT OF ***CONCRETE,*** NOT ***WOOD*** LIKE THEY DO NOW.

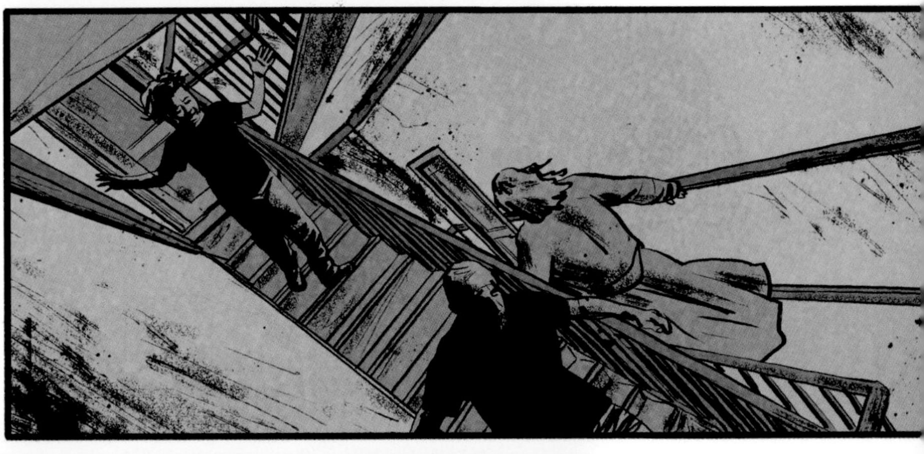

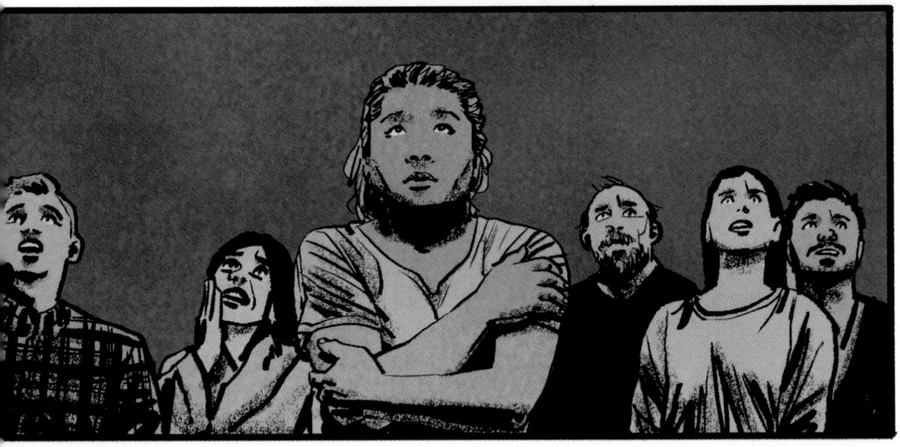

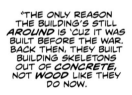

"IF IT WAS MADE OF ***WOOD,*** THERE WOULDN'T BE ***ANYTHING*** LEFT OF..."

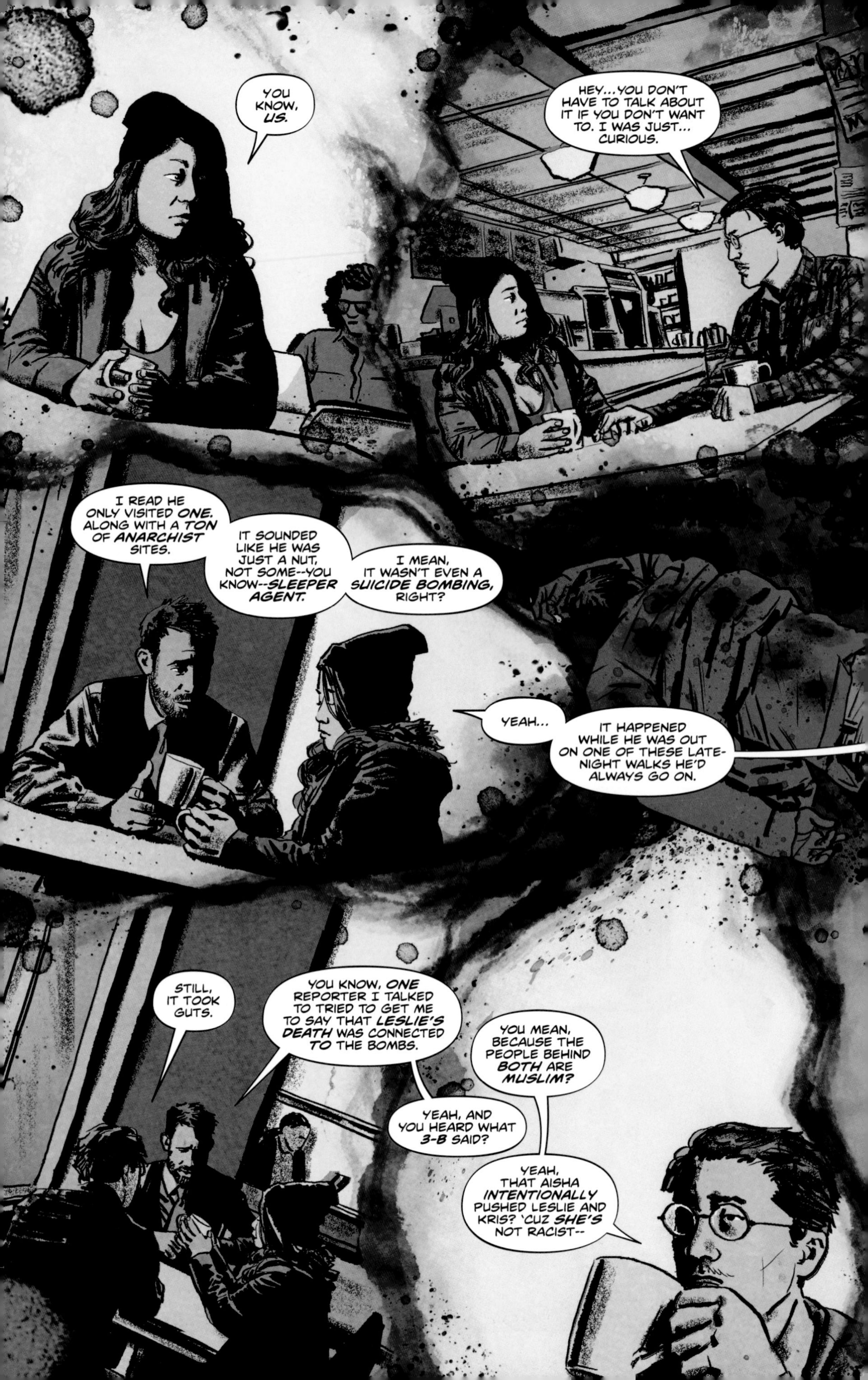
YOU KNOW, US.
HEY... YOU DON'T HAVE TO TALK ABOUT IT IF YOU DON'T WANT TO. I WAS JUST... CURIOUS.
I READ HE ONLY VISITED ONE. ALONG WITH A TON OF ANARCHIST SITES.
IT SOUNDED LIKE HE WAS JUST A NUT, NOT SOME--YOU KNOW--SLEEPER AGENT.
I MEAN, IT WASN'T EVEN A SUICIDE BOMBING, RIGHT?
YEAH...
IT HAPPENED WHILE HE WAS OUT ON ONE OF THESE LATE-NIGHT WALKS HE'D ALWAYS GO ON.
STILL, IT TOOK GUTS.
YOU KNOW, ONE REPORTER I TALKED TO TRIED TO GET ME TO SAY THAT LESLIE'S DEATH WAS CONNECTED TO THE BOMBS.
YOU MEAN, BECAUSE THE PEOPLE BEHIND BOTH ARE MUSLIM?
YEAH, AND YOU HEARD WHAT 3-B SAID?
YEAH, THAT AISHA INTENTIONALLY PUSHED LESLIE AND KRIS? 'CUZ SHE'S NOT RACIST--

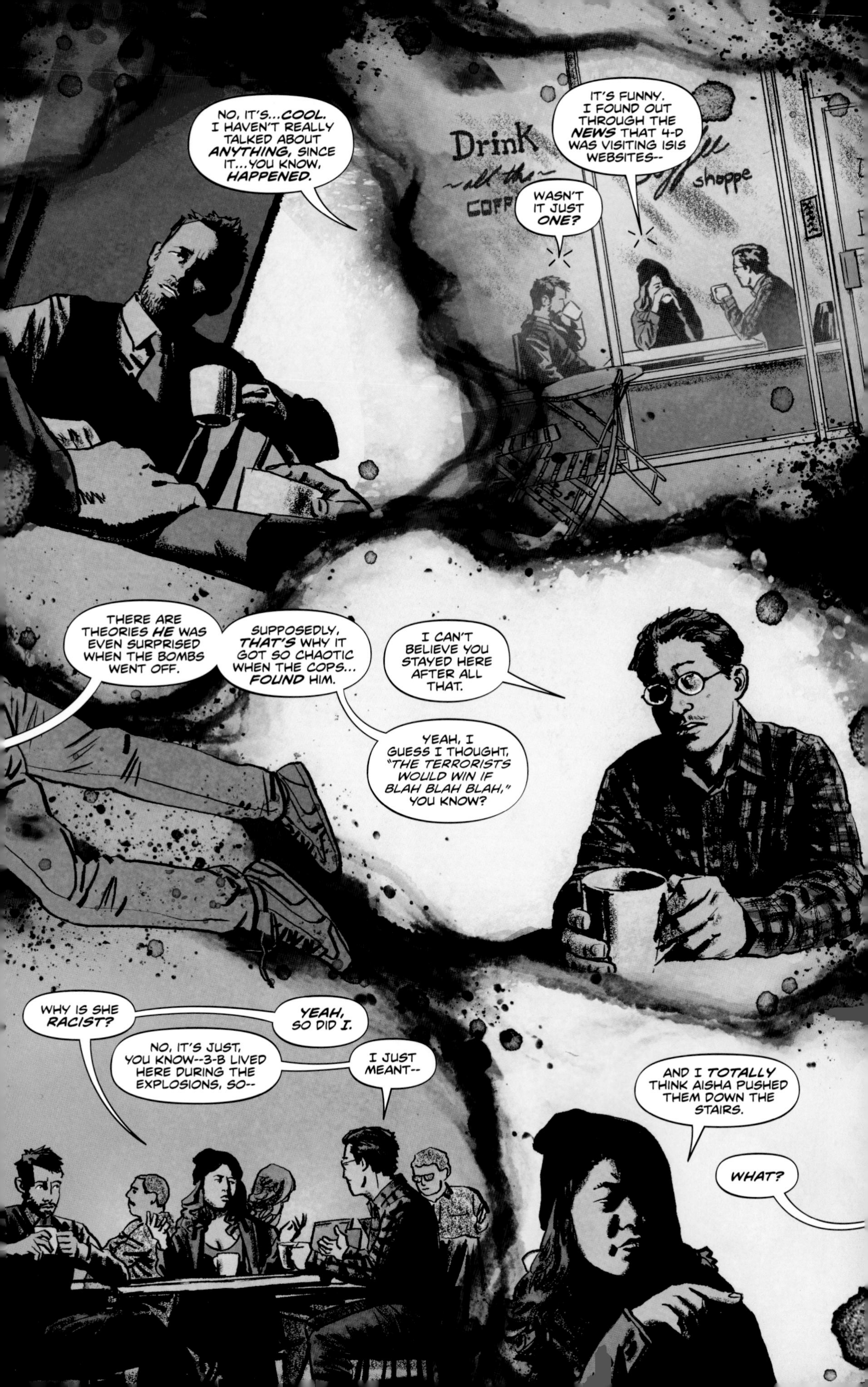

NO, IT'S...*COOL.* I HAVEN'T REALLY TALKED ABOUT *ANYTHING,* SINCE IT...YOU KNOW, *HAPPENED.*
Drink
shoppe
IT'S FUNNY. I FOUND OUT THROUGH THE *NEWS* THAT 4-D WAS VISITING ISIS WEBSITES--
WASN'T IT JUST *ONE?*
THERE ARE THEORIES *HE* WAS EVEN SURPRISED WHEN THE BOMBS WENT OFF.
SUPPOSEDLY, *THAT'S* WHY IT GOT SO CHAOTIC WHEN THE COPS... *FOUND* HIM.
I CAN'T BELIEVE YOU STAYED HERE AFTER ALL THAT.
YEAH, I GUESS I THOUGHT, *"THE TERRORISTS WOULD WIN IF BLAH BLAH BLAH,"* YOU KNOW?
WHY IS SHE *RACIST?*
YEAH, SO DID *I.*
NO, IT'S JUST, YOU KNOW--3-B LIVED HERE DURING THE EXPLOSIONS, SO--
I JUST MEANT--
AND I *TOTALLY* THINK AISHA PUSHED THEM DOWN THE STAIRS.
WHAT?

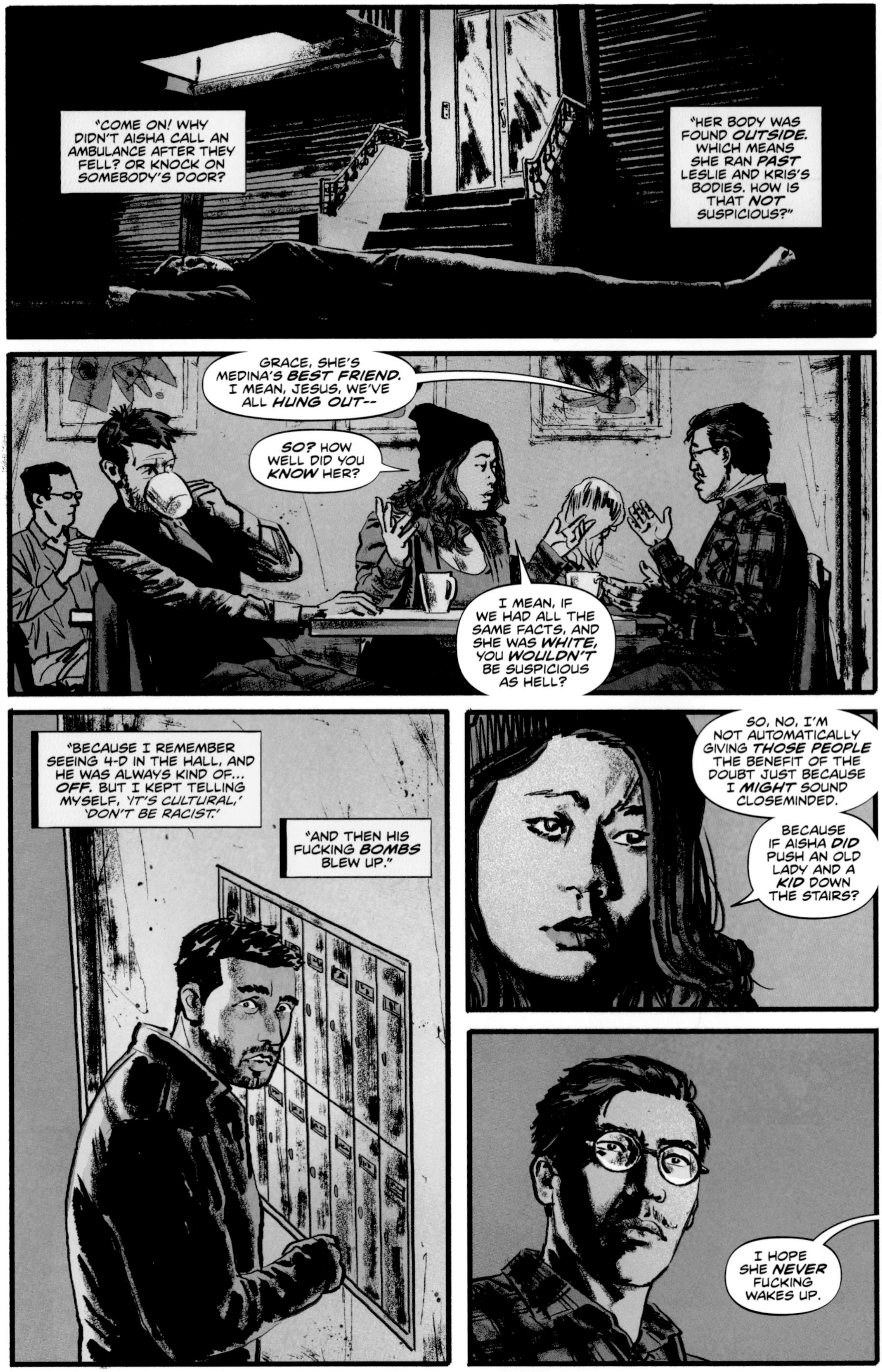

"COME ON! WHY DIDN'T AISHA CALL AN AMBULANCE AFTER THEY FELL? OR KNOCK ON SOMEBODY'S DOOR?
"HER BODY WAS FOUND OUTSIDE. WHICH MEANS SHE RAN PAST LESLIE AND KRIS'S BODIES. HOW IS THAT NOT SUSPICIOUS?"
GRACE, SHE'S MEDINA'S BEST FRIEND. I MEAN, JESUS, WE'VE ALL HUNG OUT--
SO? HOW WELL DID YOU KNOW HER?
I MEAN, IF WE HAD ALL THE SAME FACTS, AND SHE WAS WHITE, YOU WOULDN'T BE SUSPICIOUS AS HELL?
"BECAUSE I REMEMBER SEEING 4-D IN THE HALL, AND HE WAS ALWAYS KIND OF... OFF. BUT I KEPT TELLING MYSELF, 'IT'S CULTURAL,' 'DON'T BE RACIST.'
"AND THEN HIS FUCKING BOMBS BLEW UP."
SO, NO, I'M NOT AUTOMATICALLY GIVING THOSE PEOPLE THE BENEFIT OF THE DOUBT JUST BECAUSE I MIGHT SOUND CLOSEMINDED.
BECAUSE IF AISHA DID PUSH AN OLD LADY AND A KID DOWN THE STAIRS?
I HOPE SHE NEVER FUCKING WAKES UP.

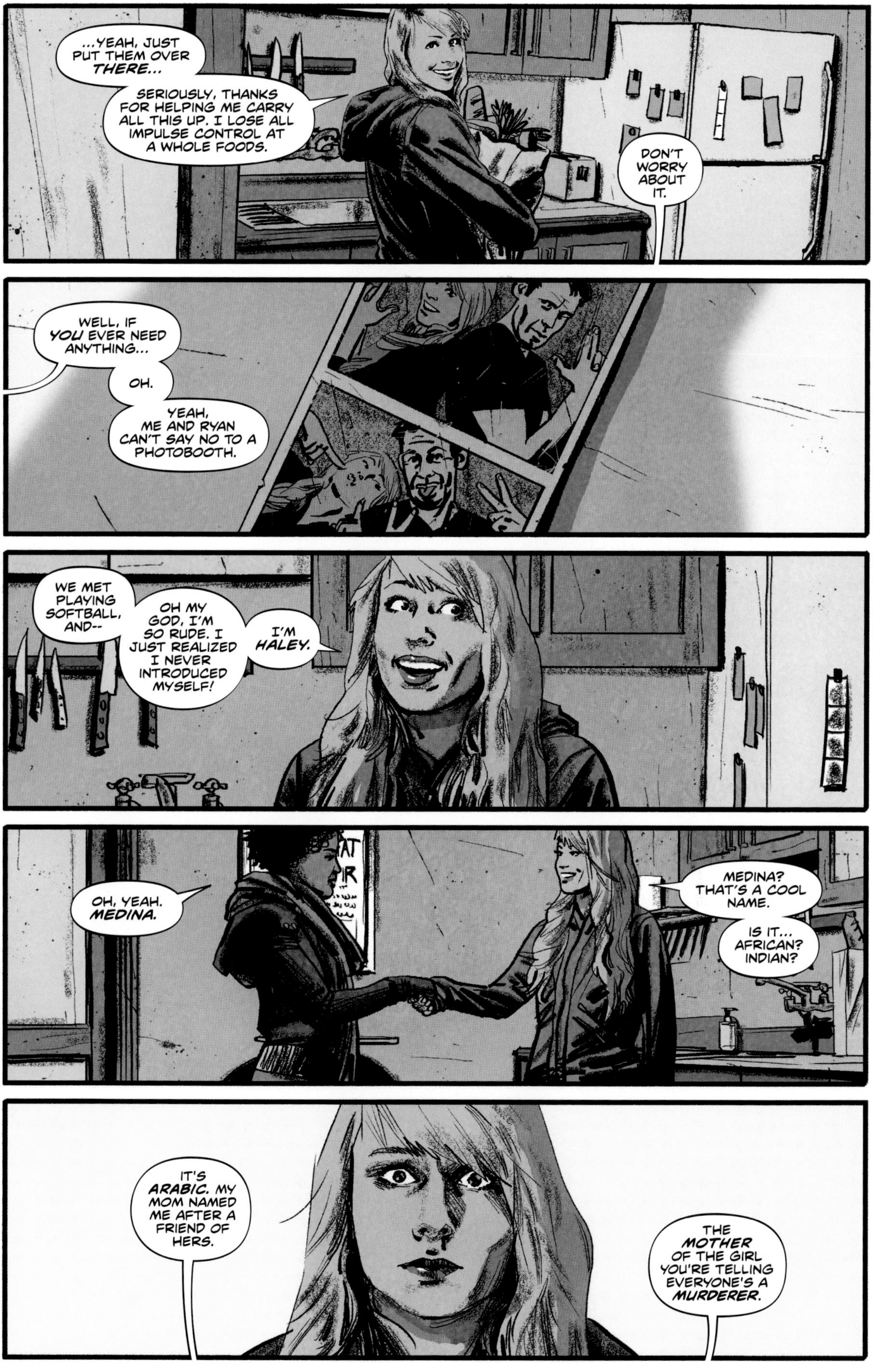
...YEAH, JUST PUT THEM OVER *THERE*...
SERIOUSLY, THANKS FOR HELPING ME CARRY ALL THIS UP. I LOSE ALL IMPULSE CONTROL AT A WHOLE FOODS.
DON'T WORRY ABOUT IT.
WELL, IF *YOU* EVER NEED ANYTHING...
OH.
YEAH, ME AND RYAN CAN'T SAY NO TO A PHOTOBOOTH.
WE MET PLAYING SOFTBALL, AND--
OH MY GOD, I'M SO RUDE. I JUST REALIZED I NEVER INTRODUCED MYSELF!
I'M *HALEY*.
OH, YEAH. *MEDINA*.
MEDINA? THAT'S A COOL NAME.
IS IT... AFRICAN? INDIAN?
IT'S *ARABIC*. MY MOM NAMED ME AFTER A FRIEND OF HERS.
THE *MOTHER* OF THE GIRL YOU'RE TELLING EVERYONE'S A *MURDERER*.

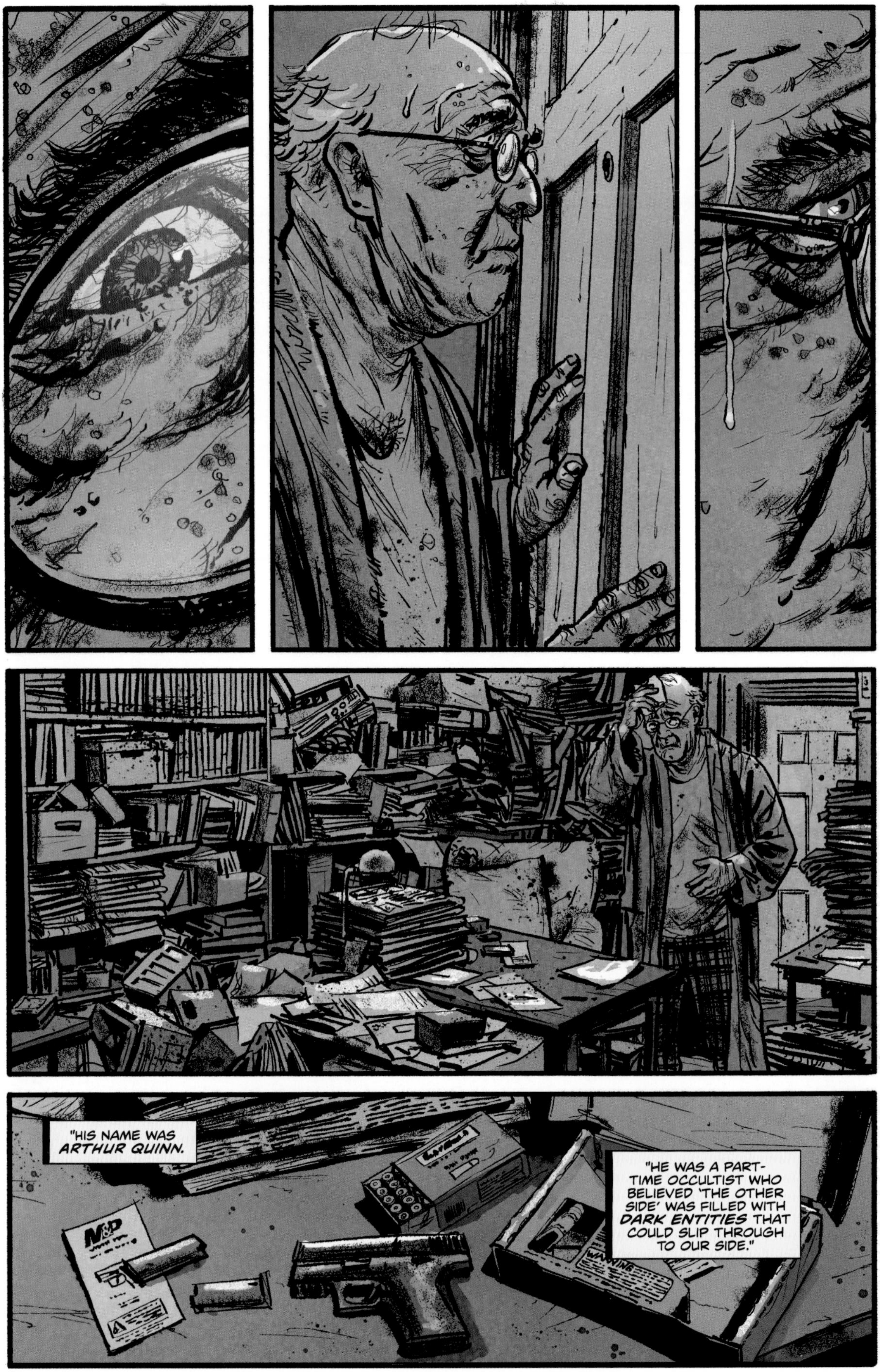
"HIS NAME WAS ARTHUR QUINN.
"HE WAS A PART-TIME OCCULTIST WHO BELIEVED 'THE OTHER SIDE' WAS FILLED WITH DARK ENTITIES THAT COULD SLIP THROUGH TO OUR SIDE."

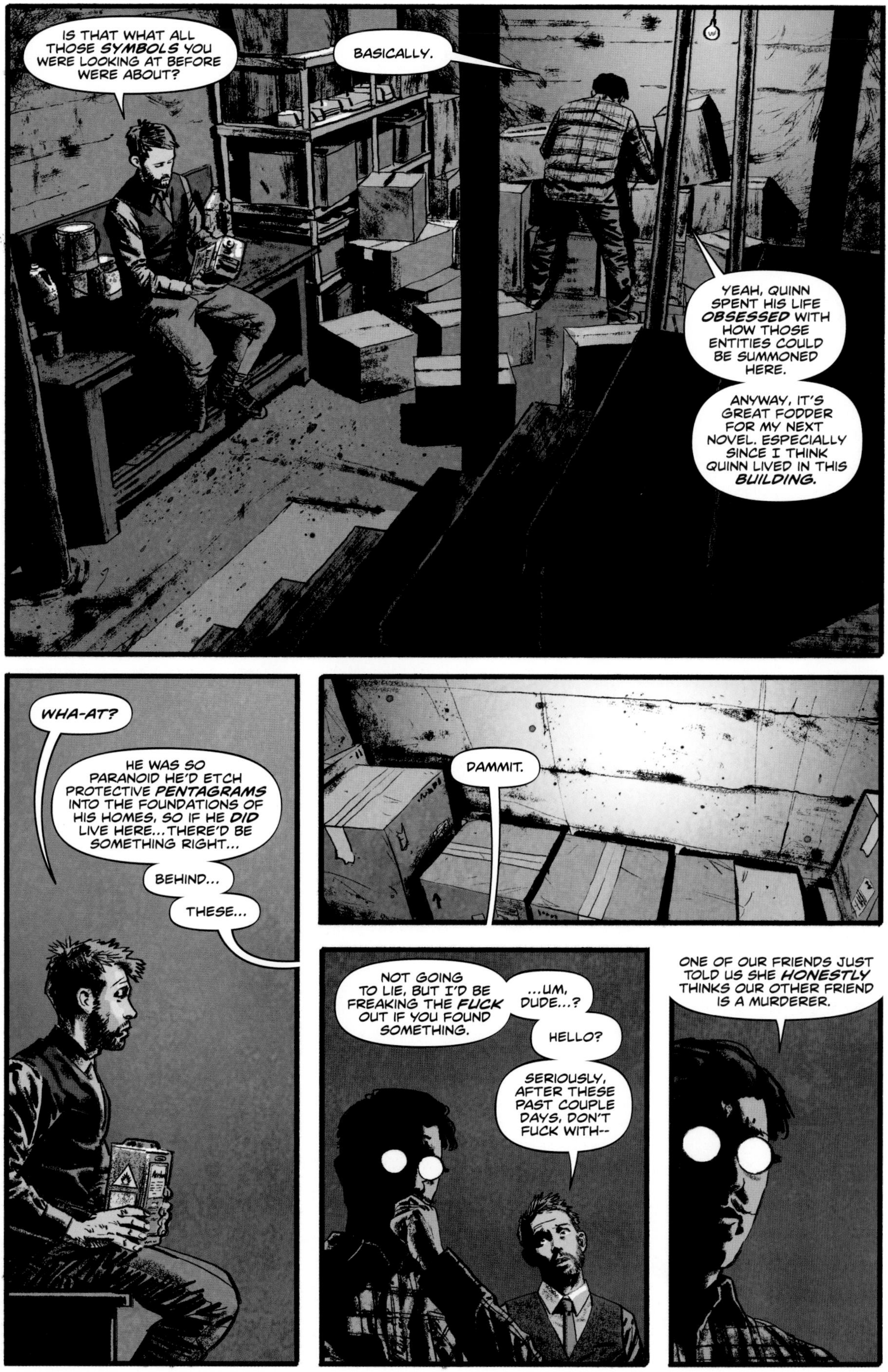
IS THAT WHAT ALL THOSE SYMBOLS YOU WERE LOOKING AT BEFORE WERE ABOUT?
BASICALLY.
YEAH, QUINN SPENT HIS LIFE OBSESSED WITH HOW THOSE ENTITIES COULD BE SUMMONED HERE.
ANYWAY, IT'S GREAT FODDER FOR MY NEXT NOVEL. ESPECIALLY SINCE I THINK QUINN LIVED IN THIS BUILDING.
WHA-AT?
HE WAS SO PARANOID HE'D ETCH PROTECTIVE PENTAGRAMS INTO THE FOUNDATIONS OF HIS HOMES, SO IF HE DID LIVE HERE...THERE'D BE SOMETHING RIGHT...
BEHIND...
THESE...
DAMMIT.
NOT GOING TO LIE, BUT I'D BE FREAKING THE FUCK OUT IF YOU FOUND SOMETHING.
...UM, DUDE...?
HELLO?
SERIOUSLY, AFTER THESE PAST COUPLE DAYS, DON'T FUCK WITH--
ONE OF OUR FRIENDS JUST TOLD US SHE HONESTLY THINKS OUR OTHER FRIEND IS A MURDERER.

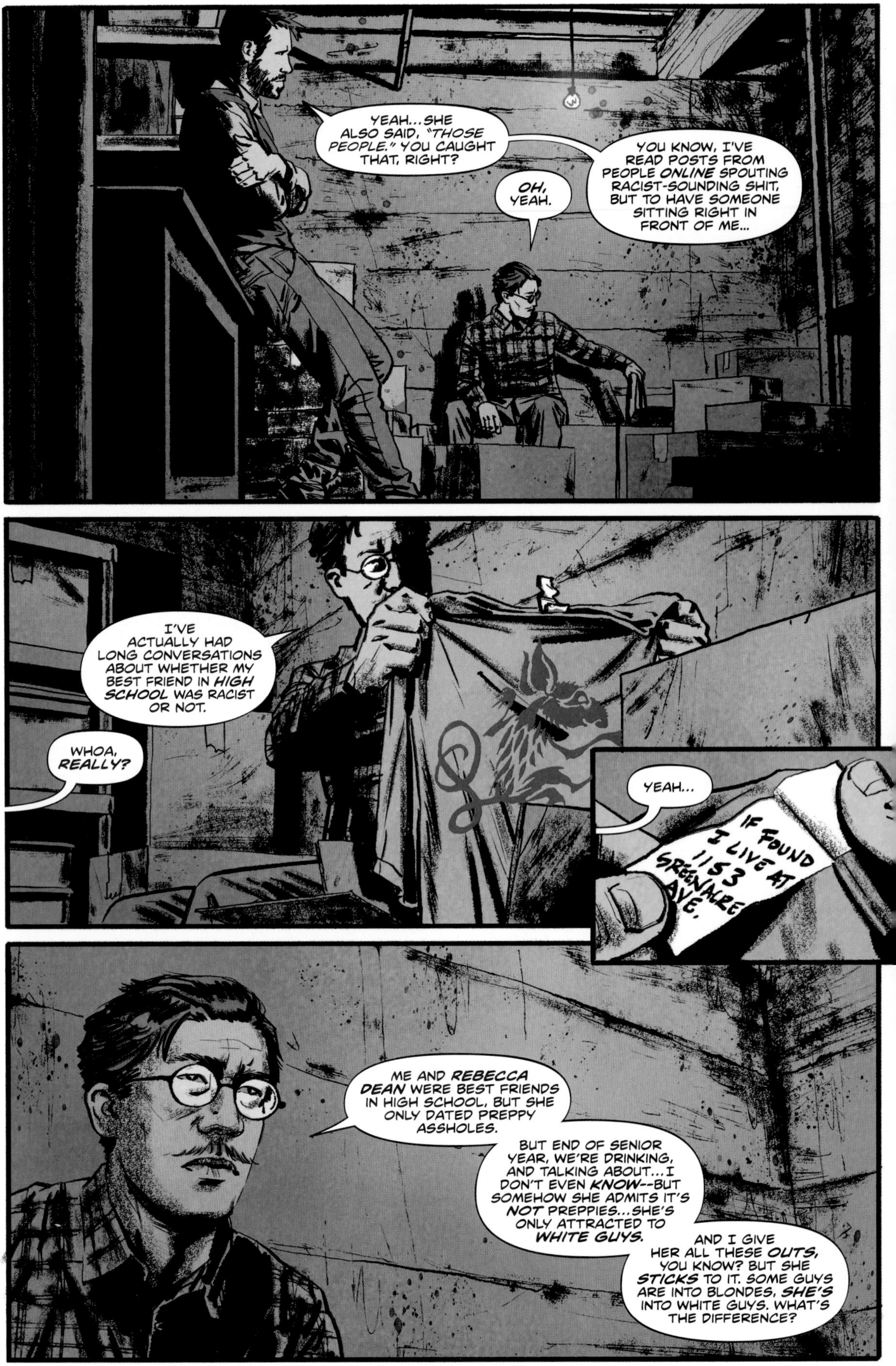

YEAH...SHE ALSO SAID, "THOSE PEOPLE." YOU CAUGHT THAT, RIGHT?
YOU KNOW, I'VE READ POSTS FROM PEOPLE ONLINE SPOUTING RACIST-SOUNDING SHIT, BUT TO HAVE SOMEONE SITTING RIGHT IN FRONT OF ME...
OH, YEAH.
I'VE ACTUALLY HAD LONG CONVERSATIONS ABOUT WHETHER MY BEST FRIEND IN HIGH SCHOOL WAS RACIST OR NOT.
WHOA, REALLY?
YEAH...
IF FOUND I LIVE AT 1153 GREENACRE AVE.
ME AND REBECCA DEAN WERE BEST FRIENDS IN HIGH SCHOOL, BUT SHE ONLY DATED PREPPY ASSHOLES.
BUT END OF SENIOR YEAR, WE'RE DRINKING, AND TALKING ABOUT...I DON'T EVEN KNOW--BUT SOMEHOW SHE ADMITS IT'S NOT PREPPIES...SHE'S ONLY ATTRACTED TO WHITE GUYS.
AND I GIVE HER ALL THESE OUTS, YOU KNOW? BUT SHE STICKS TO IT. SOME GUYS ARE INTO BLONDES, SHE'S INTO WHITE GUYS. WHAT'S THE DIFFERENCE?

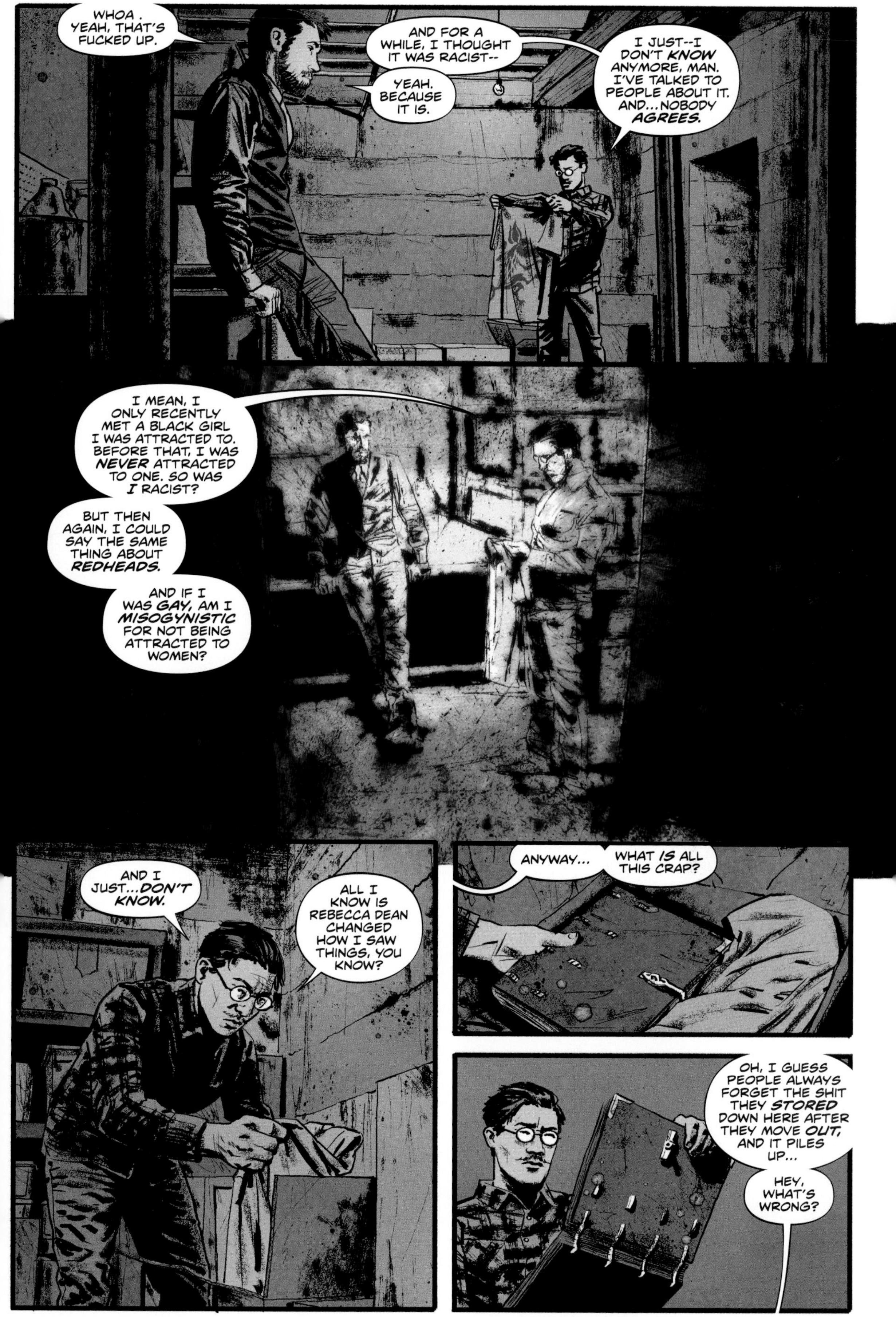
WHOA . YEAH, THAT'S FUCKED UP.
AND FOR A WHILE, I THOUGHT IT WAS RACIST--
YEAH. BECAUSE IT IS.
I JUST--I DON'T KNOW ANYMORE, MAN. I'VE TALKED TO PEOPLE ABOUT IT. AND... NOBODY AGREES.
I MEAN, I ONLY RECENTLY MET A BLACK GIRL I WAS ATTRACTED TO. BEFORE THAT, I WAS NEVER ATTRACTED TO ONE. SO WAS I RACIST?
BUT THEN AGAIN, I COULD SAY THE SAME THING ABOUT REDHEADS.
AND IF I WAS GAY, AM I MISOGYNISTIC FOR NOT BEING ATTRACTED TO WOMEN?
AND I JUST... DON'T KNOW.
ALL I KNOW IS REBECCA DEAN CHANGED HOW I SAW THINGS, YOU KNOW?
ANYWAY...
WHAT IS ALL THIS CRAP?
OH, I GUESS PEOPLE ALWAYS FORGET THE SHIT THEY STORED DOWN HERE AFTER THEY MOVE OUT, AND IT PILES UP...
HEY, WHAT'S WRONG?

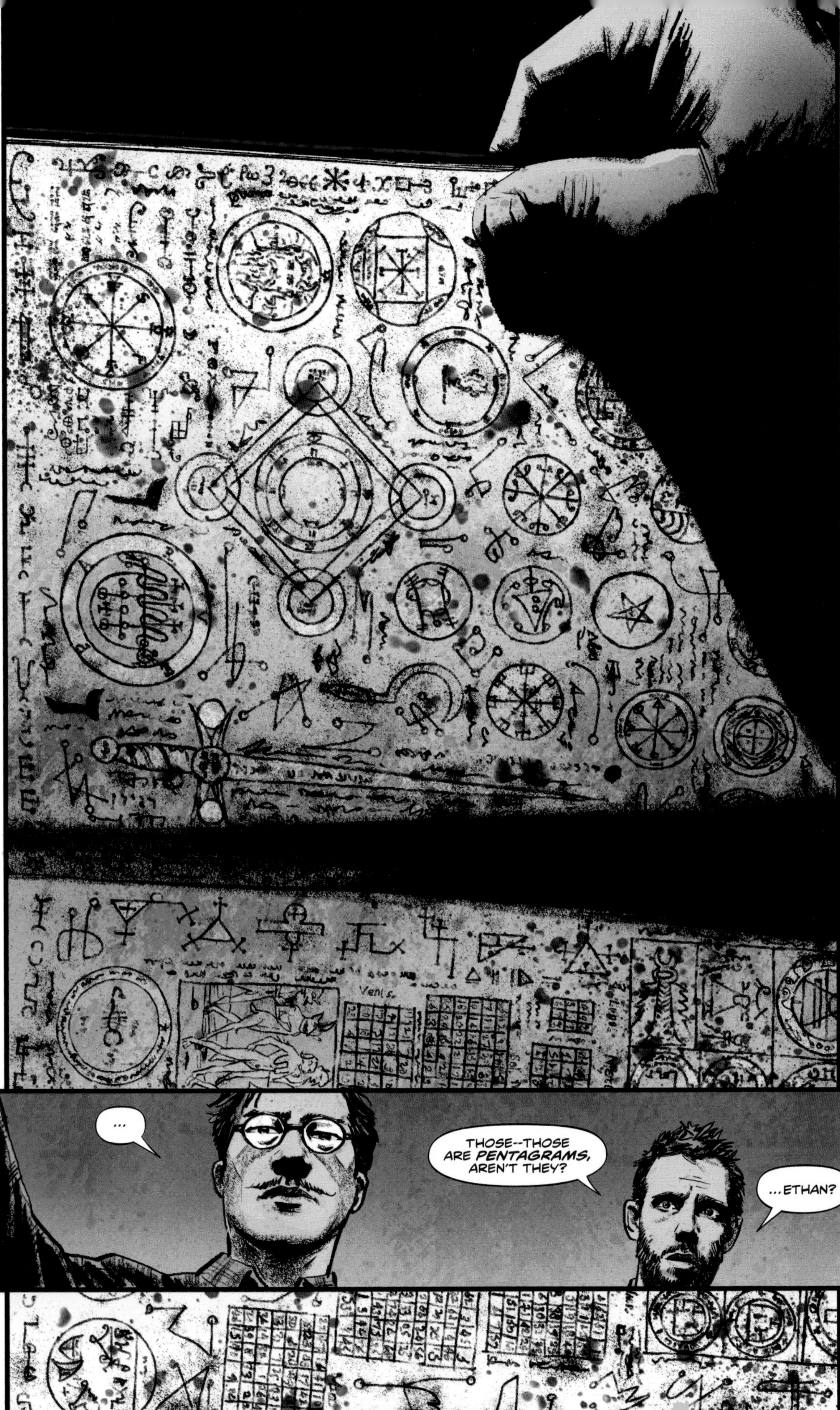
Venus
...
THOSE--THOSE ARE PENTAGRAMS, AREN'T THEY?
...ETHAN?

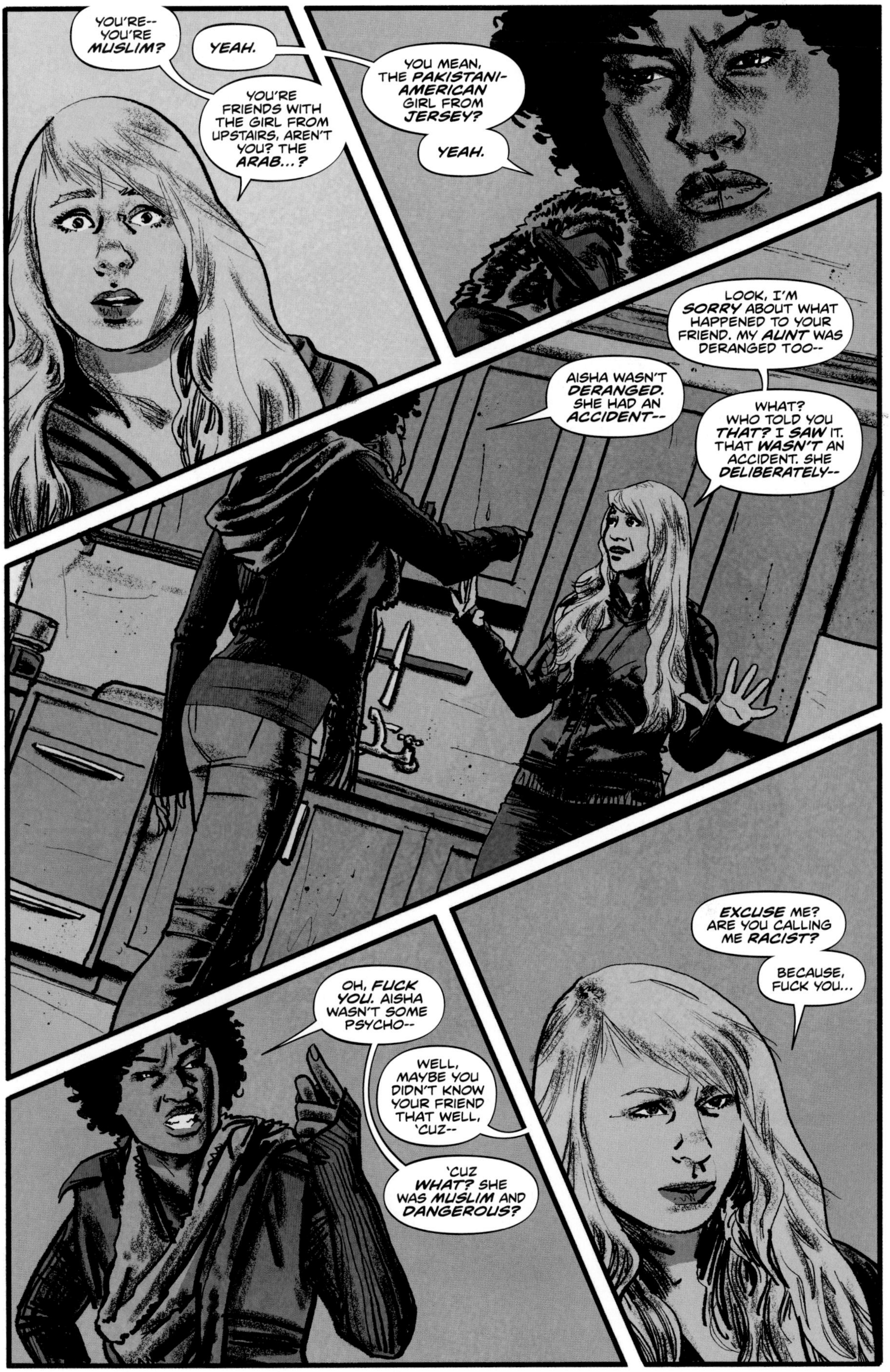
YOU'RE-- YOU'RE MUSLIM?
YEAH.
YOU'RE FRIENDS WITH THE GIRL FROM UPSTAIRS, AREN'T YOU? THE ARAB...?
YOU MEAN, THE PAKISTANI-AMERICAN GIRL FROM JERSEY?
YEAH.
LOOK, I'M SORRY ABOUT WHAT HAPPENED TO YOUR FRIEND. MY AUNT WAS DERANGED TOO--
AISHA WASN'T DERANGED. SHE HAD AN ACCIDENT--
WHAT? WHO TOLD YOU THAT? I SAW IT. THAT WASN'T AN ACCIDENT. SHE DELIBERATELY--
OH, FUCK YOU. AISHA WASN'T SOME PSYCHO--
WELL, MAYBE YOU DIDN'T KNOW YOUR FRIEND THAT WELL, 'CUZ--
'CUZ WHAT? SHE WAS MUSLIM AND DANGEROUS?
EXCUSE ME? ARE YOU CALLING ME RACIST?
BECAUSE, FUCK YOU...

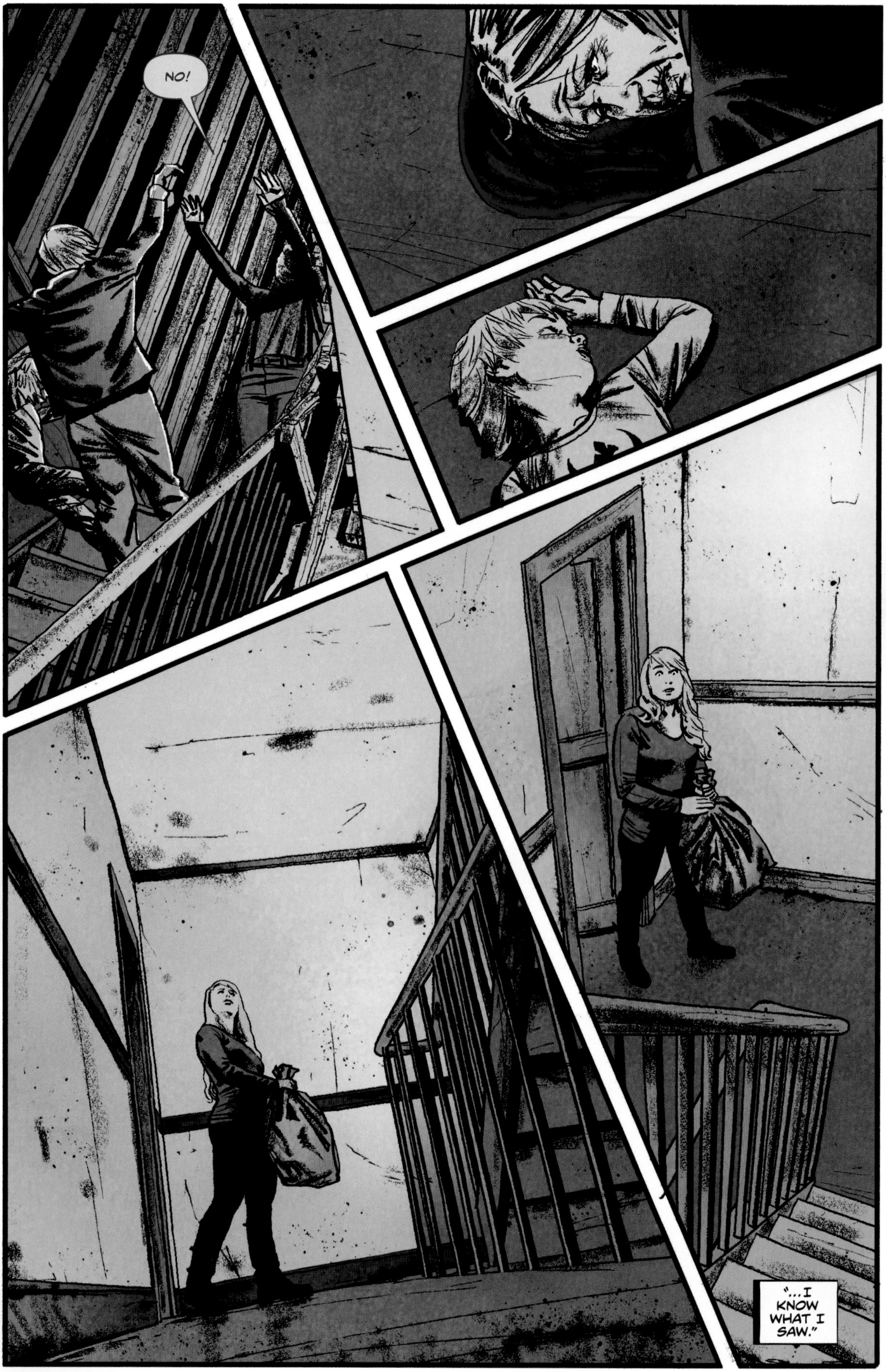
NO!
"...I KNOW WHAT I SAW."

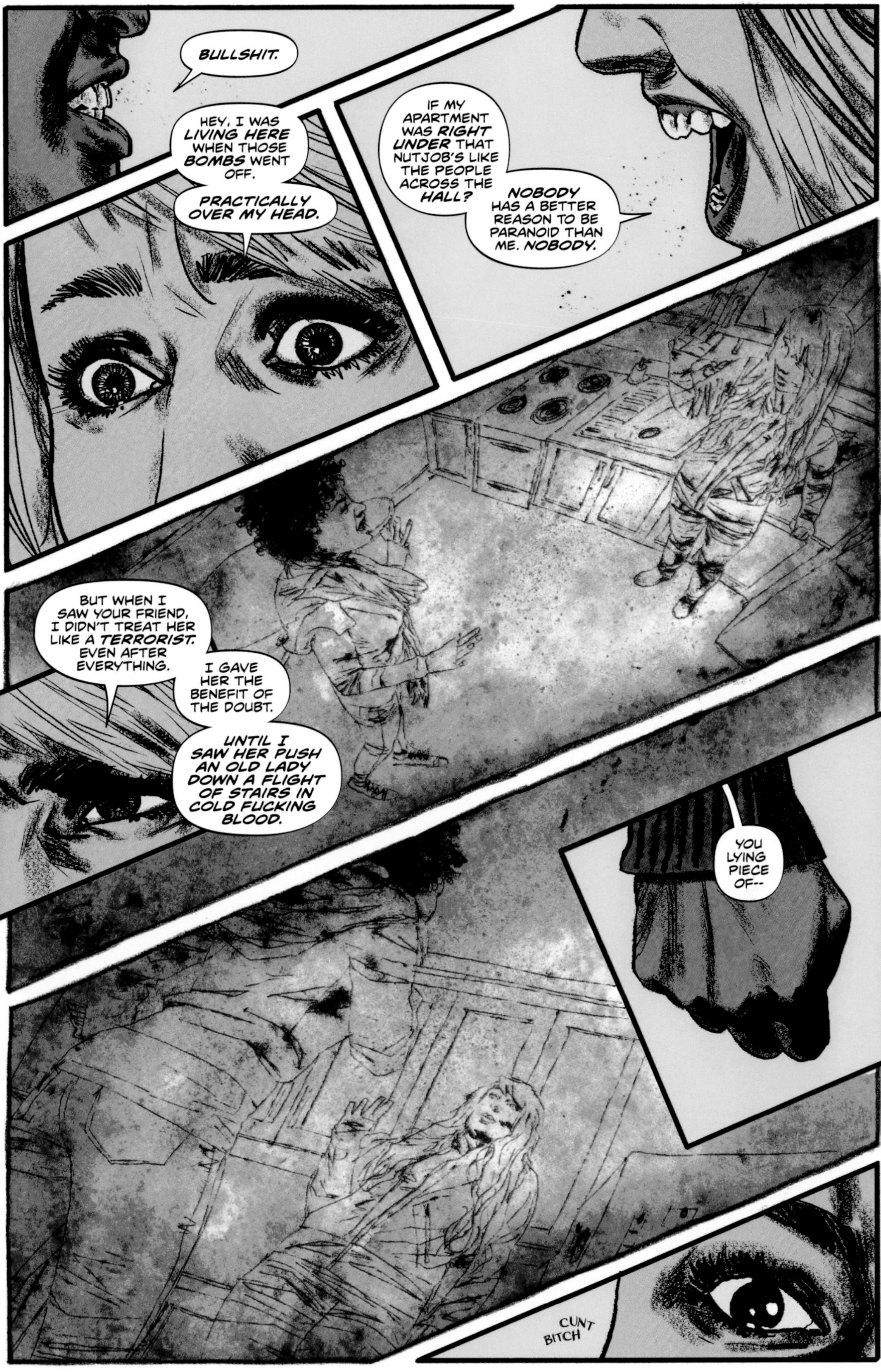
BULLSHIT.
HEY, I WAS LIVING HERE WHEN THOSE BOMBS WENT OFF.
PRACTICALLY OVER MY HEAD.
IF MY APARTMENT WAS RIGHT UNDER THAT NUTJOB'S LIKE THE PEOPLE ACROSS THE HALL?
NOBODY HAS A BETTER REASON TO BE PARANOID THAN ME. NOBODY.
BUT WHEN I SAW YOUR FRIEND, I DIDN'T TREAT HER LIKE A TERRORIST. EVEN AFTER EVERYTHING.
I GAVE HER THE BENEFIT OF THE DOUBT.
UNTIL I SAW HER PUSH AN OLD LADY DOWN A FLIGHT OF STAIRS IN COLD FUCKING BLOOD.
YOU LYING PIECE OF--
CUNT
BITCH

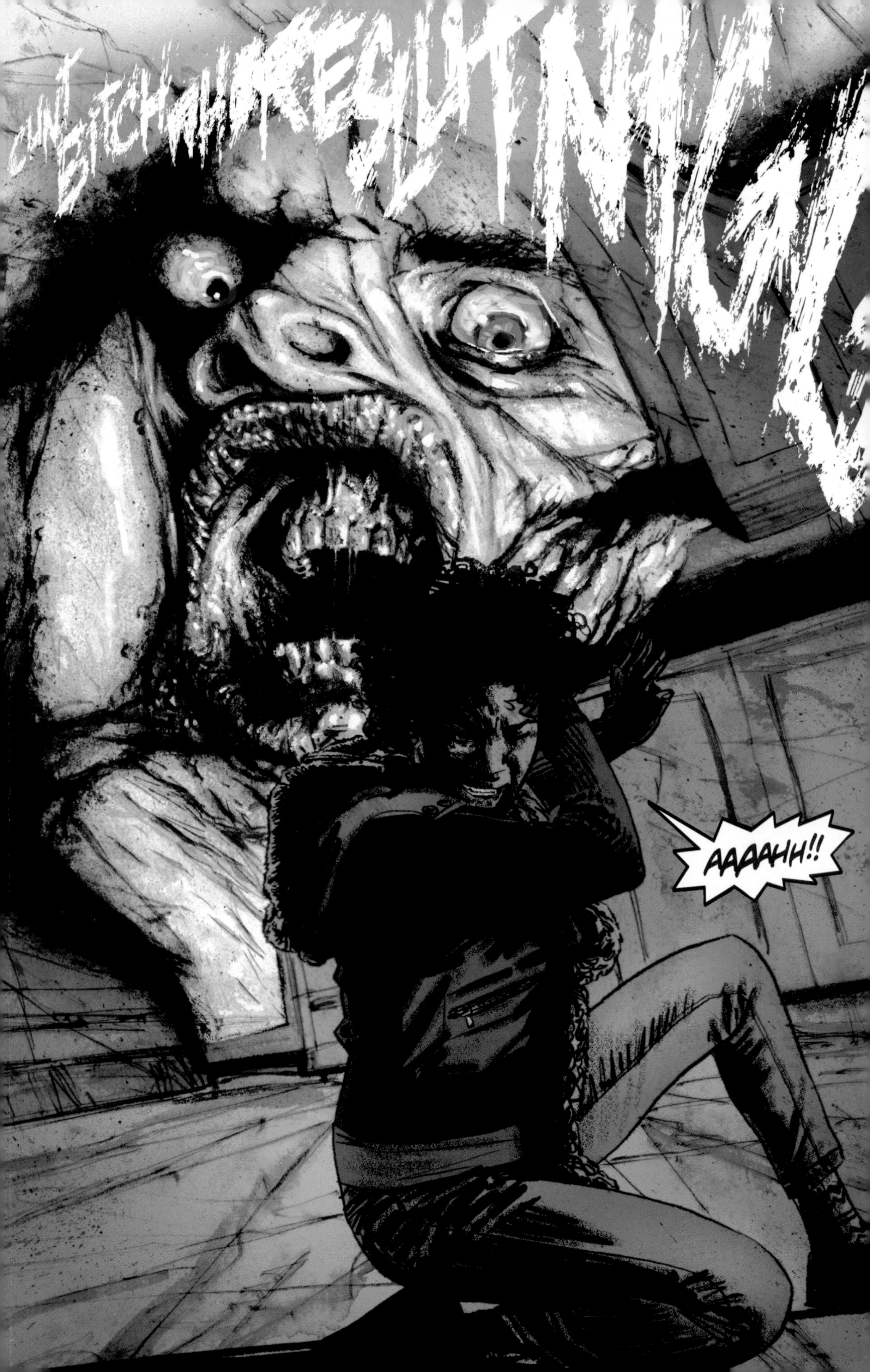
CUNT
BITCH
AAAAHH!!

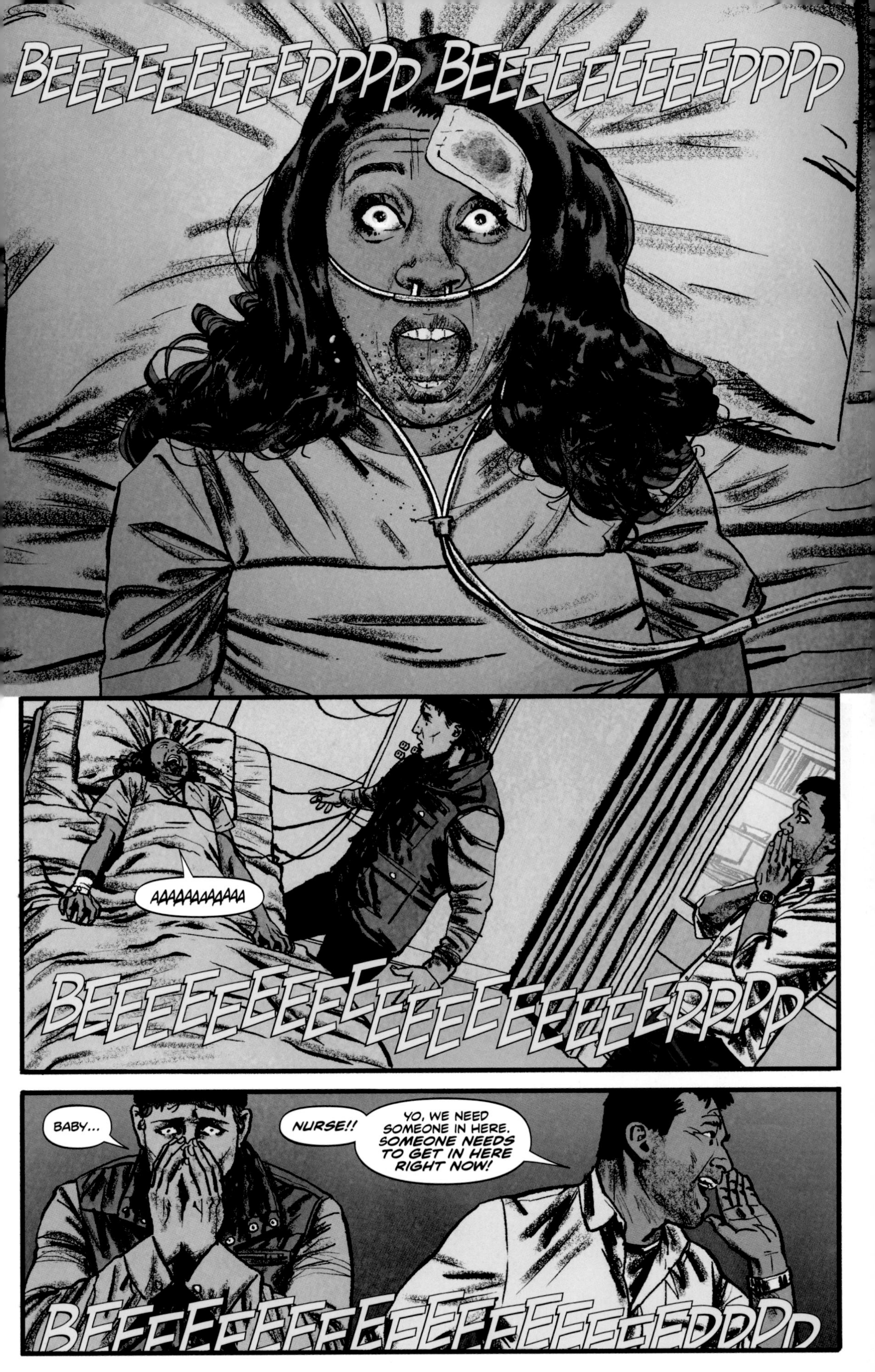
BEEEEEEEEEEEPPPPP BEEEEEEEEEEEPPPPP
AAAAAAAAAAA
BEEEEEEEEEEEEEEEEEEEEEPPPPP
BABY...
NURSE!!
YO, WE NEED SOMEONE IN HERE. SOMEONE NEEDS TO GET IN HERE RIGHT NOW!
BEEEEEEEEEEEEEEEEEEEPPPPP

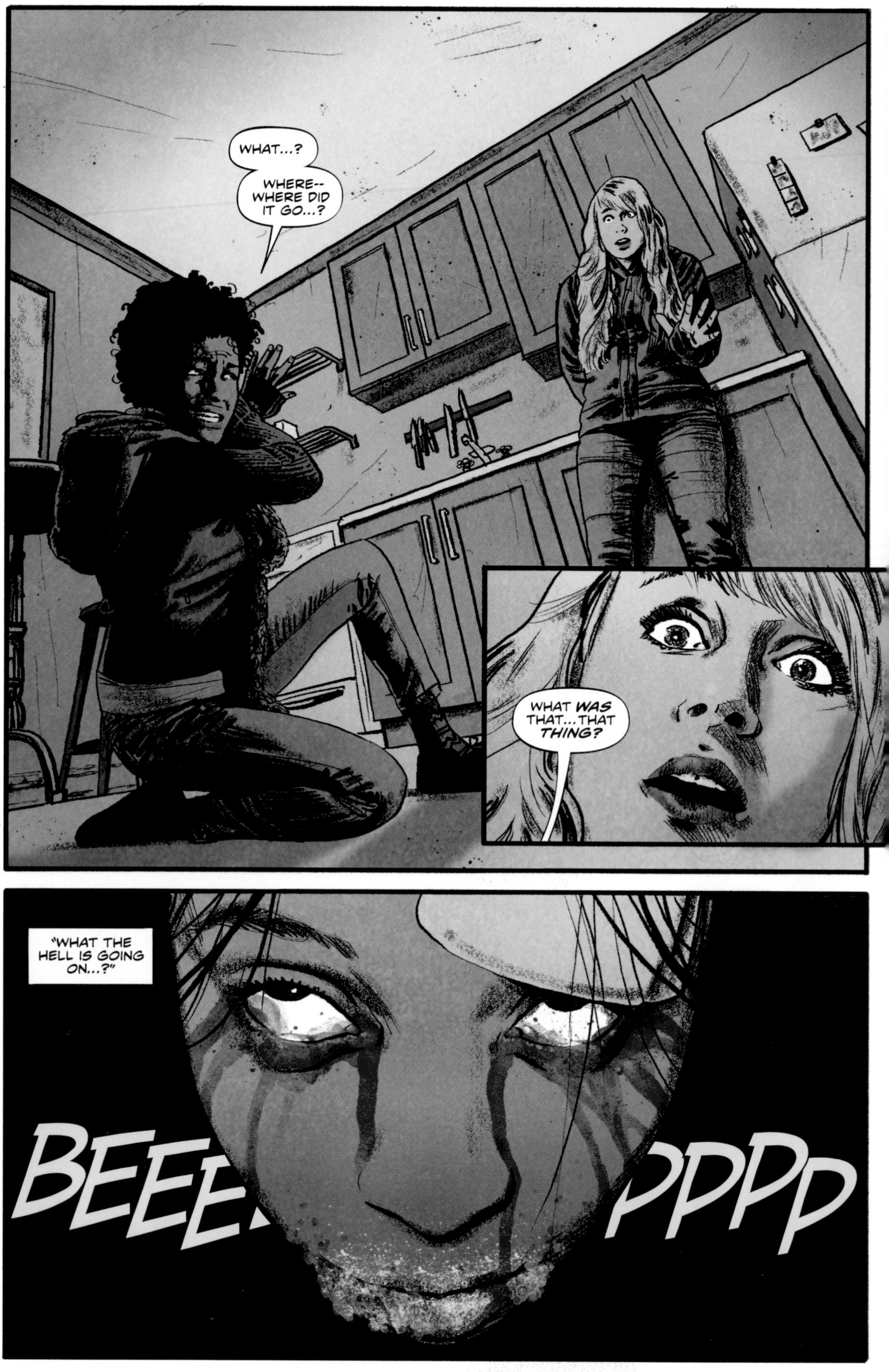
WHAT...?
WHERE-- WHERE DID IT GO...?
WHAT WAS THAT...THAT THING?
"WHAT THE HELL IS GOING ON...?"
BEEE PPPP

chapter 4

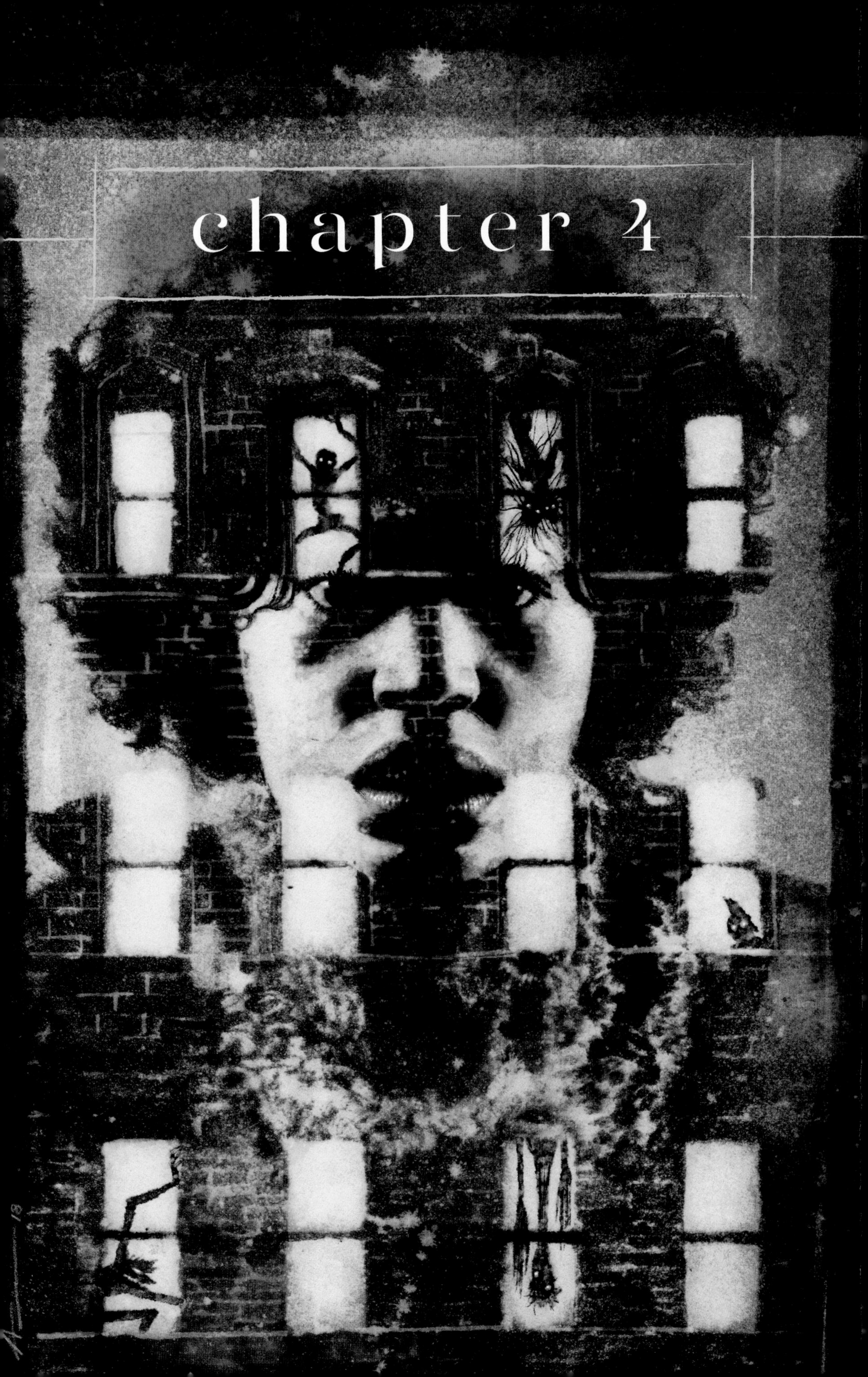

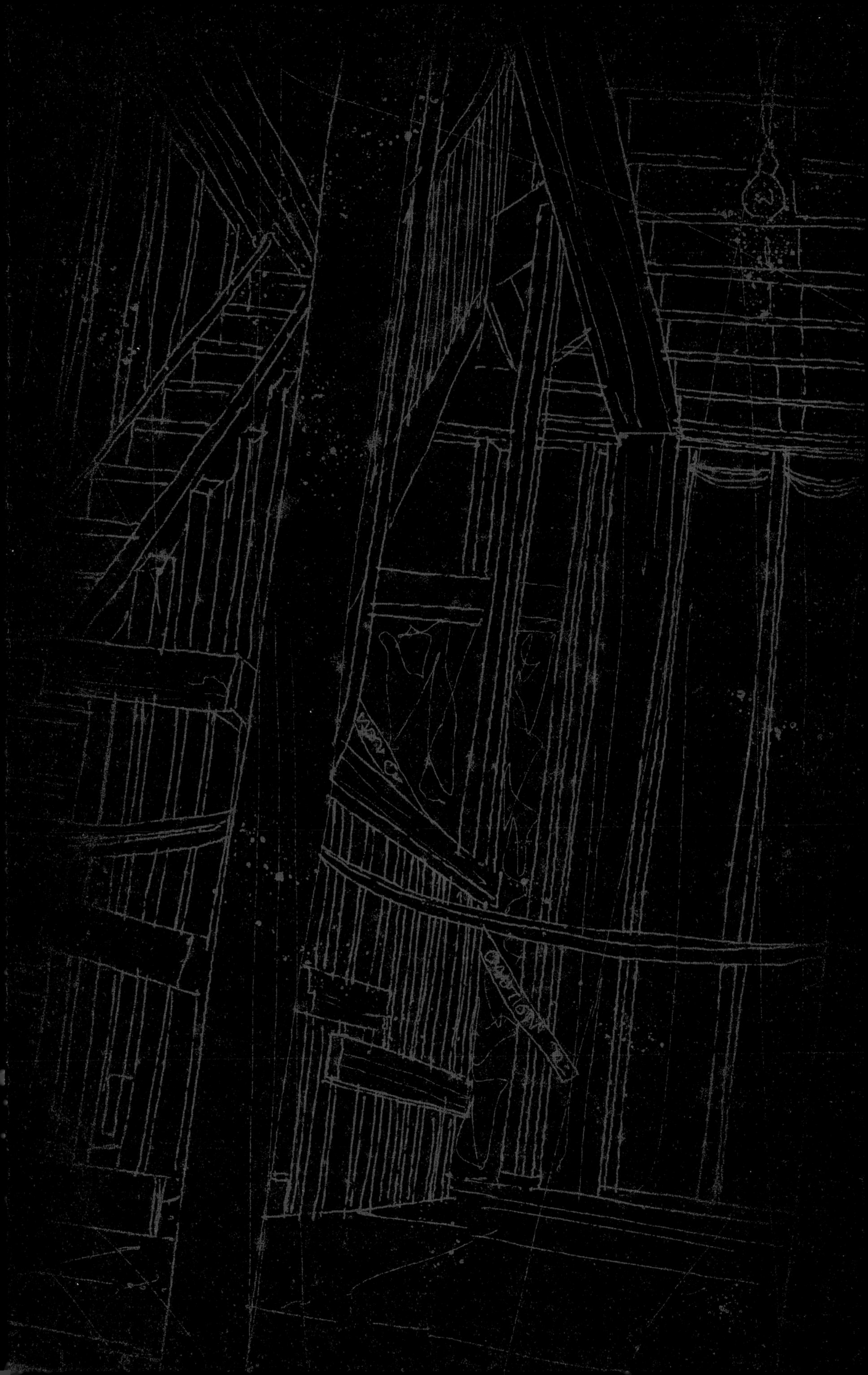

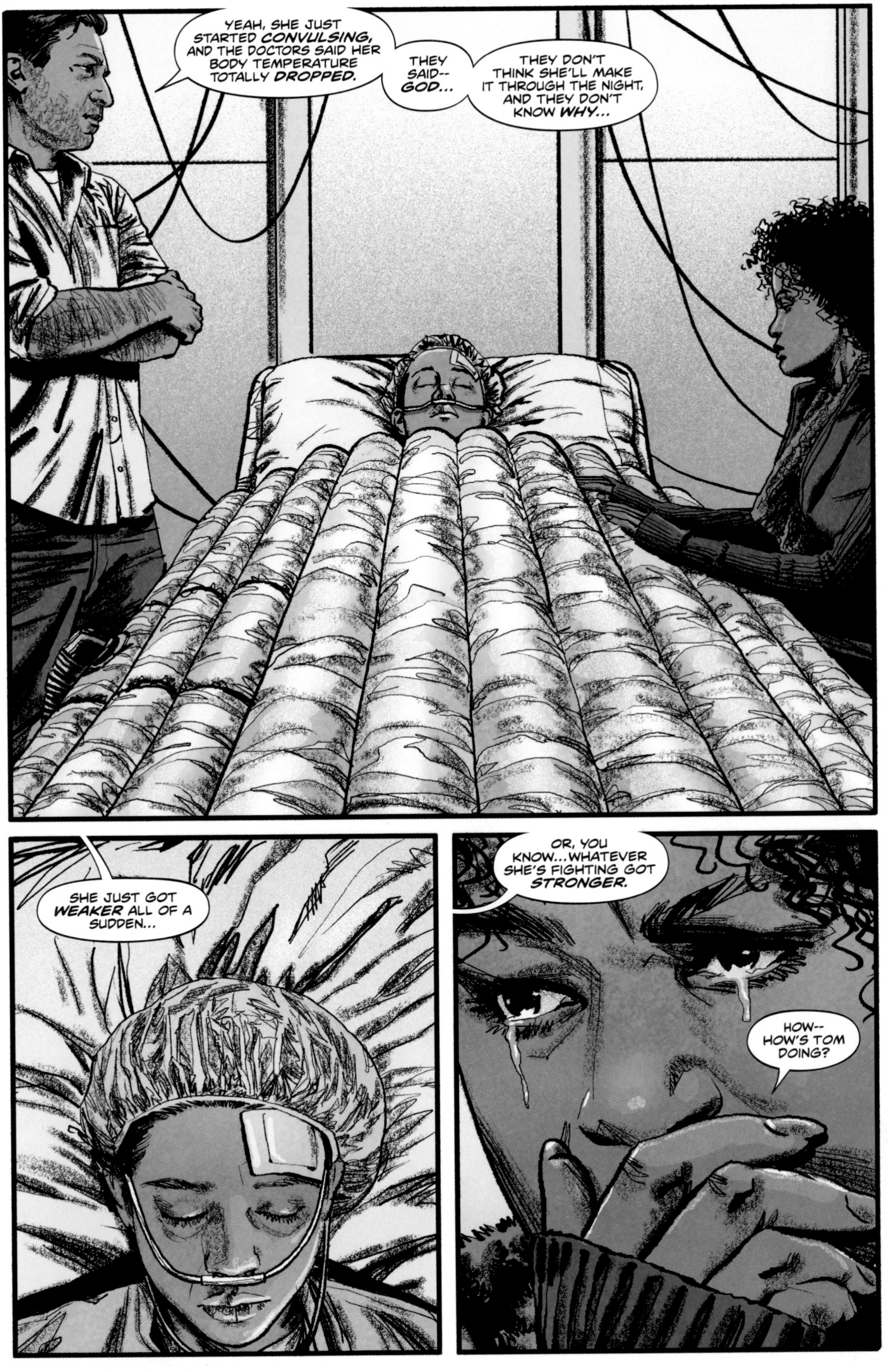
YEAH, SHE JUST STARTED CONVULSING, AND THE DOCTORS SAID HER BODY TEMPERATURE TOTALLY DROPPED.
THEY SAID-- GOD...
THEY DON'T THINK SHE'LL MAKE IT THROUGH THE NIGHT, AND THEY DON'T KNOW WHY...
SHE JUST GOT WEAKER ALL OF A SUDDEN...
OR, YOU KNOW...WHATEVER SHE'S FIGHTING GOT STRONGER.
HOW-- HOW'S TOM DOING?

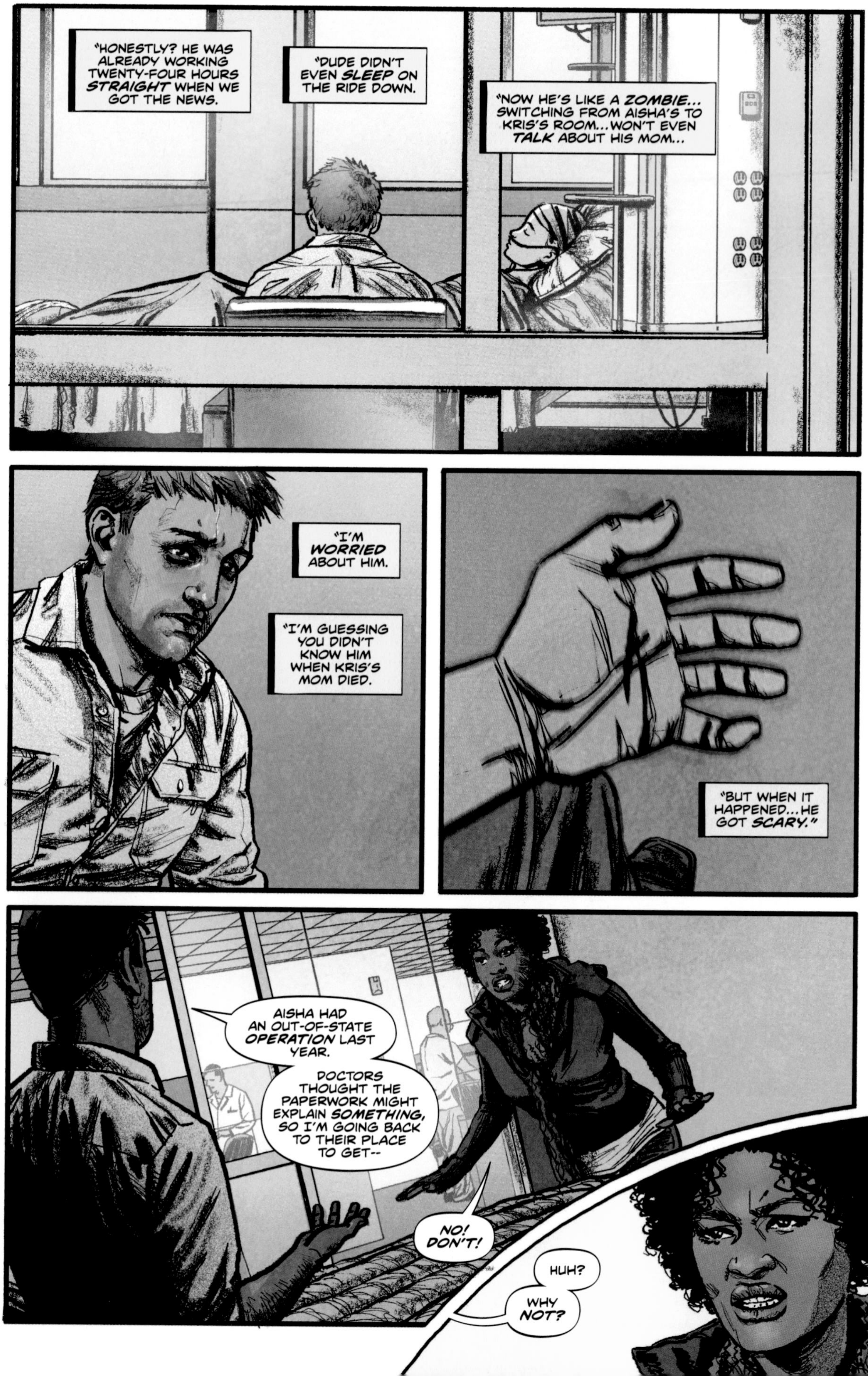

"HONESTLY? HE WAS ALREADY WORKING TWENTY-FOUR HOURS STRAIGHT WHEN WE GOT THE NEWS.
"DUDE DIDN'T EVEN SLEEP ON THE RIDE DOWN.
"NOW HE'S LIKE A ZOMBIE... SWITCHING FROM AISHA'S TO KRIS'S ROOM...WON'T EVEN TALK ABOUT HIS MOM...
"I'M WORRIED ABOUT HIM.
"I'M GUESSING YOU DIDN'T KNOW HIM WHEN KRIS'S MOM DIED.
"BUT WHEN IT HAPPENED...HE GOT SCARY."
AISHA HAD AN OUT-OF-STATE OPERATION LAST YEAR.
DOCTORS THOUGHT THE PAPERWORK MIGHT EXPLAIN SOMETHING, SO I'M GOING BACK TO THEIR PLACE TO GET--
NO! DON'T!
HUH?
WHY NOT?

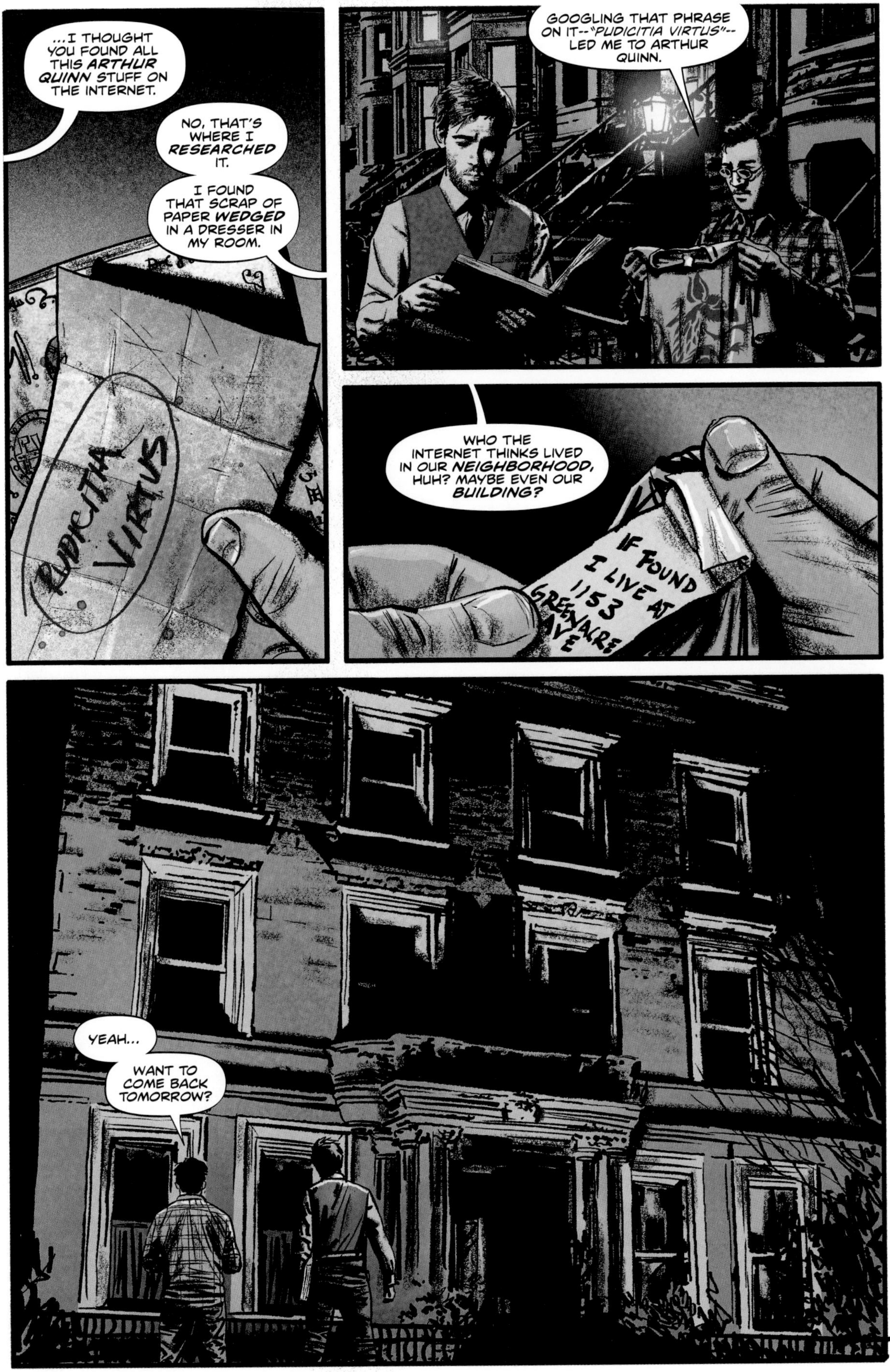
...I THOUGHT YOU FOUND ALL THIS *ARTHUR QUINN* STUFF ON THE INTERNET.
NO, THAT'S WHERE I *RESEARCHED* IT.
I FOUND THAT SCRAP OF PAPER *WEDGED* IN A DRESSER IN MY ROOM.
PUDICITIA VIRTUS
GOOGLING THAT PHRASE ON IT--"*PUDICITIA VIRTUS*"--LED ME TO ARTHUR QUINN.
WHO THE INTERNET THINKS LIVED IN OUR *NEIGHBORHOOD*, HUH? MAYBE EVEN OUR *BUILDING*?
IF FOUND I LIVE AT 1153 GREENACRE AVE
YEAH...
WANT TO COME BACK TOMORROW?

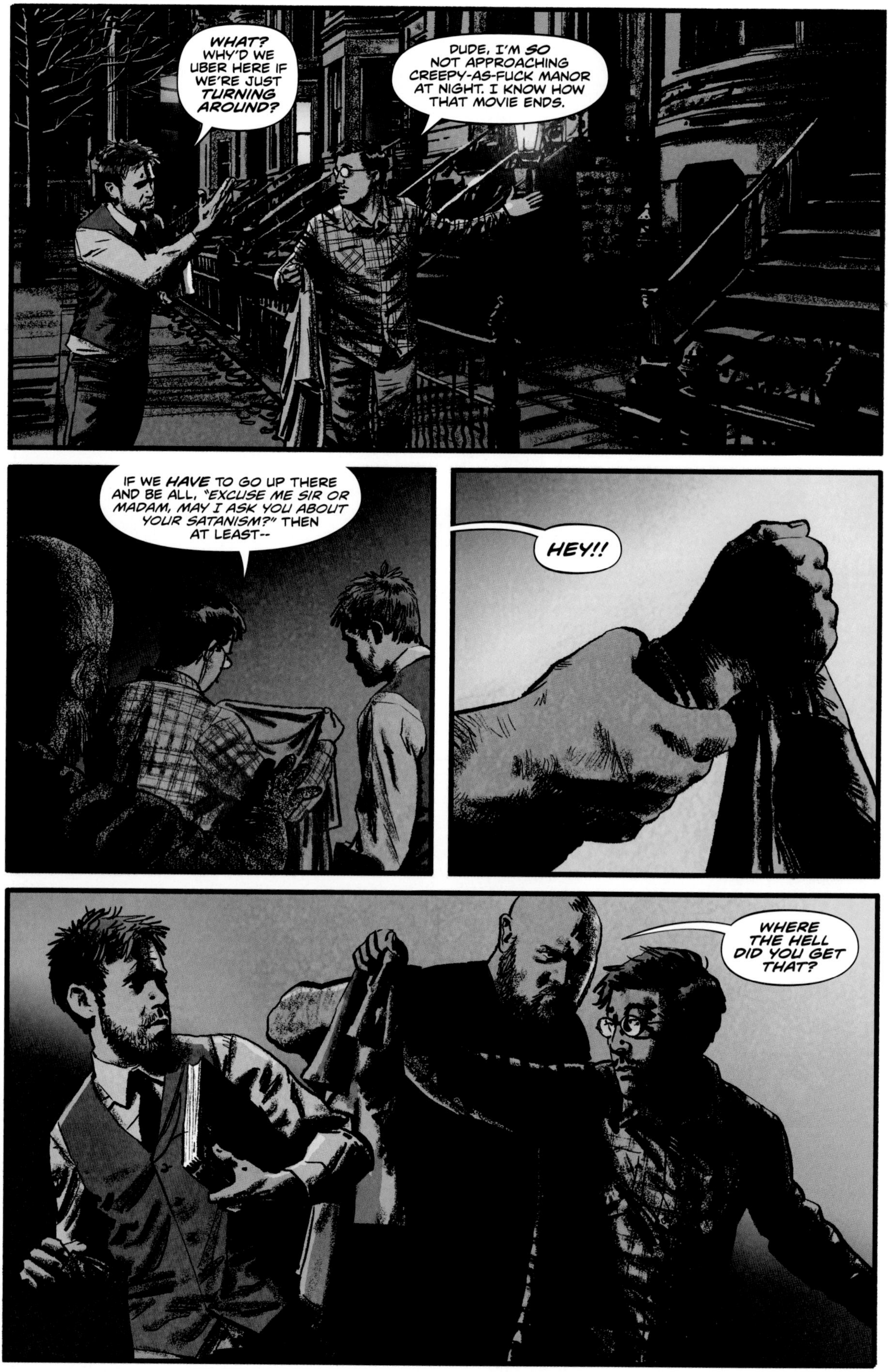
WHAT? WHY'D WE UBER HERE IF WE'RE JUST TURNING AROUND?
DUDE, I'M SO NOT APPROACHING CREEPY-AS-FUCK MANOR AT NIGHT. I KNOW HOW THAT MOVIE ENDS.
IF WE HAVE TO GO UP THERE AND BE ALL, "EXCUSE ME SIR OR MADAM, MAY I ASK YOU ABOUT YOUR SATANISM?" THEN AT LEAST--
HEY!!
WHERE THE HELL DID YOU GET THAT?

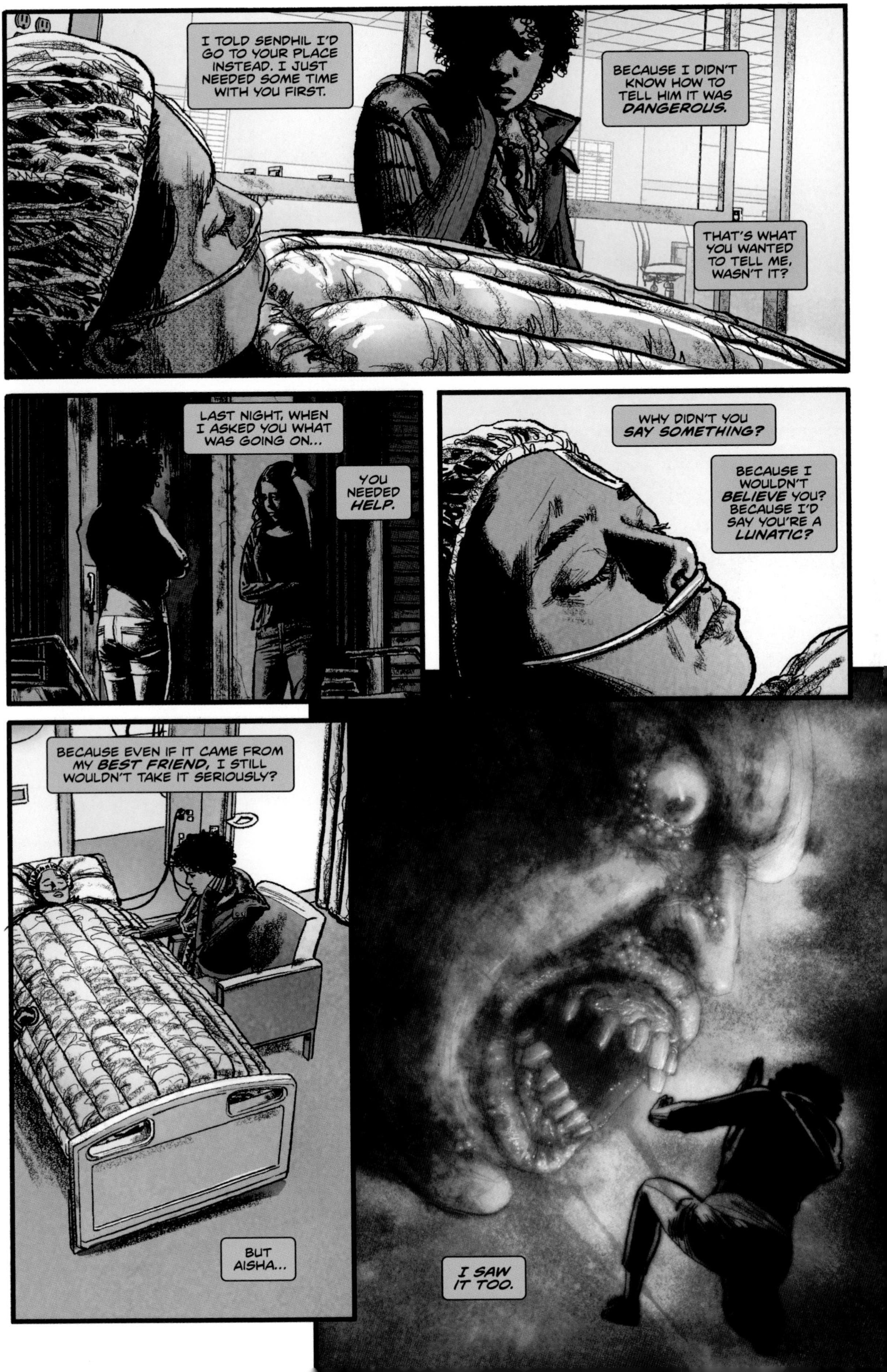
I TOLD SENDHIL I'D GO TO YOUR PLACE INSTEAD. I JUST NEEDED SOME TIME WITH YOU FIRST.
BECAUSE I DIDN'T KNOW HOW TO TELL HIM IT WAS *DANGEROUS.*
THAT'S WHAT YOU WANTED TO TELL ME, WASN'T IT?
LAST NIGHT, WHEN I ASKED YOU WHAT WAS GOING ON...
YOU NEEDED *HELP.*
WHY DIDN'T YOU *SAY SOMETHING?*
BECAUSE I WOULDN'T *BELIEVE* YOU? BECAUSE I'D SAY YOU'RE A *LUNATIC?*
BECAUSE EVEN IF IT CAME FROM MY *BEST FRIEND,* I STILL WOULDN'T TAKE IT SERIOUSLY?
BUT AISHA...
I SAW IT TOO.

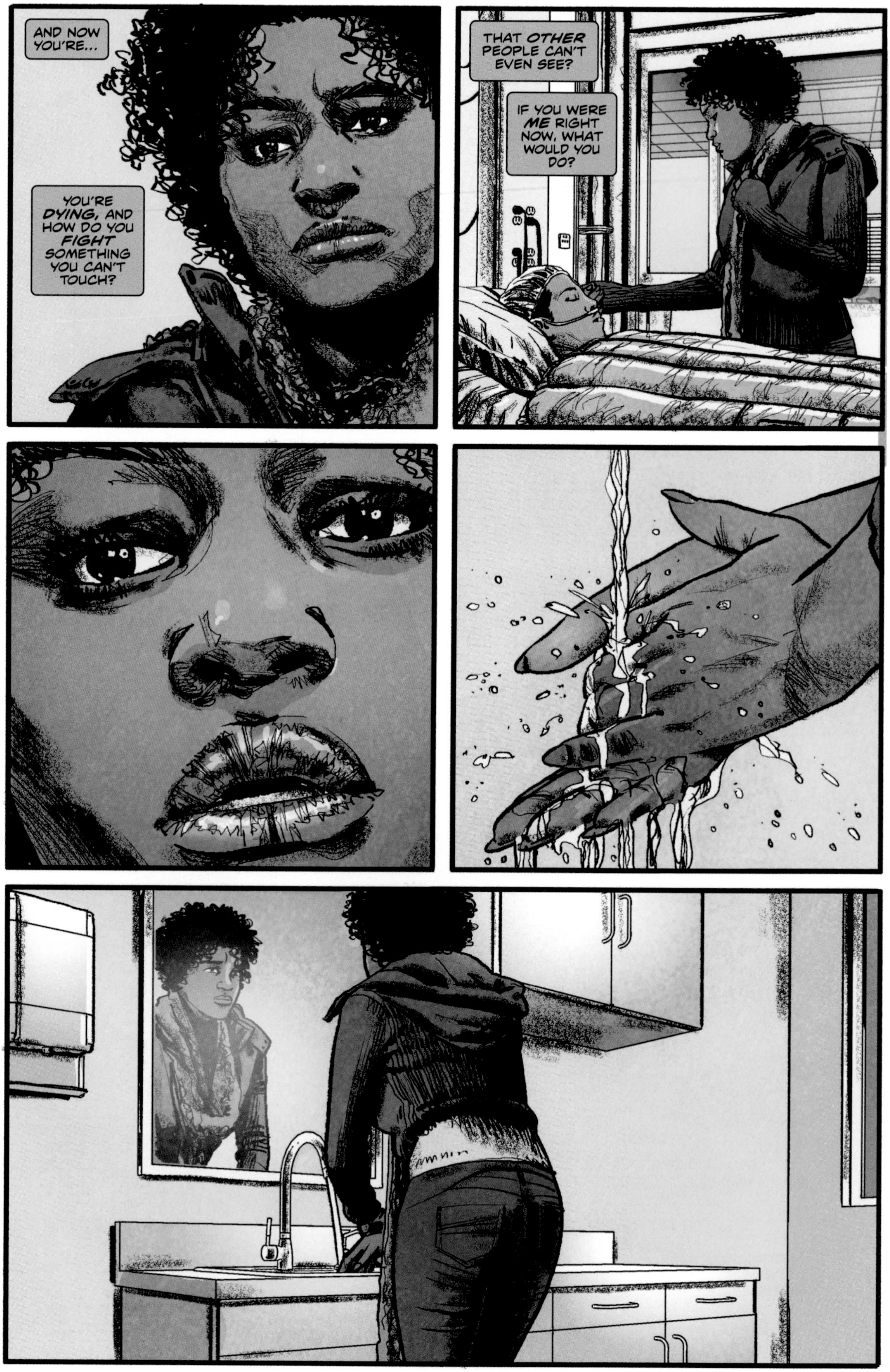
AND NOW YOU'RE...
YOU'RE DYING, AND HOW DO YOU FIGHT SOMETHING YOU CAN'T TOUCH?
THAT OTHER PEOPLE CAN'T EVEN SEE?
IF YOU WERE ME RIGHT NOW, WHAT WOULD YOU DO?

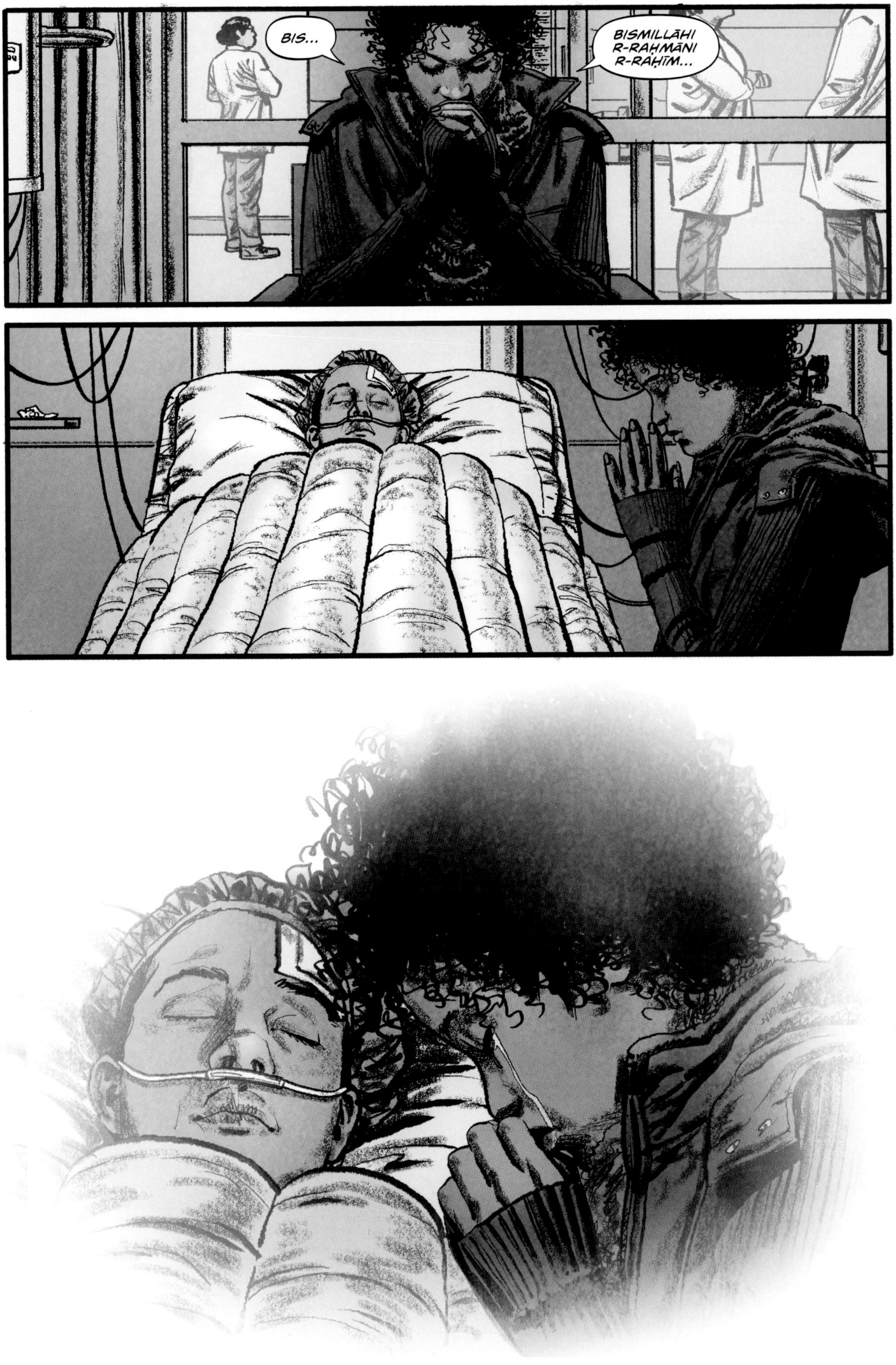
BIS...
BISMILLĀHI R-RAḤMĀNI R-RAḤĪM...

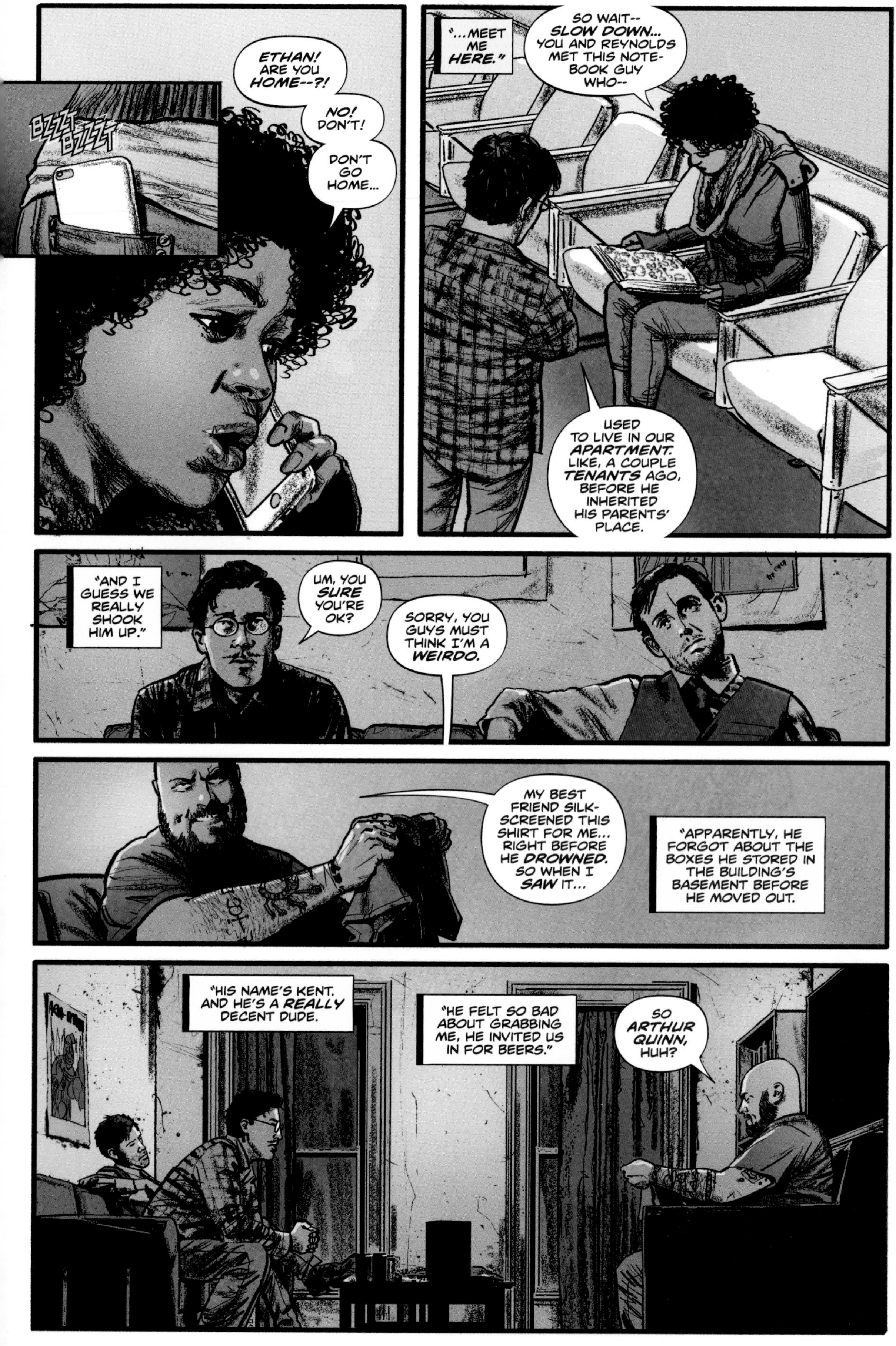
BZZZT BZZZT
ETHAN! ARE YOU HOME--?!
NO! DON'T!
DON'T GO HOME...
"...MEET ME HERE."
SO WAIT-- SLOW DOWN... YOU AND REYNOLDS MET THIS NOTE-BOOK GUY WHO--
USED TO LIVE IN OUR APARTMENT. LIKE, A COUPLE TENANTS AGO, BEFORE HE INHERITED HIS PARENTS' PLACE.
"AND I GUESS WE REALLY SHOOK HIM UP."
UM, YOU SURE YOU'RE OK?
SORRY, YOU GUYS MUST THINK I'M A WEIRDO.
MY BEST FRIEND SILK-SCREENED THIS SHIRT FOR ME... RIGHT BEFORE HE DROWNED. SO WHEN I SAW IT...
"APPARENTLY, HE FORGOT ABOUT THE BOXES HE STORED IN THE BUILDING'S BASEMENT BEFORE HE MOVED OUT.
"HIS NAME'S KENT. AND HE'S A REALLY DECENT DUDE.
"HE FELT SO BAD ABOUT GRABBING ME, HE INVITED US IN FOR BEERS."
SO ARTHUR QUINN, HUH?

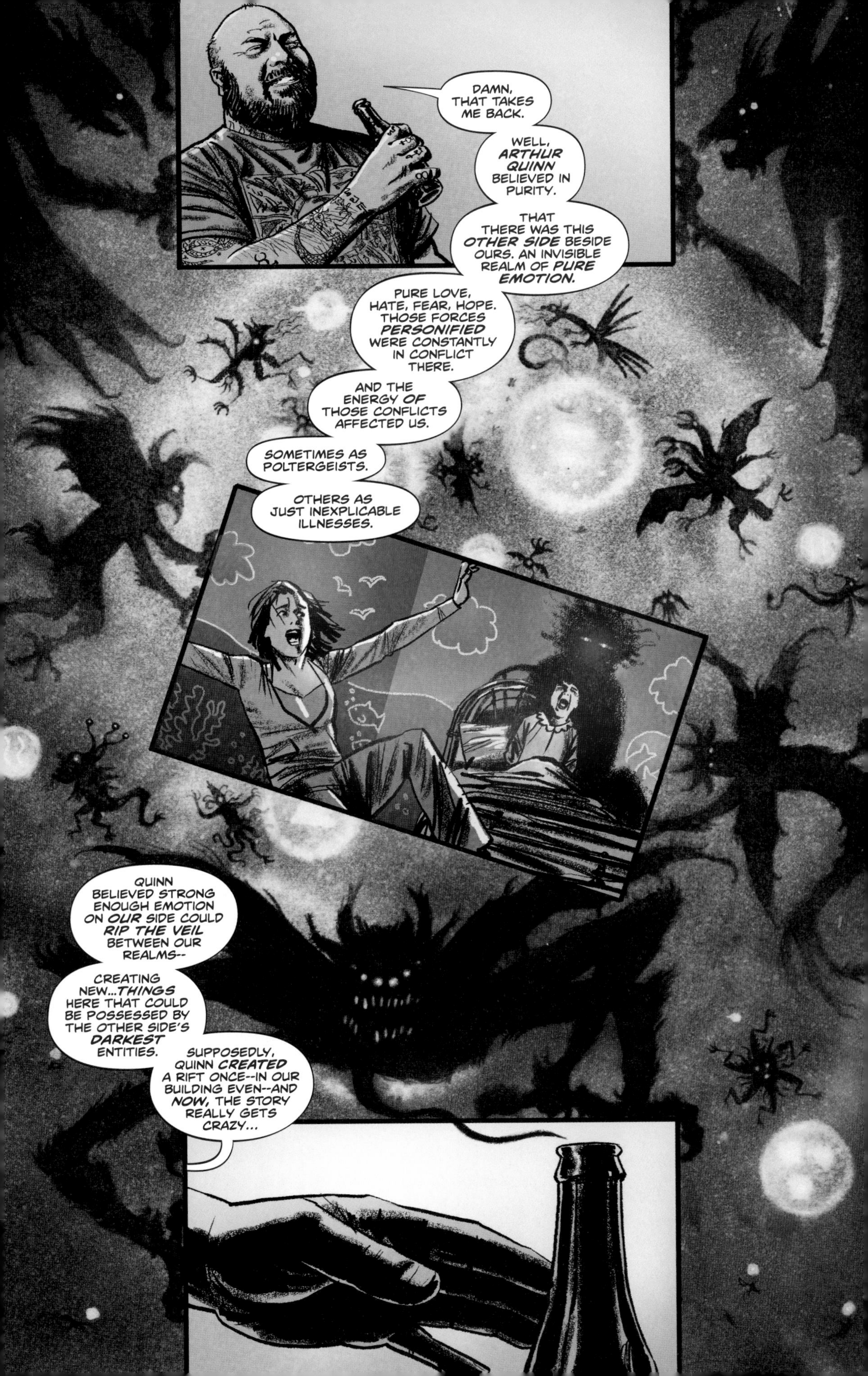
DAMN, THAT TAKES ME BACK.
WELL, ARTHUR QUINN BELIEVED IN PURITY.
THAT THERE WAS THIS OTHER SIDE BESIDE OURS. AN INVISIBLE REALM OF PURE EMOTION.
PURE LOVE, HATE, FEAR, HOPE. THOSE FORCES PERSONIFIED WERE CONSTANTLY IN CONFLICT THERE.
AND THE ENERGY OF THOSE CONFLICTS AFFECTED US.
SOMETIMES AS POLTERGEISTS.
OTHERS AS JUST INEXPLICABLE ILLNESSES.
QUINN BELIEVED STRONG ENOUGH EMOTION ON OUR SIDE COULD RIP THE VEIL BETWEEN OUR REALMS--
CREATING NEW...THINGS HERE THAT COULD BE POSSESSED BY THE OTHER SIDE'S DARKEST ENTITIES.
SUPPOSEDLY, QUINN CREATED A RIFT ONCE--IN OUR BUILDING EVEN--AND NOW, THE STORY REALLY GETS CRAZY...

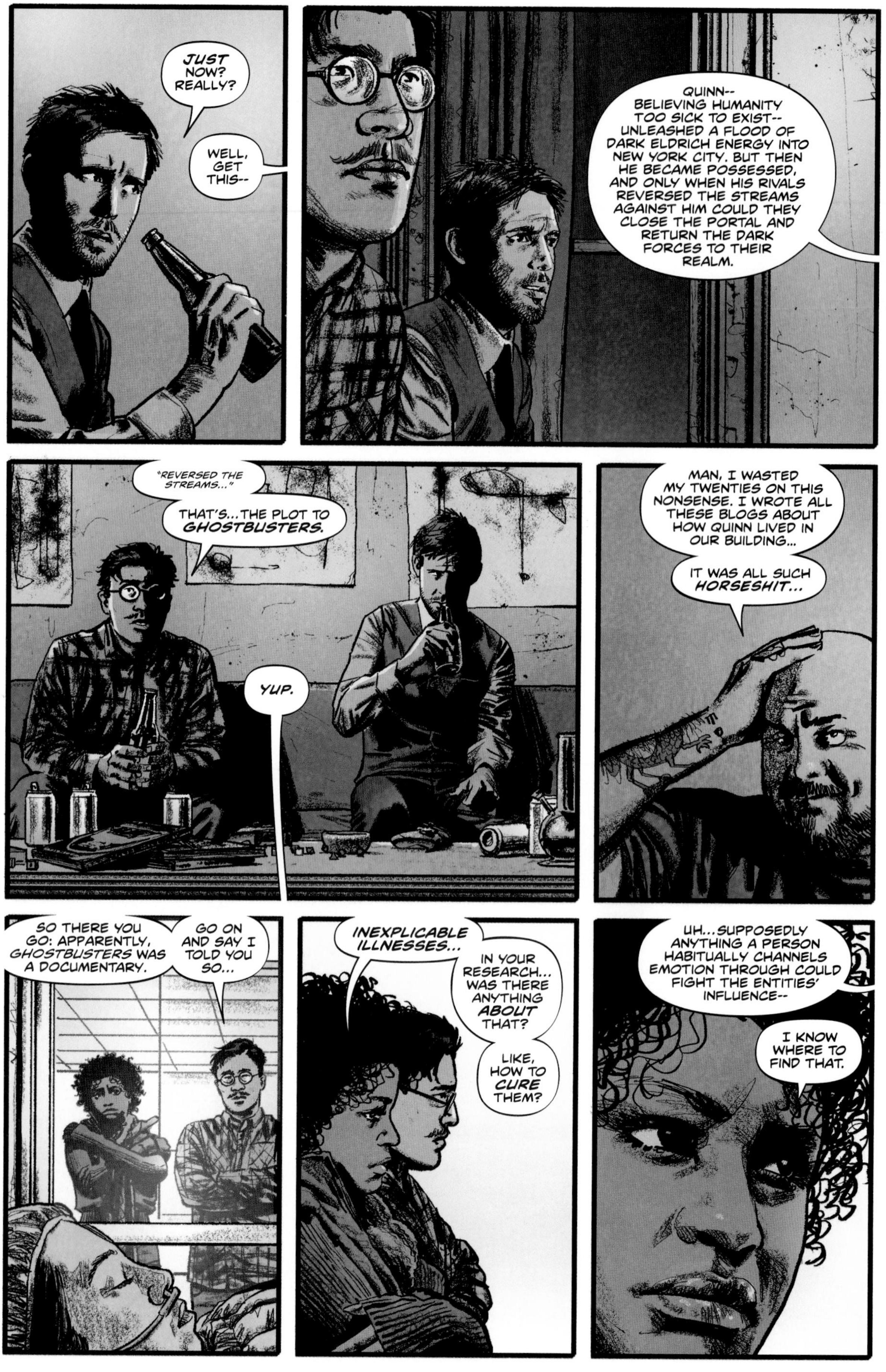
JUST NOW? REALLY?
WELL, GET THIS--
QUINN-- BELIEVING HUMANITY TOO SICK TO EXIST-- UNLEASHED A FLOOD OF DARK ELDRICH ENERGY INTO NEW YORK CITY. BUT THEN HE BECAME POSSESSED, AND ONLY WHEN HIS RIVALS REVERSED THE STREAMS AGAINST HIM COULD THEY CLOSE THE PORTAL AND RETURN THE DARK FORCES TO THEIR REALM.
"REVERSED THE STREAMS..."
THAT'S...THE PLOT TO GHOSTBUSTERS.
YUP.
MAN, I WASTED MY TWENTIES ON THIS NONSENSE. I WROTE ALL THESE BLOGS ABOUT HOW QUINN LIVED IN OUR BUILDING...
IT WAS ALL SUCH HORSESHIT...
SO THERE YOU GO: APPARENTLY, GHOSTBUSTERS WAS A DOCUMENTARY.
GO ON AND SAY I TOLD YOU SO...
INEXPLICABLE ILLNESSES...
IN YOUR RESEARCH... WAS THERE ANYTHING ABOUT THAT?
LIKE, HOW TO CURE THEM?
UH...SUPPOSEDLY ANYTHING A PERSON HABITUALLY CHANNELS EMOTION THROUGH COULD FIGHT THE ENTITIES' INFLUENCE--
I KNOW WHERE TO FIND THAT.

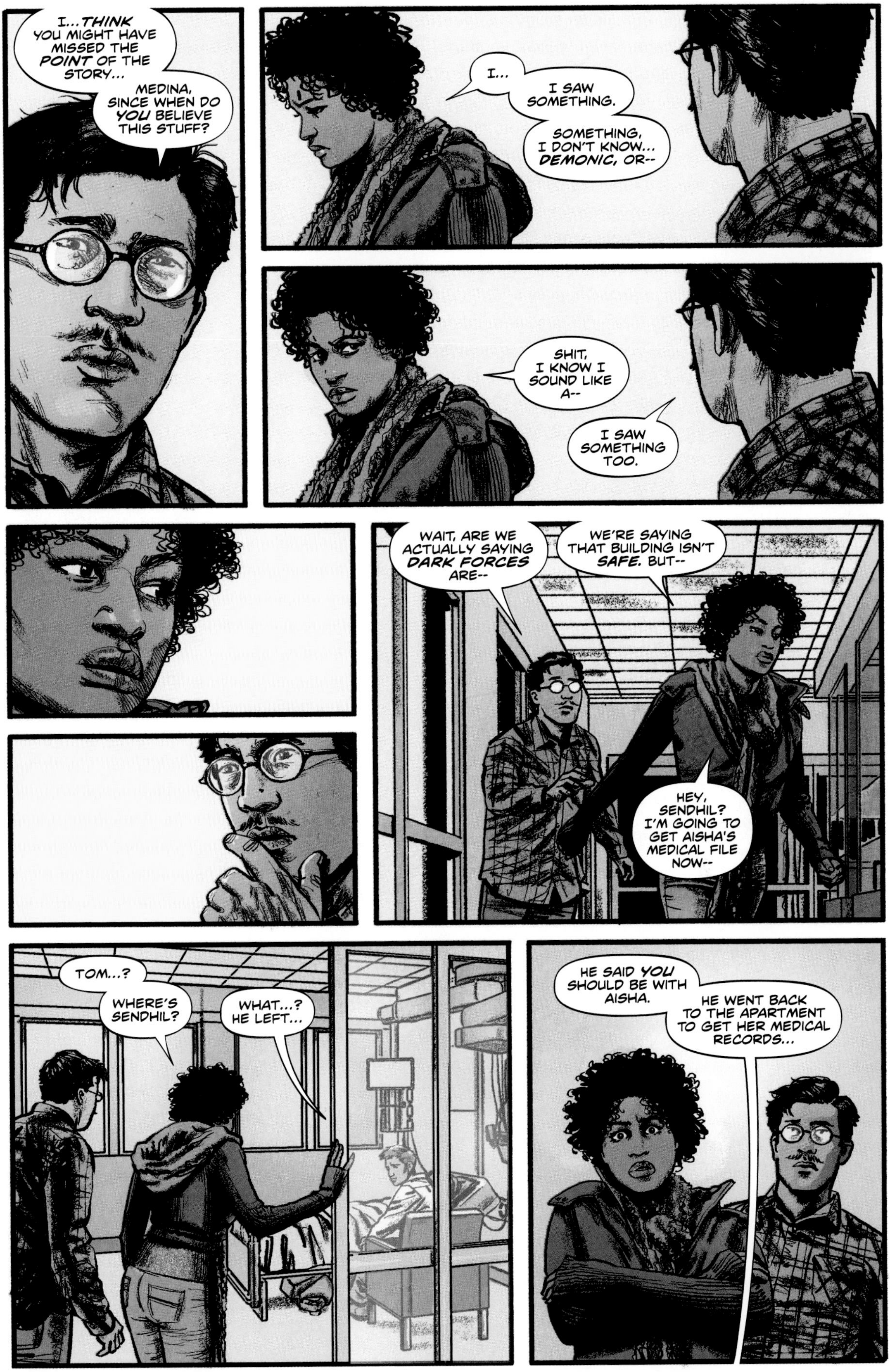

I... THINK YOU MIGHT HAVE MISSED THE POINT OF THE STORY...
MEDINA, SINCE WHEN DO YOU BELIEVE THIS STUFF?
I...
I SAW SOMETHING.
SOMETHING, I DON'T KNOW... DEMONIC, OR--
SHIT, I KNOW I SOUND LIKE A--
I SAW SOMETHING TOO.
WAIT, ARE WE ACTUALLY SAYING DARK FORCES ARE--
WE'RE SAYING THAT BUILDING ISN'T SAFE. BUT--
HEY, SENDHIL? I'M GOING TO GET AISHA'S MEDICAL FILE NOW--
TOM...?
WHERE'S SENDHIL?
WHAT...? HE LEFT...
HE SAID YOU SHOULD BE WITH AISHA.
HE WENT BACK TO THE APARTMENT TO GET HER MEDICAL RECORDS...

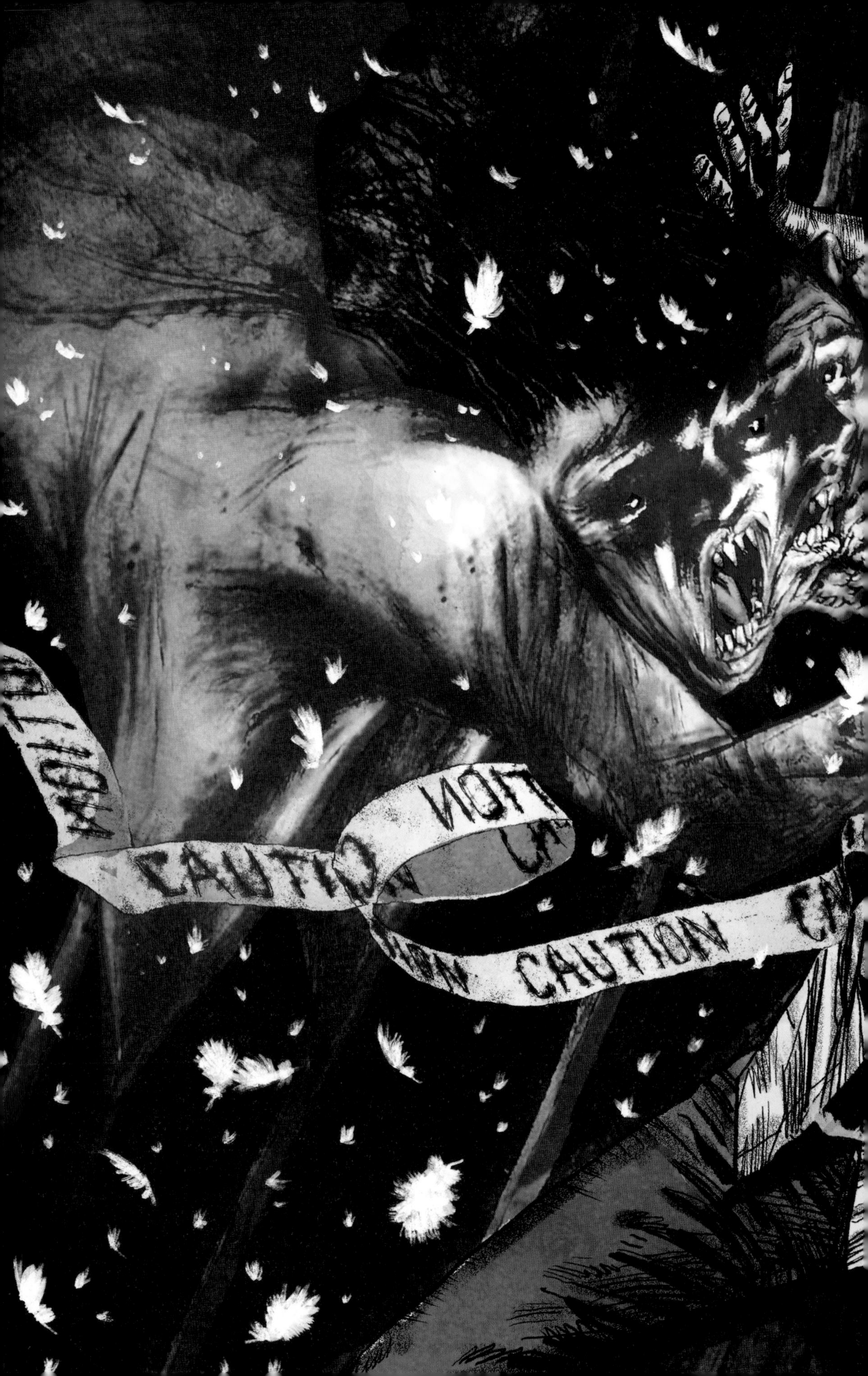
CAUTION
CAUTION

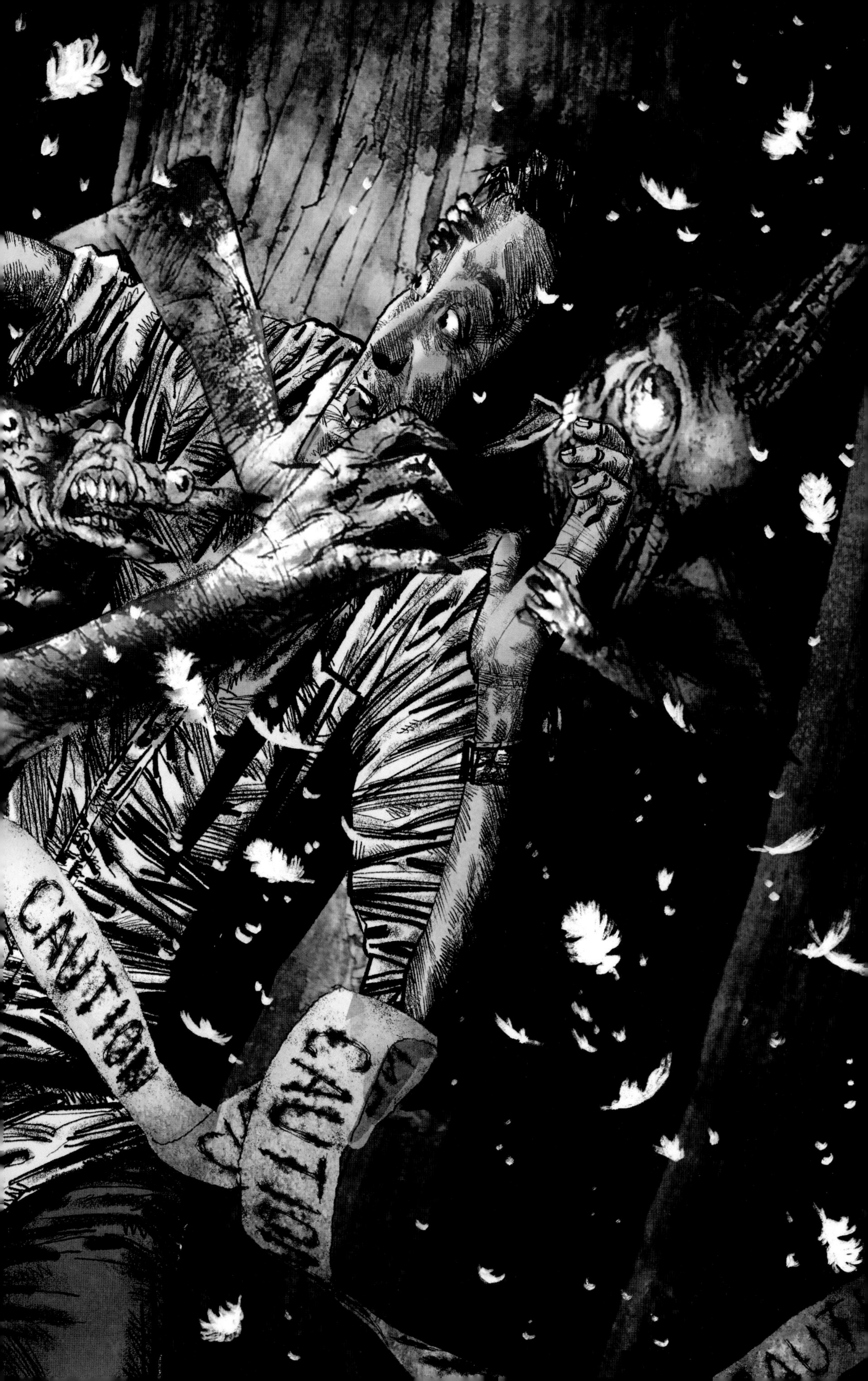
CAUTION
CAUTION

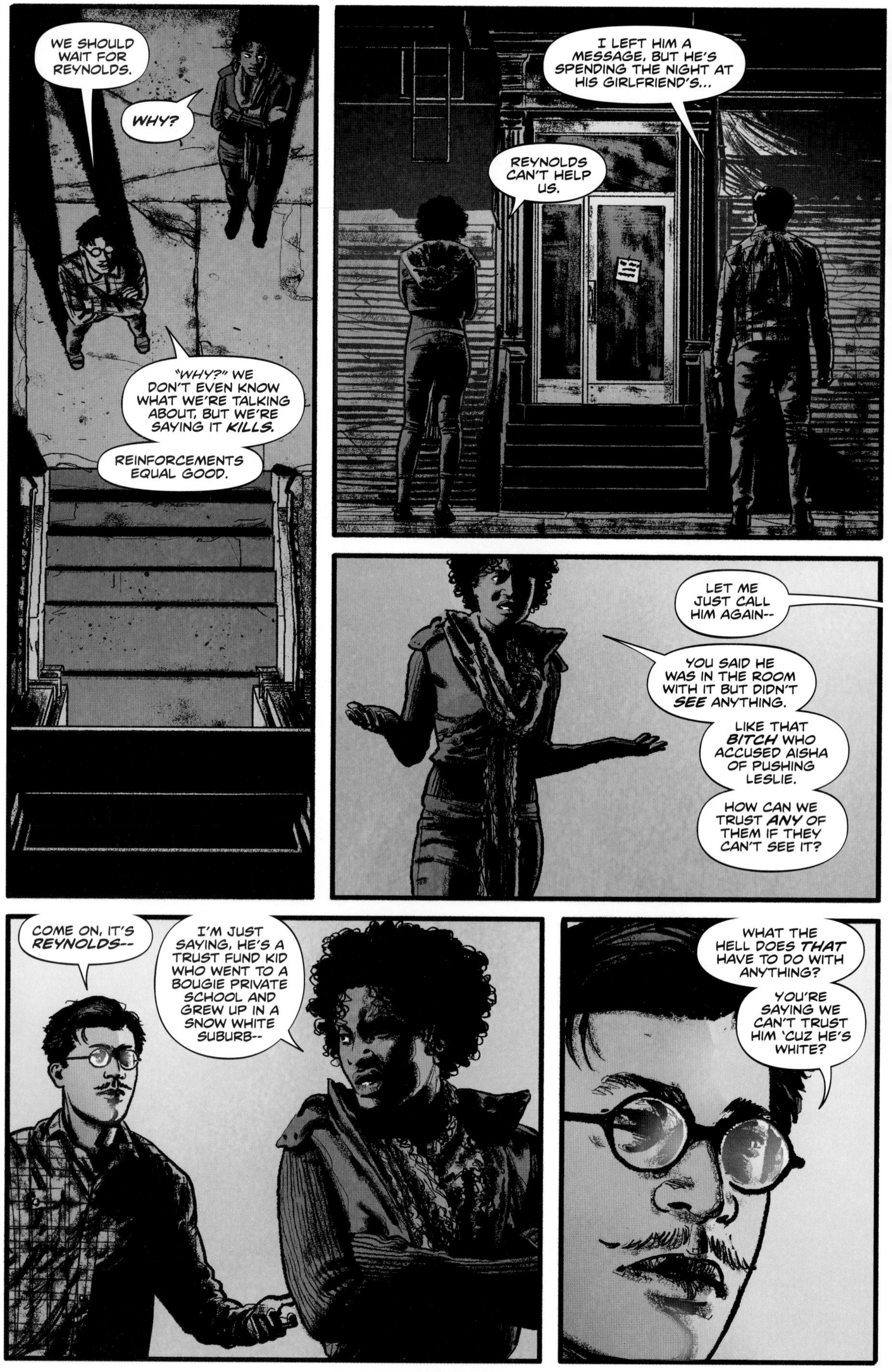
WE SHOULD WAIT FOR REYNOLDS.
WHY?
"WHY?" WE DON'T EVEN KNOW WHAT WE'RE TALKING ABOUT, BUT WE'RE SAYING IT KILLS.
REINFORCEMENTS EQUAL GOOD.
I LEFT HIM A MESSAGE, BUT HE'S SPENDING THE NIGHT AT HIS GIRLFRIEND'S...
REYNOLDS CAN'T HELP US.
LET ME JUST CALL HIM AGAIN--
YOU SAID HE WAS IN THE ROOM WITH IT BUT DIDN'T SEE ANYTHING.
LIKE THAT BITCH WHO ACCUSED AISHA OF PUSHING LESLIE.
HOW CAN WE TRUST ANY OF THEM IF THEY CAN'T SEE IT?
COME ON, IT'S REYNOLDS--
I'M JUST SAYING, HE'S A TRUST FUND KID WHO WENT TO A BOUGIE PRIVATE SCHOOL AND GREW UP IN A SNOW WHITE SUBURB--
WHAT THE HELL DOES THAT HAVE TO DO WITH ANYTHING?
YOU'RE SAYING WE CAN'T TRUST HIM 'CUZ HE'S WHITE?

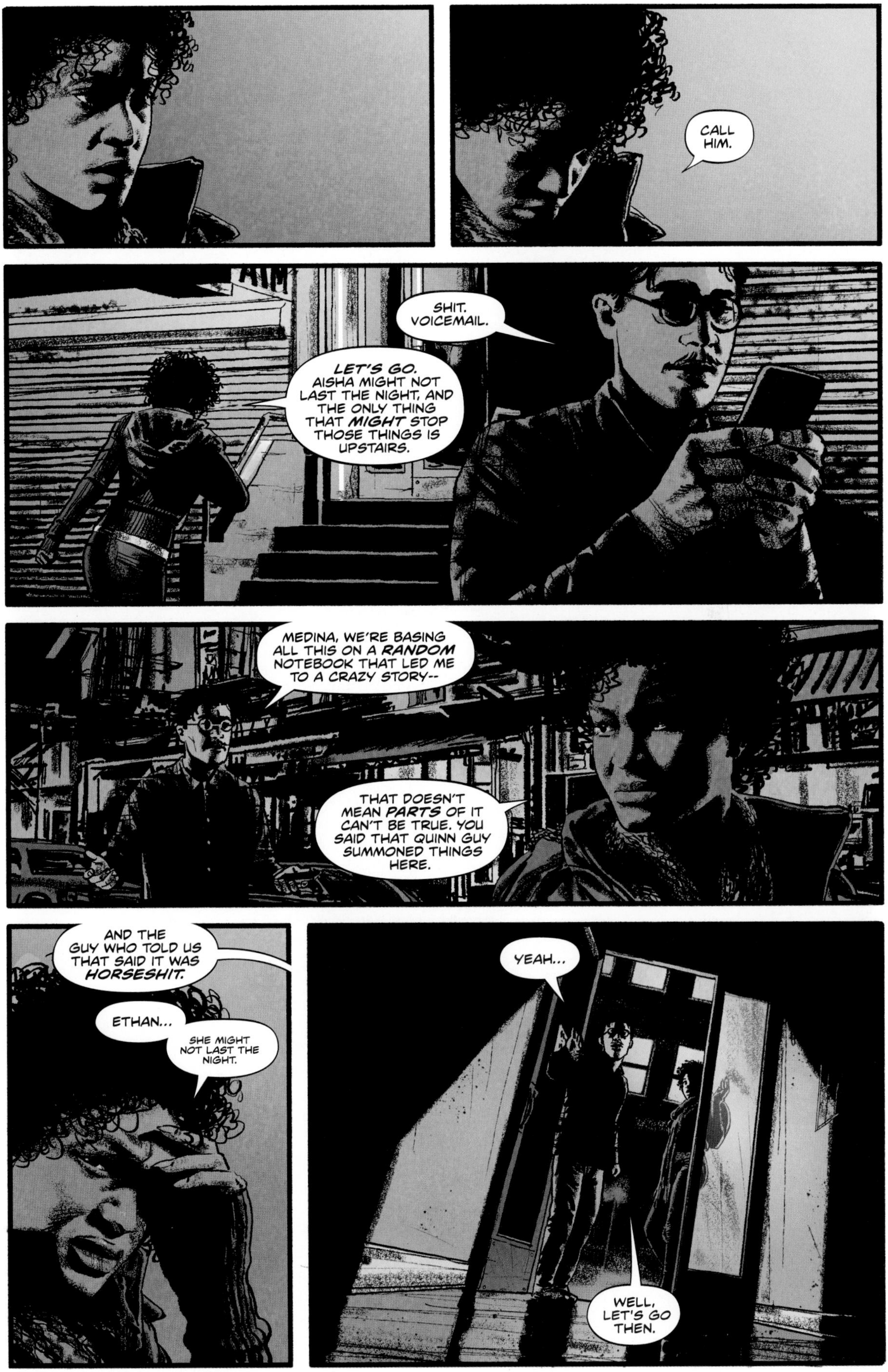
CALL HIM.
SHIT. VOICEMAIL.
LET'S GO. AISHA MIGHT NOT LAST THE NIGHT, AND THE ONLY THING THAT MIGHT STOP THOSE THINGS IS UPSTAIRS.
MEDINA, WE'RE BASING ALL THIS ON A RANDOM NOTEBOOK THAT LED ME TO A CRAZY STORY--
THAT DOESN'T MEAN PARTS OF IT CAN'T BE TRUE. YOU SAID THAT QUINN GUY SUMMONED THINGS HERE.
AND THE GUY WHO TOLD US THAT SAID IT WAS HORSESHIT.
ETHAN...
SHE MIGHT NOT LAST THE NIGHT.
YEAH...
WELL, LET'S GO THEN.

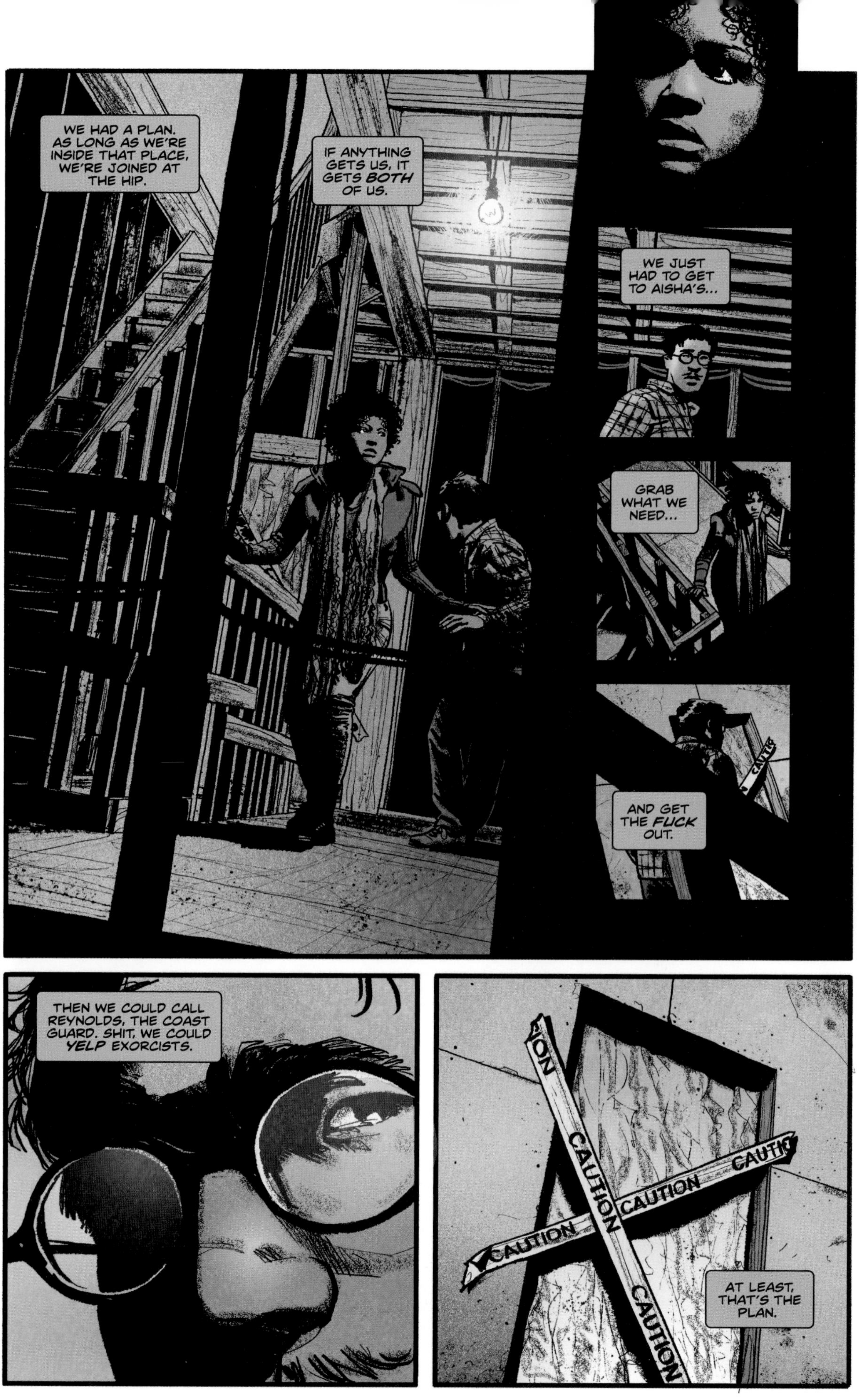

WE HAD A PLAN. AS LONG AS WE'RE INSIDE THAT PLACE, WE'RE JOINED AT THE HIP.
IF ANYTHING GETS US, IT GETS *BOTH* OF US.
WE JUST HAD TO GET TO AISHA'S...
GRAB WHAT WE NEED...
AND GET THE *FUCK* OUT.
THEN WE COULD CALL REYNOLDS, THE COAST GUARD. SHIT, WE COULD *YELP* EXORCISTS.
CAUTION
CAUTION
CAUTION
CAUTION
AT LEAST, THAT'S THE PLAN.

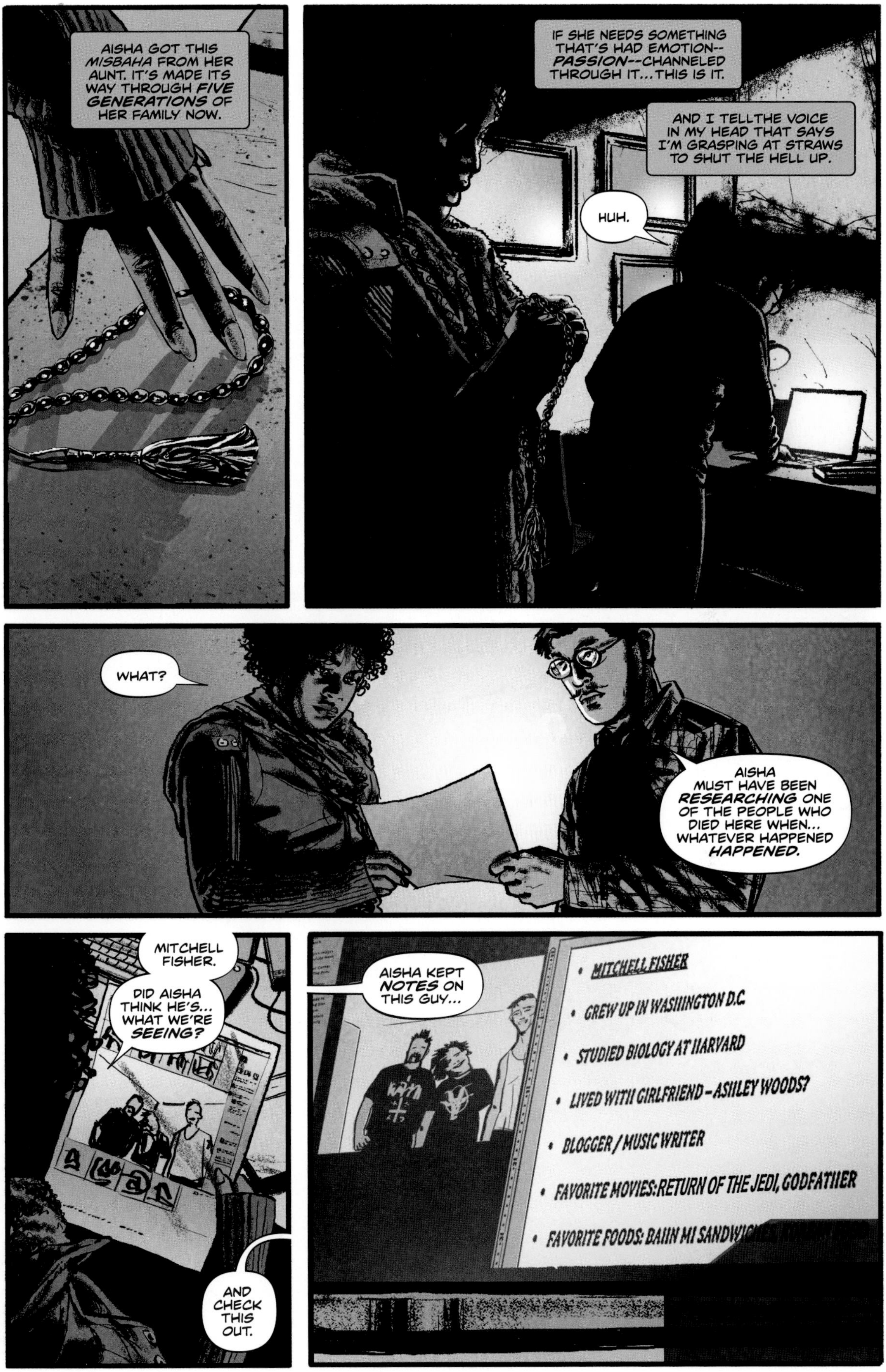
AISHA GOT THIS *MISBAHA* FROM HER AUNT. IT'S MADE ITS WAY THROUGH *FIVE GENERATIONS* OF HER FAMILY NOW.
IF SHE NEEDS SOMETHING THAT'S HAD EMOTION-- *PASSION*--CHANNELED THROUGH IT... THIS IS IT.
AND I TELLTHE VOICE IN MY HEAD THAT SAYS I'M GRASPING AT STRAWS TO SHUT THE HELL UP.
HUH.
WHAT?
AISHA MUST HAVE BEEN ***RESEARCHING*** ONE OF THE PEOPLE WHO DIED HERE WHEN... WHATEVER HAPPENED ***HAPPENED.***
MITCHELL FISHER.
DID AISHA THINK HE'S... WHAT WE'RE *SEEING?*
AISHA KEPT *NOTES* ON THIS GUY...
MITCHELL FISHER
GREW UP IN WASHINGTON D.C.
STUDIED BIOLOGY AT HARVARD
LIVED WITH GIRLFRIEND - ASHLEY WOODS?
BLOGGER / MUSIC WRITER
FAVORITE MOVIES: RETURN OF THE JEDI, GODFATHER
FAVORITE FOODS: BAHN MI SANDWI
AND CHECK THIS OUT.

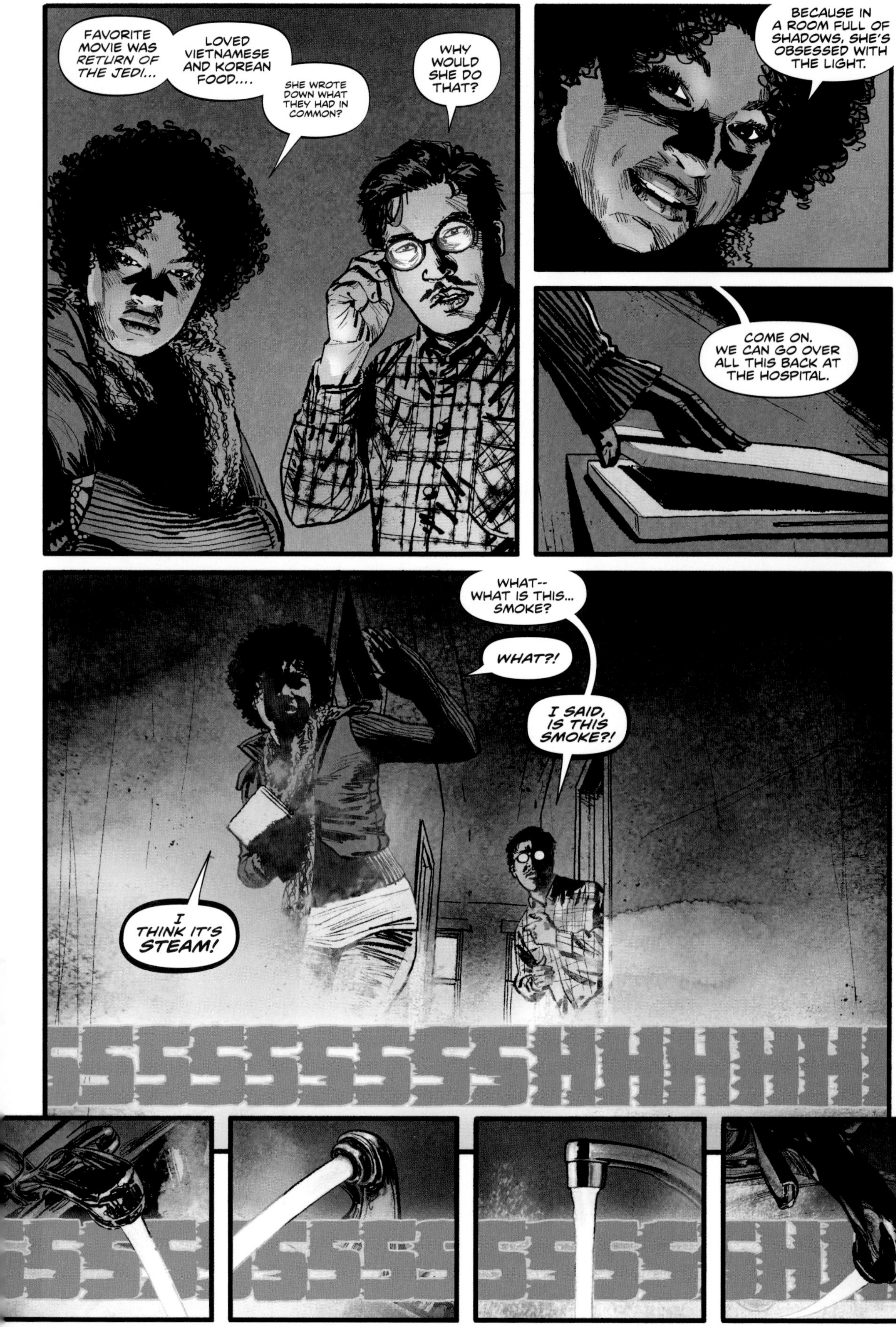
FAVORITE MOVIE WAS RETURN OF THE JEDI...
LOVED VIETNAMESE AND KOREAN FOOD....
SHE WROTE DOWN WHAT THEY HAD IN COMMON?
WHY WOULD SHE DO THAT?
BECAUSE IN A ROOM FULL OF SHADOWS, SHE'S OBSESSED WITH THE LIGHT.
COME ON. WE CAN GO OVER ALL THIS BACK AT THE HOSPITAL.
WHAT-- WHAT IS THIS... SMOKE?
WHAT?!
I SAID, IS THIS SMOKE?!
I THINK IT'S STEAM!
SSSSSSSSHHHHH
SSSSSSSSSSSSH

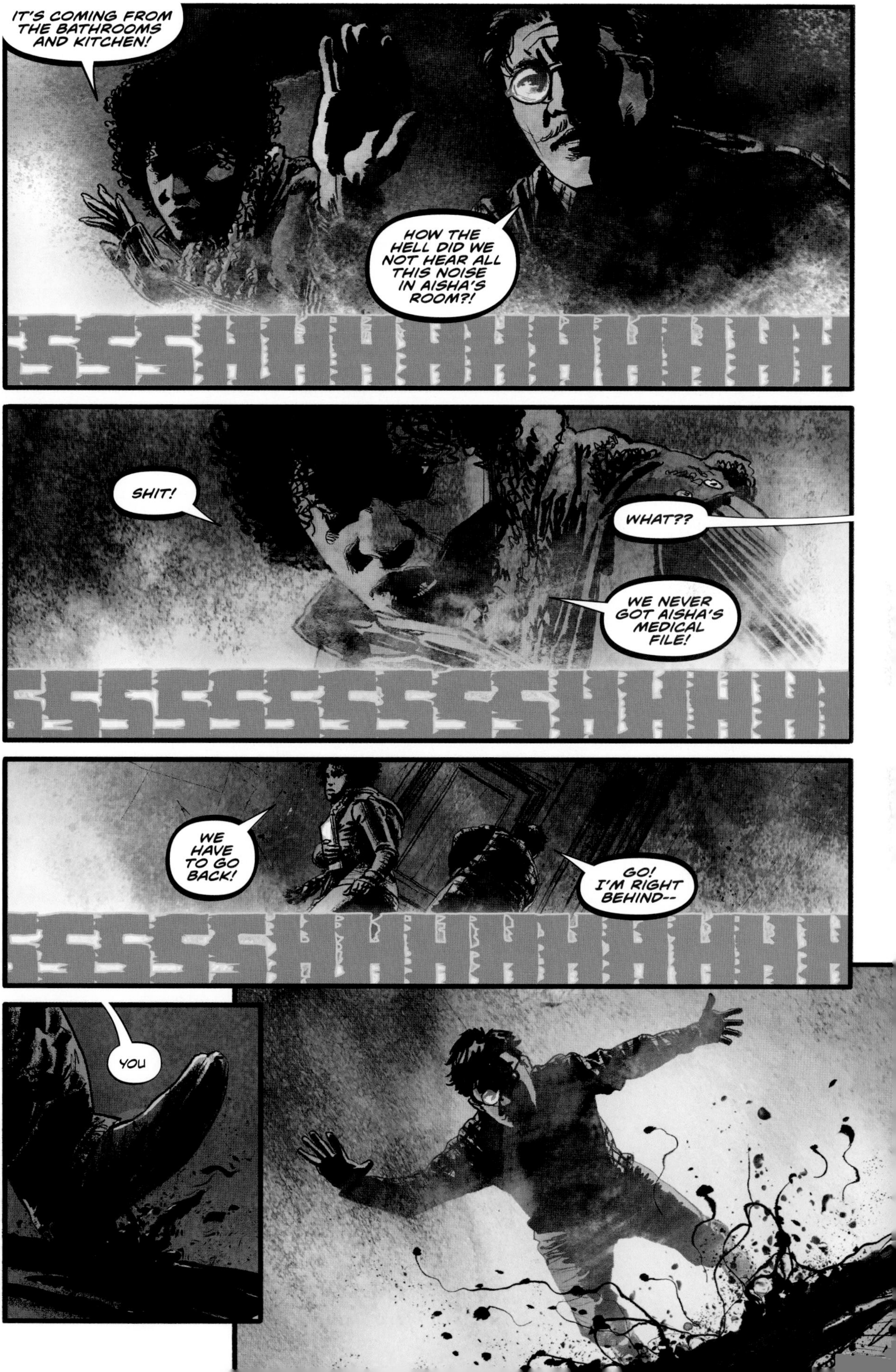
IT'S COMING FROM THE BATHROOMS AND KITCHEN!
HOW THE HELL DID WE NOT HEAR ALL THIS NOISE IN AISHA'S ROOM?!
SSSHHHHHHHHHHHH
SHIT!
WHAT??
WE NEVER GOT AISHA'S MEDICAL FILE!
SSSSSSSSSHHHH
WE HAVE TO GO BACK!
GO! I'M RIGHT BEHIND--
SSSSHHHHHHHHHHHH
YOU

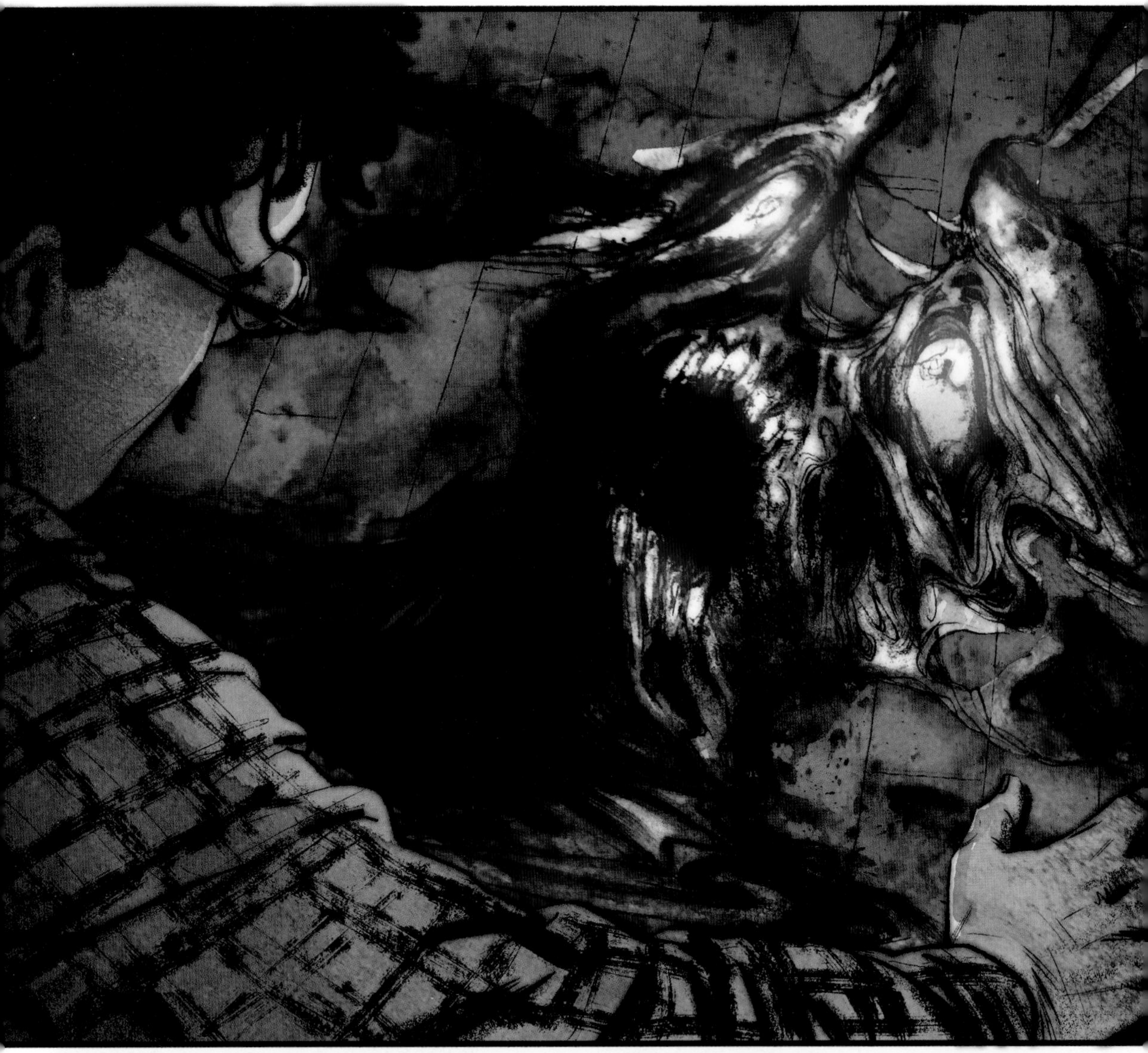

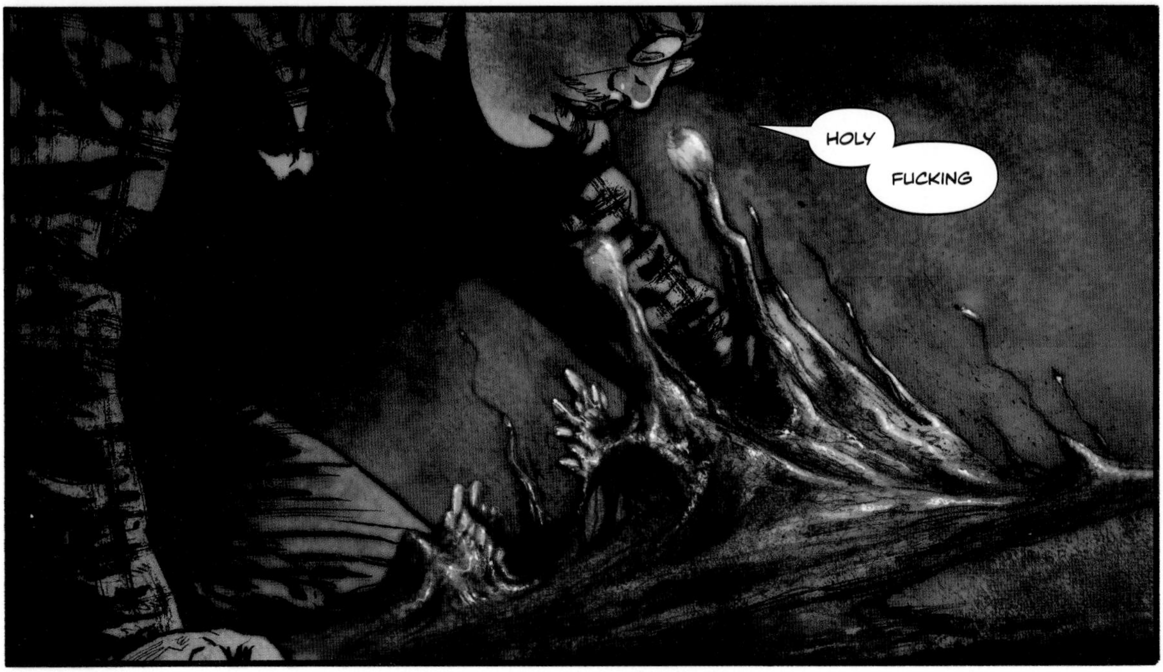
HOLY
FUCKING

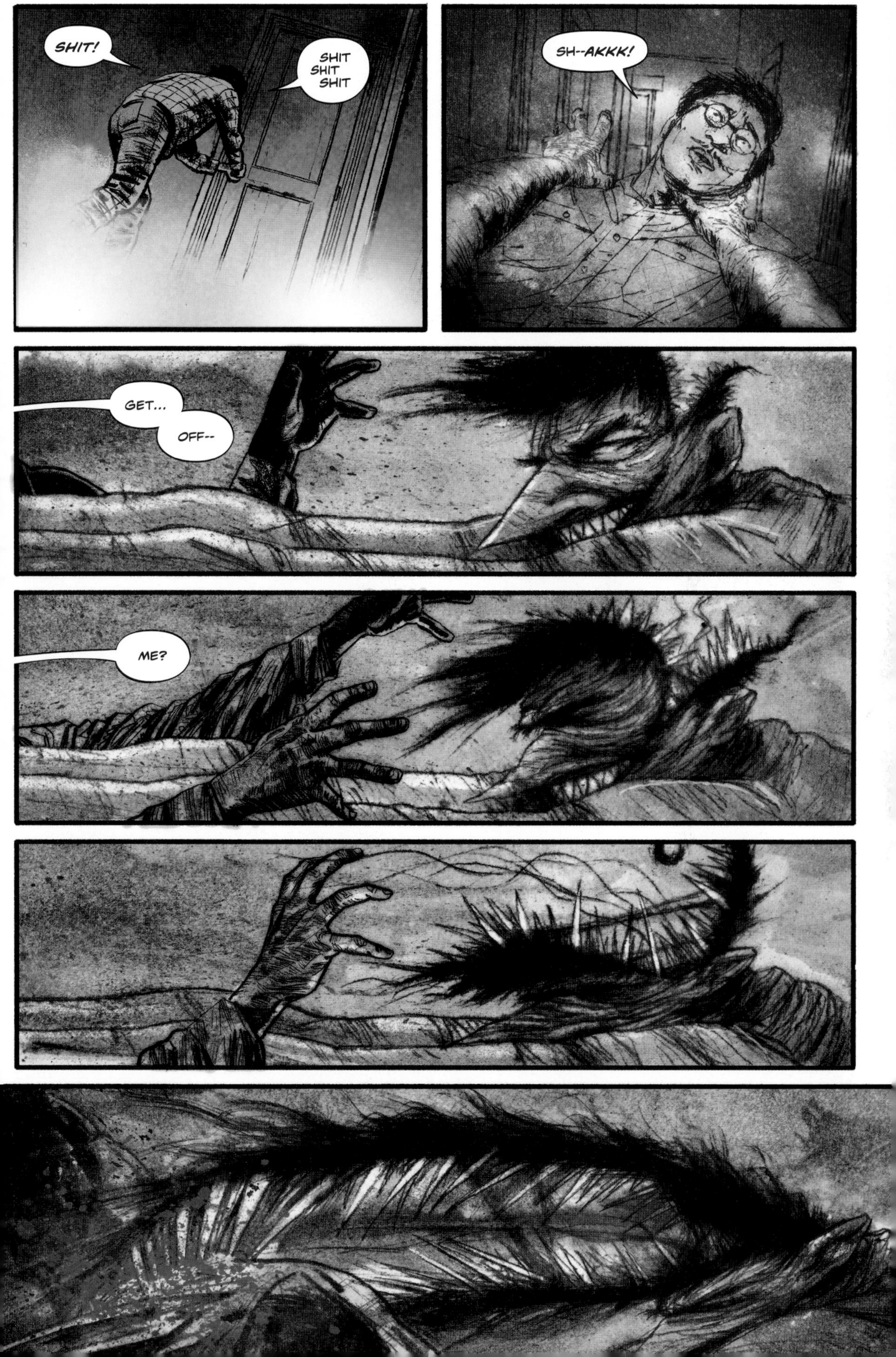
SHIT!
SHIT
SHIT
SHIT
SH--AKKK!
GET...
OFF--
ME?

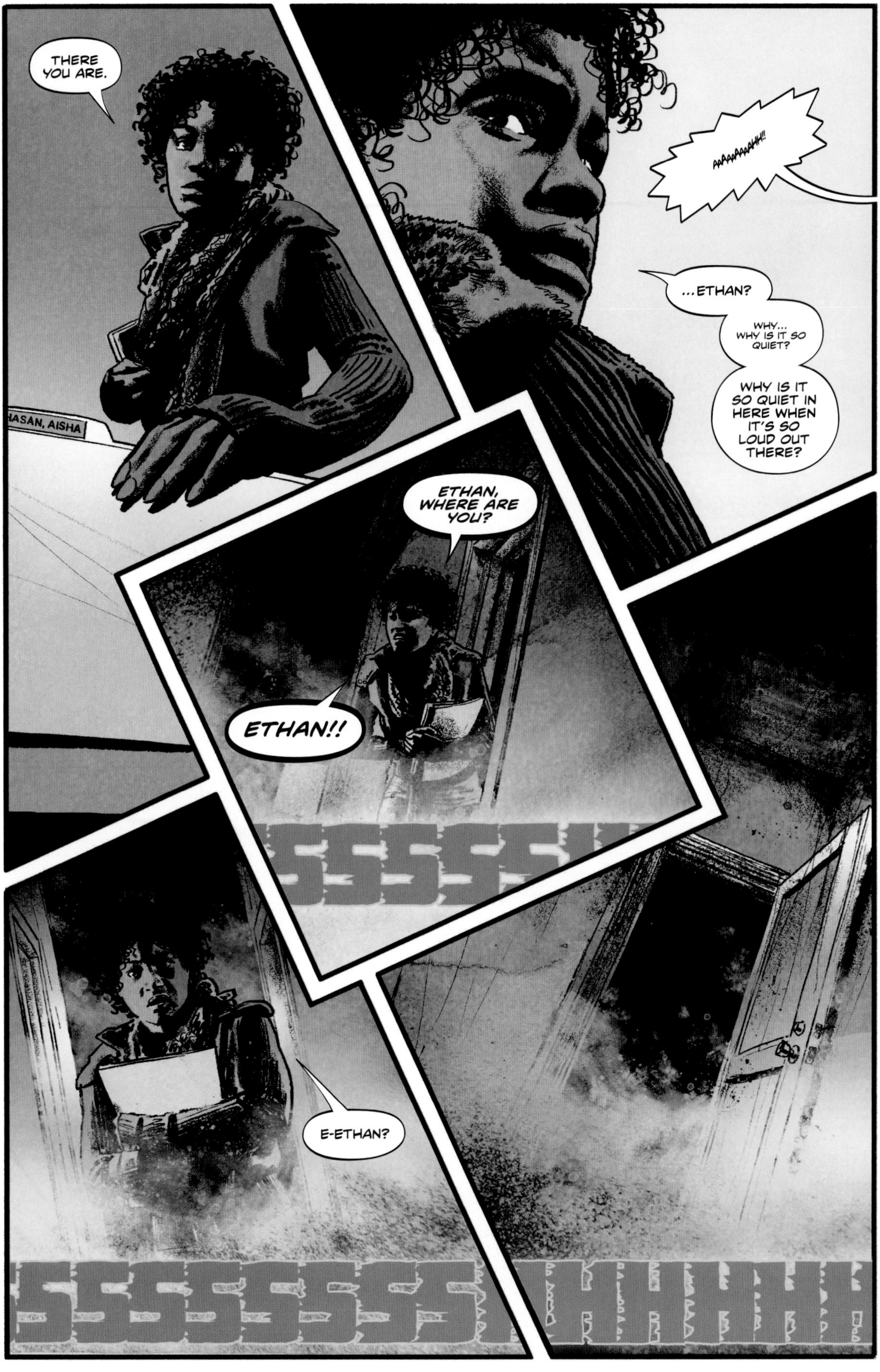
THERE YOU ARE.
HASAN, AISHA
AAAAAAAAAHH!!
...ETHAN?
WHY... WHY IS IT SO QUIET?
WHY IS IT SO QUIET IN HERE WHEN IT'S SO LOUD OUT THERE?
ETHAN, WHERE ARE YOU?
ETHAN!!
E-ETHAN?
SSSSSSSHHHHHH

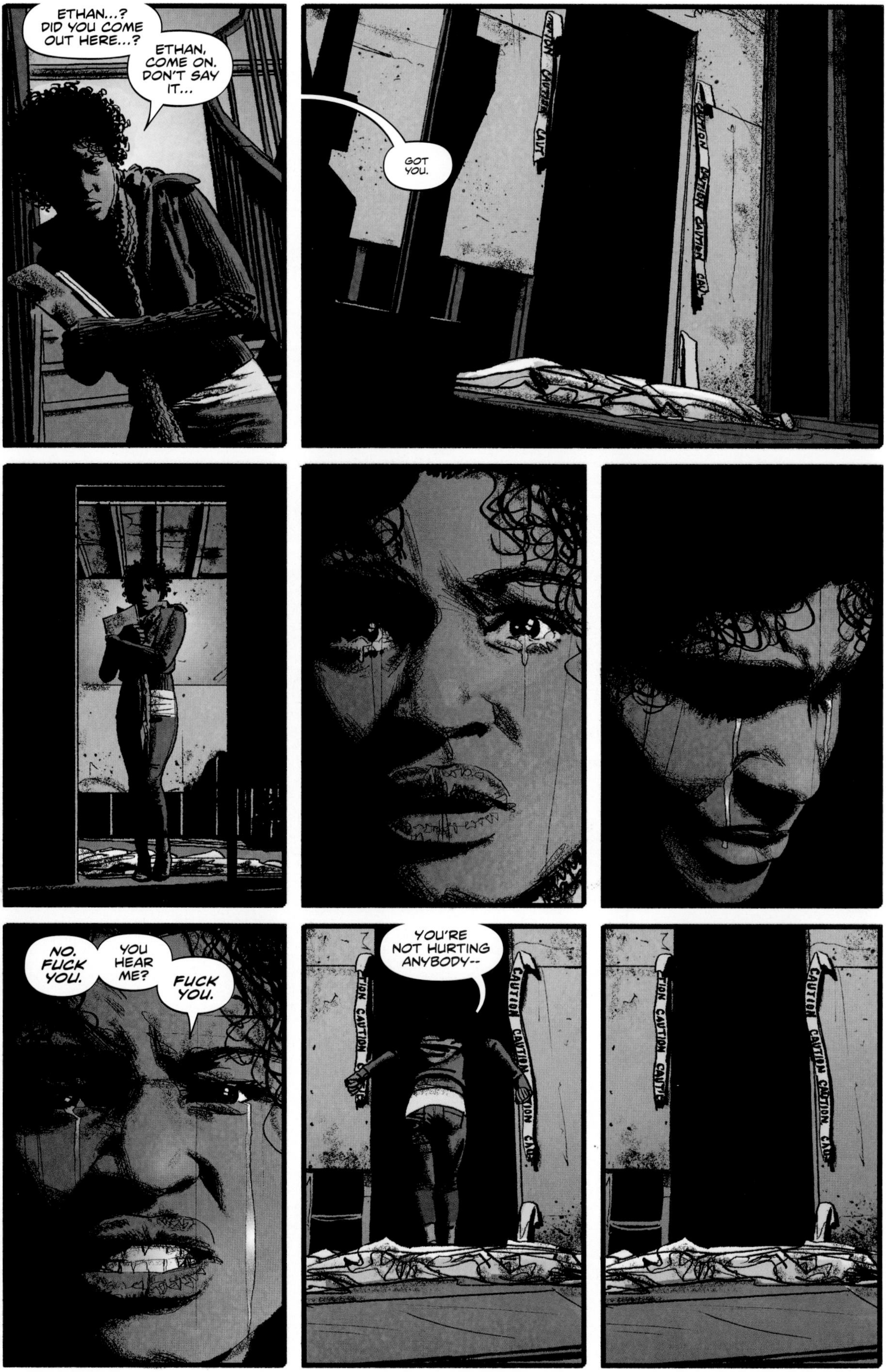
ETHAN...? DID YOU COME OUT HERE...?
ETHAN, COME ON. DON'T SAY IT...
GOT YOU.
CAUTION CAUTION CAUT
CAUTION CAUTION CAUTION CAU
NO. FUCK YOU.
YOU HEAR ME?
FUCK YOU.
YOU'RE NOT HURTING ANYBODY--

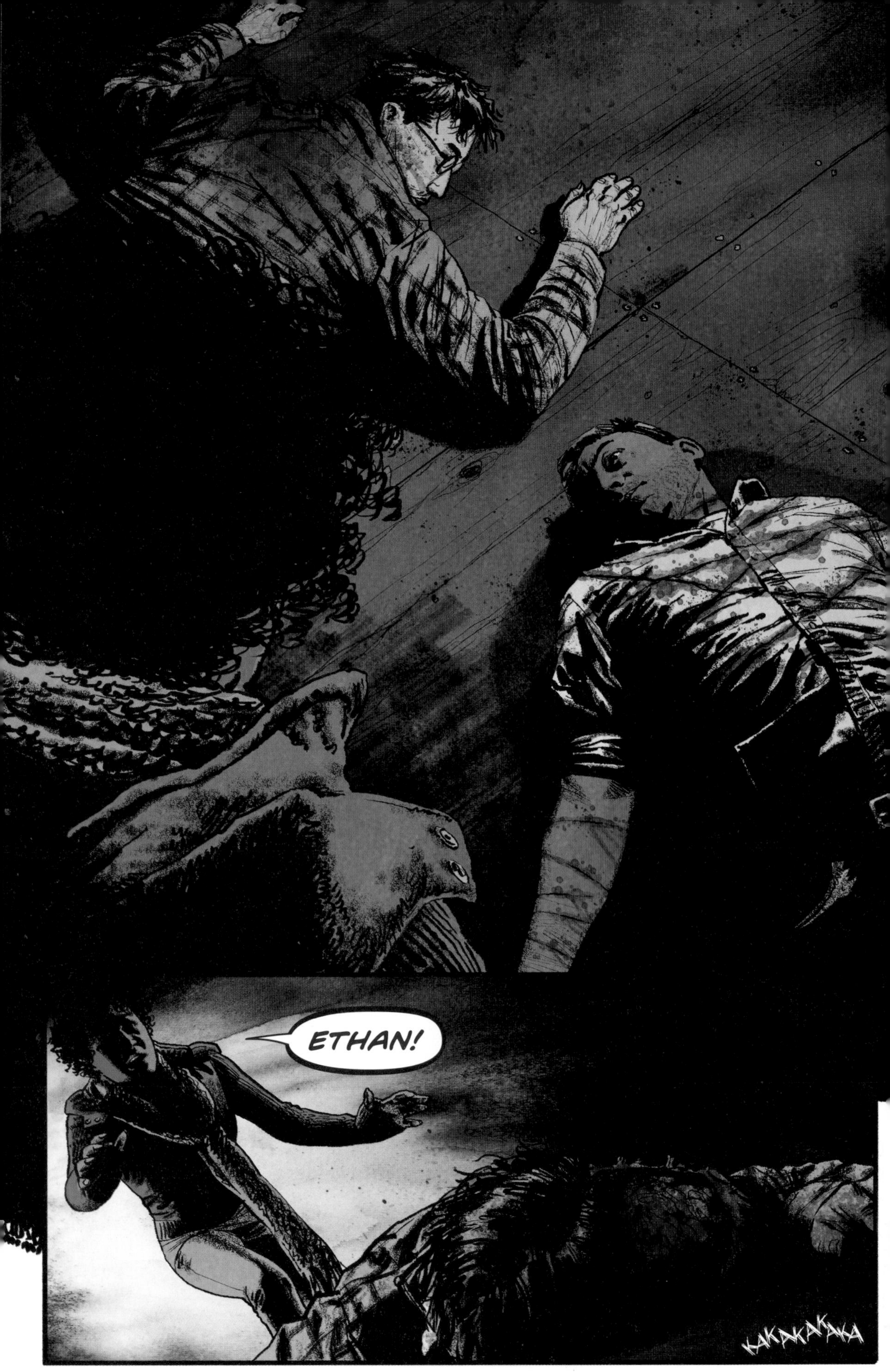
ETHAN!
KAKAKAKAKA

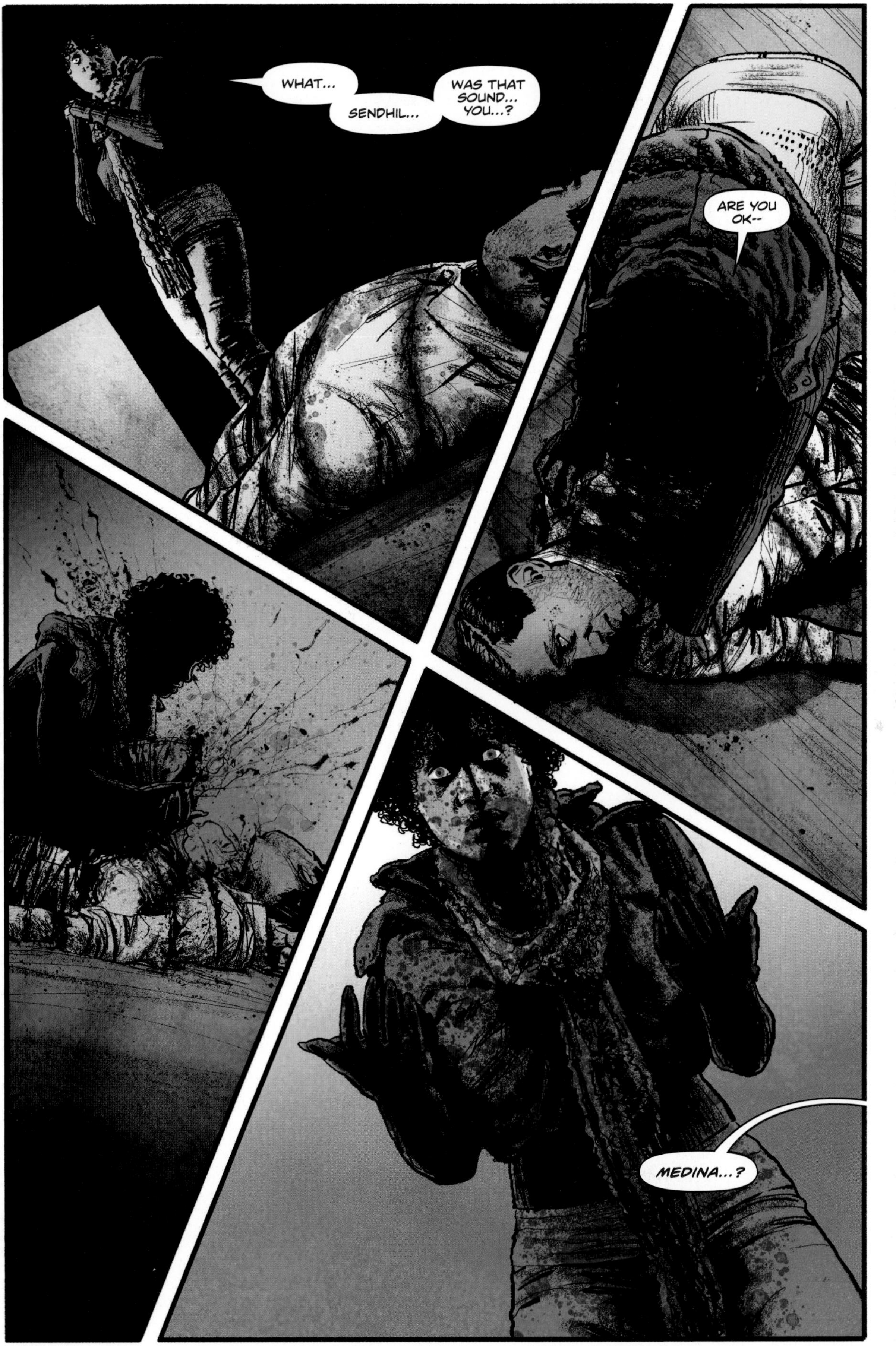
WHAT...
SENDHIL...
WAS THAT SOUND... YOU...?
ARE YOU OK--
MEDINA...?

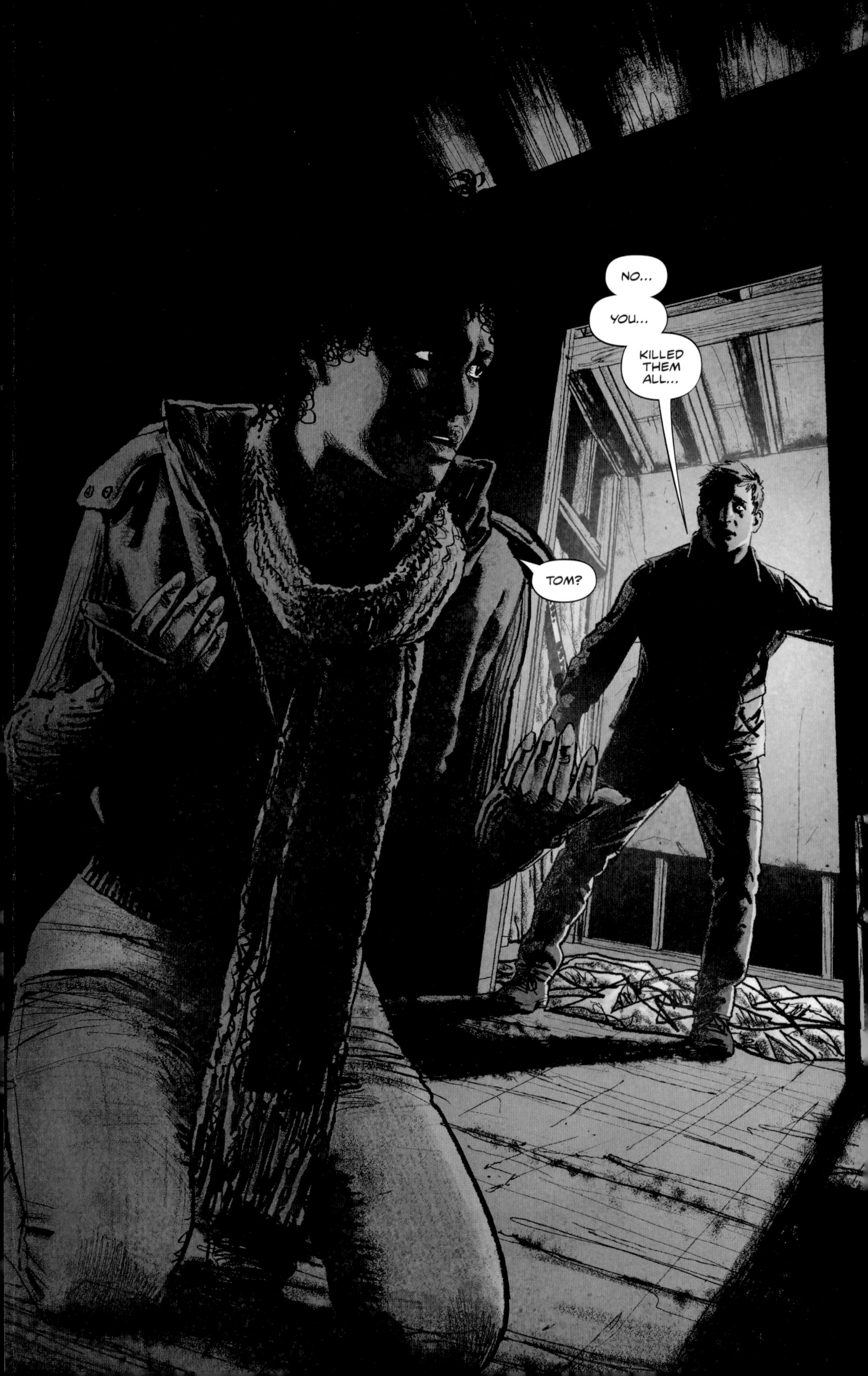
NO...
YOU...
KILLED THEM ALL...
TOM?

chapter 5

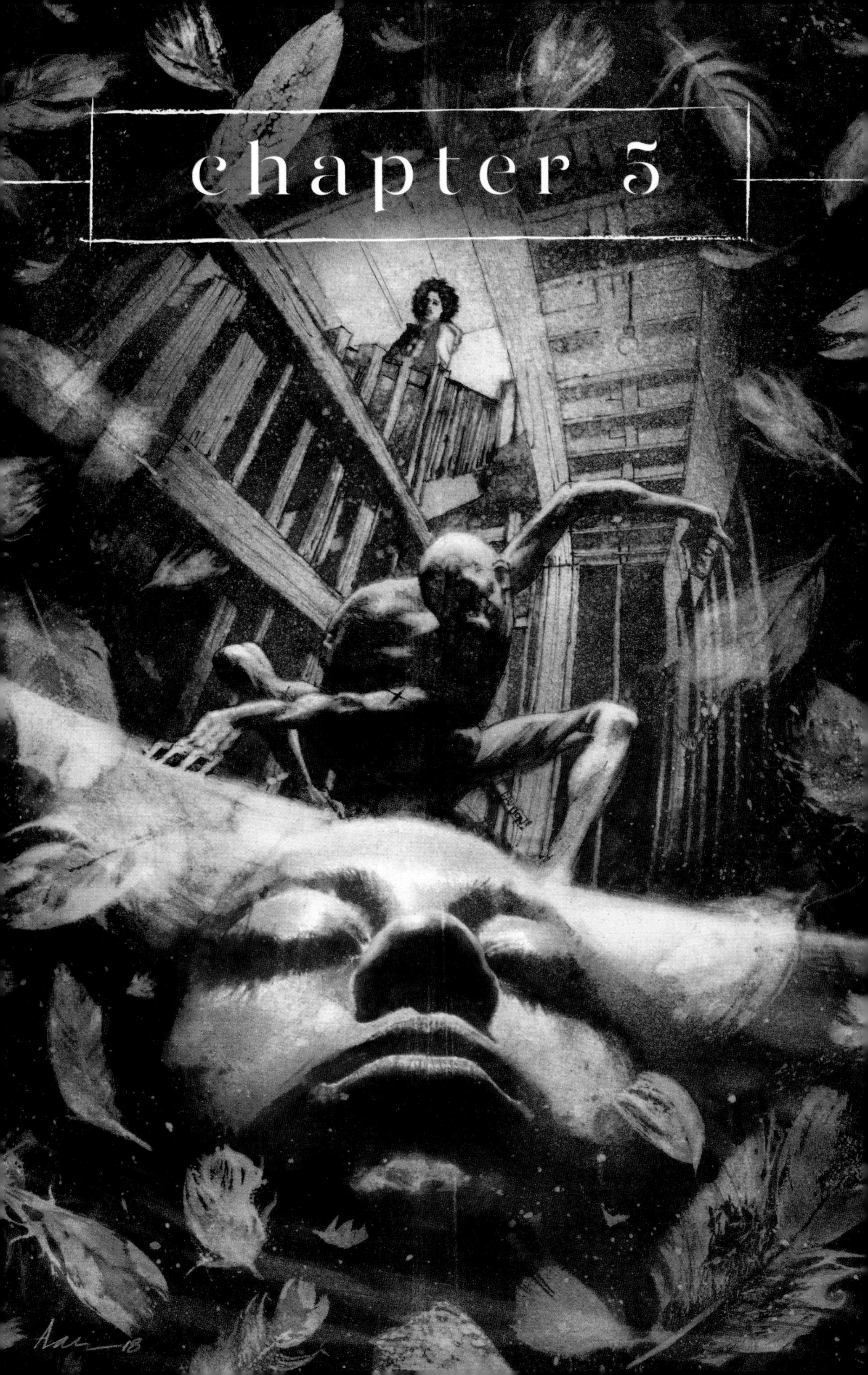

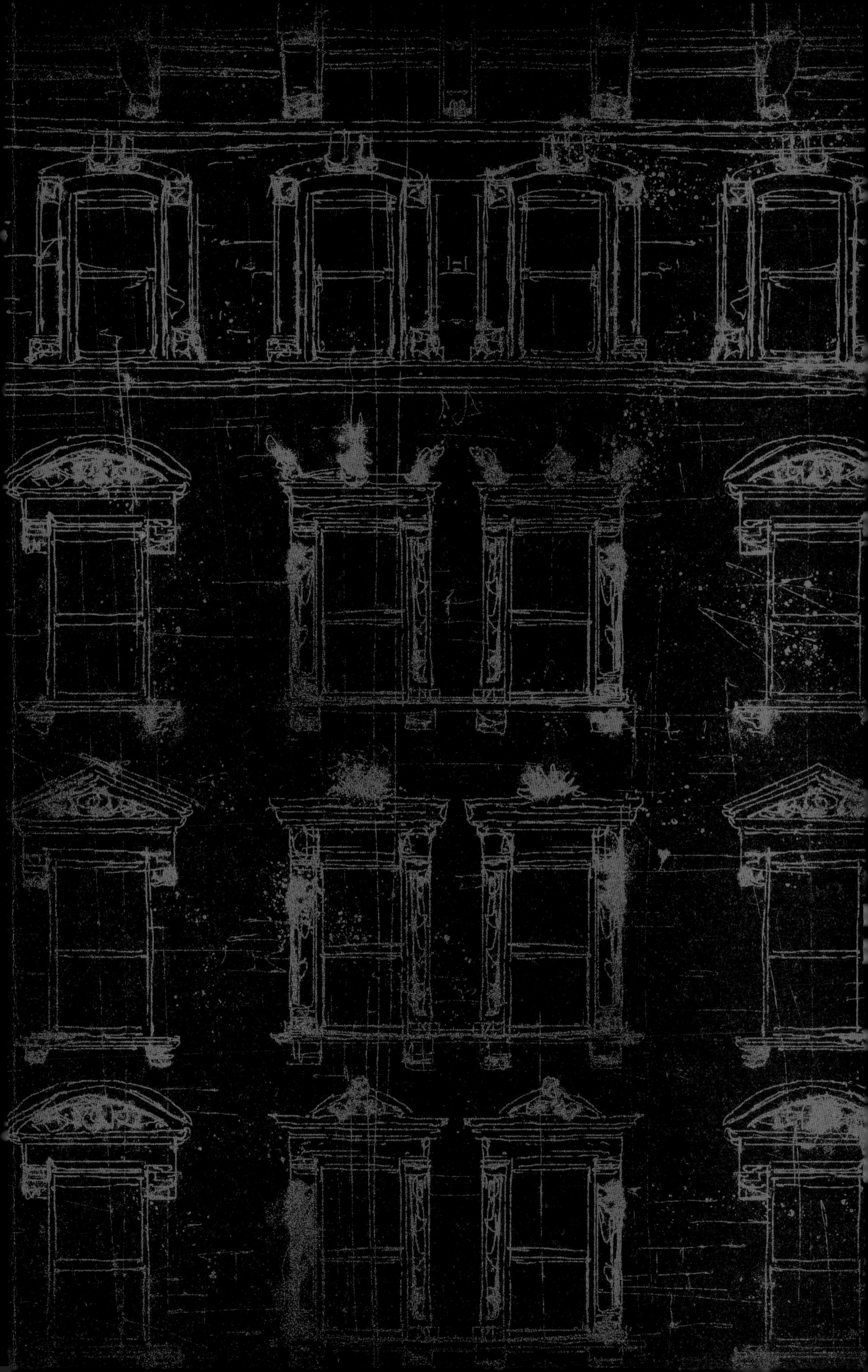

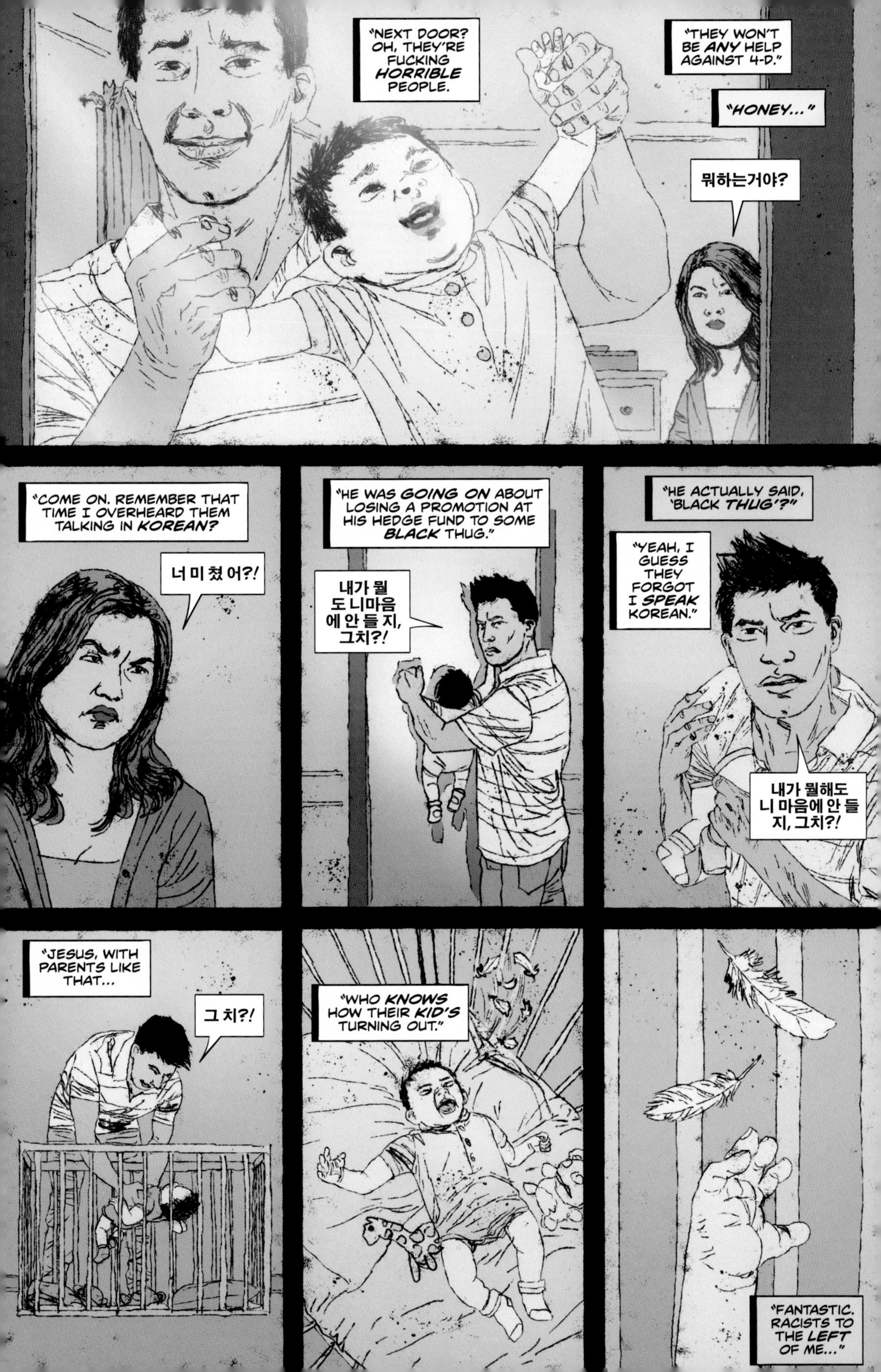
"NEXT DOOR? OH, THEY'RE FUCKING *HORRIBLE* PEOPLE.
"THEY WON'T BE *ANY* HELP AGAINST 4-D."
"HONEY..."
뭐하는거야?
"COME ON. REMEMBER THAT TIME I OVERHEARD THEM TALKING IN *KOREAN?*
너 미 쳤 어?!
"HE WAS *GOING ON* ABOUT LOSING A PROMOTION AT HIS HEDGE FUND TO SOME *BLACK* THUG."
내가 뭘 도 니마음 에 안 들 지, 그치?!
"HE ACTUALLY SAID, 'BLACK *THUG*'?"
"YEAH, I GUESS THEY FORGOT I *SPEAK* KOREAN."
내가 뭘해도 니 마음에 안 들 지, 그치?!
"JESUS, WITH PARENTS LIKE THAT...
그 치?!
"WHO *KNOWS* HOW THEIR *KID'S* TURNING OUT."
"FANTASTIC. RACISTS TO THE *LEFT* OF ME..."

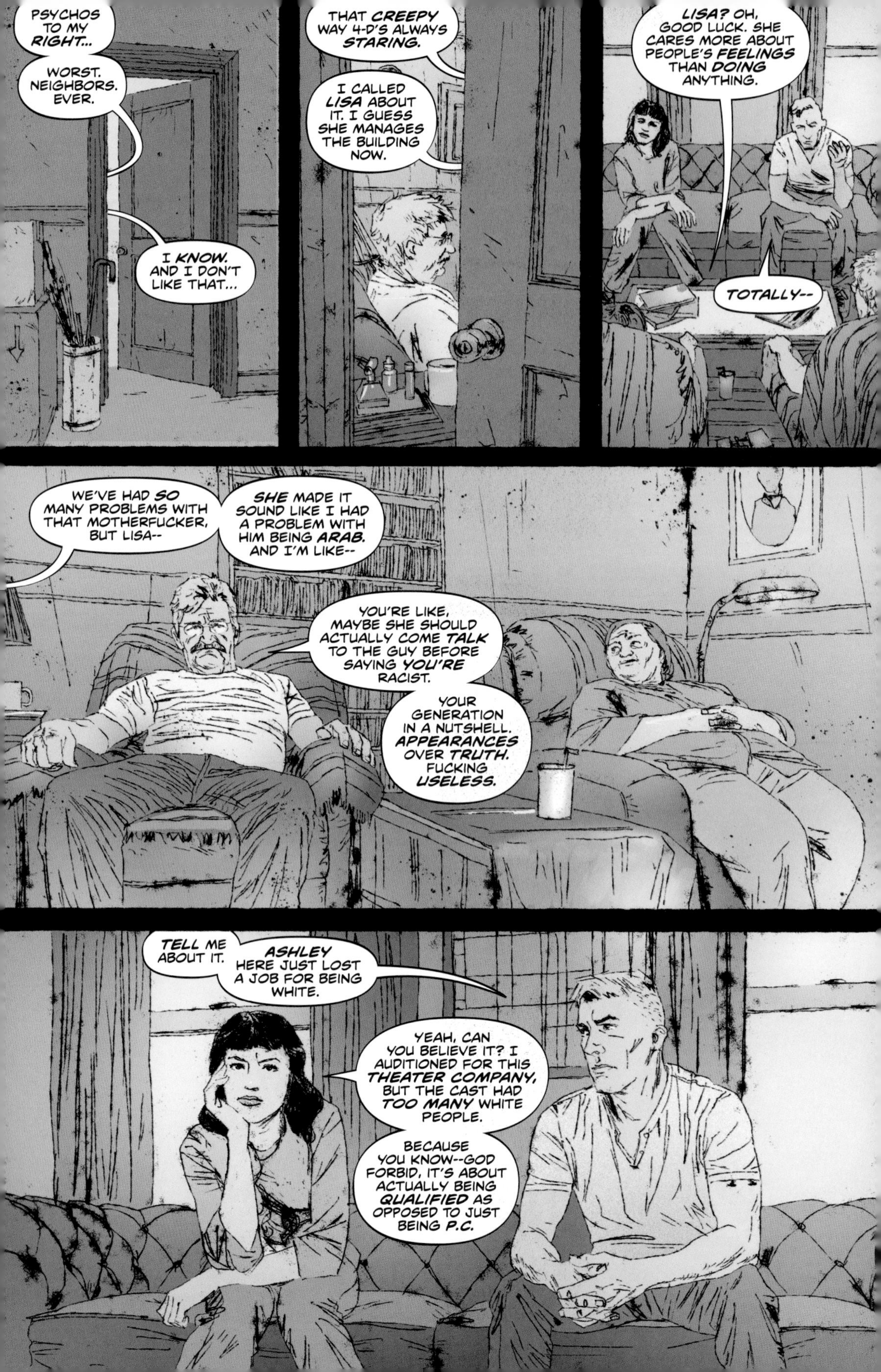
PSYCHOS TO MY RIGHT...
WORST. NEIGHBORS. EVER.
I KNOW. AND I DON'T LIKE THAT...
THAT CREEPY WAY 4-D'S ALWAYS STARING.
I CALLED LISA ABOUT IT. I GUESS SHE MANAGES THE BUILDING NOW.
LISA? OH, GOOD LUCK. SHE CARES MORE ABOUT PEOPLE'S FEELINGS THAN DOING ANYTHING.
TOTALLY--
WE'VE HAD SO MANY PROBLEMS WITH THAT MOTHERFUCKER, BUT LISA--
SHE MADE IT SOUND LIKE I HAD A PROBLEM WITH HIM BEING ARAB. AND I'M LIKE--
YOU'RE LIKE, MAYBE SHE SHOULD ACTUALLY COME TALK TO THE GUY BEFORE SAYING YOU'RE RACIST.
YOUR GENERATION IN A NUTSHELL. APPEARANCES OVER TRUTH. FUCKING USELESS.
TELL ME ABOUT IT. ASHLEY HERE JUST LOST A JOB FOR BEING WHITE.
YEAH, CAN YOU BELIEVE IT? I AUDITIONED FOR THIS THEATER COMPANY, BUT THE CAST HAD TOO MANY WHITE PEOPLE.
BECAUSE YOU KNOW--GOD FORBID, IT'S ABOUT ACTUALLY BEING QUALIFIED AS OPPOSED TO JUST BEING P.C.

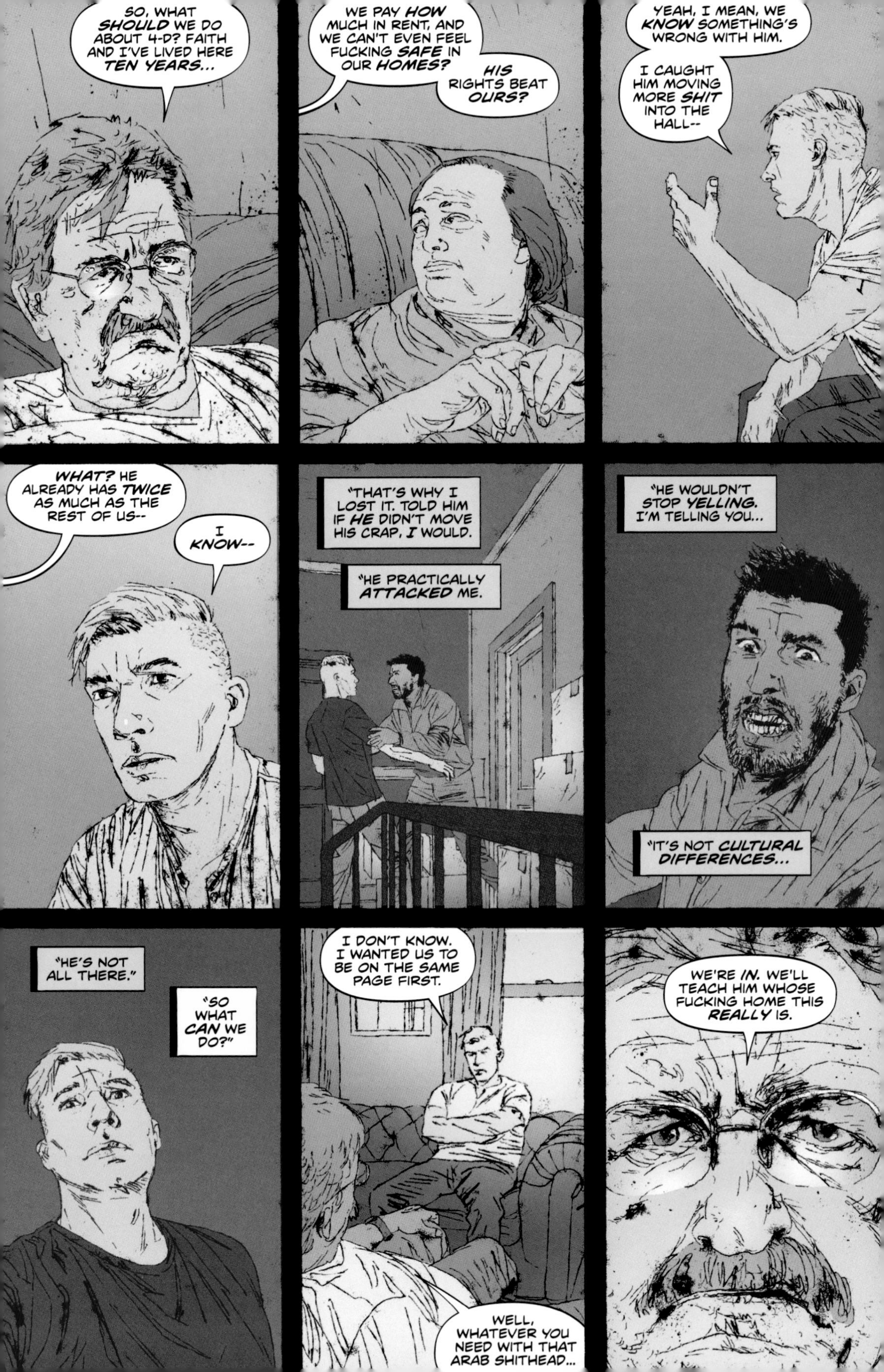
SO, WHAT SHOULD WE DO ABOUT 4-D? FAITH AND I'VE LIVED HERE TEN YEARS...
WE PAY HOW MUCH IN RENT, AND WE CAN'T EVEN FEEL FUCKING SAFE IN OUR HOMES?
HIS RIGHTS BEAT OURS?
YEAH, I MEAN, WE KNOW SOMETHING'S WRONG WITH HIM.
I CAUGHT HIM MOVING MORE SHIT INTO THE HALL--
WHAT? HE ALREADY HAS TWICE AS MUCH AS THE REST OF US--
I KNOW--
"THAT'S WHY I LOST IT. TOLD HIM IF HE DIDN'T MOVE HIS CRAP, I WOULD.
"HE PRACTICALLY ATTACKED ME.
"HE WOULDN'T STOP YELLING. I'M TELLING YOU...
"IT'S NOT CULTURAL DIFFERENCES...
"HE'S NOT ALL THERE."
"SO WHAT CAN WE DO?"
I DON'T KNOW. I WANTED US TO BE ON THE SAME PAGE FIRST.
WELL, WHATEVER YOU NEED WITH THAT ARAB SHITHEAD...
WE'RE IN. WE'LL TEACH HIM WHOSE FUCKING HOME THIS REALLY IS.

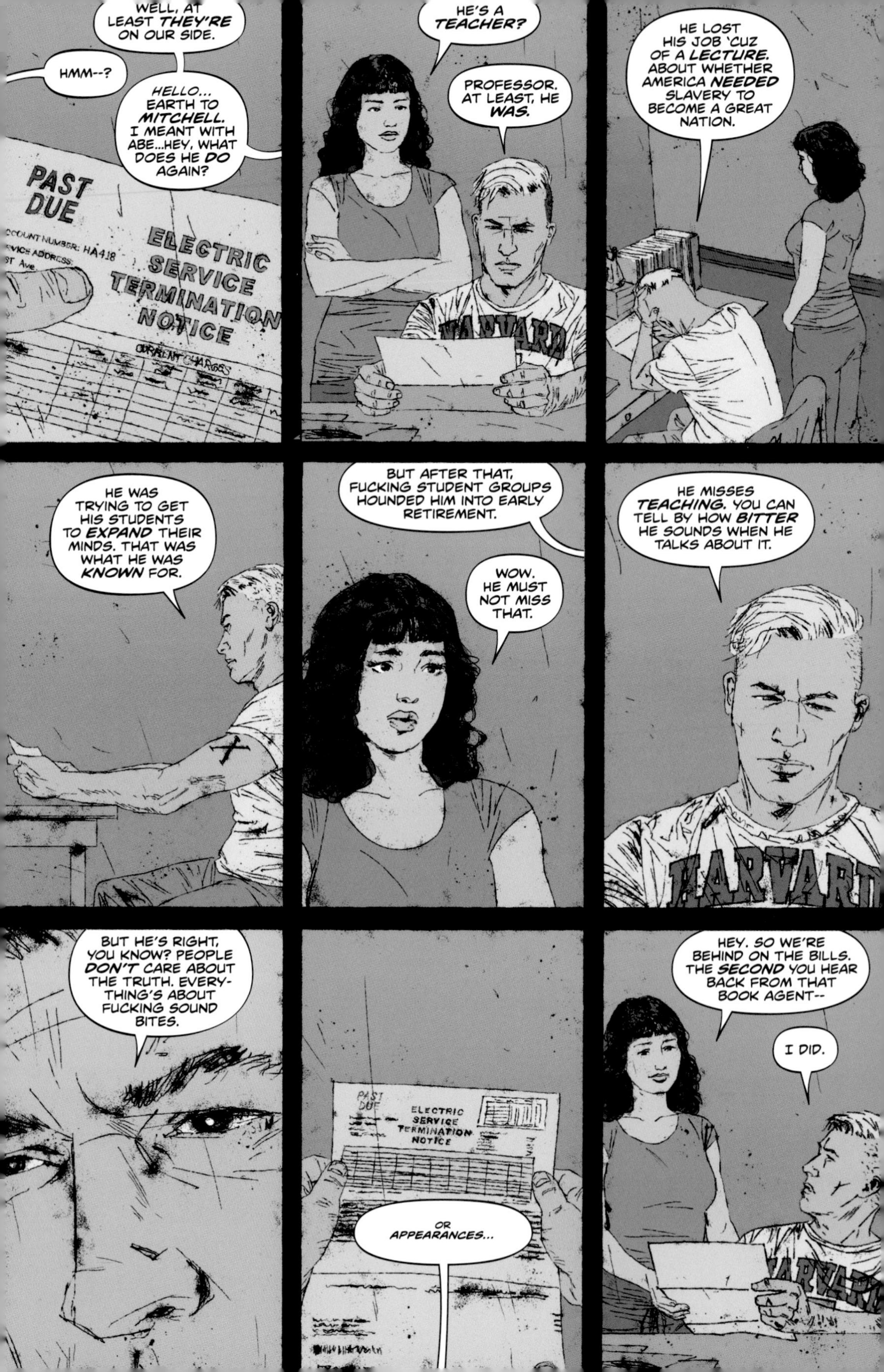
WELL, AT LEAST THEY'RE ON OUR SIDE.
HMM--?
HELLO... EARTH TO MITCHELL. I MEANT WITH ABE...HEY, WHAT DOES HE DO AGAIN?
PAST DUE
ELECTRIC SERVICE TERMINATION NOTICE
CURRENT CHARGES
HE'S A TEACHER?
PROFESSOR. AT LEAST, HE WAS.
HARVARD
HE LOST HIS JOB 'CUZ OF A LECTURE. ABOUT WHETHER AMERICA NEEDED SLAVERY TO BECOME A GREAT NATION.
HE WAS TRYING TO GET HIS STUDENTS TO EXPAND THEIR MINDS. THAT WAS WHAT HE WAS KNOWN FOR.
BUT AFTER THAT, FUCKING STUDENT GROUPS HOUNDED HIM INTO EARLY RETIREMENT.
WOW. HE MUST NOT MISS THAT.
HE MISSES TEACHING. YOU CAN TELL BY HOW BITTER HE SOUNDS WHEN HE TALKS ABOUT IT.
HARVARD
BUT HE'S RIGHT, YOU KNOW? PEOPLE DON'T CARE ABOUT THE TRUTH. EVERYTHING'S ABOUT FUCKING SOUND BITES.
PAST DUE
ELECTRIC SERVICE TERMINATION NOTICE
OR APPEARANCES...
HEY. SO WE'RE BEHIND ON THE BILLS. THE SECOND YOU HEAR BACK FROM THAT BOOK AGENT--
I DID.

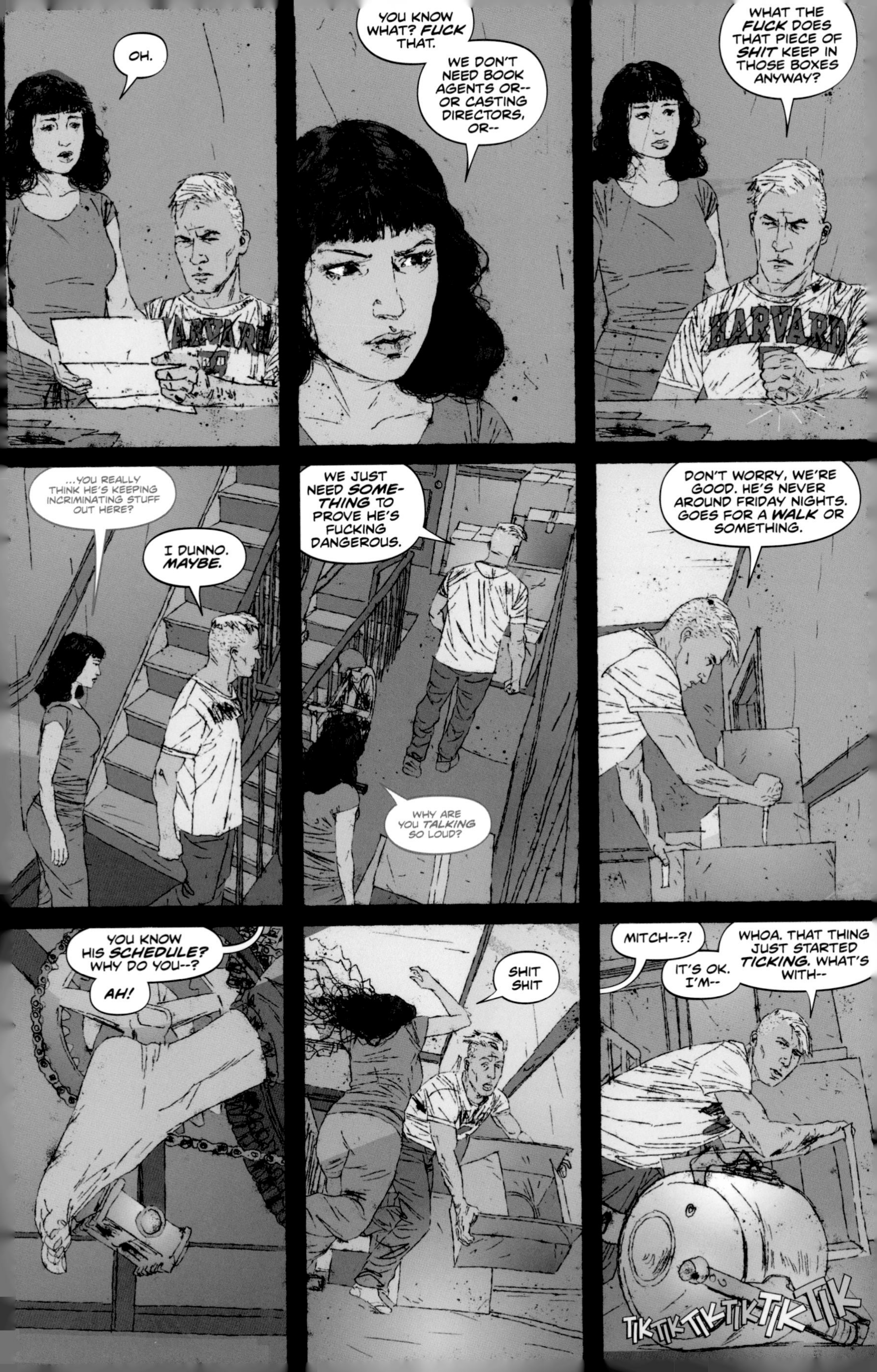
OH.
YOU KNOW WHAT? FUCK THAT.
WE DON'T NEED BOOK AGENTS OR-- OR CASTING DIRECTORS, OR--
WHAT THE FUCK DOES THAT PIECE OF SHIT KEEP IN THOSE BOXES ANYWAY?
...YOU REALLY THINK HE'S KEEPING INCRIMINATING STUFF OUT HERE?
I DUNNO. MAYBE.
WE JUST NEED SOMETHING TO PROVE HE'S FUCKING DANGEROUS.
WHY ARE YOU TALKING SO LOUD?
DON'T WORRY, WE'RE GOOD. HE'S NEVER AROUND FRIDAY NIGHTS. GOES FOR A WALK OR SOMETHING.
YOU KNOW HIS SCHEDULE? WHY DO YOU--?
AH!
SHIT SHIT
MITCH--?!
IT'S OK. I'M--
WHOA. THAT THING JUST STARTED TICKING. WHAT'S WITH--
TIK TIK TIK TIK TIK TIK TIK

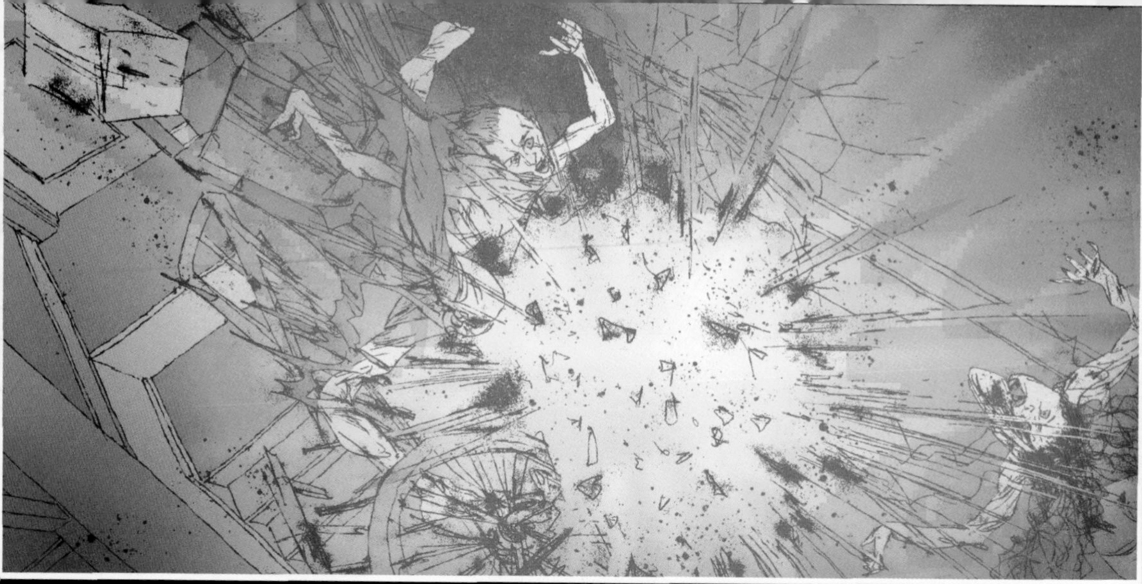

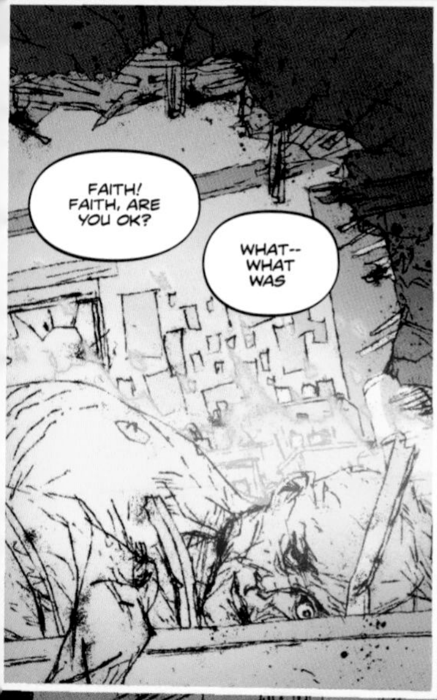
FAITH! FAITH, ARE YOU OK?
WHAT-- WHAT WAS

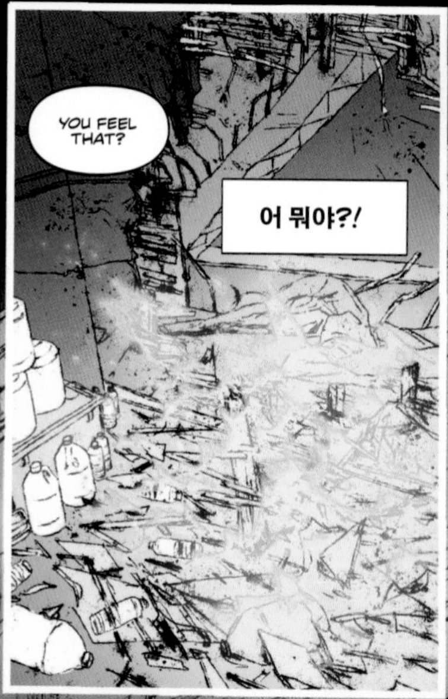
YOU FEEL THAT?
어 뭐야?!

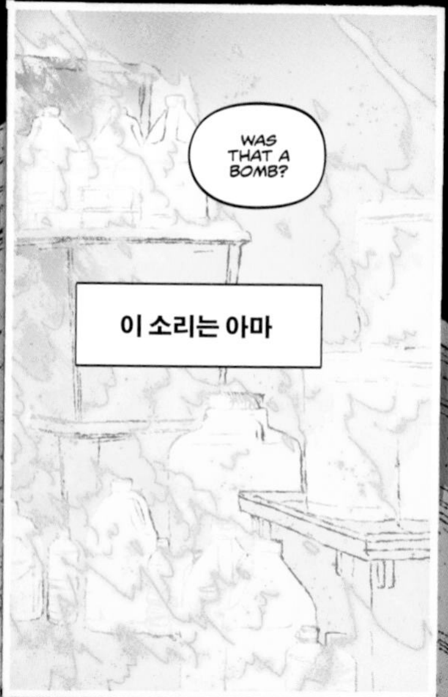
WAS THAT A BOMB?
이 소리는 아마

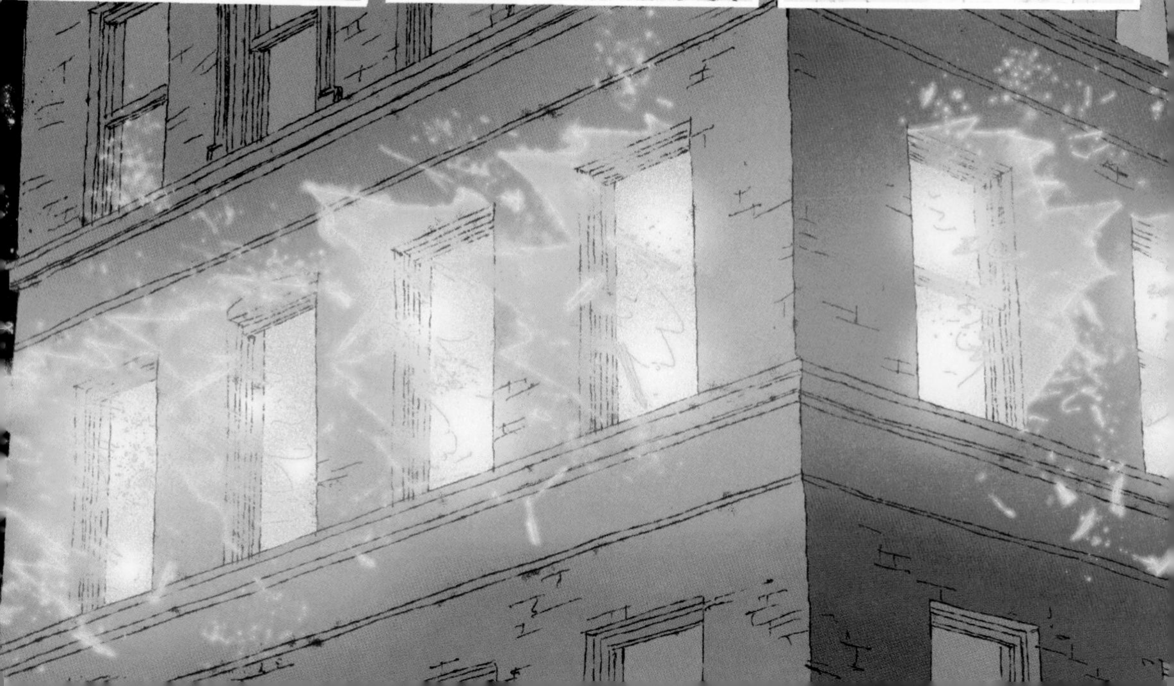

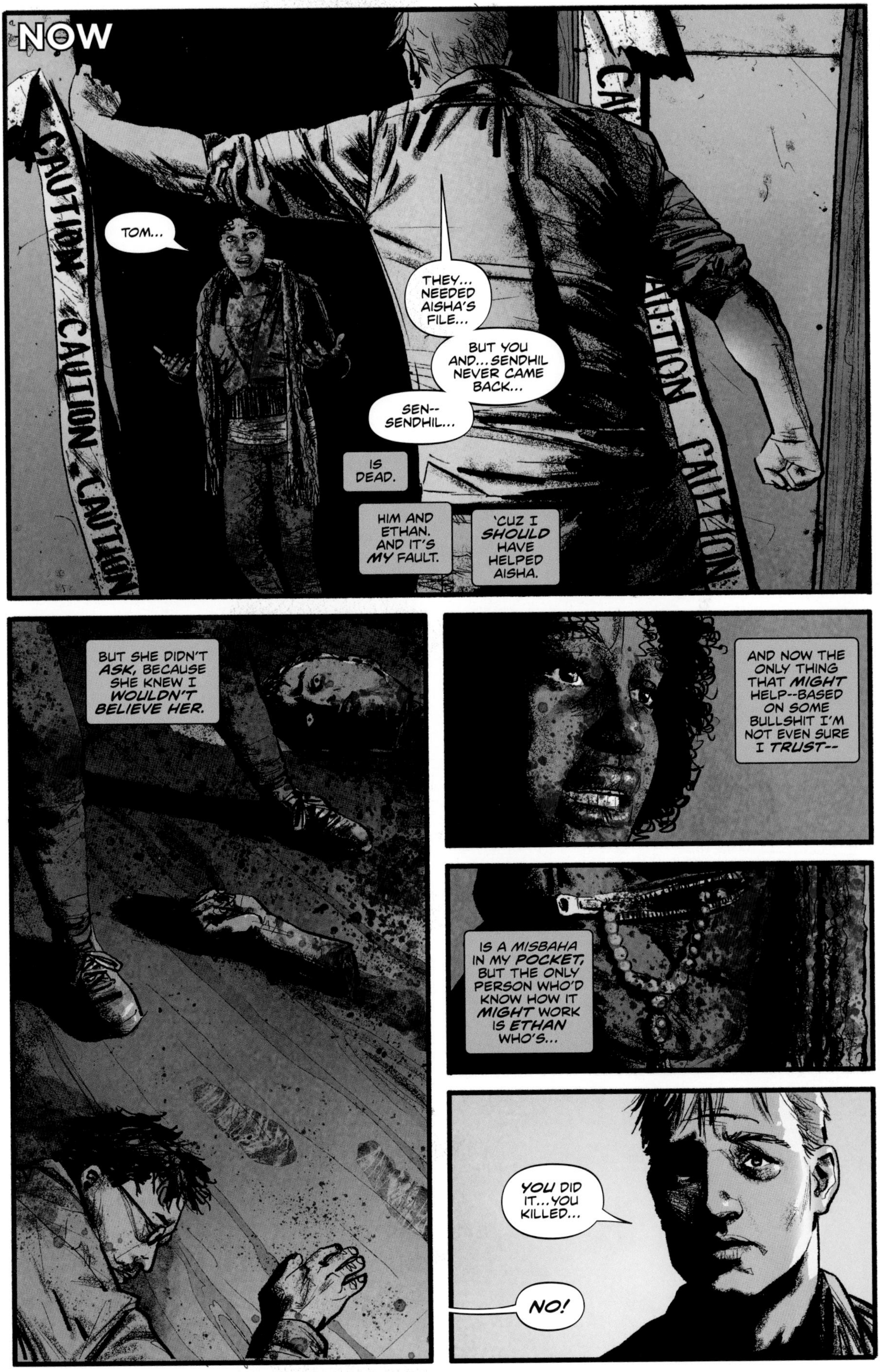
NOW
CAUTION
TOM...
THEY... NEEDED AISHA'S FILE...
BUT YOU AND... SENDHIL NEVER CAME BACK...
SEN-- SENDHIL...
IS DEAD.
HIM AND ETHAN. AND IT'S MY FAULT.
'CUZ I SHOULD HAVE HELPED AISHA.
BUT SHE DIDN'T ASK, BECAUSE SHE KNEW I WOULDN'T BELIEVE HER.
AND NOW THE ONLY THING THAT MIGHT HELP--BASED ON SOME BULLSHIT I'M NOT EVEN SURE I TRUST--
IS A MISBAHA IN MY POCKET, BUT THE ONLY PERSON WHO'D KNOW HOW IT MIGHT WORK IS ETHAN WHO'S...
YOU DID IT...YOU KILLED...
NO!

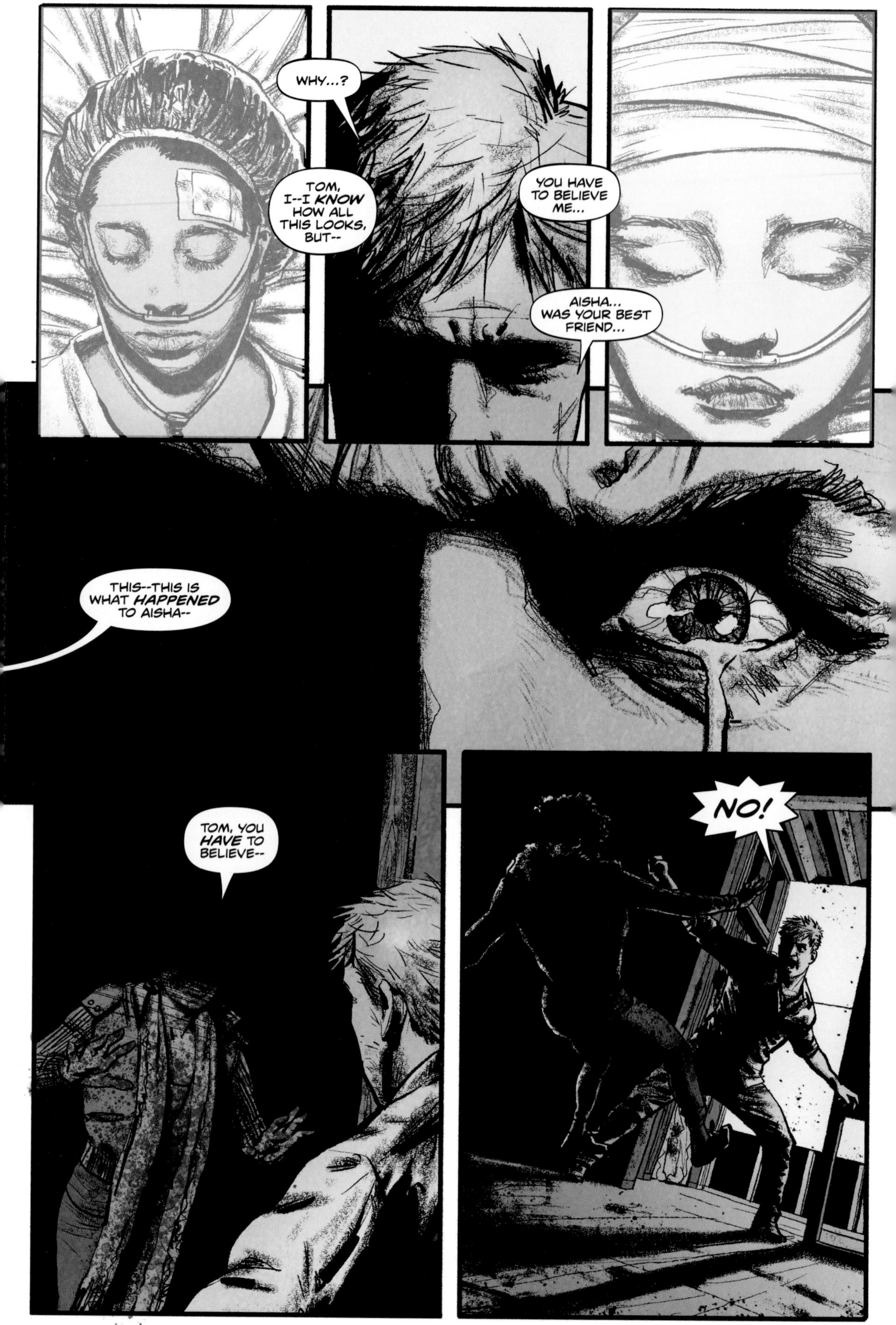
WHY...?
TOM, I--I *KNOW* HOW ALL THIS LOOKS, BUT--
YOU HAVE TO BELIEVE ME...
AISHA... WAS YOUR BEST FRIEND...
THIS--THIS IS WHAT *HAPPENED* TO AISHA--
TOM, YOU *HAVE* TO BELIEVE--
NO!

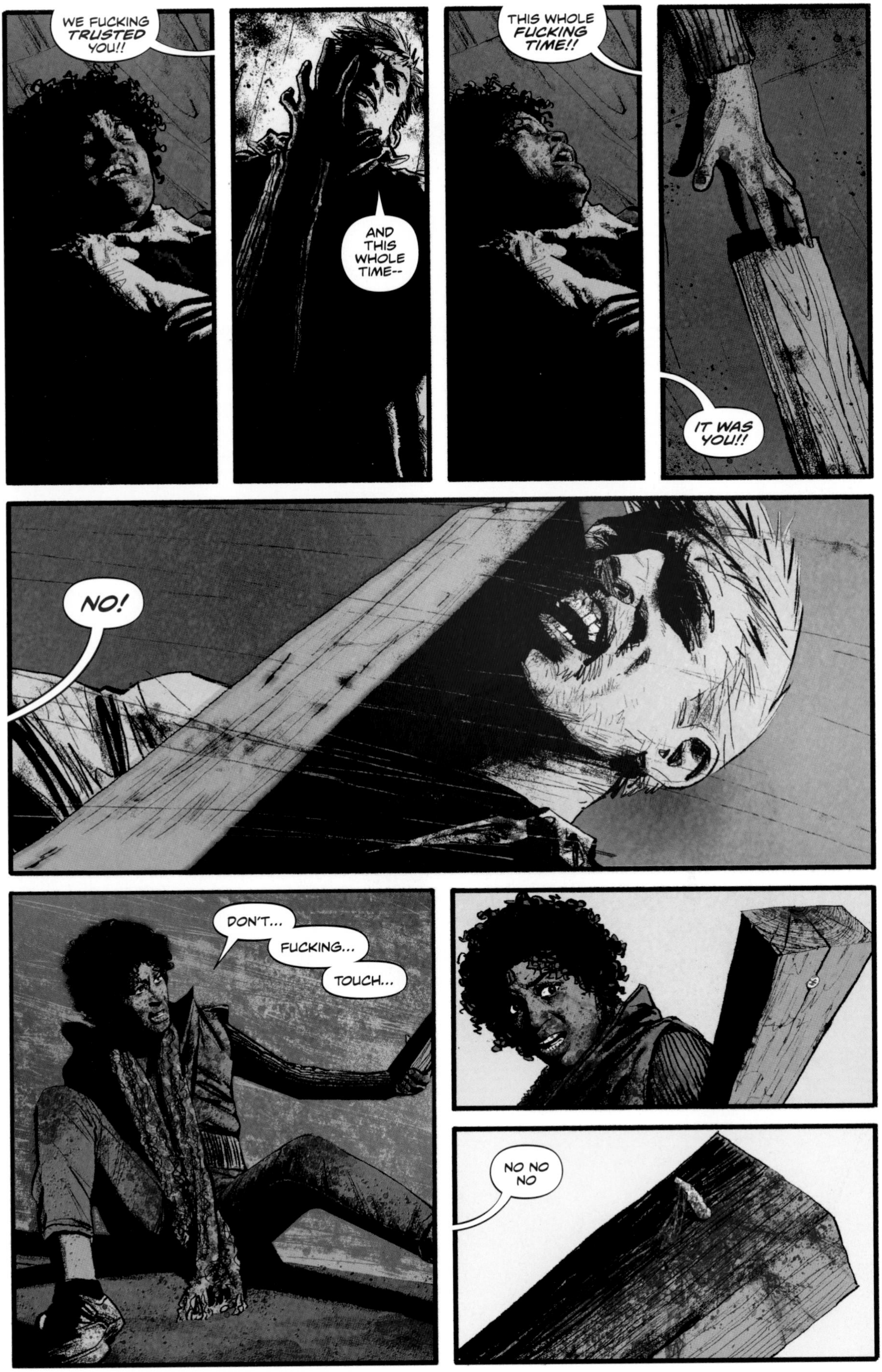
WE FUCKING TRUSTED YOU!!
AND THIS WHOLE TIME--
THIS WHOLE FUCKING TIME!!
IT WAS YOU!!
NO!
DON'T...
FUCKING...
TOUCH...
NO NO NO

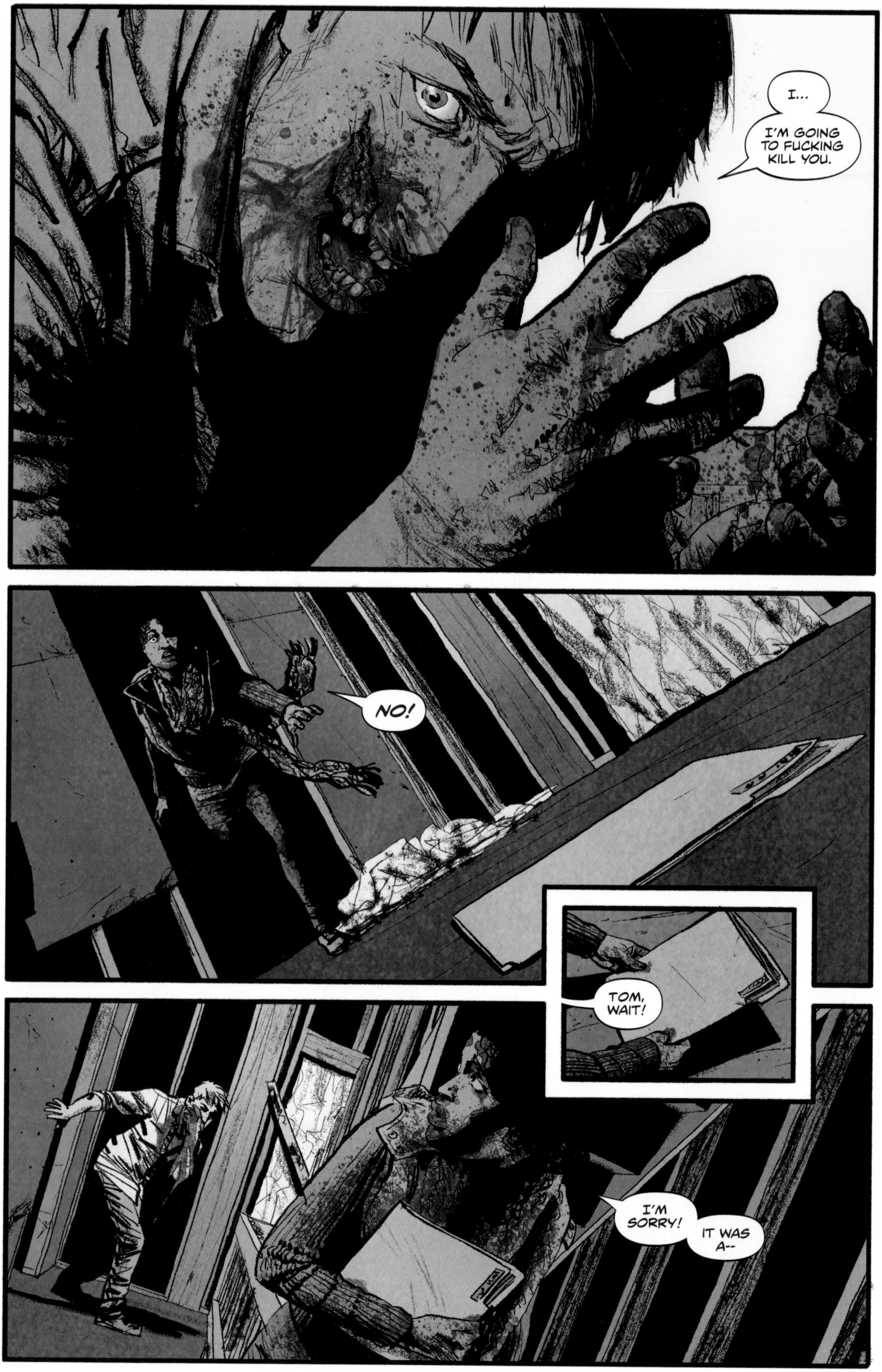
I...
I'M GOING TO FUCKING KILL YOU.
NO!
TOM, WAIT!
I'M SORRY!
IT WAS A--

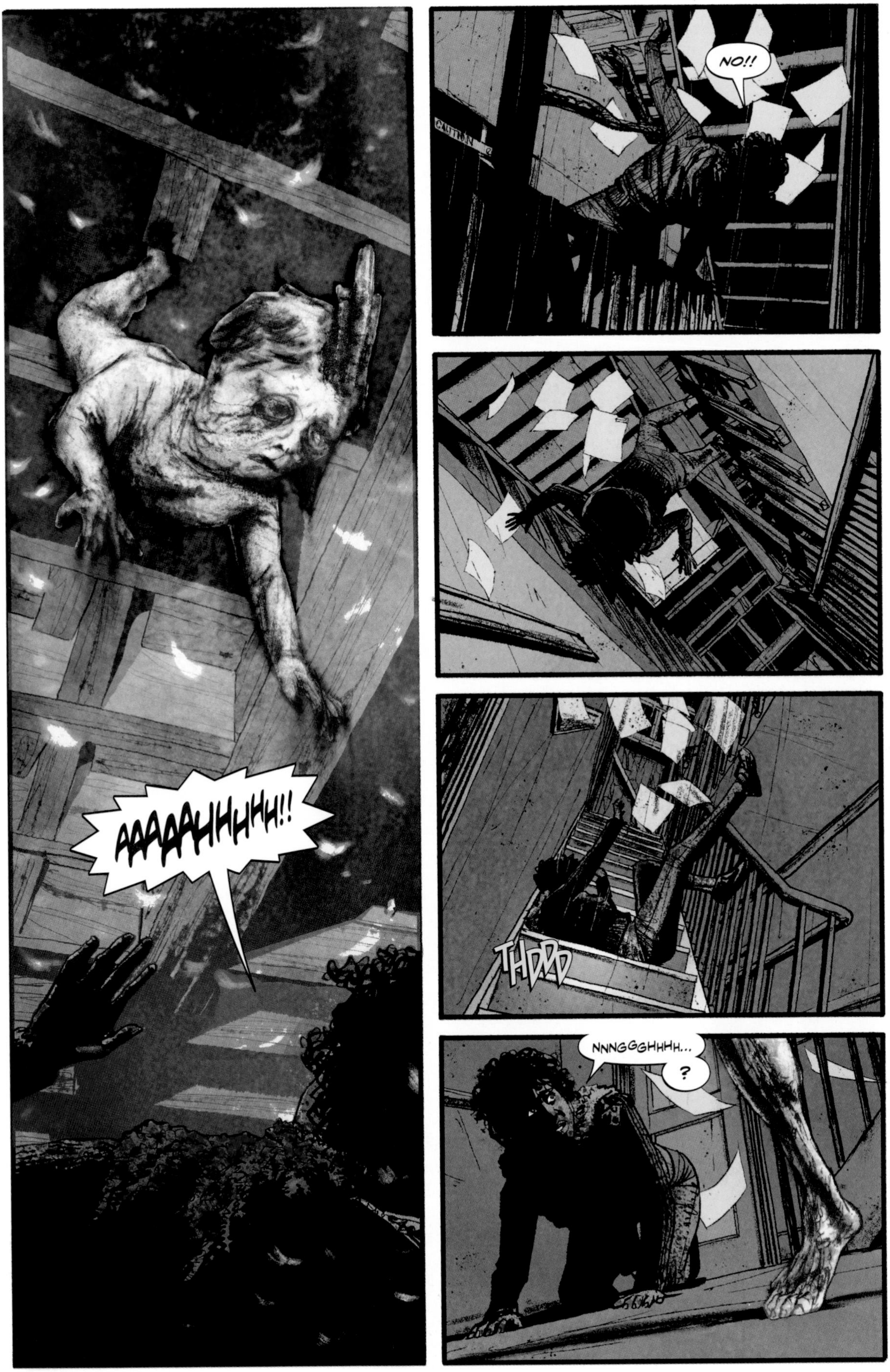
AAAAAHHHHH!!
NO!!
THDDD
NNNGGGHHHH...
?

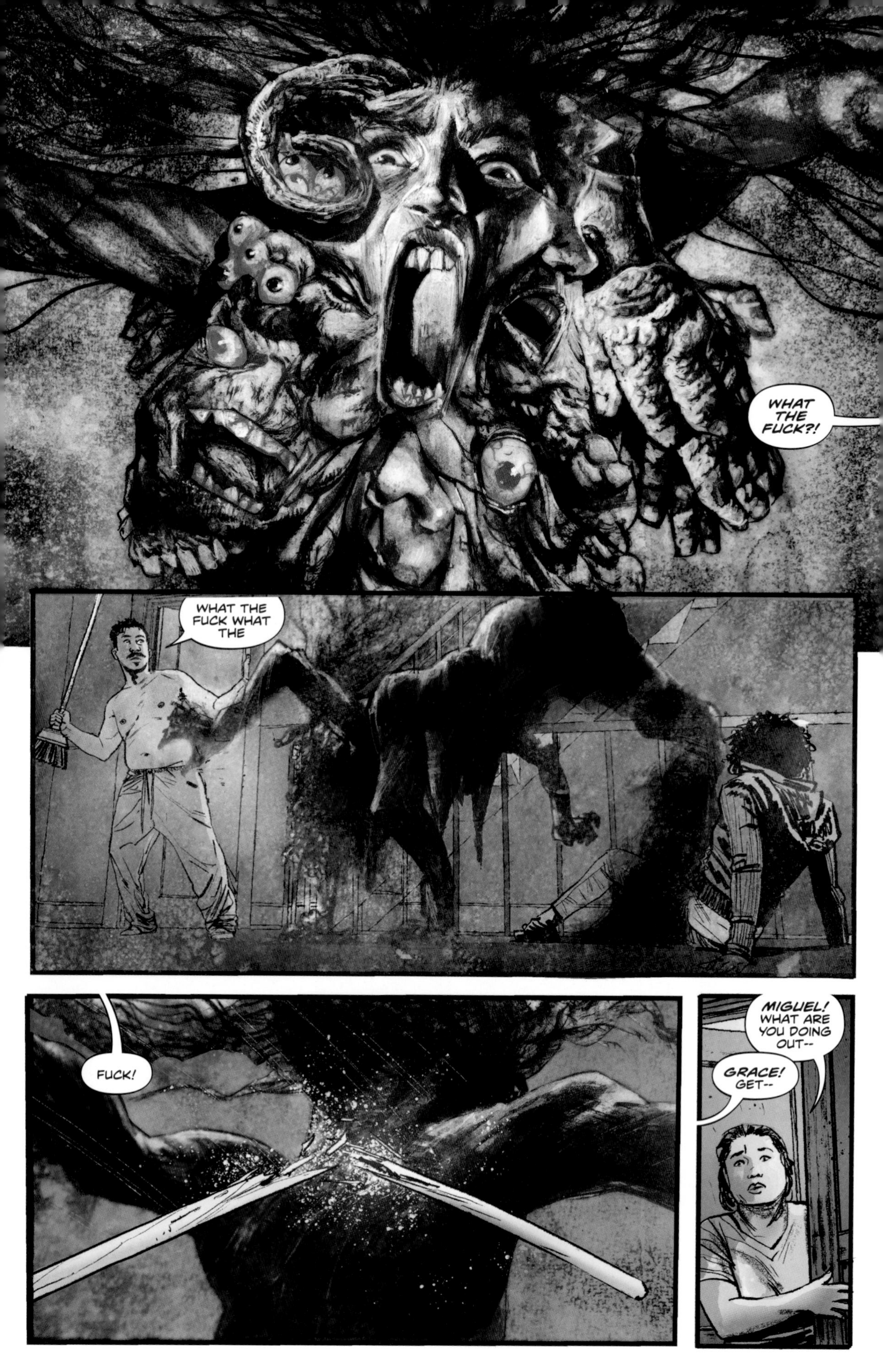
WHAT THE FUCK?!
WHAT THE FUCK WHAT THE
FUCK!
MIGUEL! WHAT ARE YOU DOING OUT--
GRACE! GET--

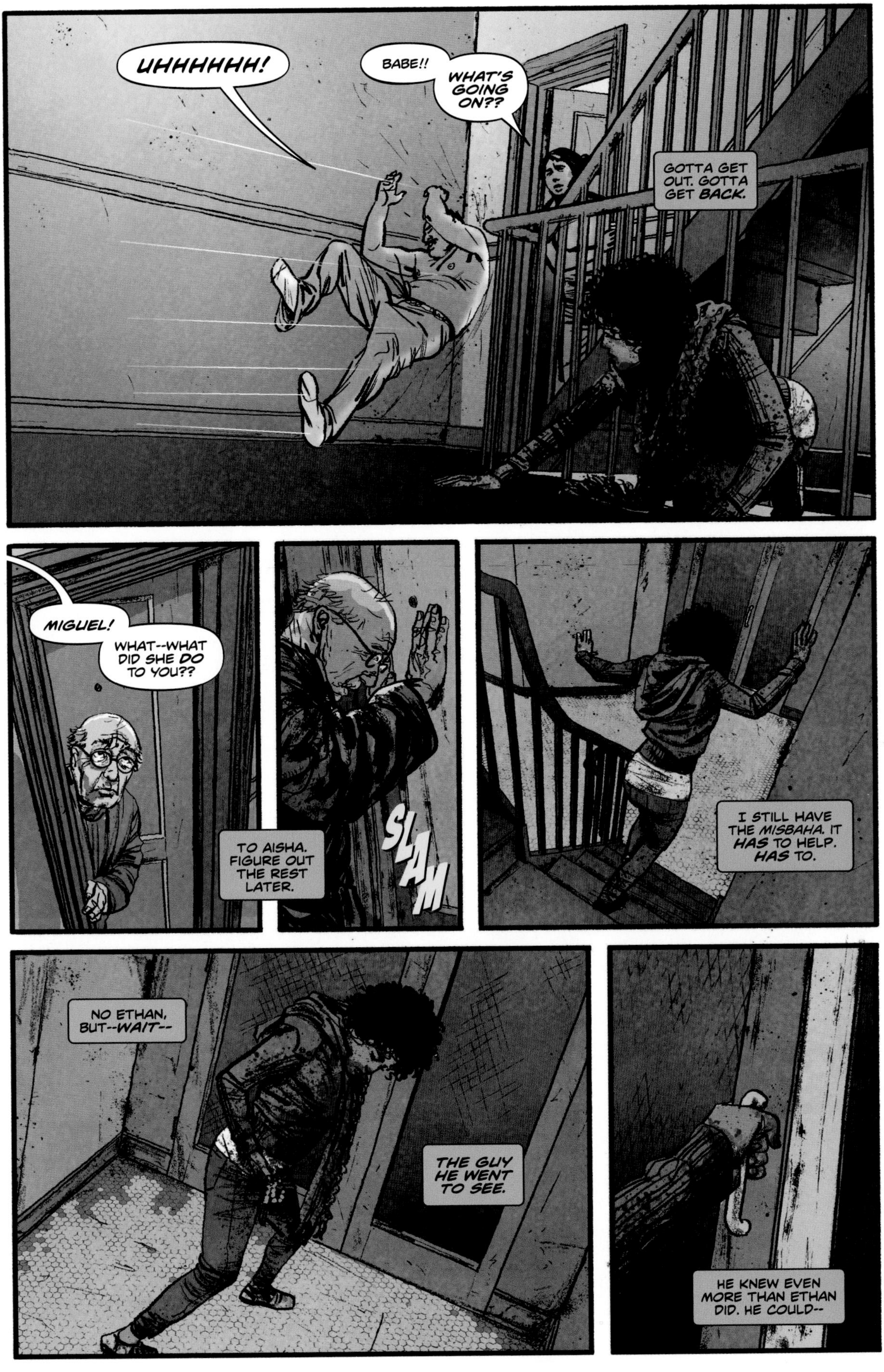
UHHHHHH!
BABE!!
WHAT'S GOING ON??
GOTTA GET OUT. GOTTA GET BACK.
MIGUEL!
WHAT--WHAT DID SHE DO TO YOU??
TO AISHA. FIGURE OUT THE REST LATER.
SLAM
I STILL HAVE THE MISBAHA. IT HAS TO HELP. HAS TO.
NO ETHAN, BUT--WAIT--
THE GUY HE WENT TO SEE.
HE KNEW EVEN MORE THAN ETHAN DID. HE COULD--

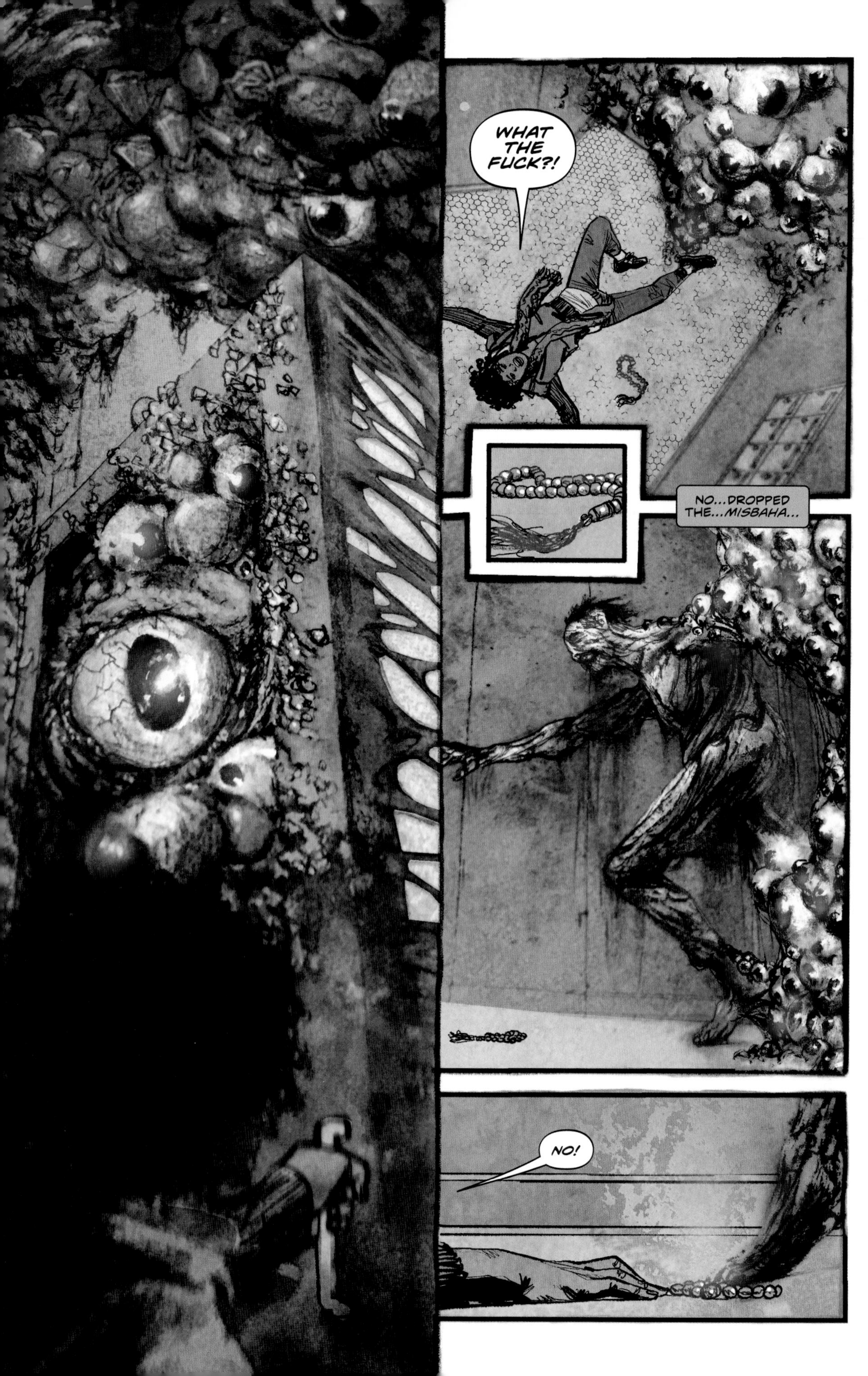
WHAT THE FUCK?!
NO...DROPPED THE...MISBAHA...
NO!

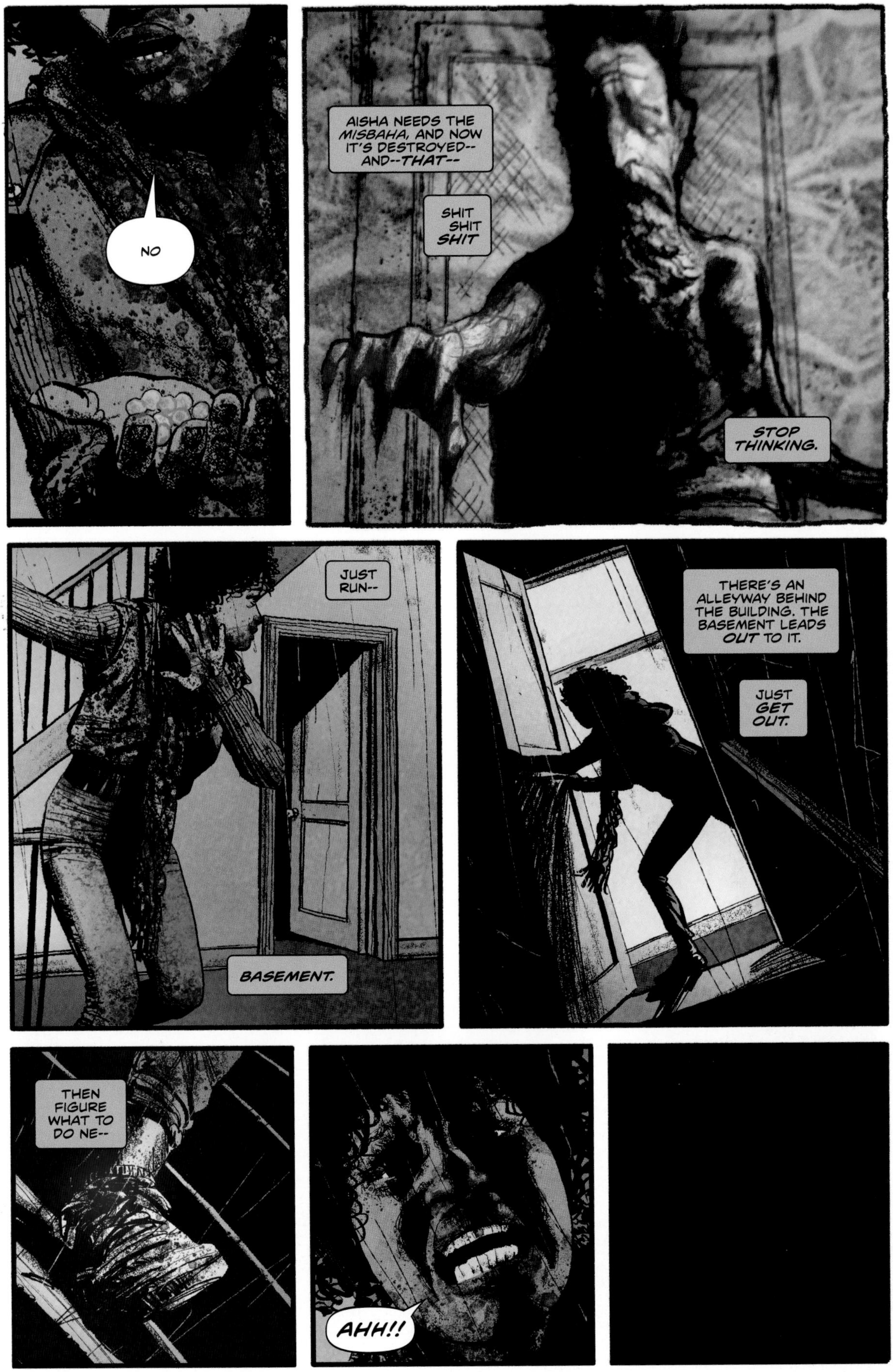
NO
AISHA NEEDS THE MISBAHA, AND NOW IT'S DESTROYED-- AND--THAT--
SHIT SHIT SHIT
STOP THINKING.
JUST RUN--
BASEMENT.
THERE'S AN ALLEYWAY BEHIND THE BUILDING. THE BASEMENT LEADS OUT TO IT.
JUST GET OUT.
THEN FIGURE WHAT TO DO NE--
AHH!!

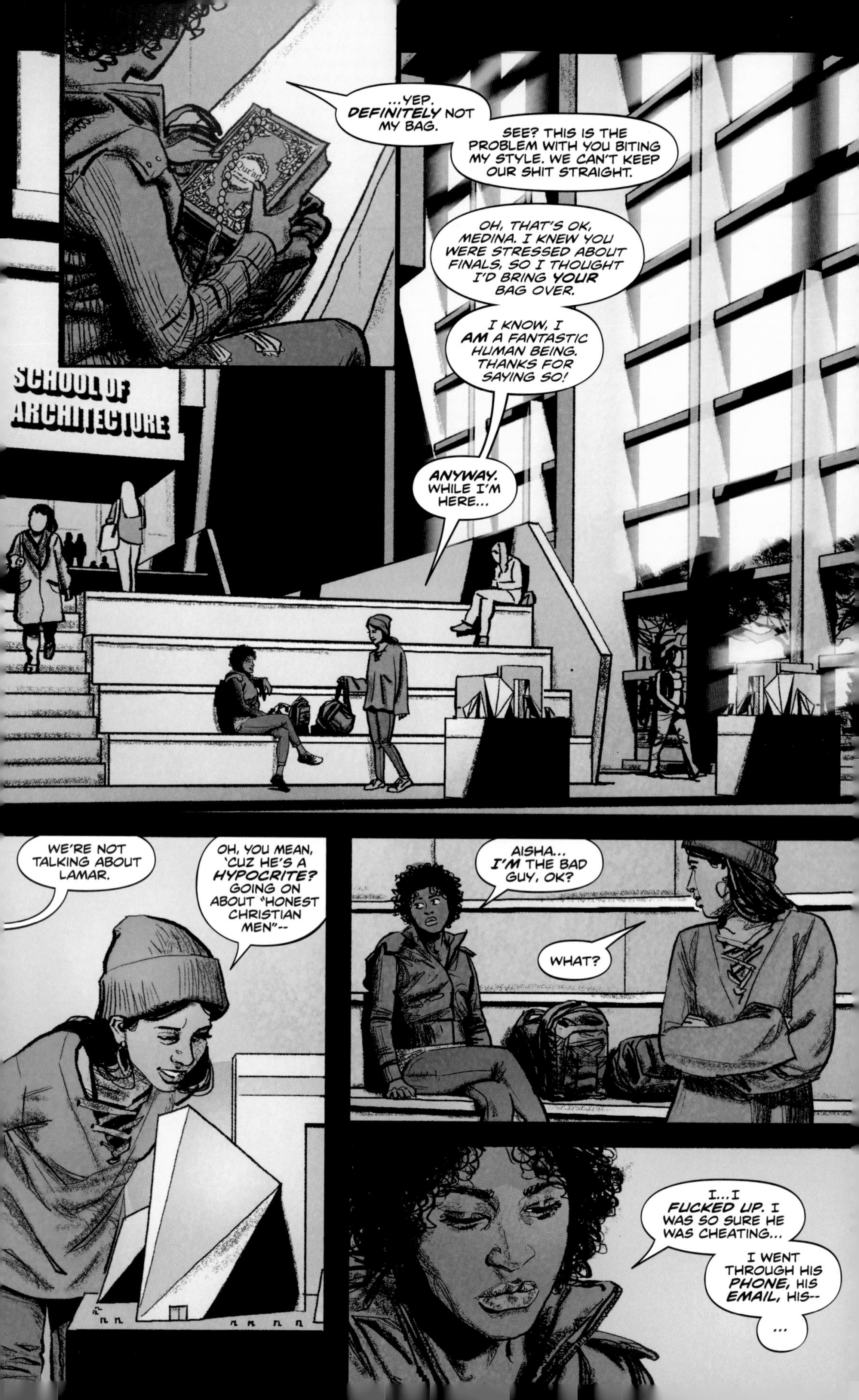
...YEP. DEFINITELY NOT MY BAG.
SEE? THIS IS THE PROBLEM WITH YOU BITING MY STYLE. WE CAN'T KEEP OUR SHIT STRAIGHT.
OH, THAT'S OK, MEDINA. I KNEW YOU WERE STRESSED ABOUT FINALS, SO I THOUGHT I'D BRING YOUR BAG OVER.
I KNOW, I AM A FANTASTIC HUMAN BEING. THANKS FOR SAYING SO!
SCHOOL OF ARCHITECTURE
ANYWAY. WHILE I'M HERE...
WE'RE NOT TALKING ABOUT LAMAR.
OH, YOU MEAN, 'CUZ HE'S A HYPOCRITE? GOING ON ABOUT "HONEST CHRISTIAN MEN"--
AISHA... I'M THE BAD GUY, OK?
WHAT?
I...I FUCKED UP. I WAS SO SURE HE WAS CHEATING...
I WENT THROUGH HIS PHONE, HIS EMAIL, HIS--
...

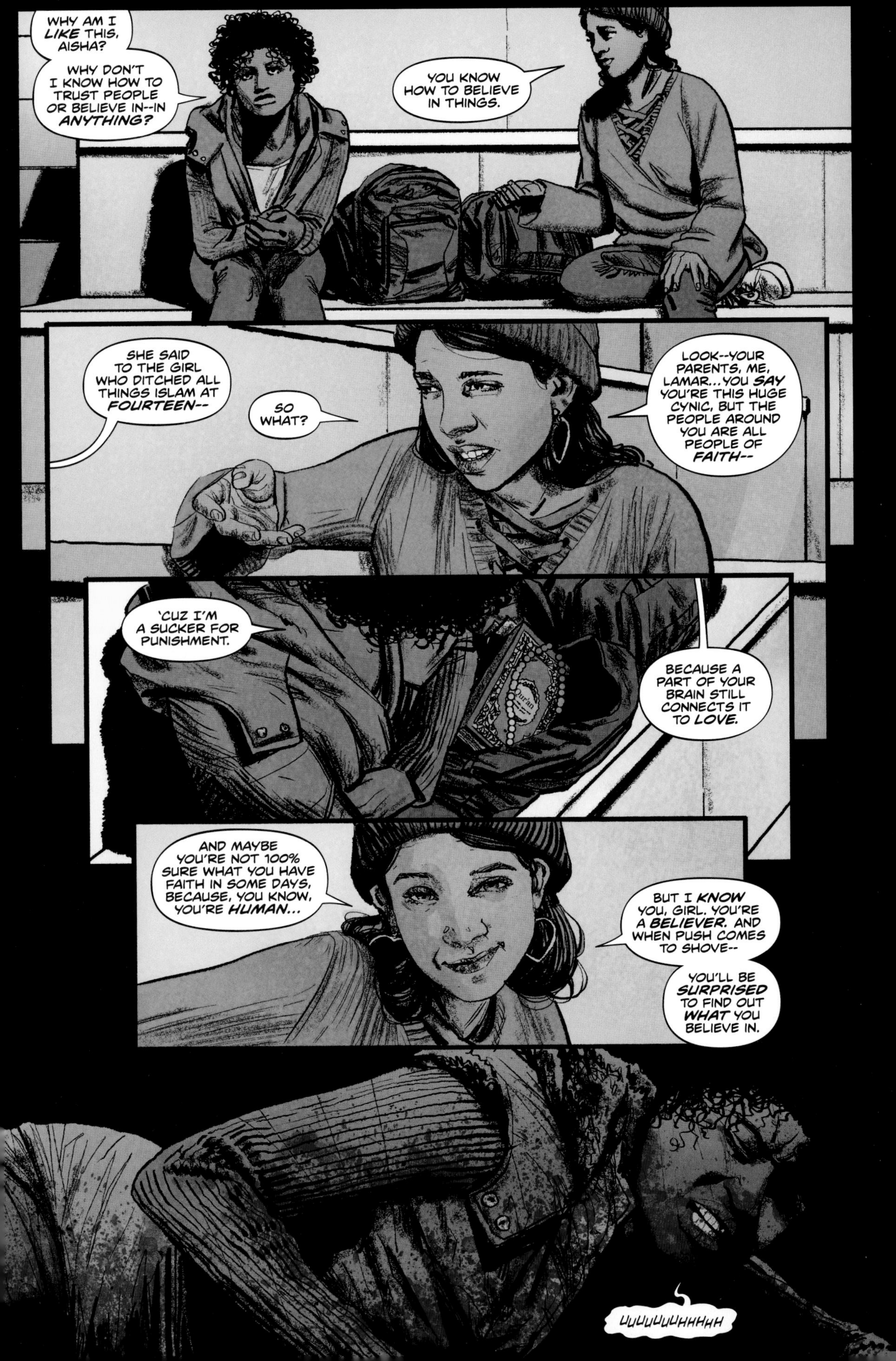
WHY AM I LIKE THIS, AISHA?
WHY DON'T I KNOW HOW TO TRUST PEOPLE OR BELIEVE IN--IN ANYTHING?
YOU KNOW HOW TO BELIEVE IN THINGS.
SHE SAID TO THE GIRL WHO DITCHED ALL THINGS ISLAM AT FOURTEEN--
SO WHAT?
LOOK--YOUR PARENTS, ME, LAMAR...YOU SAY YOU'RE THIS HUGE CYNIC, BUT THE PEOPLE AROUND YOU ARE ALL PEOPLE OF FAITH--
'CUZ I'M A SUCKER FOR PUNISHMENT.
BECAUSE A PART OF YOUR BRAIN STILL CONNECTS IT TO LOVE.
AND MAYBE YOU'RE NOT 100% SURE WHAT YOU HAVE FAITH IN SOME DAYS, BECAUSE, YOU KNOW, YOU'RE HUMAN...
BUT I KNOW YOU, GIRL. YOU'RE A BELIEVER. AND WHEN PUSH COMES TO SHOVE--
YOU'LL BE SURPRISED TO FIND OUT WHAT YOU BELIEVE IN.
UUUUUUUHHHHH

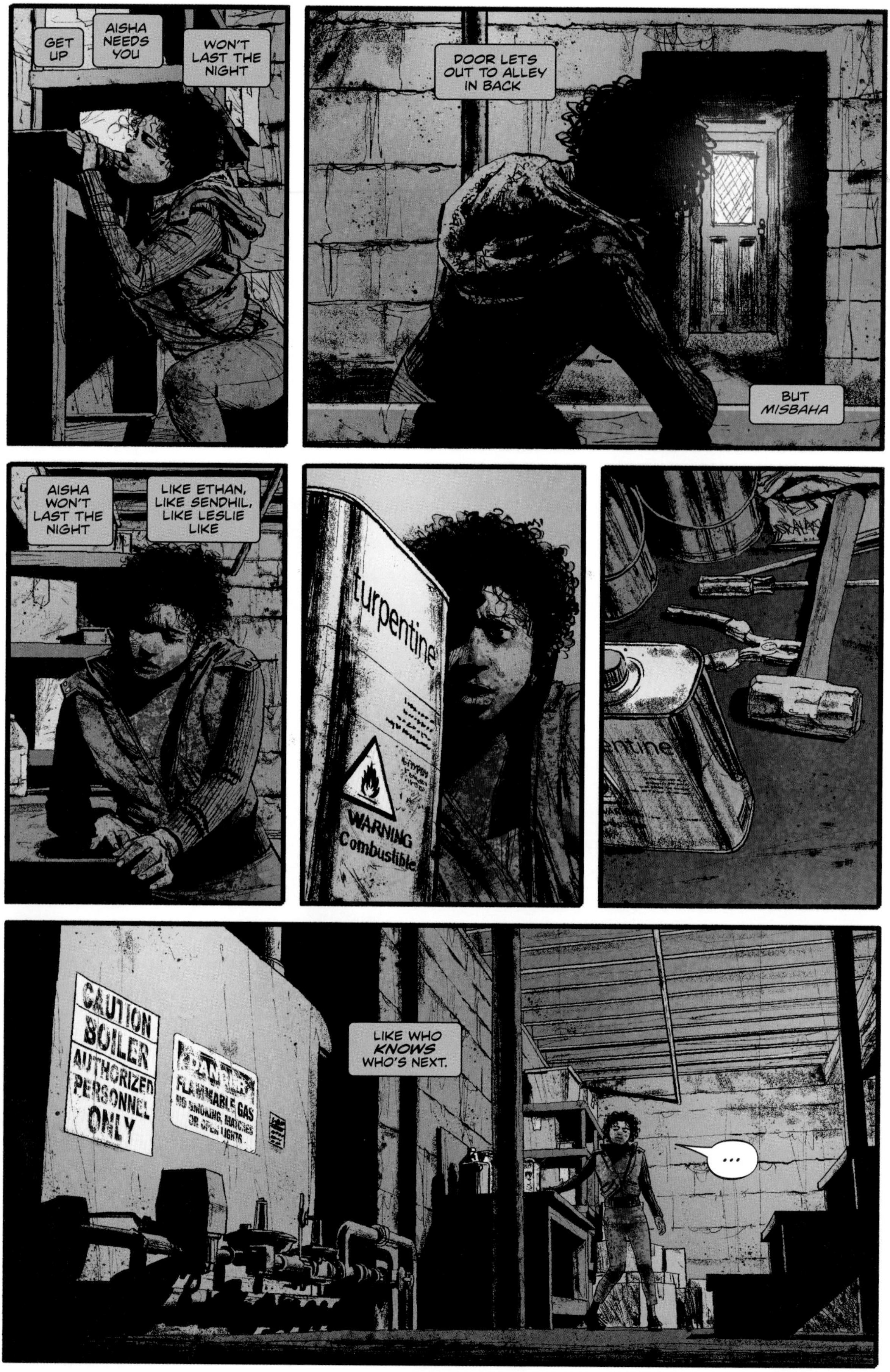
GET UP
AISHA NEEDS YOU
WON'T LAST THE NIGHT
DOOR LETS OUT TO ALLEY IN BACK
BUT *MISBAHA*
AISHA WON'T LAST THE NIGHT
LIKE ETHAN, LIKE SENDHIL, LIKE LESLIE LIKE
turpentine
WARNING
Combustible
CAUTION
BOILER
AUTHORIZED PERSONNEL ONLY
FLAMMABLE GAS
NO SMOKING, MATCHES OR OPEN LIGHTS
LIKE WHO *KNOWS* WHO'S NEXT.
...

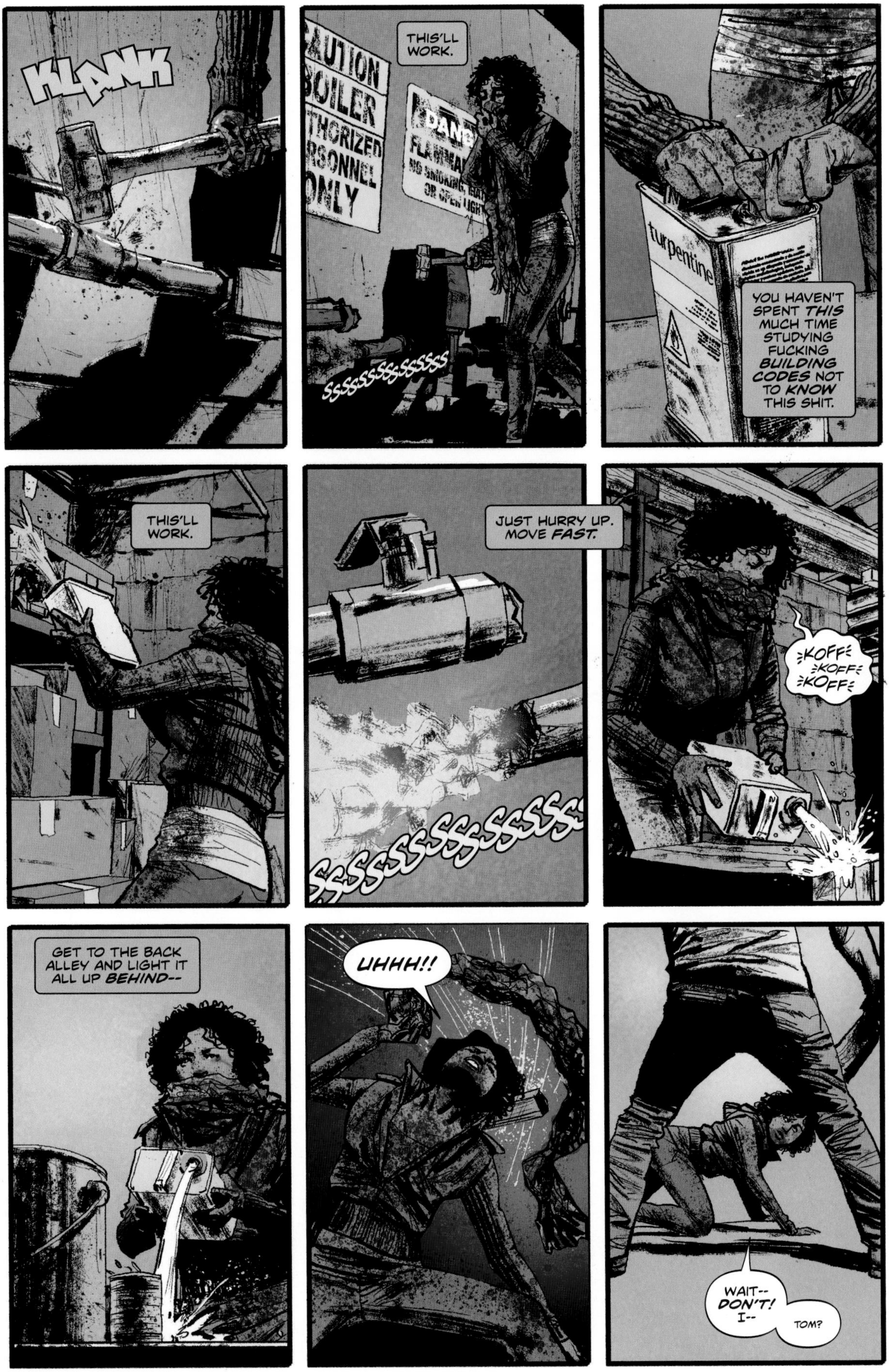
KLANK
THIS'LL WORK.
CAUTION BOILER AUTHORIZED PERSONNEL ONLY
DANG
FLAMMA
NO SMOKING, OR OPEN LIGHT
SSSSSSSSSSSSSS
turpentine
YOU HAVEN'T SPENT *THIS* MUCH TIME STUDYING FUCKING *BUILDING CODES* NOT TO *KNOW* THIS SHIT.
THIS'LL WORK.
JUST HURRY UP. MOVE *FAST.*
SSSSSSSSSSSSSSSS
KOFF KOFF KOFF
GET TO THE BACK ALLEY AND LIGHT IT ALL UP *BEHIND--*
UHHH!!
WAIT-- *DON'T!* I--
TOM?

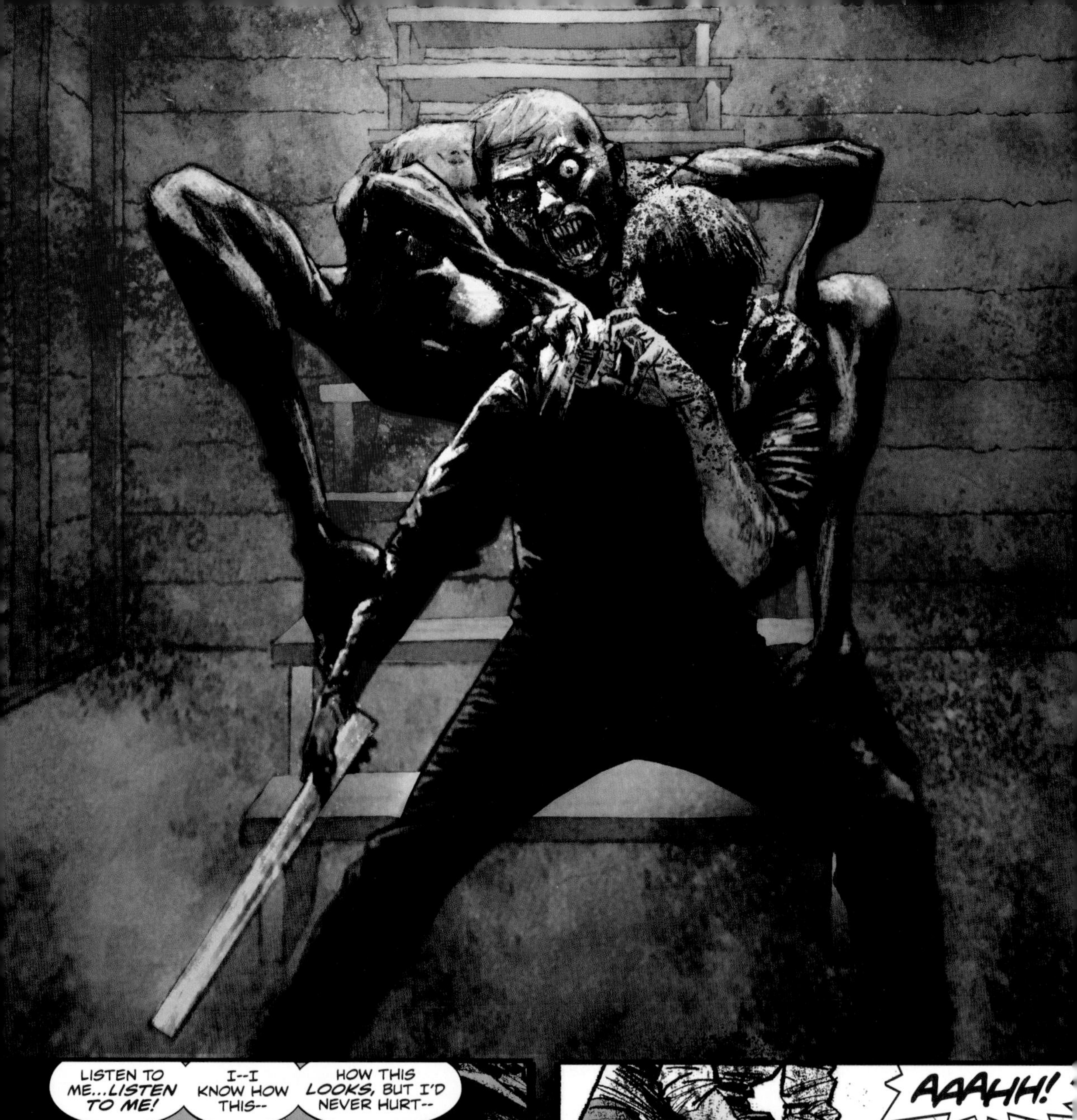
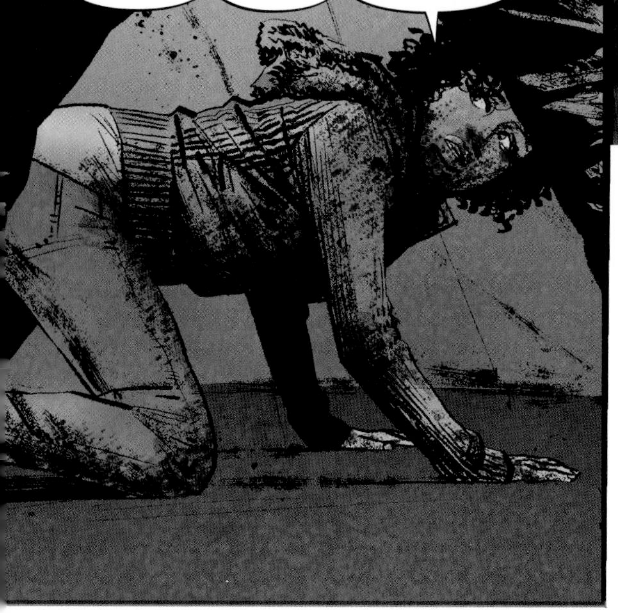
LISTEN TO ME...LISTEN TO ME!
I--I KNOW HOW THIS--
HOW THIS LOOKS, BUT I'D NEVER HURT--
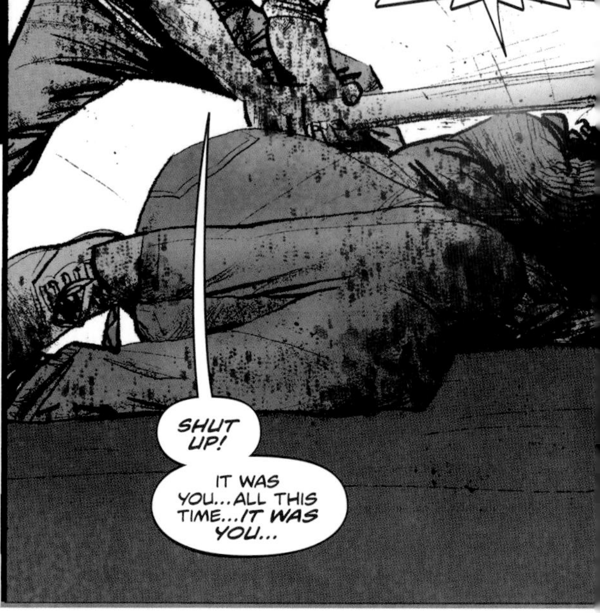
AAAHH!
SHUT UP!
IT WAS YOU...ALL THIS TIME...IT WAS YOU...

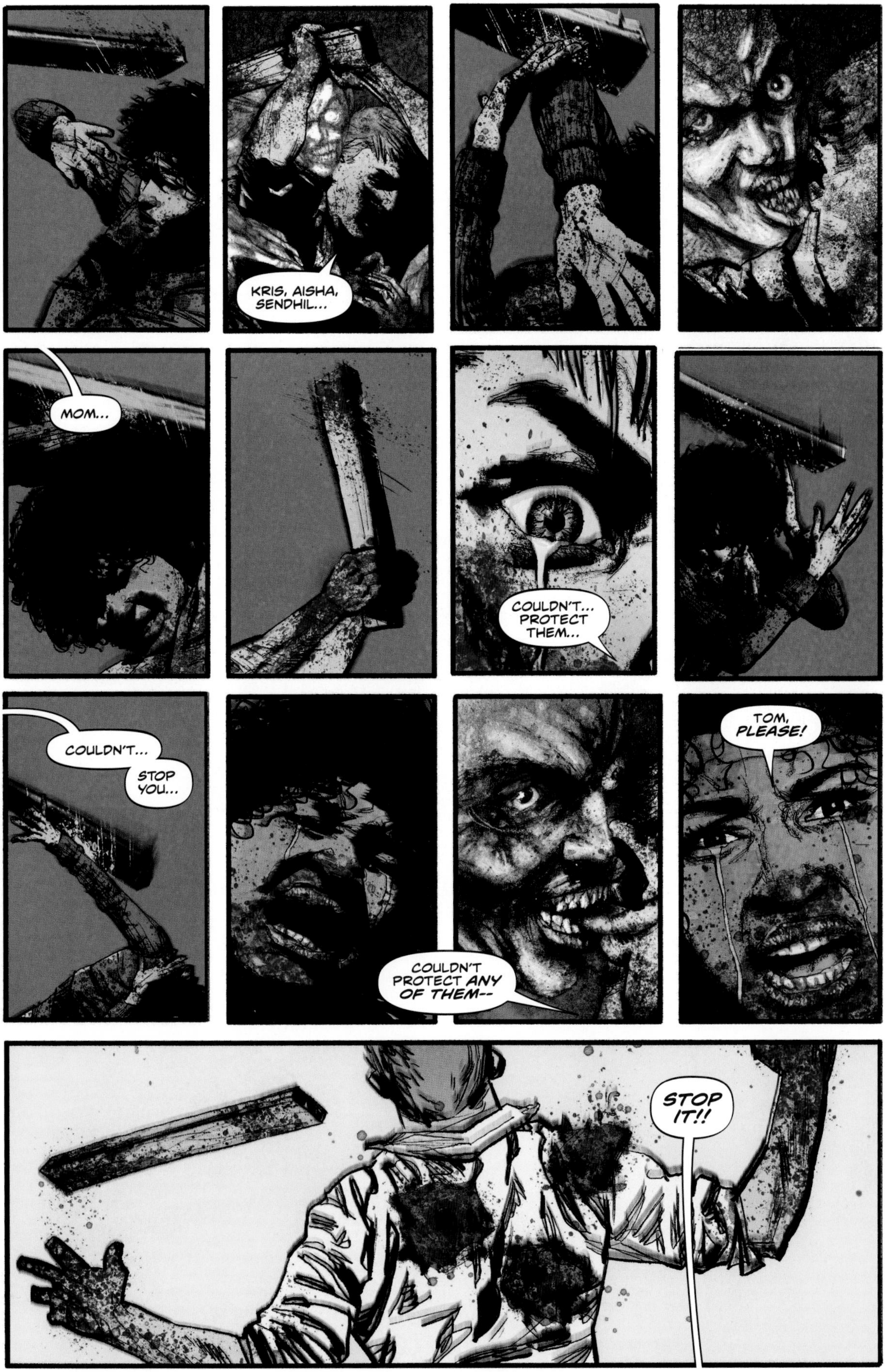
KRIS, AISHA, SENDHIL...
MOM...
COULDN'T... PROTECT THEM...
COULDN'T...
STOP YOU...
TOM, PLEASE!
COULDN'T PROTECT ANY OF THEM--
STOP IT!!

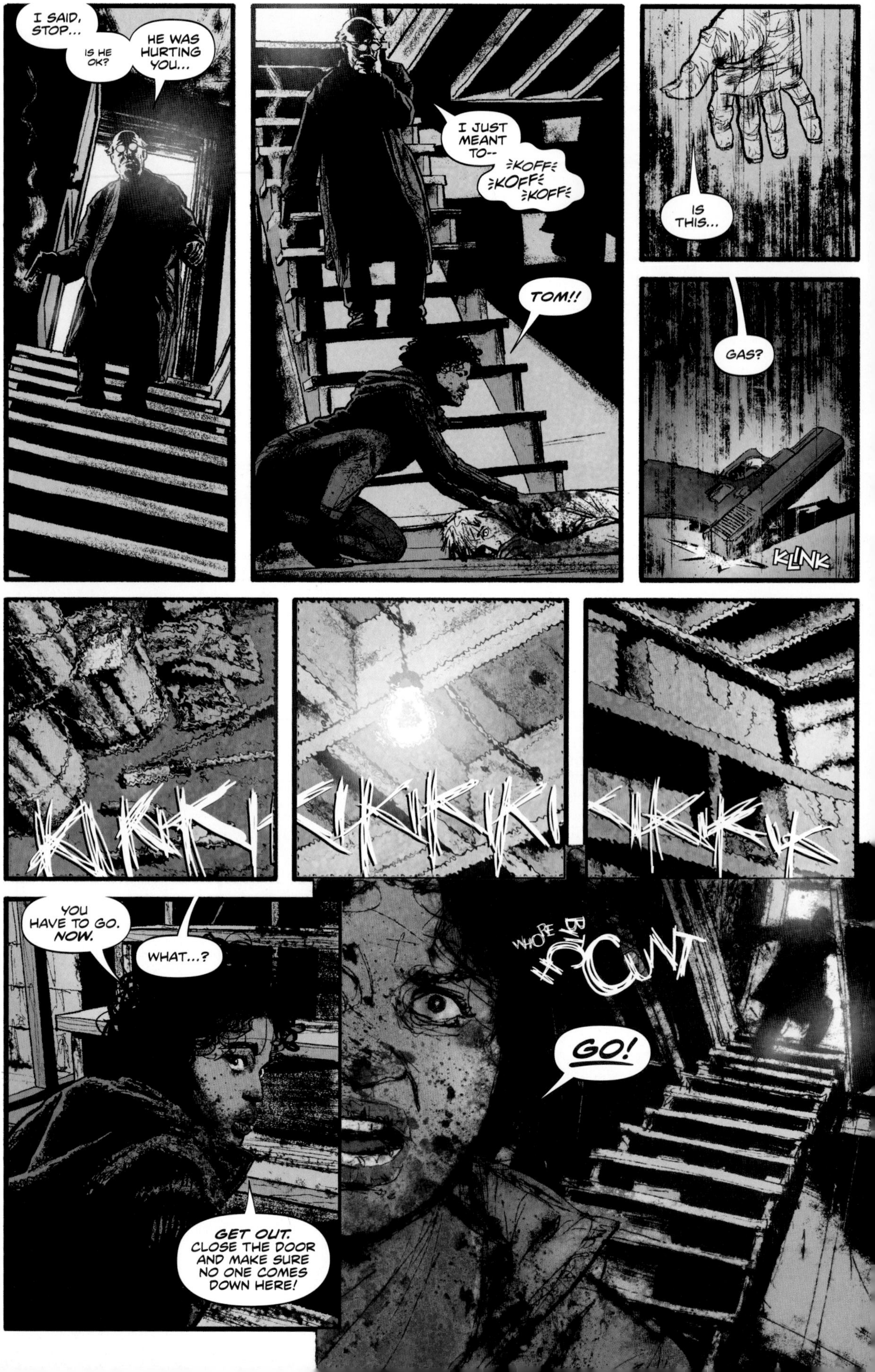
I SAID, STOP...
IS HE OK?
HE WAS HURTING YOU...
I JUST MEANT TO--
KOFF KOFF KOFF
TOM!!
IS THIS...
GAS?
KLINK
YOU HAVE TO GO. NOW.
WHAT...?
GET OUT. CLOSE THE DOOR AND MAKE SURE NO ONE COMES DOWN HERE!
WHORE BITCH CUNT
GO!

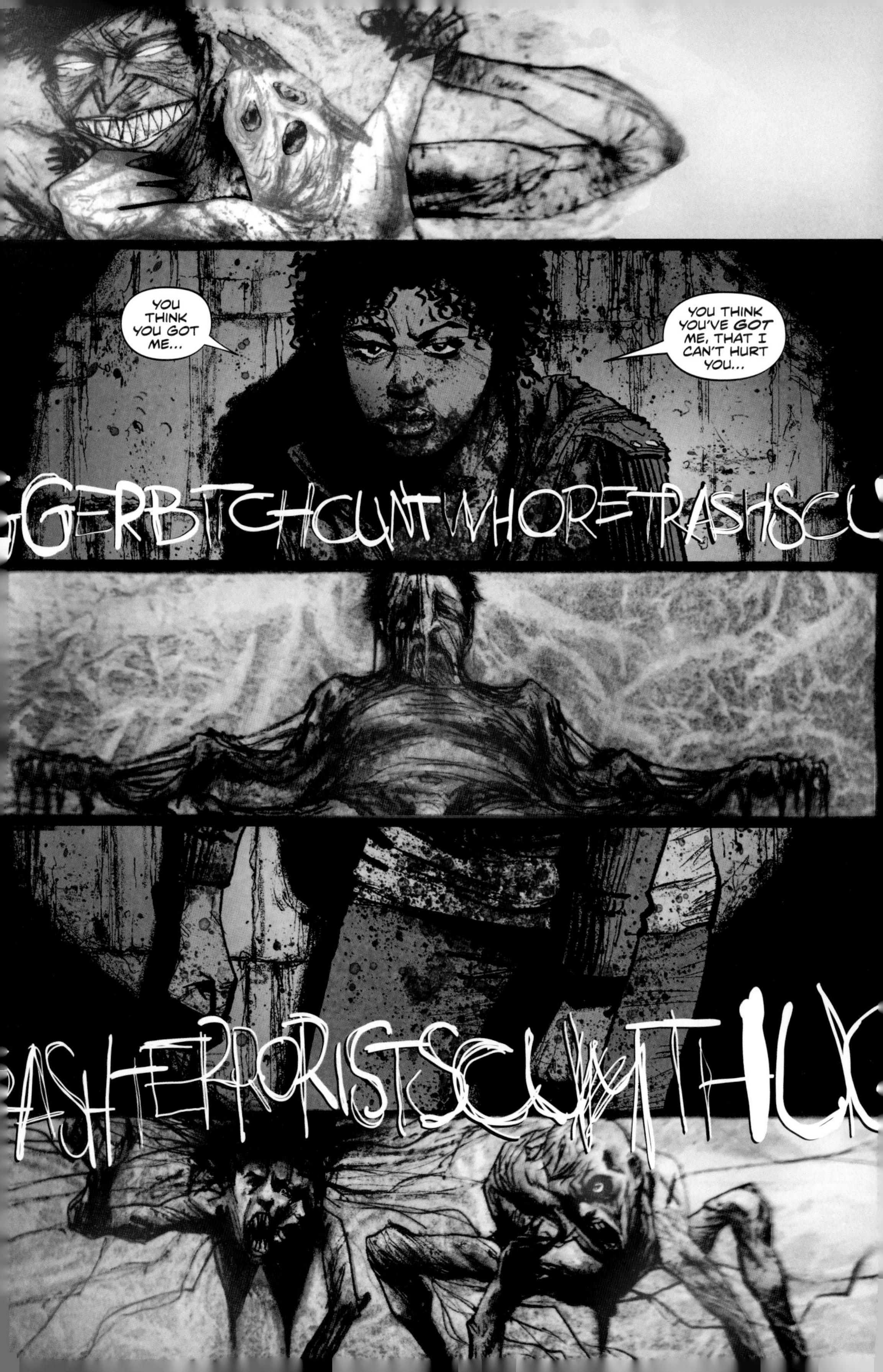
YOU THINK YOU GOT ME...
YOU THINK YOU'VE GOT ME, THAT I CAN'T HURT YOU...
GERBITCHCUNTWHORETRASHSCU
RASHTERRORISTSCUMTHU

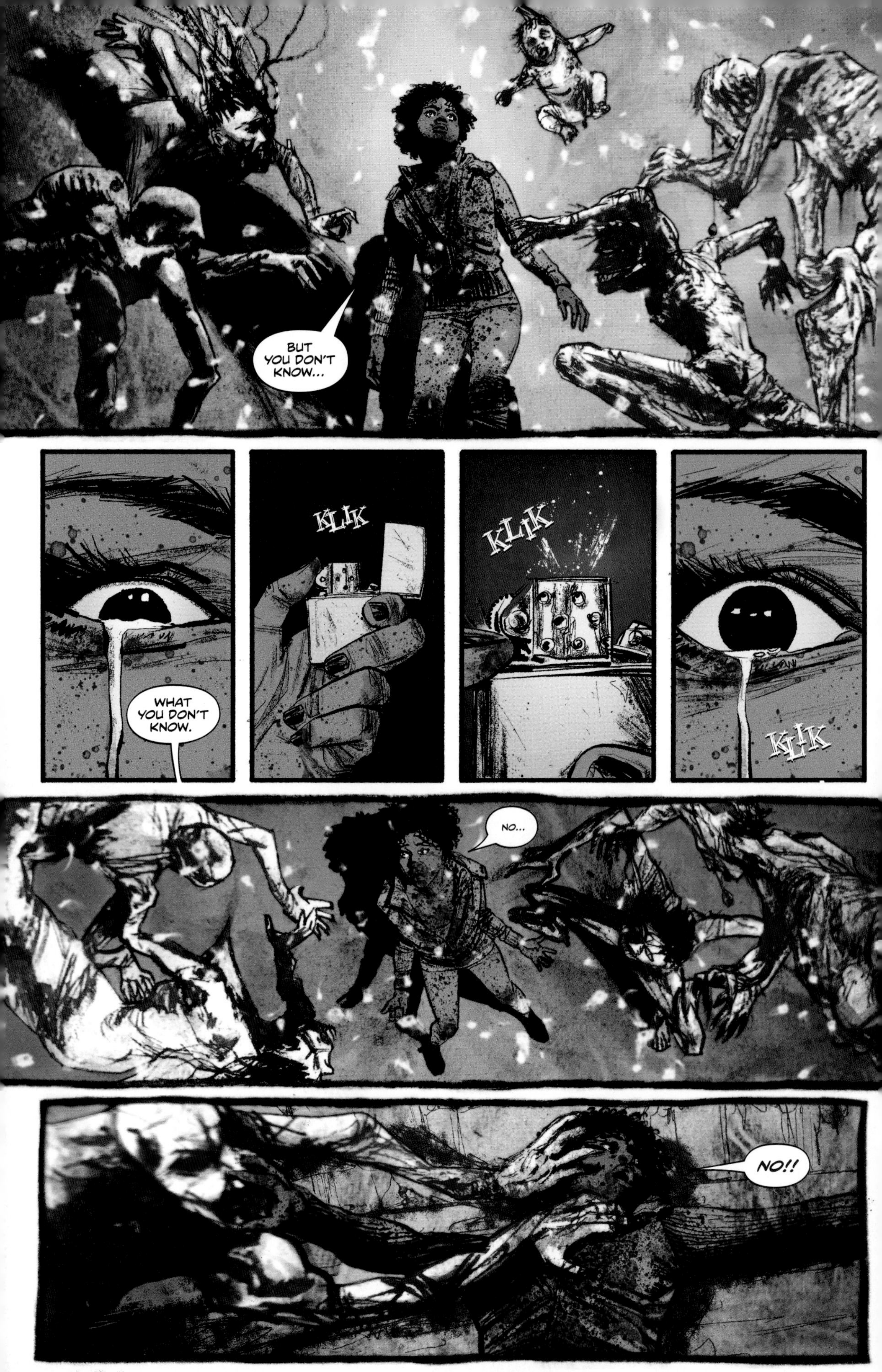
BUT YOU DON'T KNOW...
WHAT YOU DON'T KNOW.
KLIK
KLIK
KLIK
NO...
NO!!

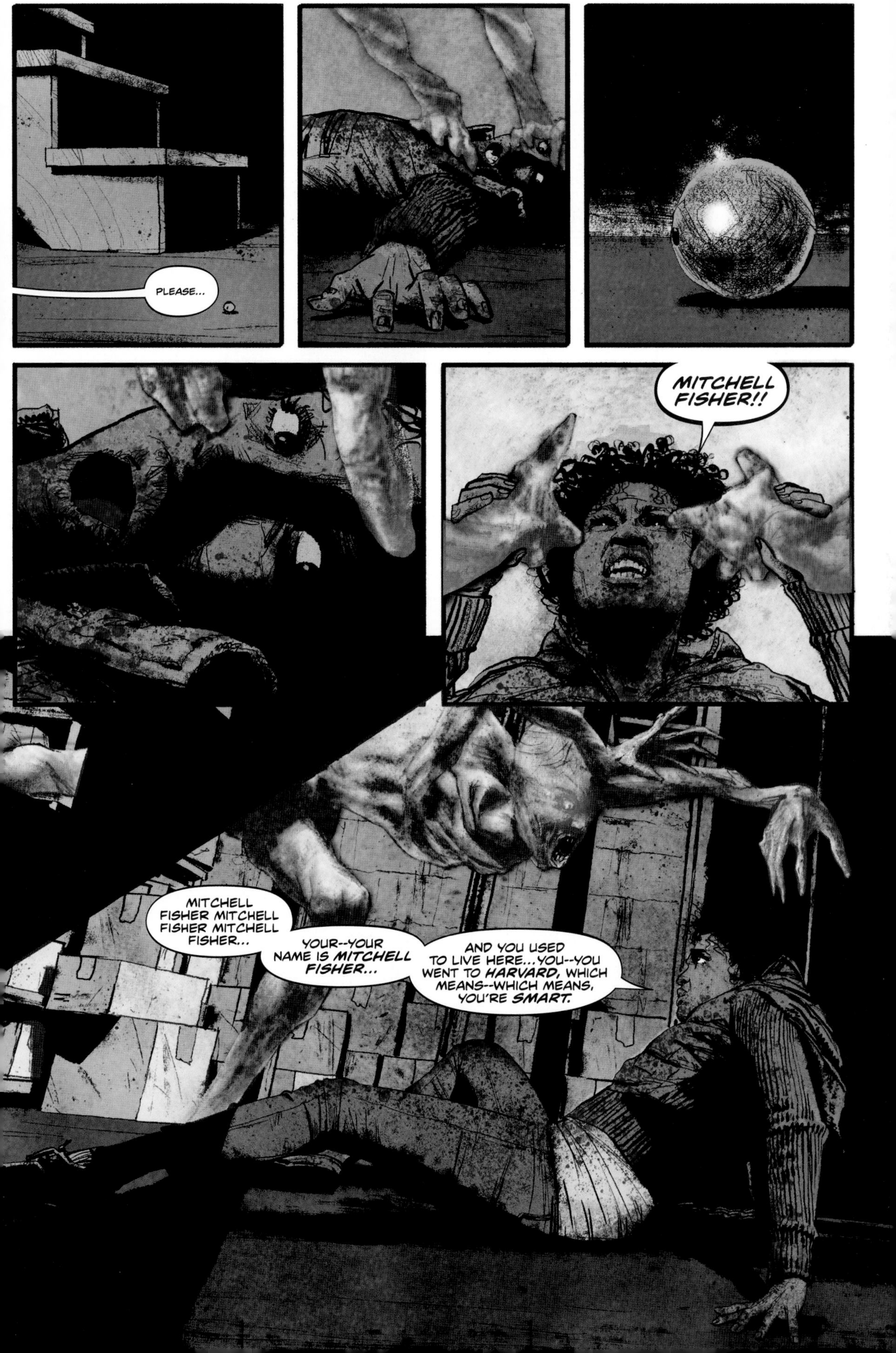
PLEASE...
MITCHELL FISHER!!
MITCHELL FISHER MITCHELL FISHER MITCHELL FISHER...
YOUR--YOUR NAME IS MITCHELL FISHER...
AND YOU USED TO LIVE HERE...YOU--YOU WENT TO HARVARD, WHICH MEANS--WHICH MEANS, YOU'RE SMART.

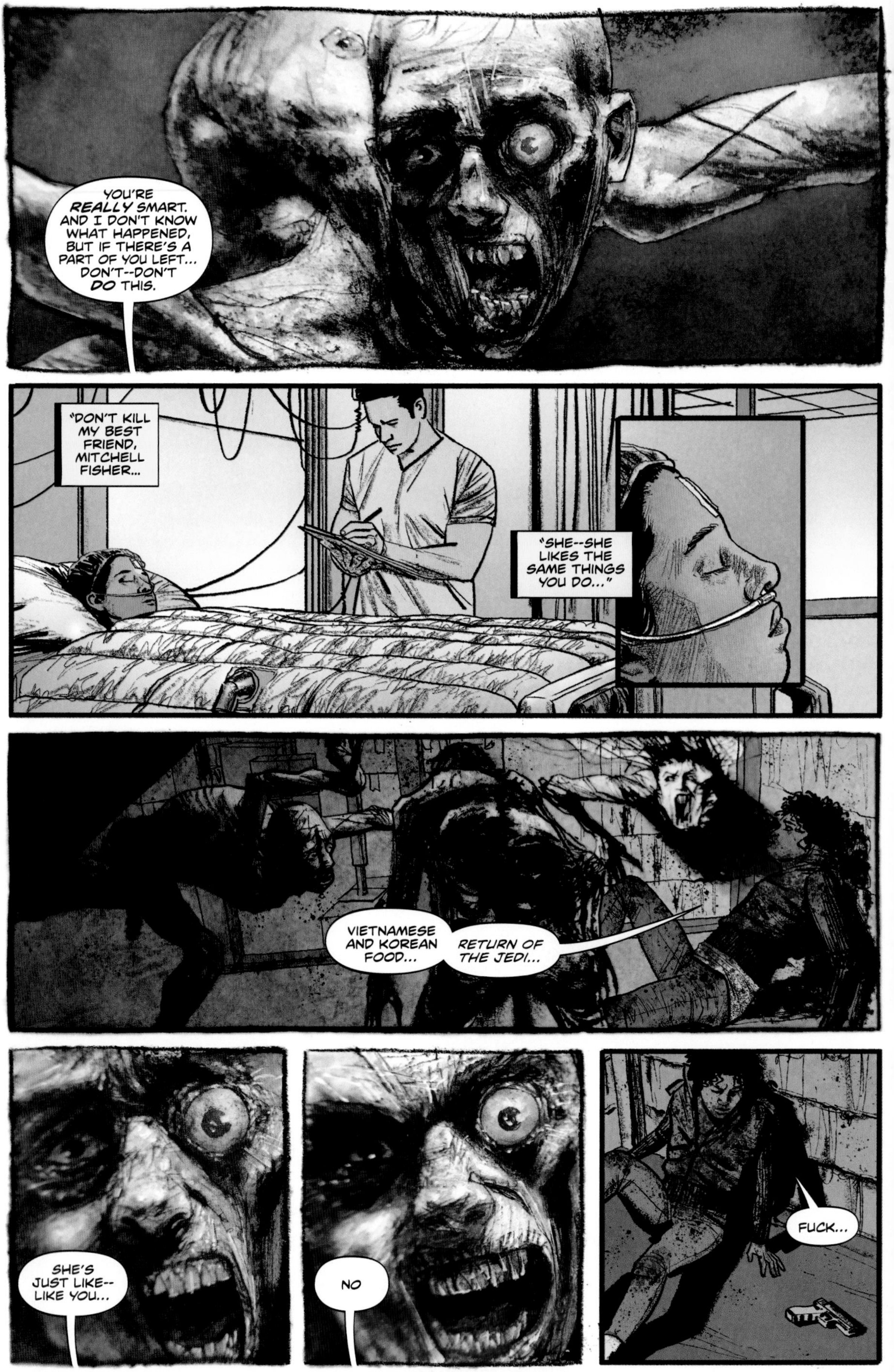
YOU'RE REALLY SMART. AND I DON'T KNOW WHAT HAPPENED, BUT IF THERE'S A PART OF YOU LEFT... DON'T--DON'T DO THIS.
"DON'T KILL MY BEST FRIEND, MITCHELL FISHER...
"SHE--SHE LIKES THE SAME THINGS YOU DO..."
VIETNAMESE AND KOREAN FOOD...
RETURN OF THE JEDI...
SHE'S JUST LIKE--LIKE YOU...
NO
FUCK...

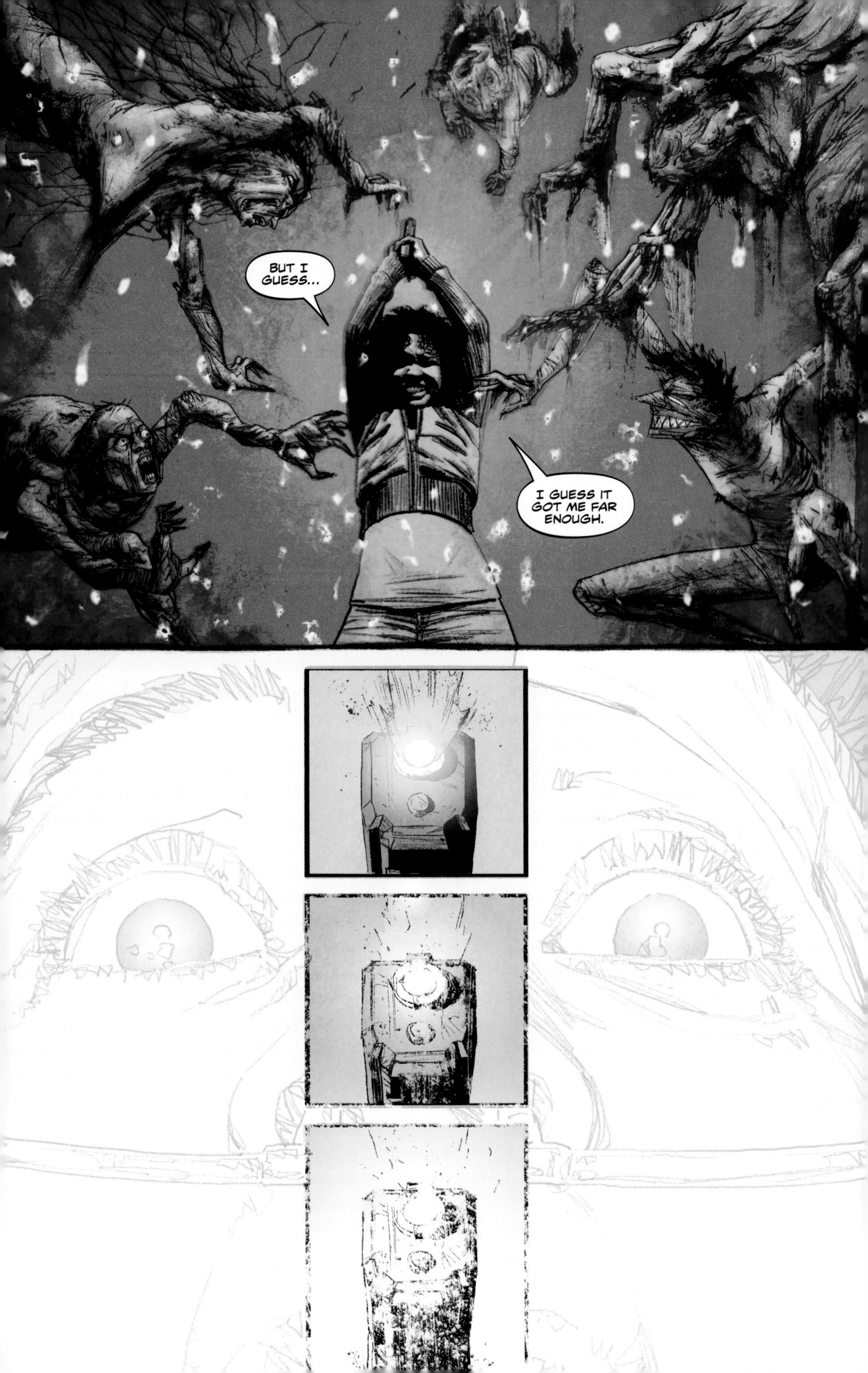
BUT I GUESS...
I GUESS IT GOT ME FAR ENOUGH.

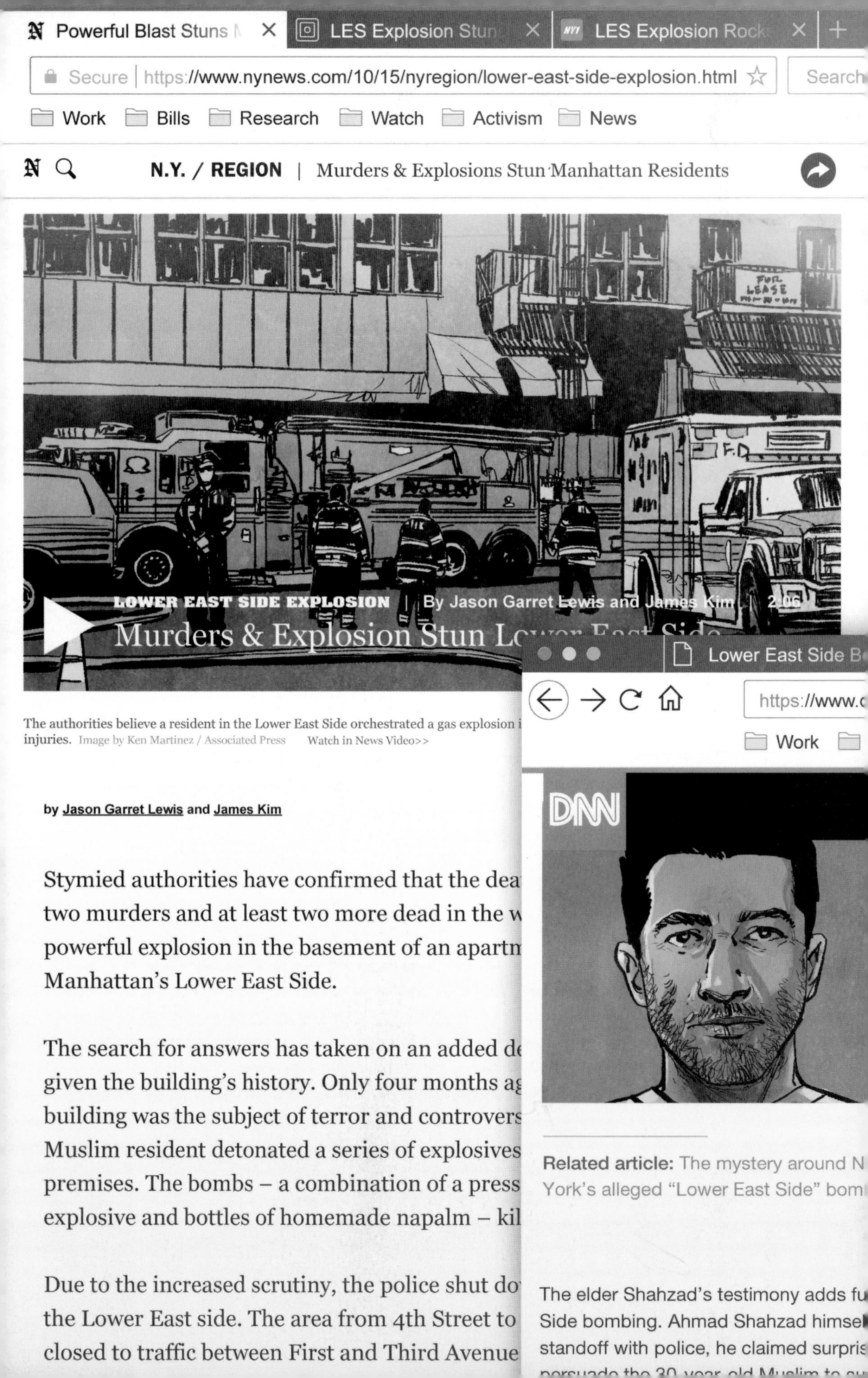
Powerful Blast Stuns M
LES Explosion Stun
LES Explosion Rock
Secure | https://www.nynews.com/10/15/nyregion/lower-east-side-explosion.html
Search
Work
Bills
Research
Watch
Activism
News
N.Y. / REGION | Murders & Explosions Stun Manhattan Residents
FOR LEASE
LOWER EAST SIDE EXPLOSION | By Jason Garret Lewis and James Kim | 2:06
Murders & Explosion Stun Lower East Side
The authorities believe a resident in the Lower East Side orchestrated a gas explosion i
injuries. Image by Ken Martinez / Associated Press Watch in News Video>>
by Jason Garret Lewis and James Kim
Stymied authorities have confirmed that the dea
two murders and at least two more dead in the w
powerful explosion in the basement of an apartm
Manhattan's Lower East Side.
The search for answers has taken on an added de
given the building's history. Only four months ag
building was the subject of terror and controvers
Muslim resident detonated a series of explosives
premises. The bombs – a combination of a press
explosive and bottles of homemade napalm – kil
Due to the increased scrutiny, the police shut do
the Lower East side. The area from 4th Street to
closed to traffic between First and Third Avenue
Lower East Side B
https://www.
Work
DNN
Related article: The mystery around N
York's alleged "Lower East Side" bom
The elder Shahzad's testimony adds fu
Side bombing. Ahmad Shahzad himse
standoff with police, he claimed surpris

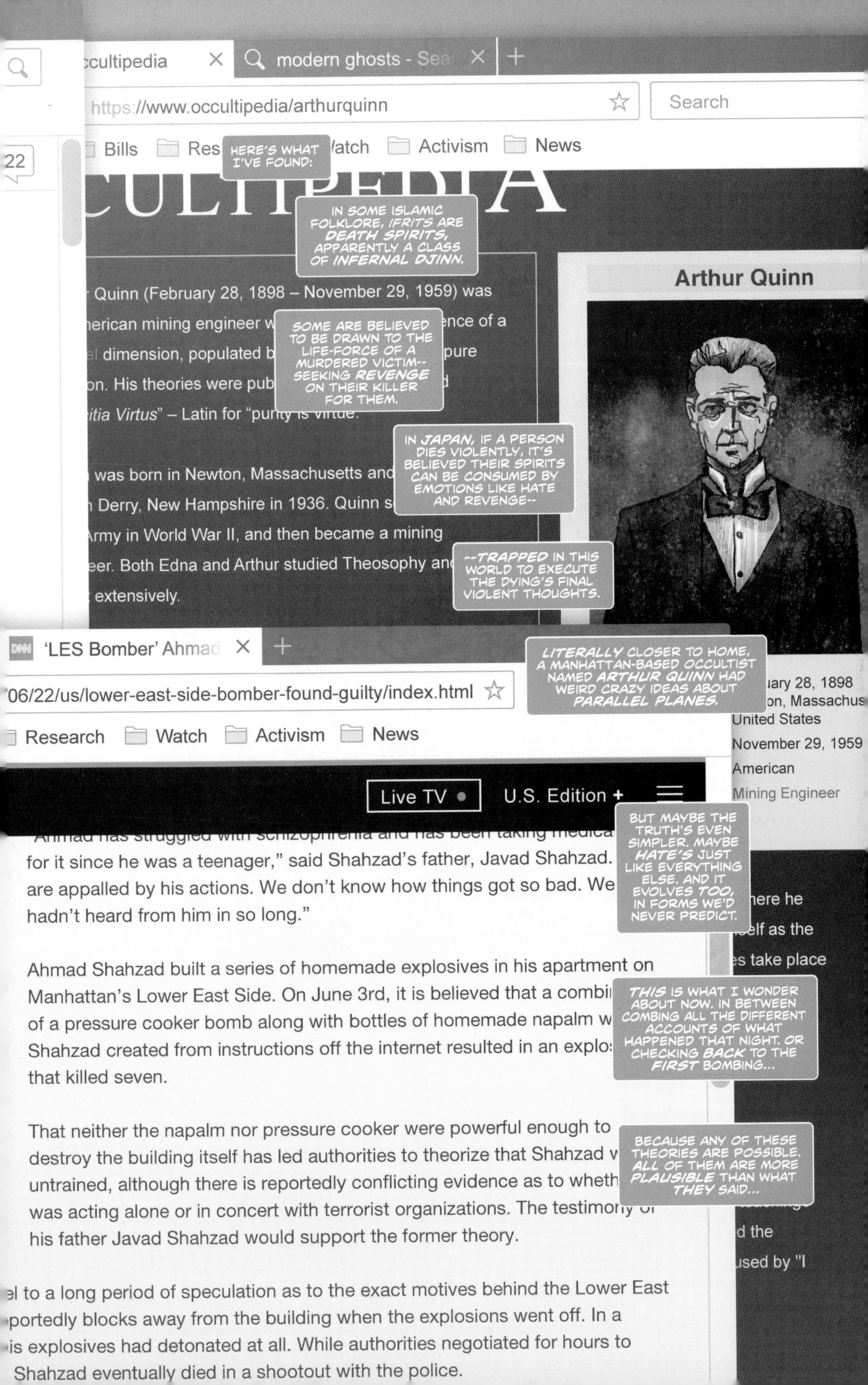

ccultipedia
modern ghosts - Sea
https://www.occultipedia/arthurquinn
Search
Bills
Res
Watch
Activism
News
HERE'S WHAT I'VE FOUND:
CULTIPEDIA
IN SOME ISLAMIC FOLKLORE, IFRITS ARE DEATH SPIRITS, APPARENTLY A CLASS OF INFERNAL DJINN.
Arthur Quinn
Quinn (February 28, 1898 – November 29, 1959) was
erican mining engineer w
ence of a
dimension, populated b
pure
on. His theories were pub
itia Virtus" – Latin for "pu
SOME ARE BELIEVED TO BE DRAWN TO THE LIFE-FORCE OF A MURDERED VICTIM--SEEKING REVENGE ON THEIR KILLER FOR THEM.
IN JAPAN, IF A PERSON DIES VIOLENTLY, IT'S BELIEVED THEIR SPIRITS CAN BE CONSUMED BY EMOTIONS LIKE HATE AND REVENGE--
was born in Newton, Massachusetts and
Derry, New Hampshire in 1936. Quinn s
Army in World War II, and then became a mining
eer. Both Edna and Arthur studied Theosophy an
extensively.
--TRAPPED IN THIS WORLD TO EXECUTE THE DYING'S FINAL VIOLENT THOUGHTS.
'LES Bomber' Ahmad
06/22/us/lower-east-side-bomber-found-guilty/index.html
Research
Watch
Activism
News
LITERALLY CLOSER TO HOME, A MANHATTAN-BASED OCCULTIST NAMED ARTHUR QUINN HAD WEIRD CRAZY IDEAS ABOUT PARALLEL PLANES.
United States
November 29, 1959
American
Mining Engineer
Live TV
U.S. Edition +
for it since he was a teenager," said Shahzad's father, Javad Shahzad.
are appalled by his actions. We don't know how things got so bad. We
hadn't heard from him in so long."
BUT MAYBE THE TRUTH'S EVEN SIMPLER. MAYBE HATE'S JUST LIKE EVERYTHING ELSE. AND IT EVOLVES TOO, IN FORMS WE'D NEVER PREDICT.
Ahmad Shahzad built a series of homemade explosives in his apartment on
Manhattan's Lower East Side. On June 3rd, it is believed that a combi
of a pressure cooker bomb along with bottles of homemade napalm w
Shahzad created from instructions off the internet resulted in an explo
that killed seven.
THIS IS WHAT I WONDER ABOUT NOW. IN BETWEEN COMBING ALL THE DIFFERENT ACCOUNTS OF WHAT HAPPENED THAT NIGHT. OR CHECKING BACK TO THE FIRST BOMBING...
That neither the napalm nor pressure cooker were powerful enough to
destroy the building itself has led authorities to theorize that Shahzad w
untrained, although there is reportedly conflicting evidence as to wheth
was acting alone or in concert with terrorist organizations. The testimon
his father Javad Shahzad would support the former theory.
BECAUSE ANY OF THESE THEORIES ARE POSSIBLE. ALL OF THEM ARE MORE PLAUSIBLE THAN WHAT THEY SAID...
to a long period of speculation as to the exact motives behind the Lower East
portedly blocks away from the building when the explosions went off. In a
is explosives had detonated at all. While authorities negotiated for hours to
Shahzad eventually died in a shootout with the police.

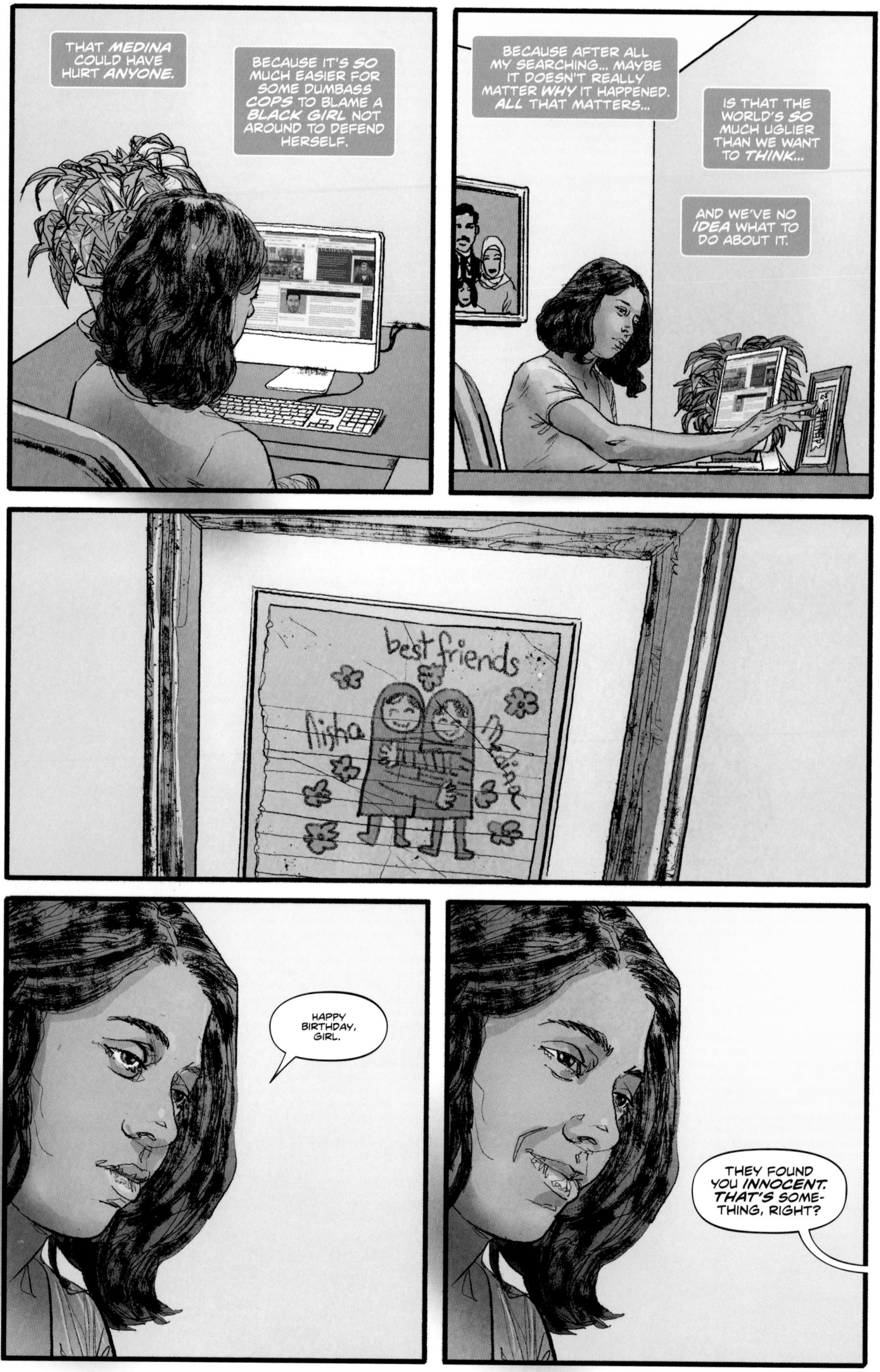
THAT MEDINA COULD HAVE HURT ANYONE.
BECAUSE IT'S SO MUCH EASIER FOR SOME DUMBASS COPS TO BLAME A BLACK GIRL NOT AROUND TO DEFEND HERSELF.
BECAUSE AFTER ALL MY SEARCHING... MAYBE IT DOESN'T REALLY MATTER WHY IT HAPPENED. ALL THAT MATTERS...
IS THAT THE WORLD'S SO MUCH UGLIER THAN WE WANT TO THINK...
AND WE'VE NO IDEA WHAT TO DO ABOUT IT.
best friends
Aisha
Medina
HAPPY BIRTHDAY, GIRL.
THEY FOUND YOU INNOCENT. THAT'S SOME-THING, RIGHT?

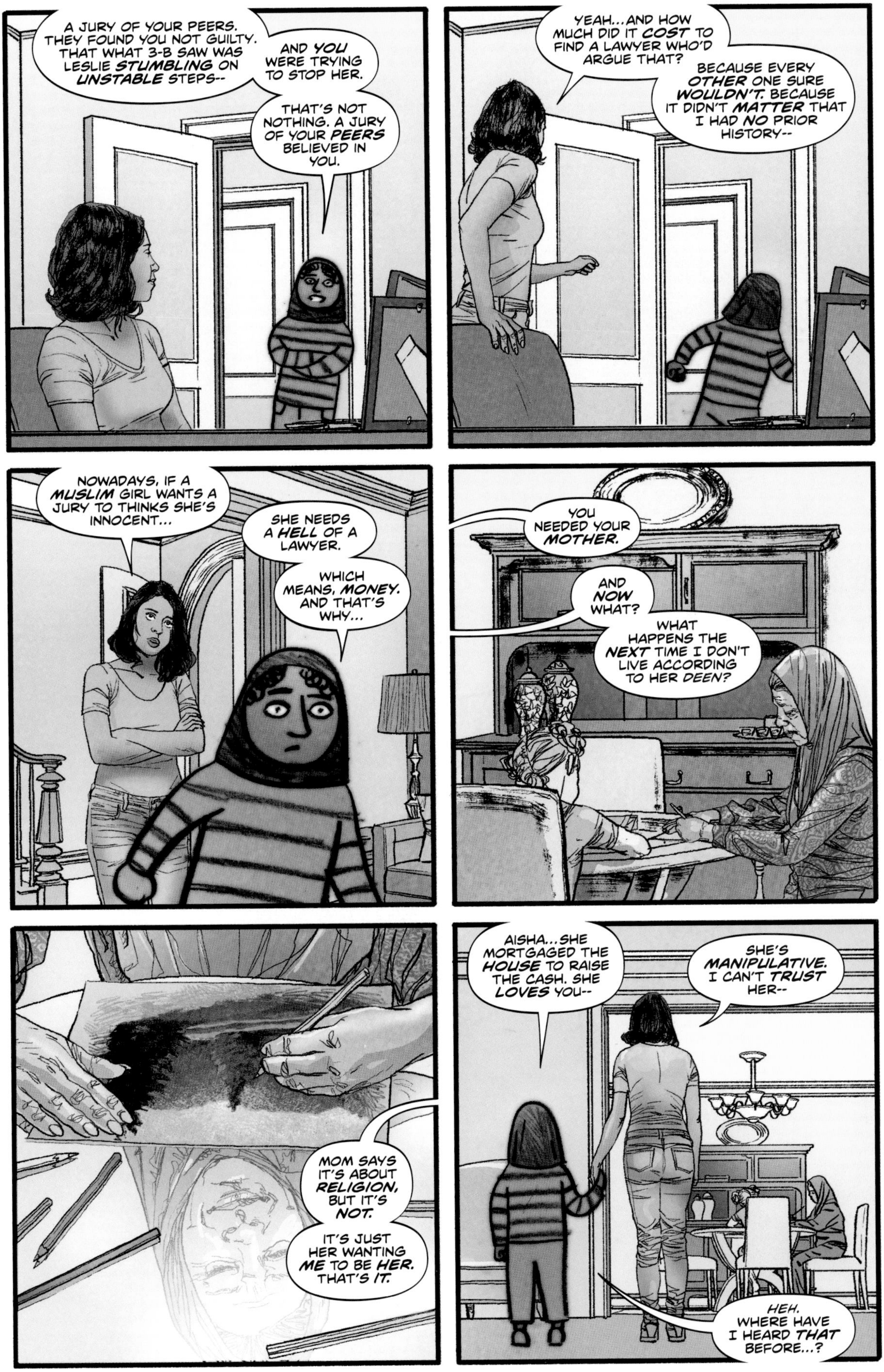
A JURY OF YOUR PEERS. THEY FOUND YOU NOT GUILTY. THAT WHAT 3-B SAW WAS LESLIE STUMBLING ON UNSTABLE STEPS--
AND YOU WERE TRYING TO STOP HER.
THAT'S NOT NOTHING. A JURY OF YOUR PEERS BELIEVED IN YOU.
YEAH...AND HOW MUCH DID IT COST TO FIND A LAWYER WHO'D ARGUE THAT?
BECAUSE EVERY OTHER ONE SURE WOULDN'T. BECAUSE IT DIDN'T MATTER THAT I HAD NO PRIOR HISTORY--
NOWADAYS, IF A MUSLIM GIRL WANTS A JURY TO THINKS SHE'S INNOCENT...
SHE NEEDS A HELL OF A LAWYER.
WHICH MEANS, MONEY. AND THAT'S WHY...
YOU NEEDED YOUR MOTHER.
AND NOW WHAT?
WHAT HAPPENS THE NEXT TIME I DON'T LIVE ACCORDING TO HER DEEN?
MOM SAYS IT'S ABOUT RELIGION, BUT IT'S NOT.
IT'S JUST HER WANTING ME TO BE HER. THAT'S IT.
AISHA...SHE MORTGAGED THE HOUSE TO RAISE THE CASH. SHE LOVES YOU--
SHE'S MANIPULATIVE. I CAN'T TRUST HER--
HEH. WHERE HAVE I HEARD THAT BEFORE...?

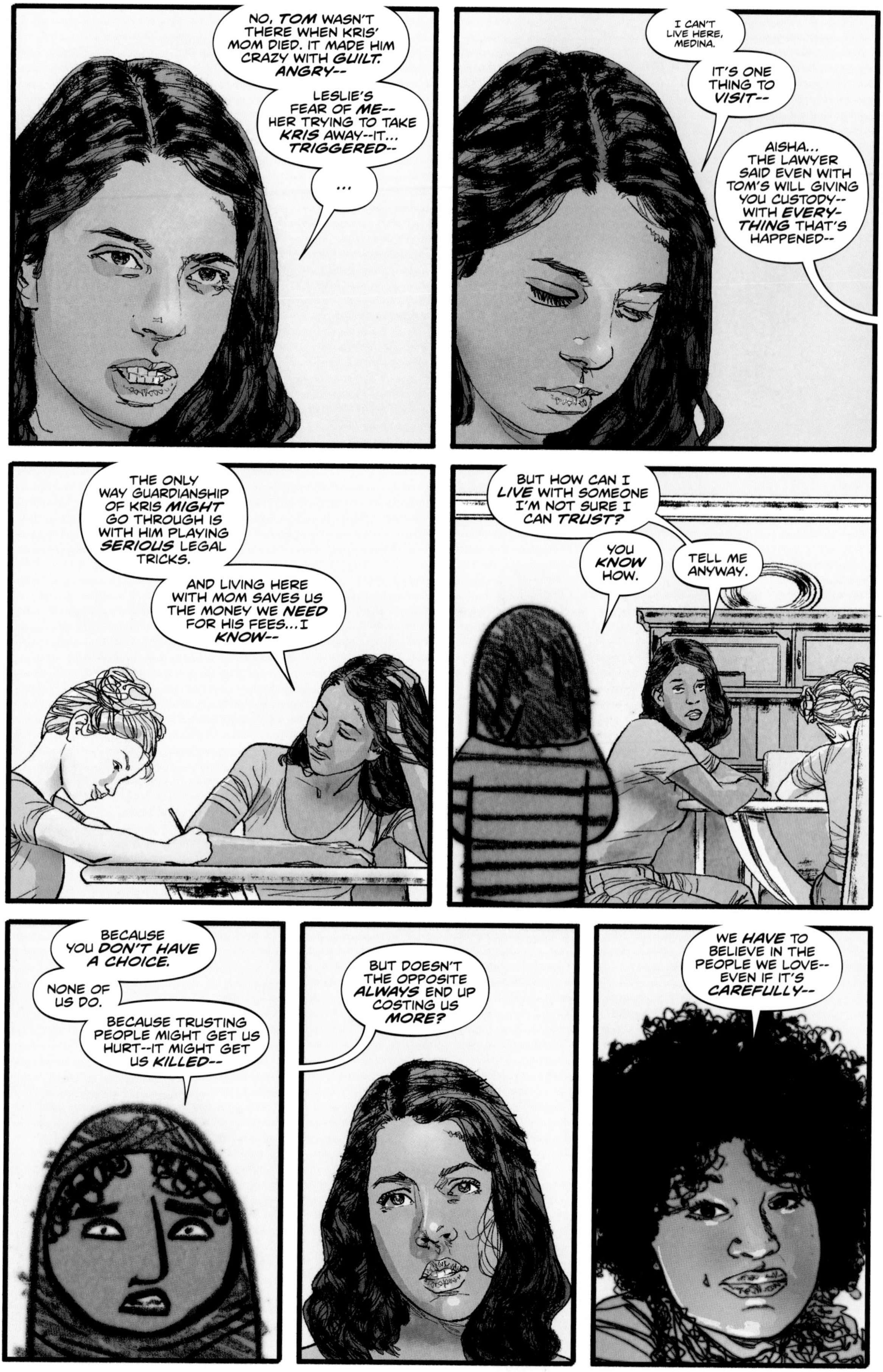
NO, TOM WASN'T THERE WHEN KRIS' MOM DIED. IT MADE HIM CRAZY WITH GUILT. ANGRY--
LESLIE'S FEAR OF ME-- HER TRYING TO TAKE KRIS AWAY--IT... TRIGGERED--
...
I CAN'T LIVE HERE, MEDINA.
IT'S ONE THING TO VISIT--
AISHA... THE LAWYER SAID EVEN WITH TOM'S WILL GIVING YOU CUSTODY-- WITH EVERYTHING THAT'S HAPPENED--
THE ONLY WAY GUARDIANSHIP OF KRIS MIGHT GO THROUGH IS WITH HIM PLAYING SERIOUS LEGAL TRICKS.
AND LIVING HERE WITH MOM SAVES US THE MONEY WE NEED FOR HIS FEES... I KNOW--
BUT HOW CAN I LIVE WITH SOMEONE I'M NOT SURE I CAN TRUST?
YOU KNOW HOW.
TELL ME ANYWAY.
BECAUSE YOU DON'T HAVE A CHOICE.
NONE OF US DO.
BECAUSE TRUSTING PEOPLE MIGHT GET US HURT--IT MIGHT GET US KILLED--
BUT DOESN'T THE OPPOSITE ALWAYS END UP COSTING US MORE?
WE HAVE TO BELIEVE IN THE PEOPLE WE LOVE-- EVEN IF IT'S CAREFULLY--

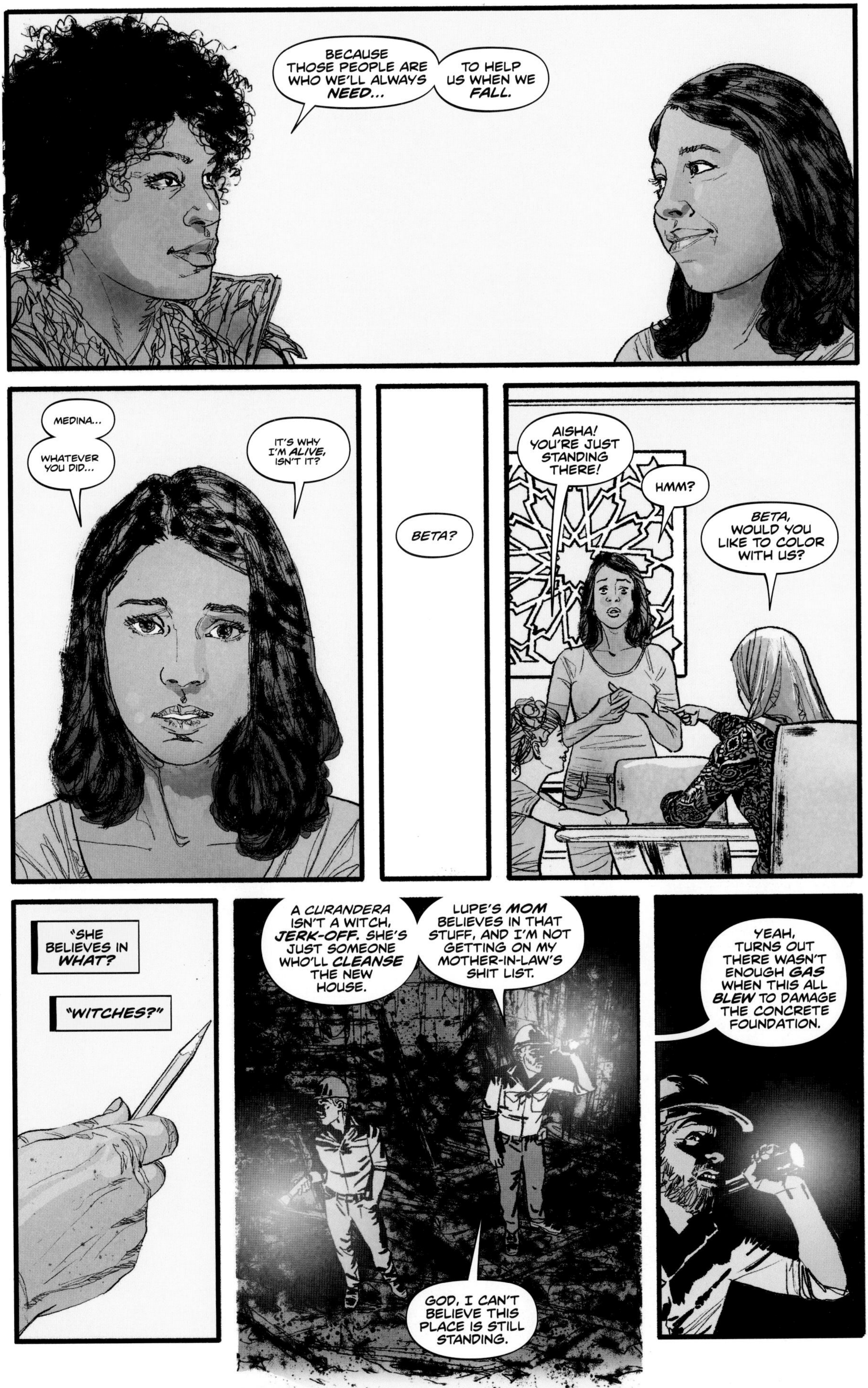
BECAUSE THOSE PEOPLE ARE WHO WE'LL ALWAYS NEED...
TO HELP US WHEN WE FALL.
MEDINA...
WHATEVER YOU DID...
IT'S WHY I'M ALIVE, ISN'T IT?
BETA?
AISHA! YOU'RE JUST STANDING THERE!
HMM?
BETA, WOULD YOU LIKE TO COLOR WITH US?
"SHE BELIEVES IN WHAT?
"WITCHES?"
A CURANDERA ISN'T A WITCH, JERK-OFF. SHE'S JUST SOMEONE WHO'LL CLEANSE THE NEW HOUSE.
LUPE'S MOM BELIEVES IN THAT STUFF, AND I'M NOT GETTING ON MY MOTHER-IN-LAW'S SHIT LIST.
GOD, I CAN'T BELIEVE THIS PLACE IS STILL STANDING.
YEAH, TURNS OUT THERE WASN'T ENOUGH GAS WHEN THIS ALL BLEW TO DAMAGE THE CONCRETE FOUNDATION.

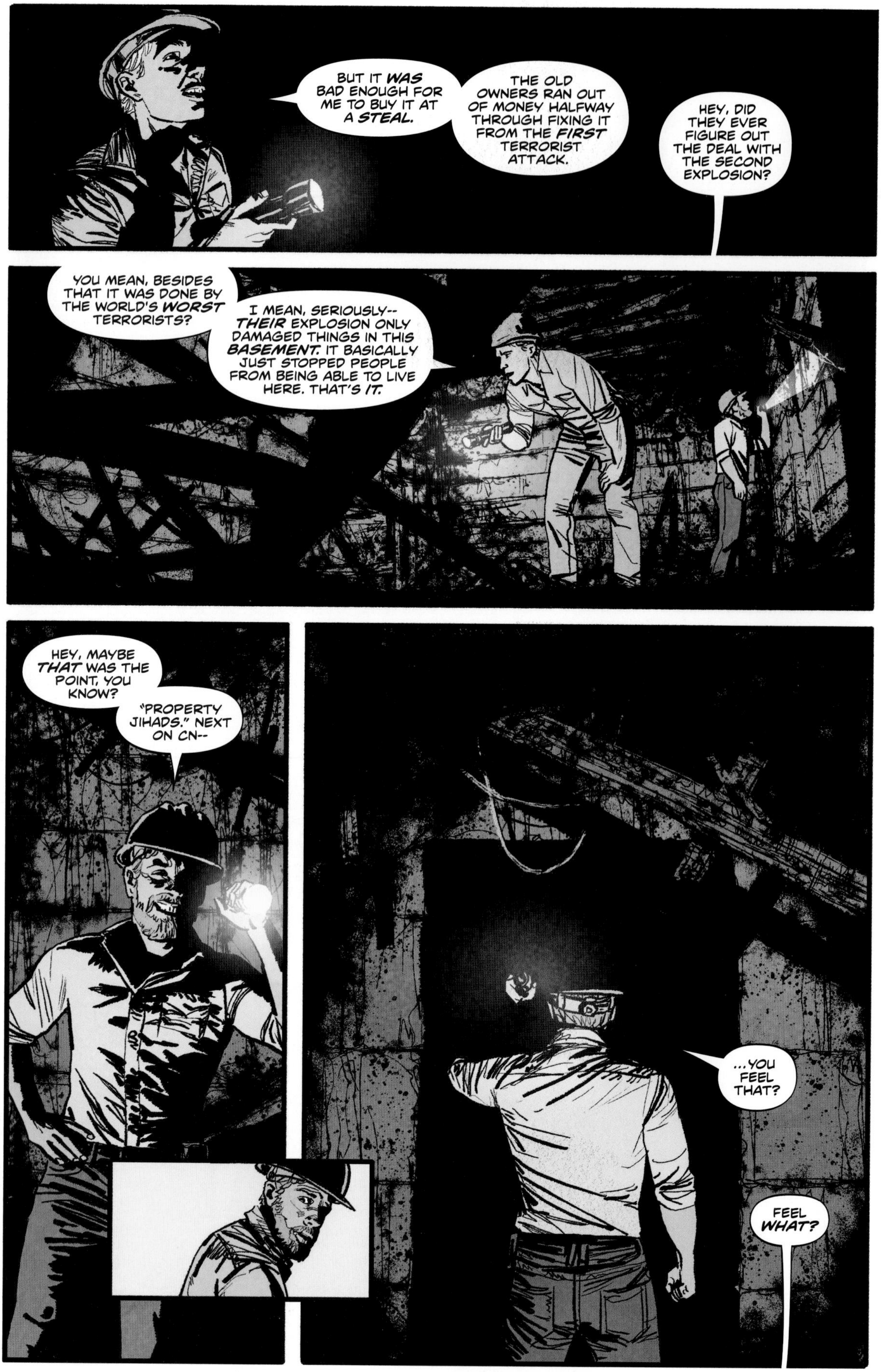
BUT IT WAS BAD ENOUGH FOR ME TO BUY IT AT A STEAL.
THE OLD OWNERS RAN OUT OF MONEY HALFWAY THROUGH FIXING IT FROM THE FIRST TERRORIST ATTACK.
HEY, DID THEY EVER FIGURE OUT THE DEAL WITH THE SECOND EXPLOSION?
YOU MEAN, BESIDES THAT IT WAS DONE BY THE WORLD'S WORST TERRORISTS?
I MEAN, SERIOUSLY-- THEIR EXPLOSION ONLY DAMAGED THINGS IN THIS BASEMENT. IT BASICALLY JUST STOPPED PEOPLE FROM BEING ABLE TO LIVE HERE. THAT'S IT.
HEY, MAYBE THAT WAS THE POINT, YOU KNOW?
"PROPERTY JIHADS." NEXT ON CN--
...YOU FEEL THAT?
FEEL WHAT?

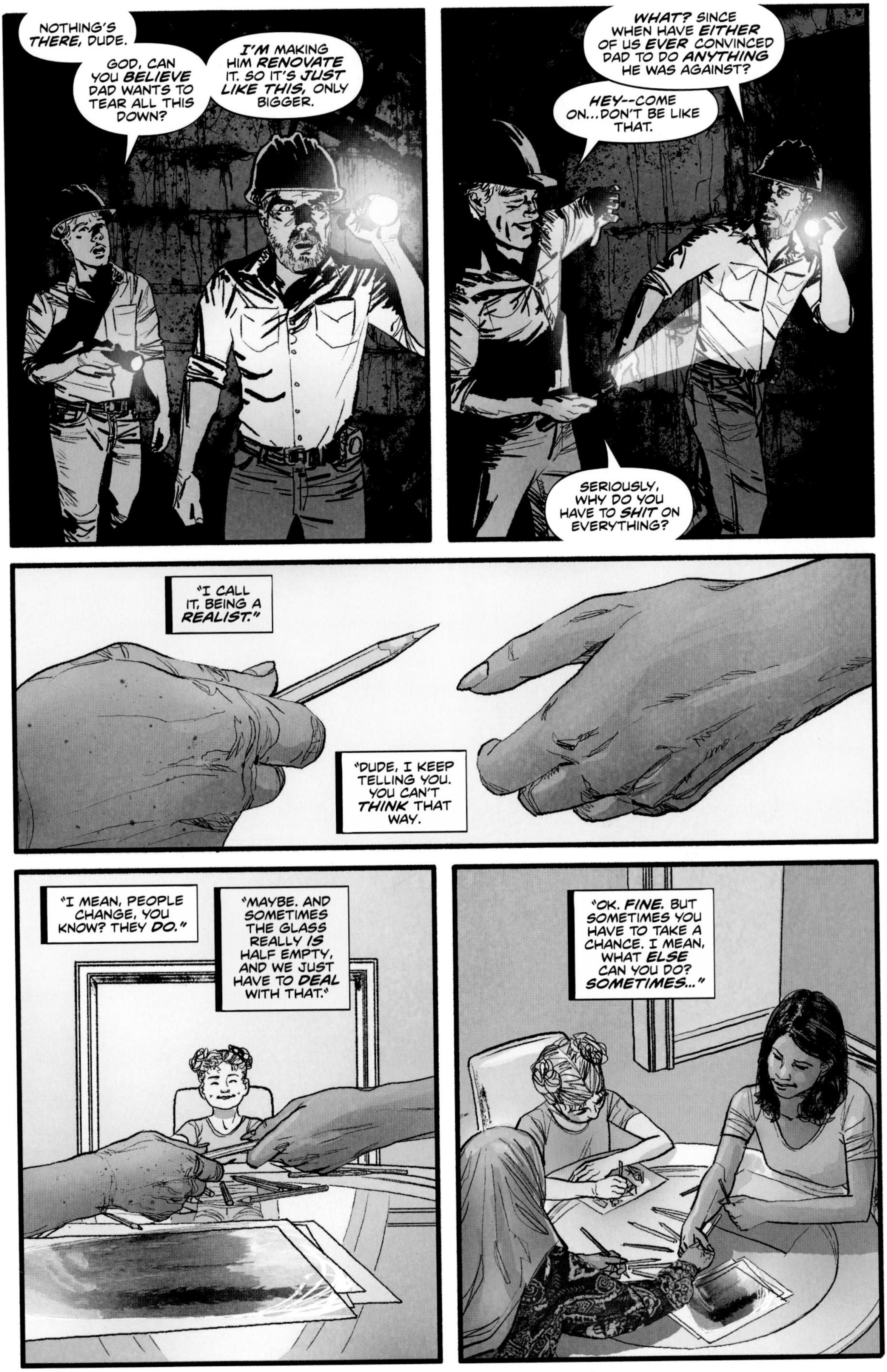
NOTHING'S *THERE*, DUDE.
GOD, CAN YOU *BELIEVE* DAD WANTS TO TEAR ALL THIS DOWN?
I'M MAKING HIM *RENOVATE* IT. SO IT'S *JUST LIKE THIS*, ONLY BIGGER.
WHAT? SINCE WHEN HAVE *EITHER* OF US *EVER* CONVINCED DAD TO DO *ANYTHING* HE WAS AGAINST?
HEY--COME ON...DON'T BE LIKE THAT.
SERIOUSLY, WHY DO YOU HAVE TO *SHIT* ON EVERYTHING?
"I CALL IT, BEING A *REALIST*."
"DUDE, I KEEP TELLING YOU. YOU CAN'T *THINK* THAT WAY.
"I MEAN, PEOPLE CHANGE, YOU KNOW? THEY *DO*."
"MAYBE. AND SOMETIMES THE GLASS REALLY *IS* HALF EMPTY, AND WE JUST HAVE TO *DEAL* WITH THAT."
"OK. *FINE*. BUT SOMETIMES YOU HAVE TO TAKE A CHANCE. I MEAN, WHAT *ELSE* CAN YOU DO? *SOMETIMES...*"

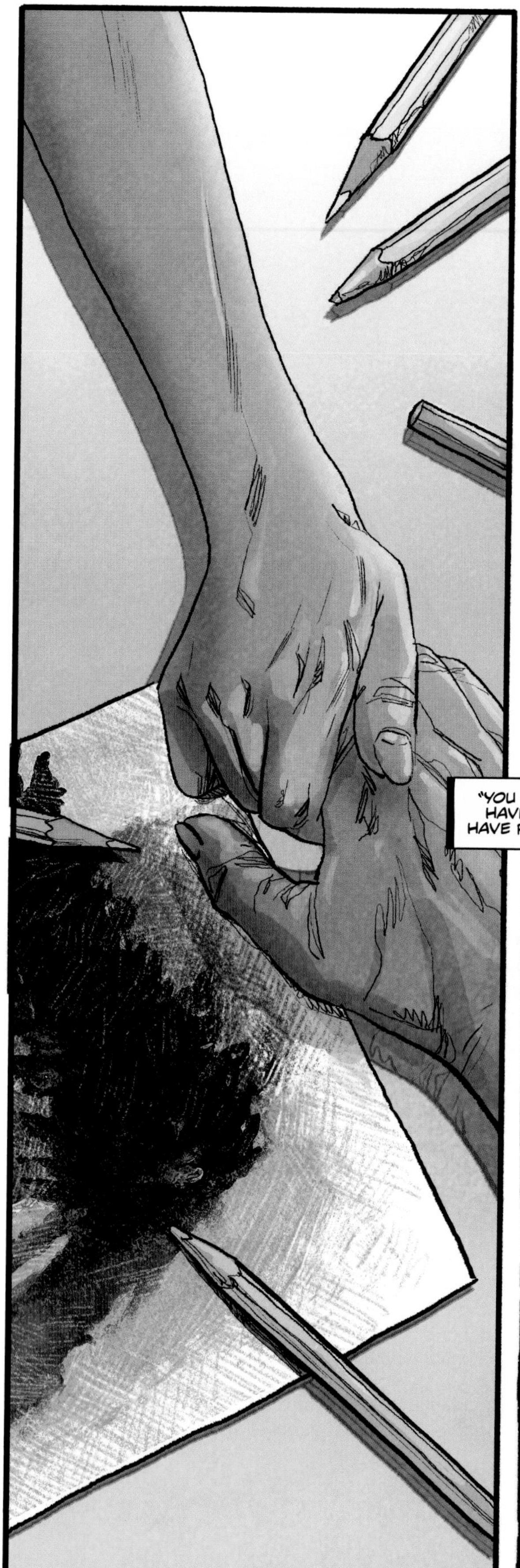
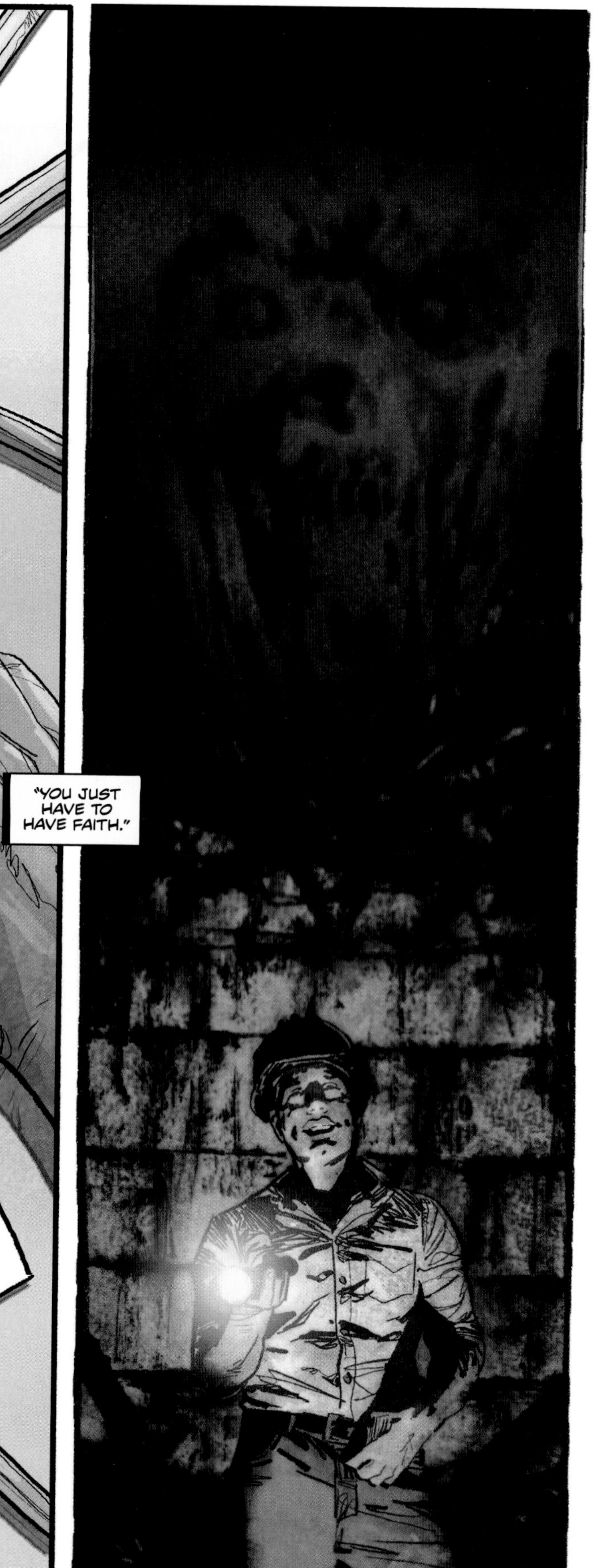
"YOU JUST HAVE TO HAVE FAITH."

infidel

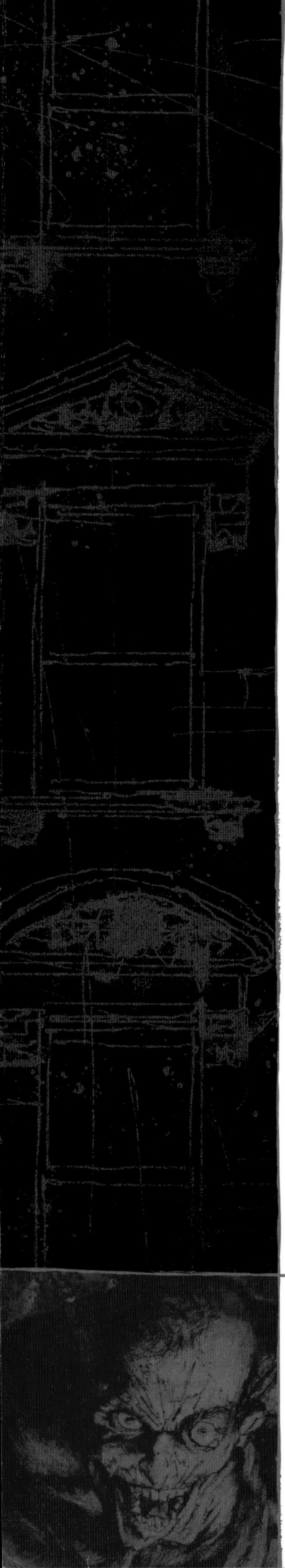

afterword

IF THERE ARE TWO THINGS that are notoriously hard to do well in comics, it is both horror stories and politically charged stories. It's really *really* easy to be heavy-handed with both and to lose the reader before you even get started.

Let's start with horror. I am of the belief that the comics medium can do anything a film or a novel can do better. But the one exception may be with horror. The huge disadvantage that comics have in this regard is that we don't have one of the very essential tools that cinema can use when rendering horror… sound. So much of what scared me in film is the atmosphere and a massive part of that is done with both music and sound design. Building terror and tension can be achieved so wonderfully with the soundtrack, and comics, like it or not, are a silent medium. The other advantage film has in scary movies is the "jump factor." Things can quite literally come on the screen out of nowhere and scare the shit out of you. We can do this to a degree in comics, if we put our scary reveal on a page turn, but even that is a bit more muted than in a film (again, sound works so well with these "jumps"). And if you don't have the foresight to place your big scares on a page turn, then it's even less effective, because the reader will see what's coming down the page before they get there.

Now let's talk politics in comics. Boy, is this a charged topic at the moment. You cannot go online, or sit in a café or do pretty much anything in today's world without seeing the massive divide in our society. People have very strong beliefs, some good, some downright evil, and they are not afraid to share them and attack you if you don't agree. And putting your politics into your art is a welcome mat for people to attack accordingly. Now, beyond the current culture wars and heated political climate, creating a comic with a "message" has always been a dicey thing. Usually the creators' hearts are in the right place, but the stories can really easily end up being heavy-handed and ham-fisted. Anyways, putting your politics in comics in subtle and entertaining way is not easy and rarely done well.

Okay… now to the point. INFIDEL! Somehow Pornsak, José, and Aaron managed to make a political comic that is also scary as fuck and entertaining as hell. So how did they do it? I am still studying it to figure that out. All I know is, I love this book. It is equal parts creepy, poignant, and beautifully drawn. And the fact that two of my dearest friends in comics created it is not why I am saying that. This book just works, and it's a testament to the talent involved. Pornsak and I go back to my days doing *Sweet Tooth* at Vertigo. He was one of four editors that book had, but easily the person who had the biggest impact on the story. I knew then that he was meant to be a writer himself. He had everything it took to tell great stories, and INFIDEL is proof. Now onto Mr. Villarrubia… There is no one in comics with better taste that José. And the evidence to support this is both his incredible colors on this series, which add so much of that mood that I spoke of earlier, but also in his choice of Aaron Campbell as the artist. I didn't know Aaron before INFIDEL, but this guy is clearly the real deal. His work here walks a beautiful and horrific line between photo-realism and phantasmagoric fantasy. This is a really powerful piece of work, and Aaron is the anchor of the whole thing.

And yes, this book is political. But do not let that turn you off. The message is sent in such a creative and scary and imaginative way that it never loses track of what is most important, a good story, well told. And this good, well-told story just happens to be *about something*. And that makes it linger in your brainstem for a lot longer than it takes to read.

INFIDEL is good comics. It's good horror. And it's about something. What more could you ask for? Well… maybe a sequel!?

– Jeff Lemire

Jeff Lemire is an Eisner-winning cartoonist and New York Times bestselling author, who has worked for every major publisher in comics, from the award-winning graphic novel Essex County *for Top Shelf; to the critically acclaimed* Sweet Tooth *for Vertigo; to* Animal Man *and* Green Arrow *for DC Comics; to* Extraordinary X-Men *and* Moon Knight*; to hit series* DESCENDER *and* GIDEON FALLS *for Image. He has won the Xeric, Joe Shuster, and Doug Wright awards, along with the American Library Association's prestigious Alex award.*

cover gallery
+ process

Featuring work from:

Jae Lee & José Villarrubia

David Mack

Alina Urusov

Yuko Shimizu

Jeff Lemire & José Villarrubia

Students from the class Fantasy Art,
Maryland Institute College of Art

JAE LEE & JOSÉ VILLARRUBIA

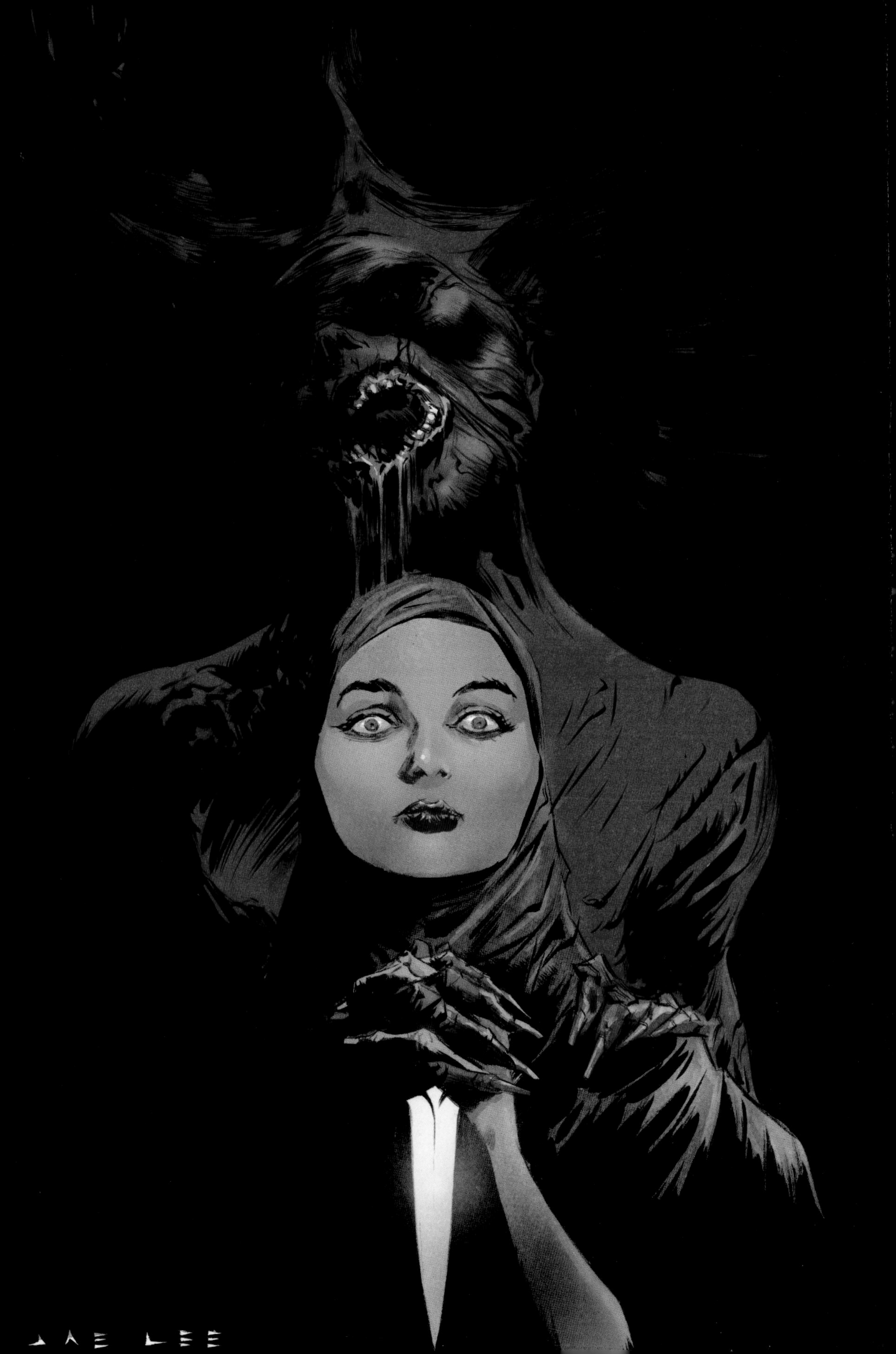

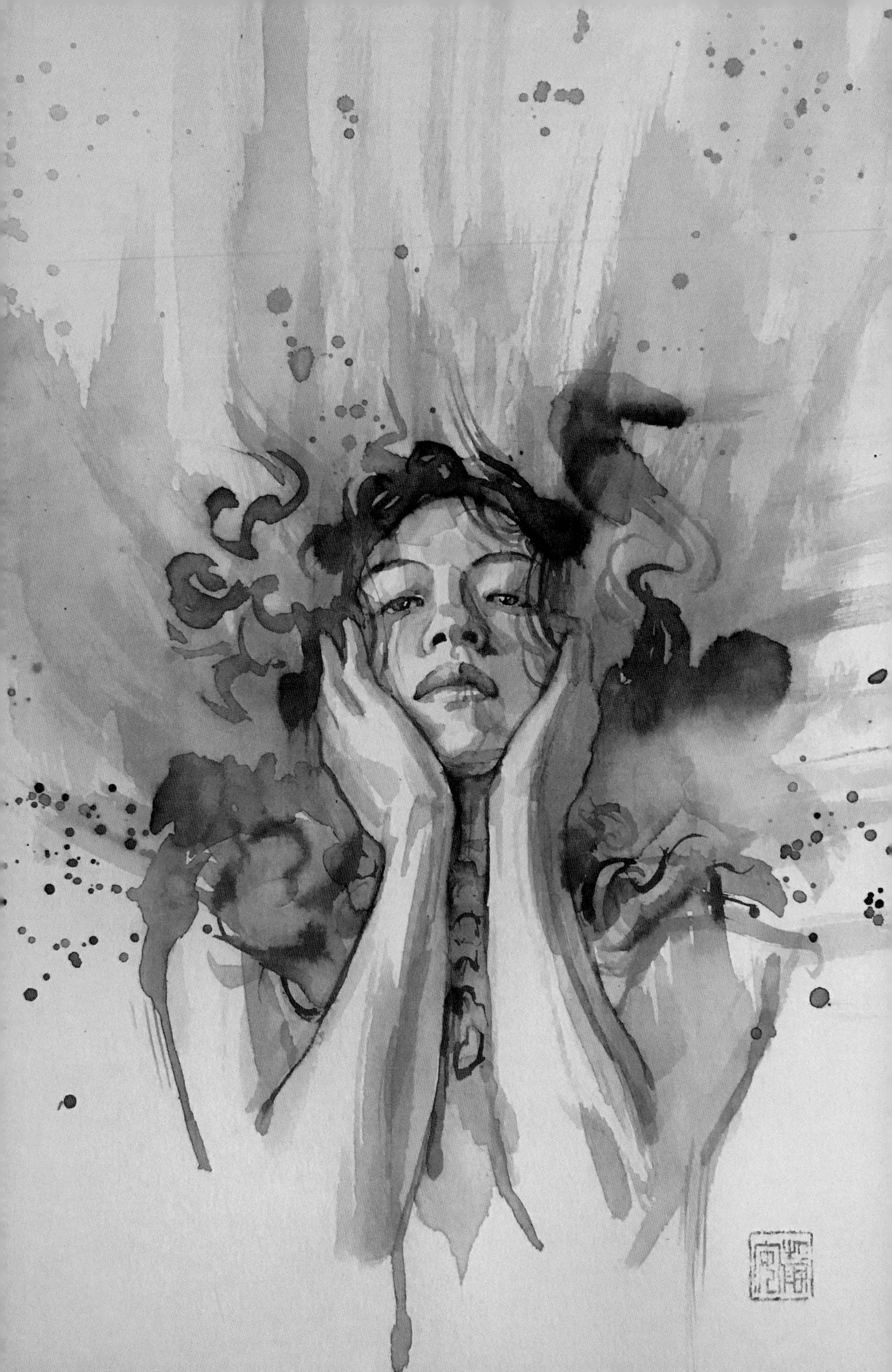

DAVID MACK

ALINA URUSOV

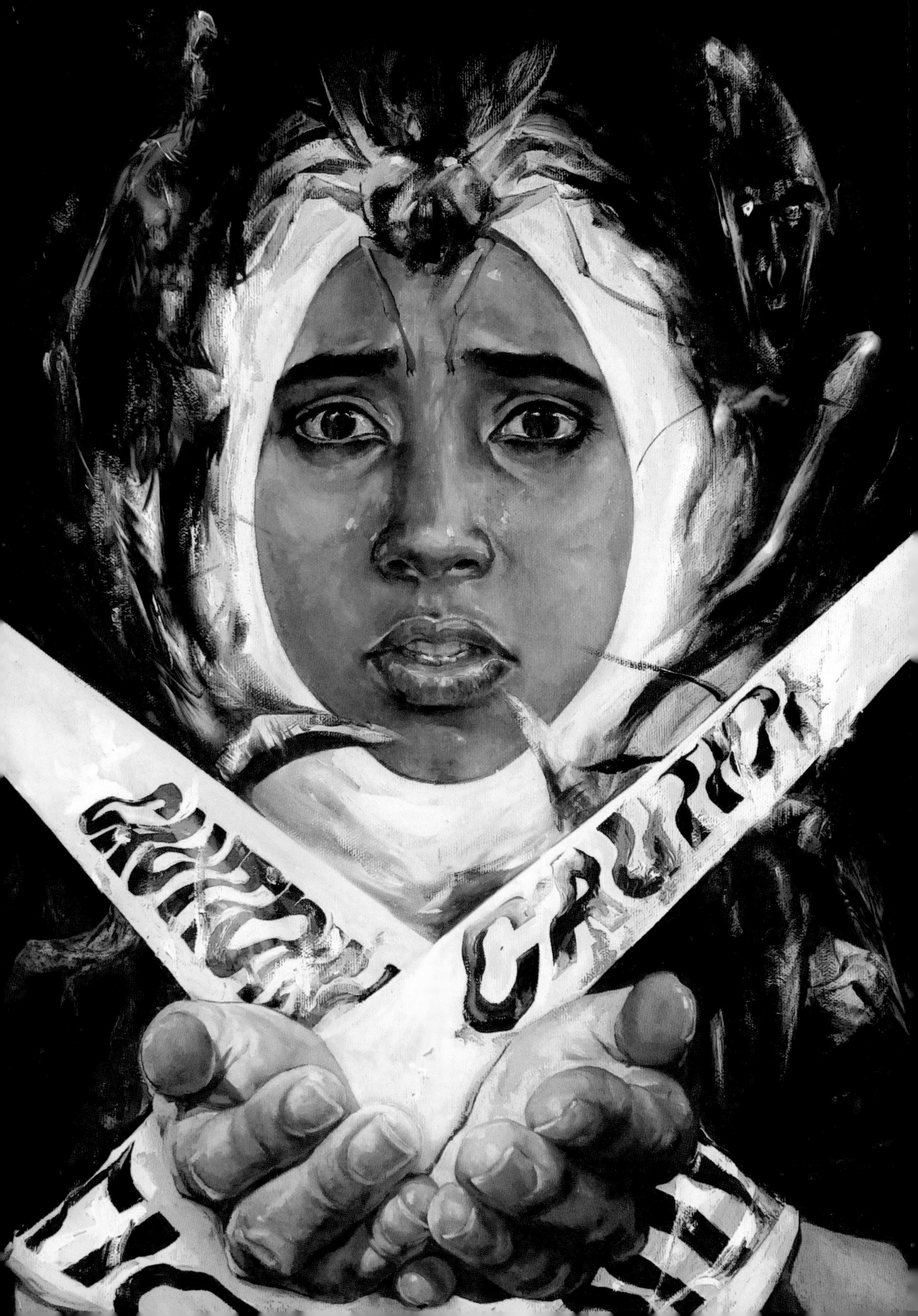

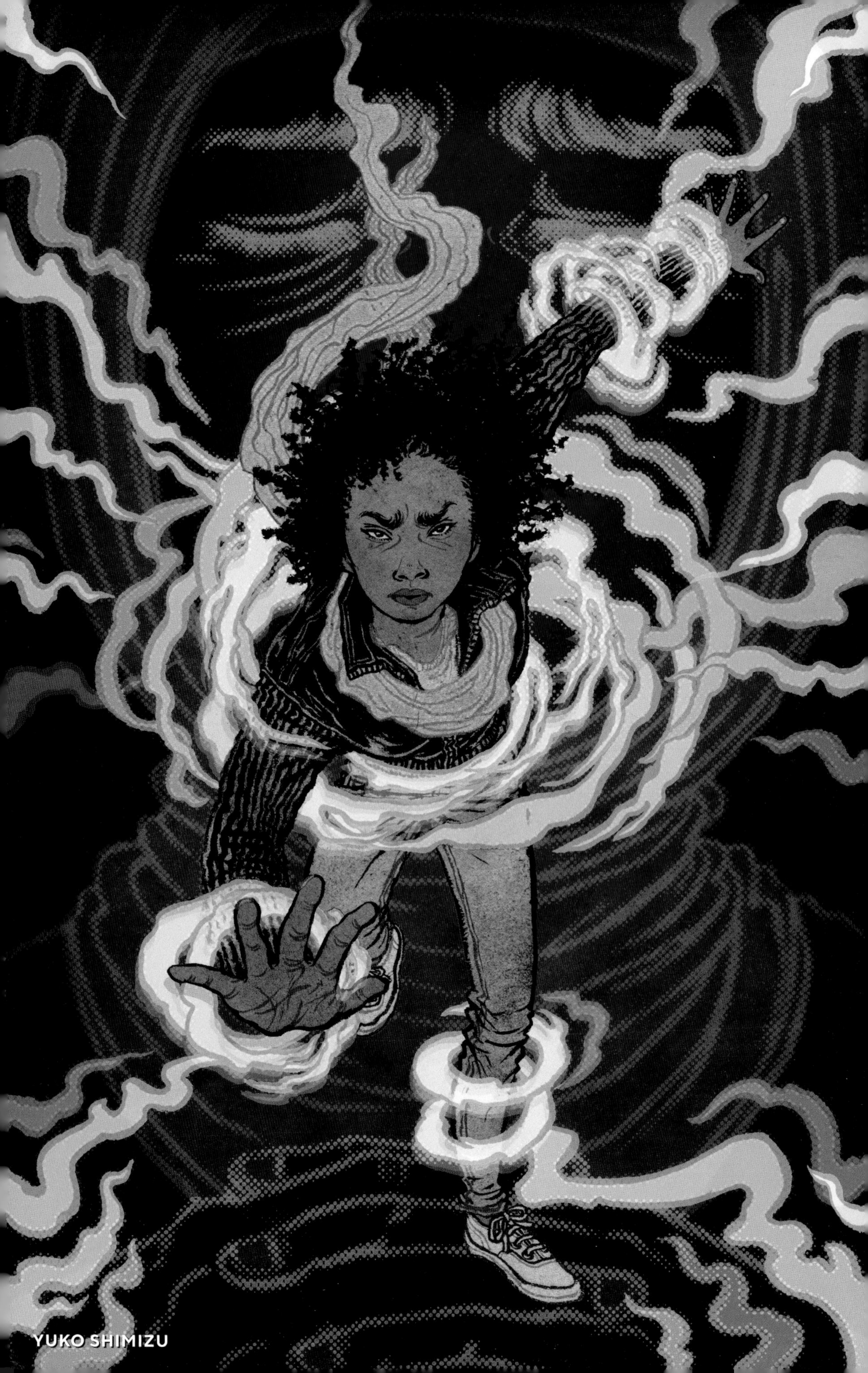
YUKO SHIMIZU

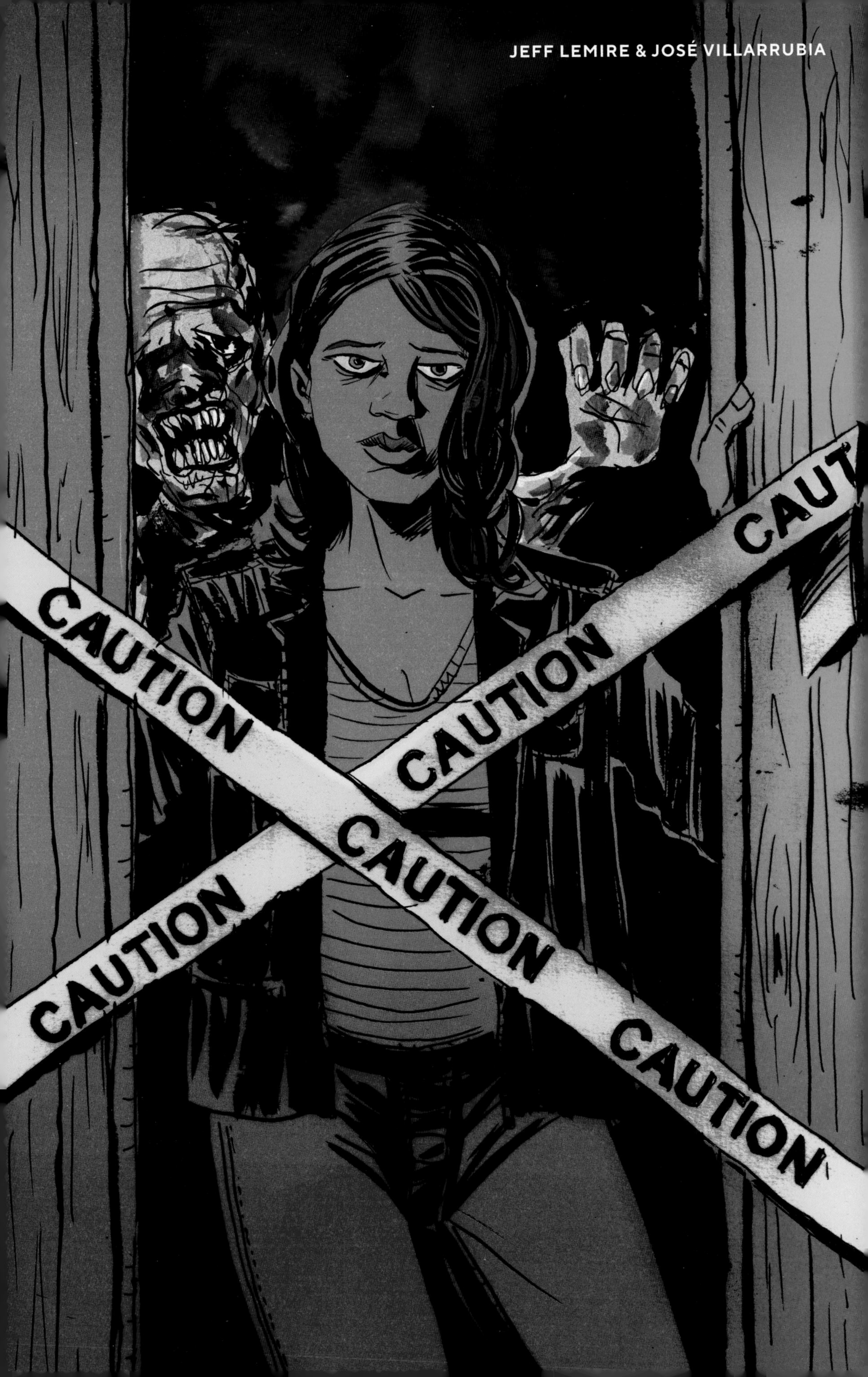

JEFF LEMIRE & JOSÉ VILLARRUBIA
CAUTION
CAUTION
CAUT
CAUTION
CAUTION
CAUTION
CAUTION

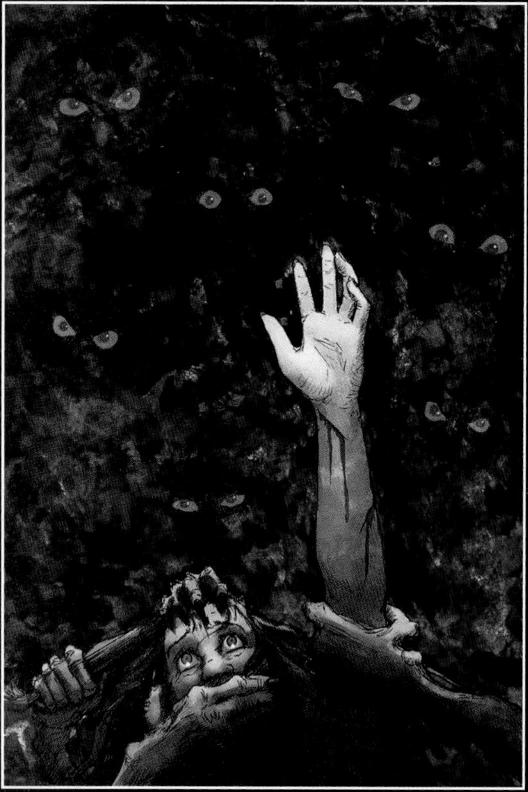

TIFFANY BURKEY

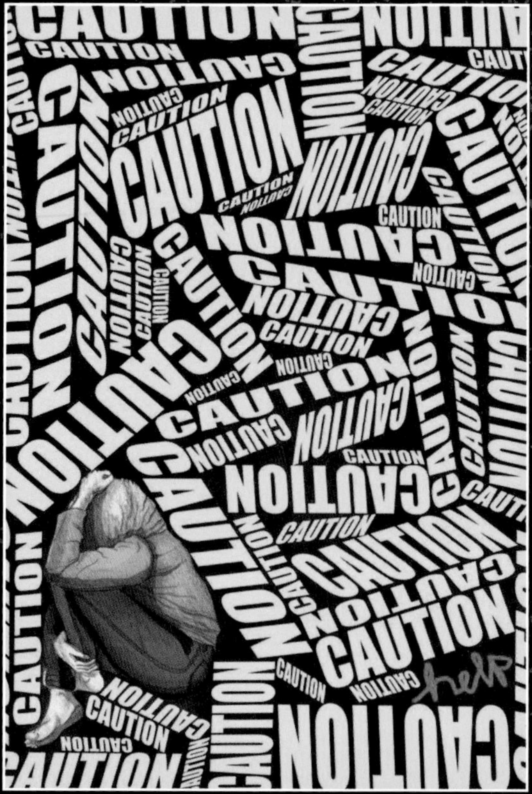
CAUTION
help

KELCEY CARBERY

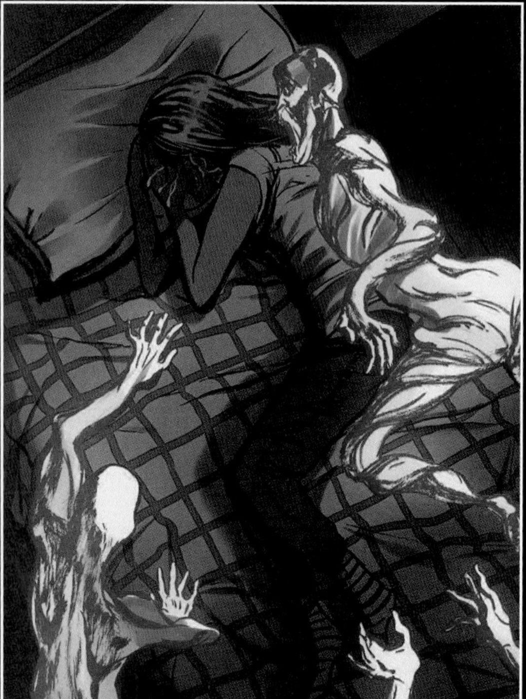

ZHIYING CHEN

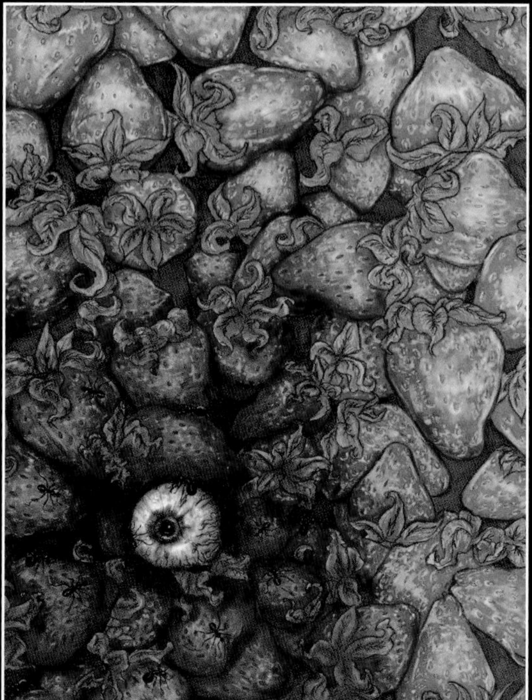

MEAGAN HOFMEISTER

STUDENTS FROM THE CLASS FANTASY ART, MARYLAND INSTITUTE COLLEGE OF ART

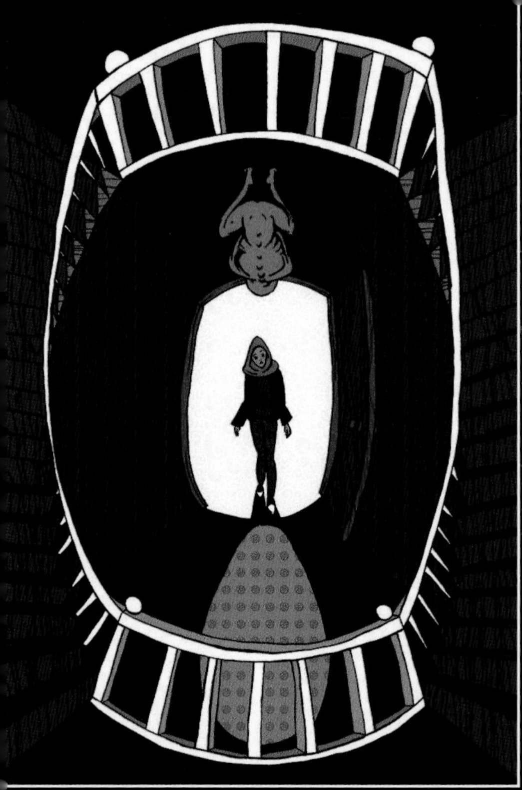

AL HONAKER

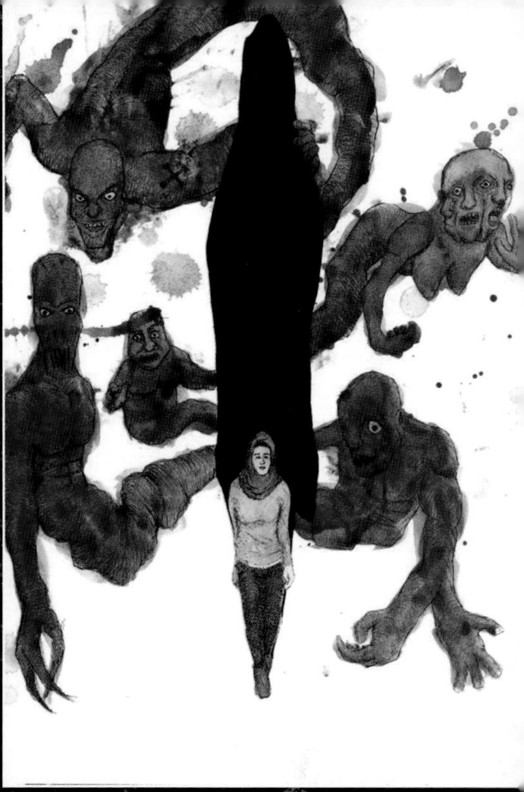

EVAN KARL

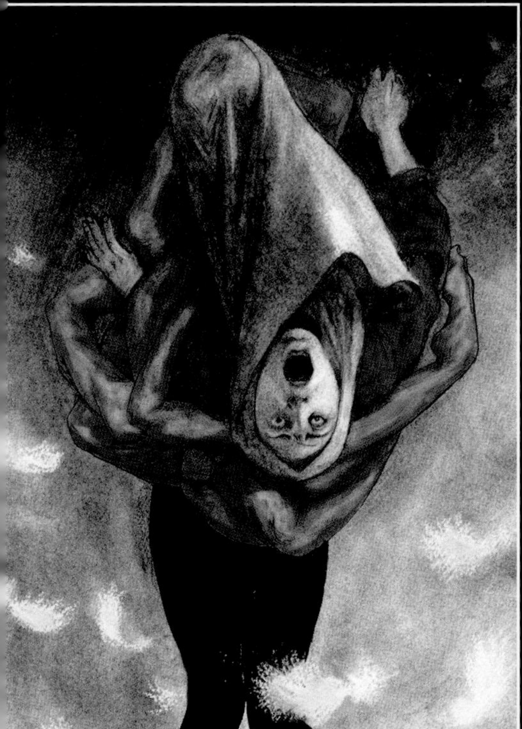

ANYA LIU

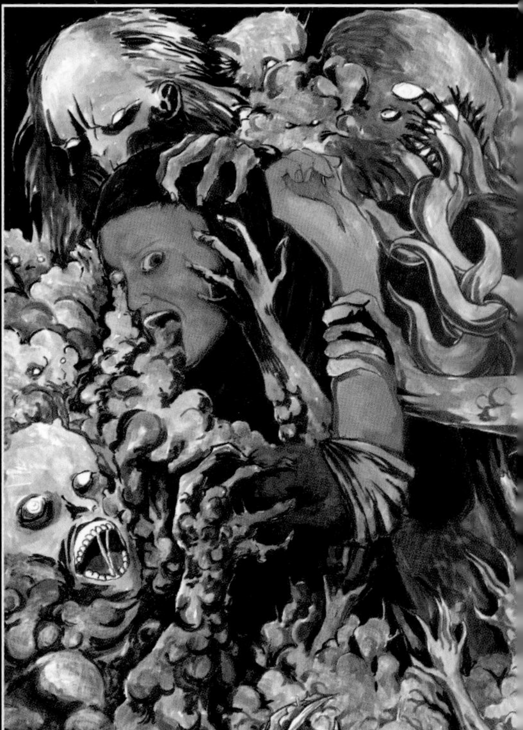

ALEX LUCAS

STUDENTS FROM THE CLASS FANTASY ART, MARYLAND INSTITUTE COLLEGE OF ART

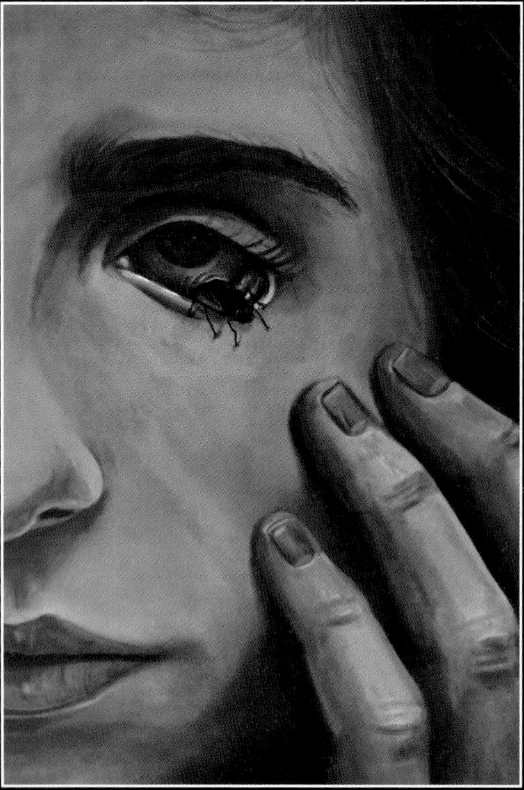

MADELEINE VENEZIANO

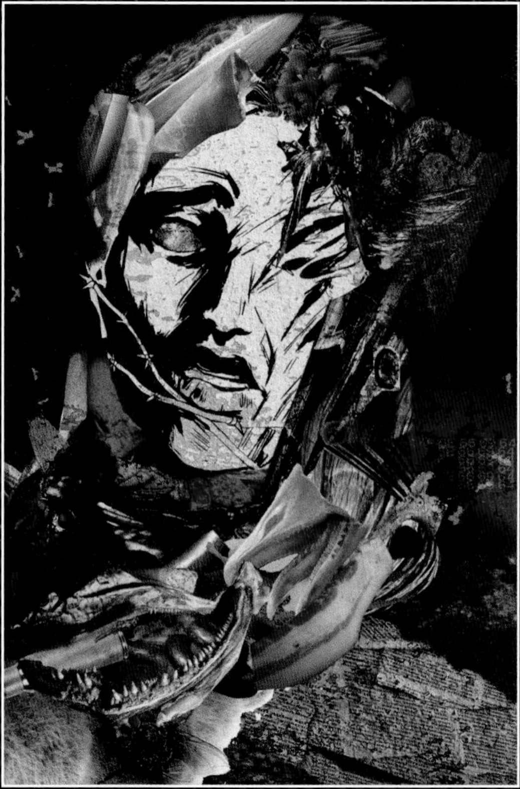

FIONA WANG

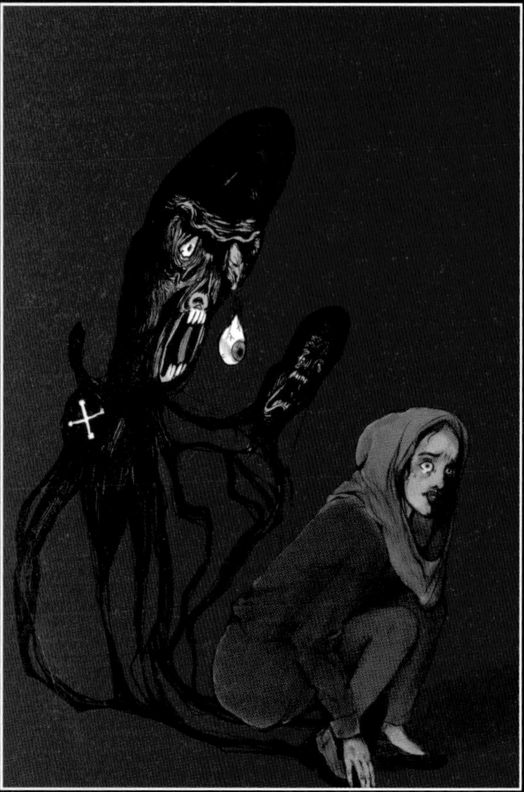

VIVIAN XIONG

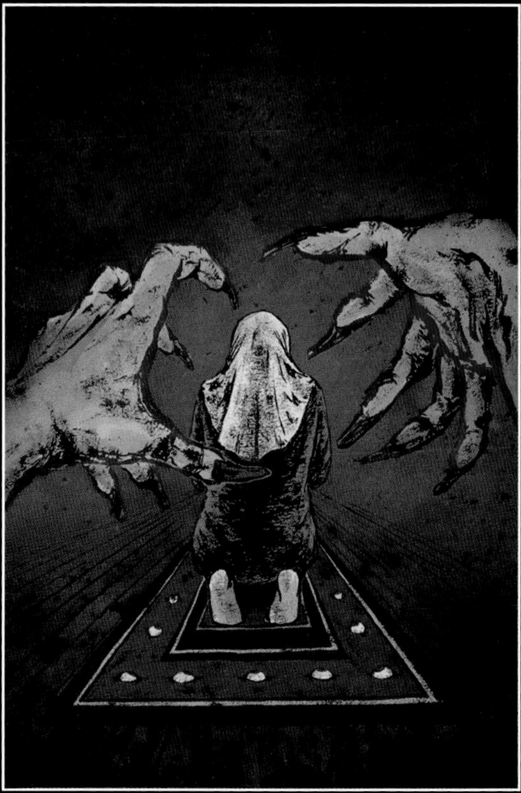

SUNNY YEN

STUDENTS FROM THE CLASS FANTASY ART, MARYLAND INSTITUTE COLLEGE OF ART

infidel cover process

To promote the launch of INFIDEL, Pornsak Pichetshote and Aaron Campbell wrote a piece for The Comics Beat, detailing the creation of the cover to INFIDEL # 1. The exchange is presented here, edited slightly for space.

Pornsak: People say "you can't judge a book by its cover," but anyone in comics knows that's a complete lie. In comics – especially creator-owned ones – books are judged entirely by their covers. After all, that cover doesn't just have to jump off the shelves of the store – it's also your book synopsis and trade ad all wrapped up into one. It's circulated more than any "elevator pitch" will ever be. So while the covers for issues 2 on up can look cool, that first cover has to do that on top of communicating what your book's about in a single image. It's something INFIDEL editor José Villarrubia and I strongly agree on.

When art directing a first issue cover, I've always believed it helps to boil the book down to its key distinguishing themes. For INFIDEL, that was Islamophobia / xenophobia and horror. Keeping the number of ideas a book represents that lean gave Aaron has more room to play with the cover's conceptual ideas. And Aaron, being a rockstar, hit us with no less than nine:

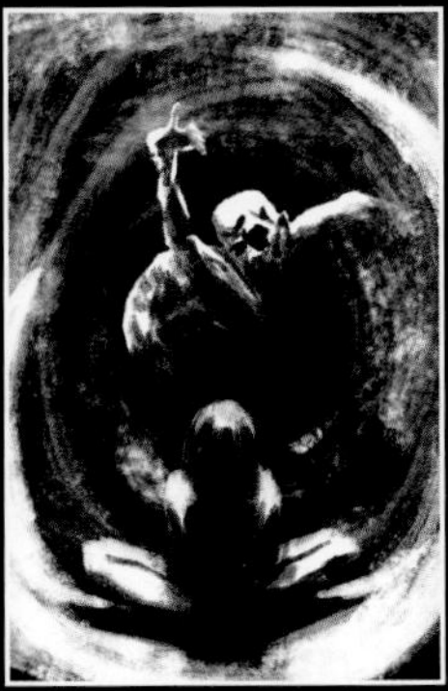
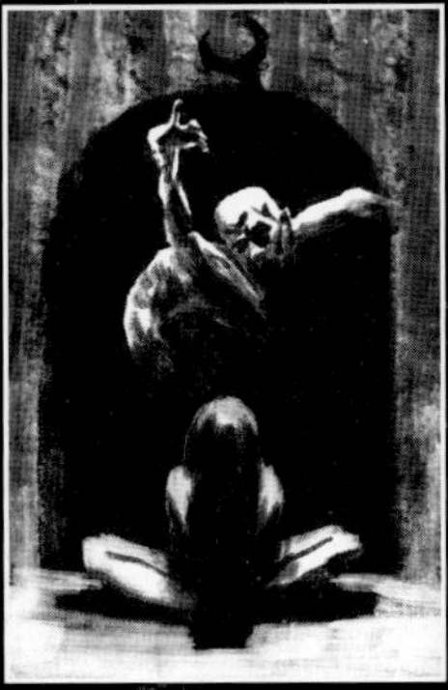
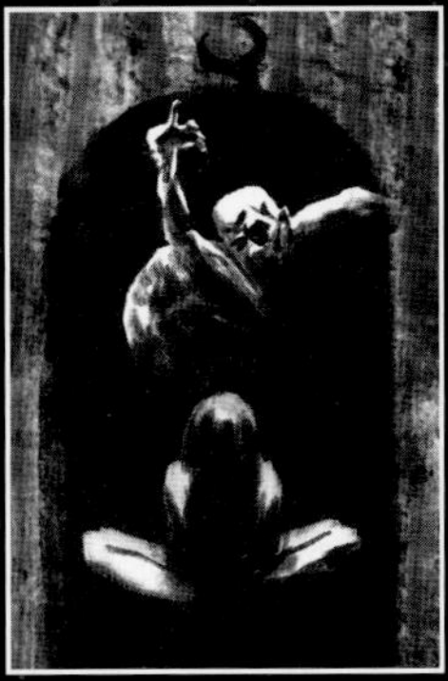
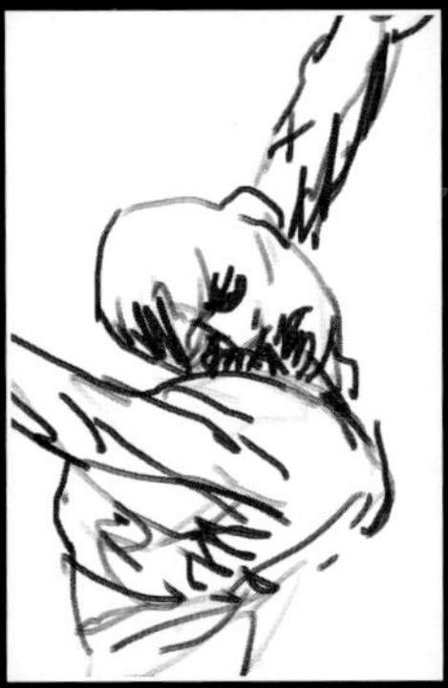
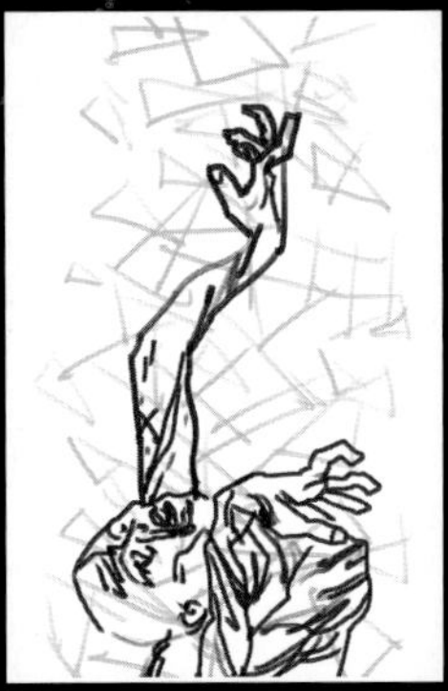
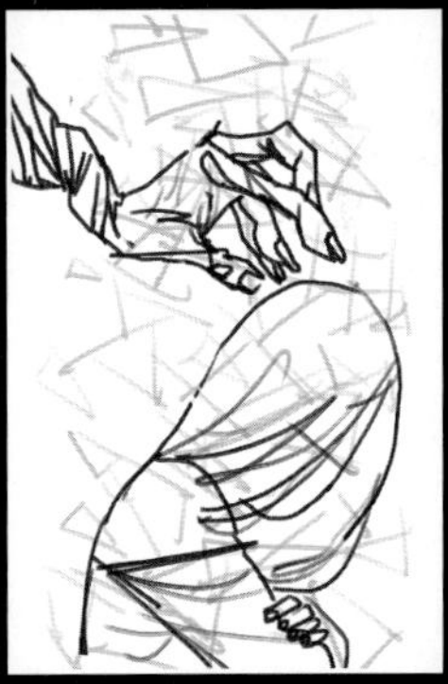
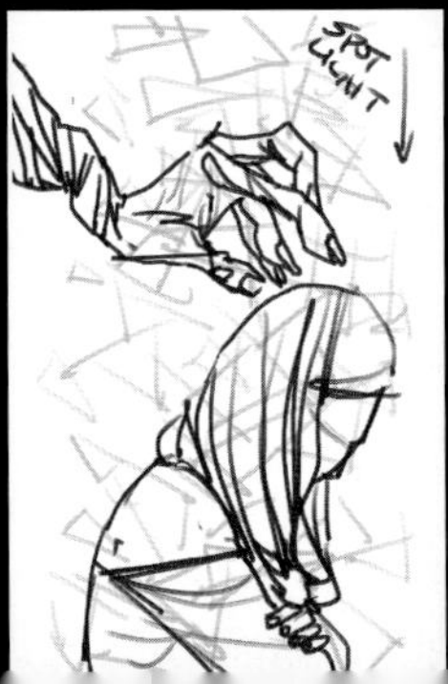
SPOT LIGHT
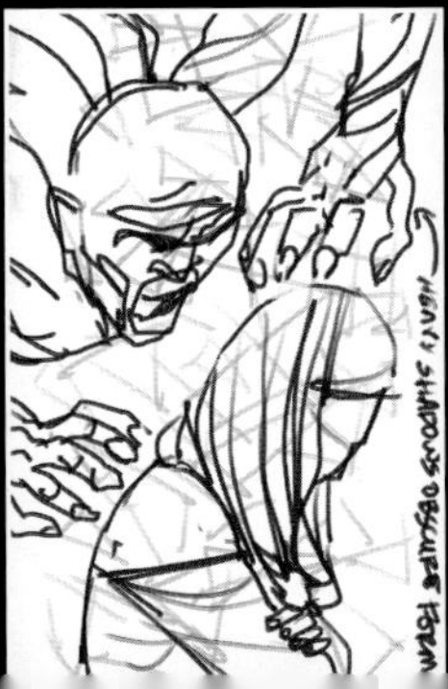
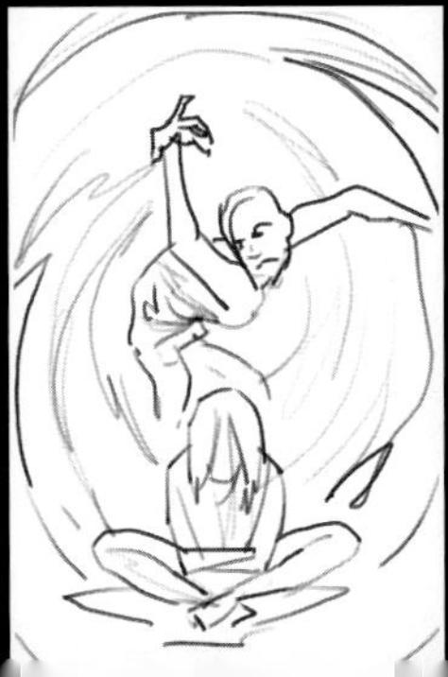

Aaron: This goes against all my instincts as an illustrator. I always try to give the least number of sketches possible to avoid decision overload. Plus, the more choices you give an editor the more likely they are to pick an idea you really don't want to do. But I felt a special tie to this project from the get-go, so I went all in.

Pornsak: And you can definitely see that passion in the work. José and I instantly fell in love with the ghostly hand reaching out to Aisha, although both of us – being us – had our own little nitpicks. José felt stronger if the image was flipped so our eye would go left to right and see the arm as it was reaching out for Aisha. I felt strongly that we should see Aisha's eye as she's about to turn. From my own editing days, I'd learned nothing helps an audience empathize with a character's emotional state more than eye contact, and I thought Aaron's decision to have her almost in mid-turn to be ingenious.

From there, Aaron proceeded to execute and man, did he. Here's 3 of the 9 stages the cover went through before Aaron finished it.

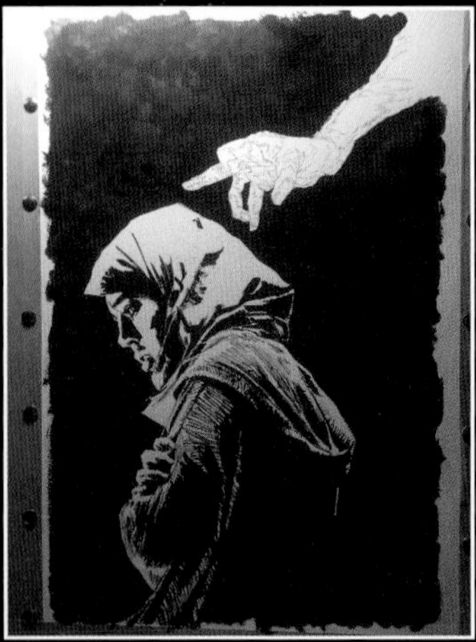

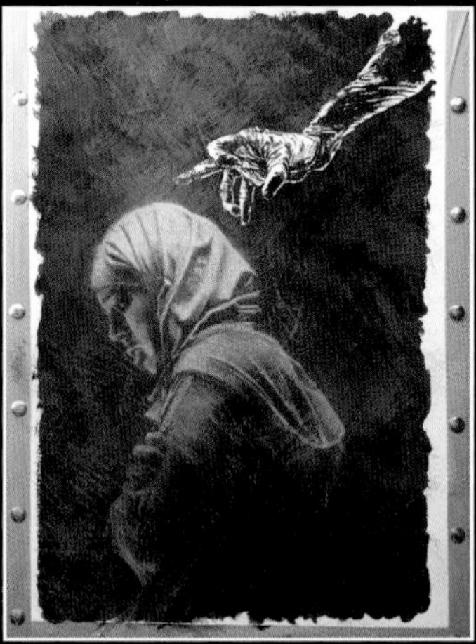

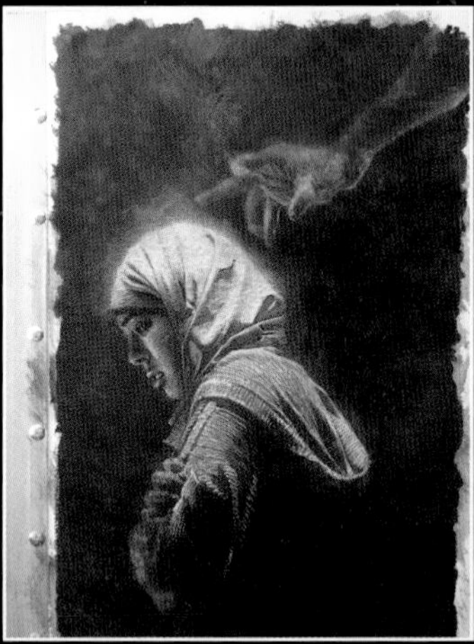

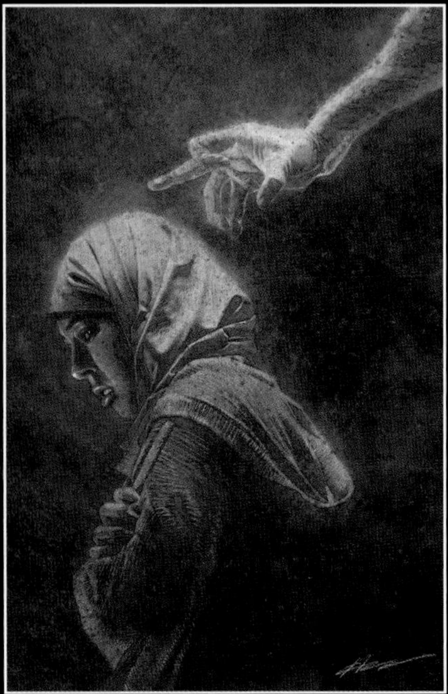

Aaron: This cover was a bit of a departure for me (well, the whole book is a departure). I decided to use similar techniques as I'm using for the supernatural elements in the series. So this was executed in a bunch of mixed media materials. There's gauche, charcoal, colored pencil, and several other mediums as well. I just wanted to stretch my artistic muscles and work towards something brimming with atmosphere and tension.

Pornsak: After Aaron finished the GORGEOUS piece above, José added his own graphic color treatment to it, wanting to make sure Aaron's art leapt from the shelves:

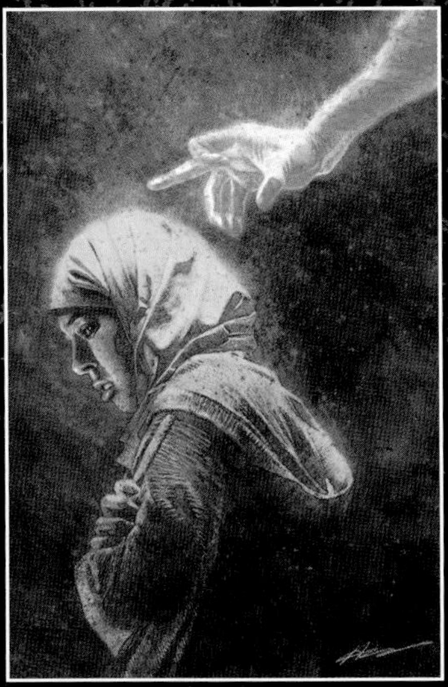

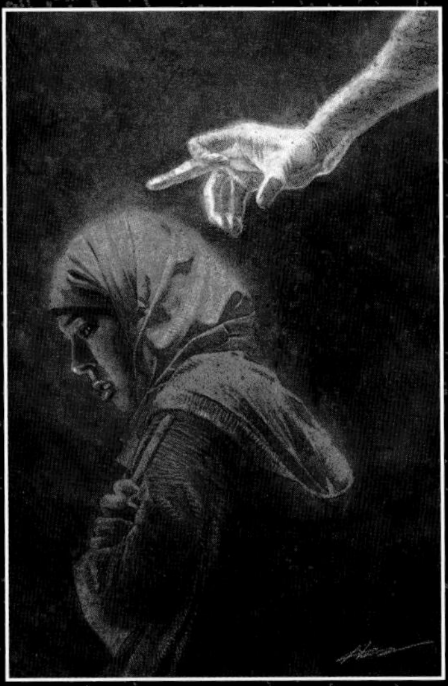

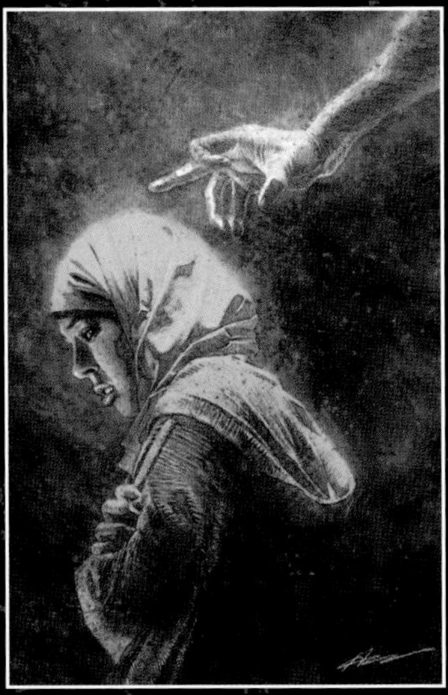

Pornsak: I believe it was Aaron and our designer extraordinaire Jeff Powell who cast the deciding vote for the red cover.

Aaron: Yeah, I really liked the coldness of the blue cover, but ultimately this cover needed to carry with it a warning: THIS BOOK IS NOT FOR THE FAINT OF HEART! So, red it was!

Pornsak: From there, José did some further tweaks on it. Jeff then cropped the image slightly for impact while adding a logo he designed, that – while yeah, I'm biased – is one of my favorite logos on anything I've ever worked on.

And voila! We had our cover, right?

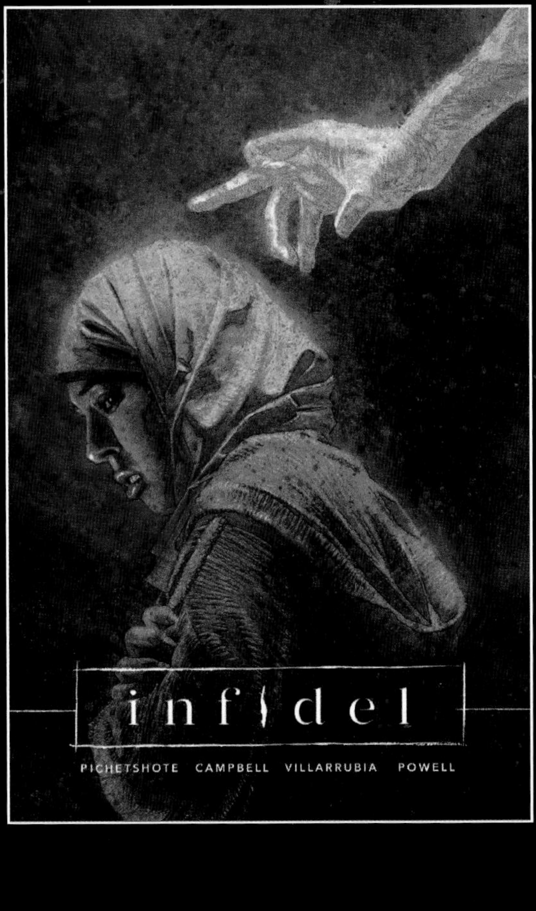
infidel
PICHETSHOTE CAMPBELL VILLARRUBIA POWELL

Well… clearly not. One of the things we found after showing that cover to people (another trick I picked up from my editing days: Whenever I had a new issue 1 cover, I'd expose it to friends outside of comics and ask them if you saw this book cover, what would you think the book was about?), we were surprised to find that a good half of them didn't realize we had a horror book. José was instantly on it – feeling the key was in that arm – playing around with no less than 15(!) different graphic treatments to give it a more horror-y vibe:

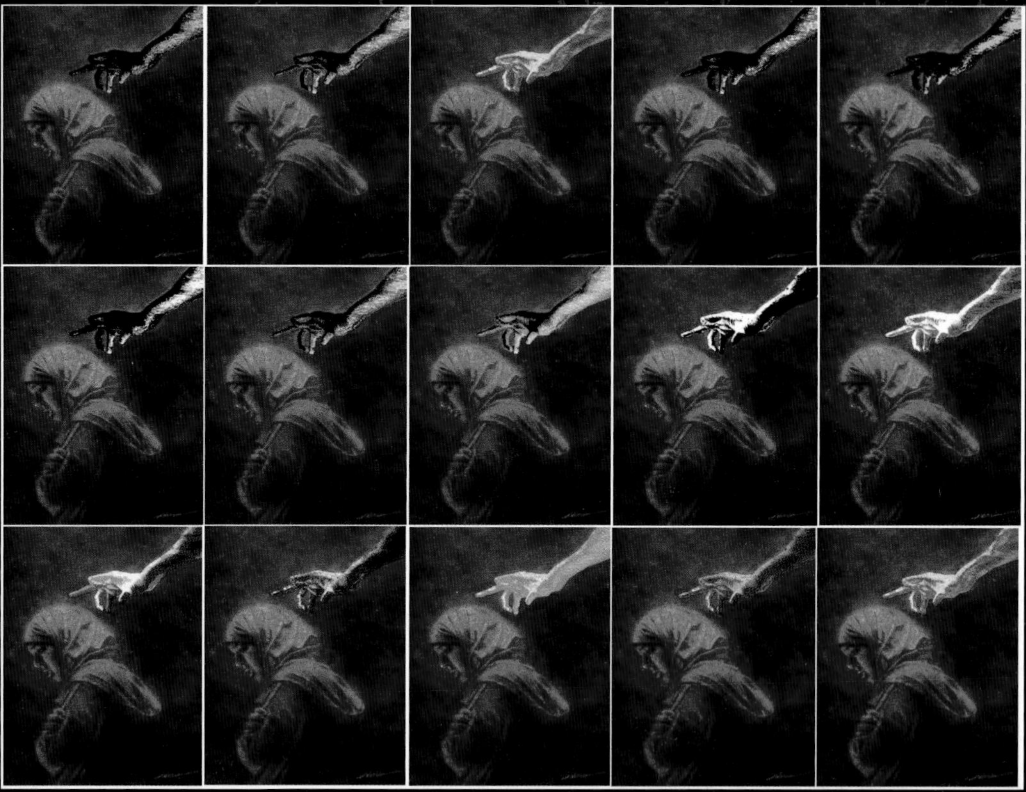

Pornsak: Ultimately, it was Aaron himself who felt that the horror feel of that arm had to be magnified separately from just rendering effects.

Aaron: Yeah, I realized that original hand was just too human. Even with the psychedelic coloring, it wasn't foreign enough. I like how the new hand almost feels like an alien mouth opening to swallow Aisha. And the impact is really driven home for me by the little charred fingertips.

Pornsak: From there, he gave us a whole new version of that cover with a new arm, one that José again applied his color wizardry to, and…now we finally had it. †

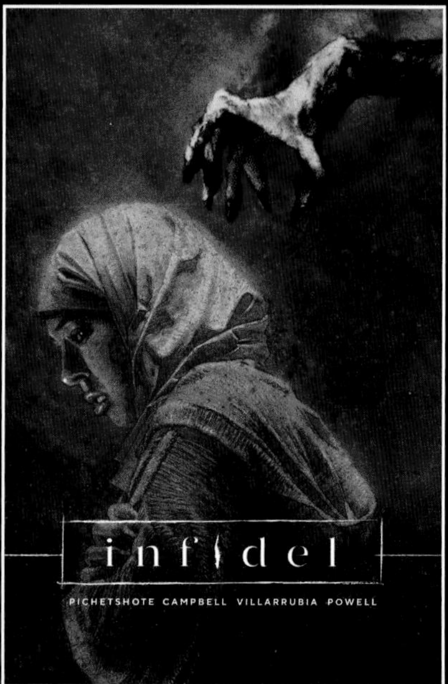
infidel
PICHETSHOTE CAMPBELL VILLARRUBIA POWELL

infidel proposal

Both as a comics editor and writer, one of the most common questions I'm asked is, what does a comics pitch look like? While there are as many different ways to fashion one as there are people in the world, our pitch to IMAGE involved a 14-page proposal that included:

- The cover to the first issue
- The first 8 pages of the comic
- A cover letter
- 3 pages of character designs
- A 2-page synopsis of the story
- Bios of the creators

While the cover and first 8 pages are obviously well-represented here – and the creator bios are presented as an bookend to the volume – the following includes a reproduction of the other material from that packet.

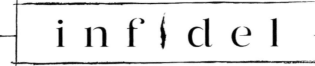

Dear Eric Stephenson:

We have not been formally introduced, but we are Pornsak Pichetshote and Jose Villarrubia. We have been working in comics for several decades; Pornsak as a former Vertigo editor and Jose as an award-winning colorist. Recently we have been putting together a new horror comic series that we would very much like you to consider for publication. IMAGE is the home of our favorite horror books, like WYTCHES and OUTCAST, and we believe ours would be a fitting addition.

The creative team is:

Pornsak Pichetshote, writer   Jose Villarrubia, editor and colorist
Aaron Campbell, artist   Jeff Powell, designer and letterer

CONCEPT: A modern update of the classic haunted house, INFIDEL follows a young American Muslim woman who moves into a building in the aftermath of a suspected terrorist bombing. Attacked by horrifying spirits, she discovers that the building's intolerance has taken on a terrifying new life of its own...

HOOK: INFIDEL takes a classic haunted house story and modernizes it with the very real fears of today. The book will appeal to horror fans – a perennial genre with a steadfast audience – while also featuring a highly diverse cast, from its two female protagonists (a Pakistani-American and an African-American) to its varied supporting characters, the story hinging upon the conflict that comes from their dissimilar backgrounds.

Aggressively topical and increasingly relevant, it should grab critical attention by incorporating its themes into a thoughtful and emotional genre tale. This pitch consists of this cover letter, a two-page story synopsis, character designs, a trade-dressed cover and the first eight colored and lettered pages of the first issue. The first issue is fully written and available upon request.

We look forward to hearing from you at your earliest convenience.

Best,

Pornsak Pichetshote   Jose Villarrubia

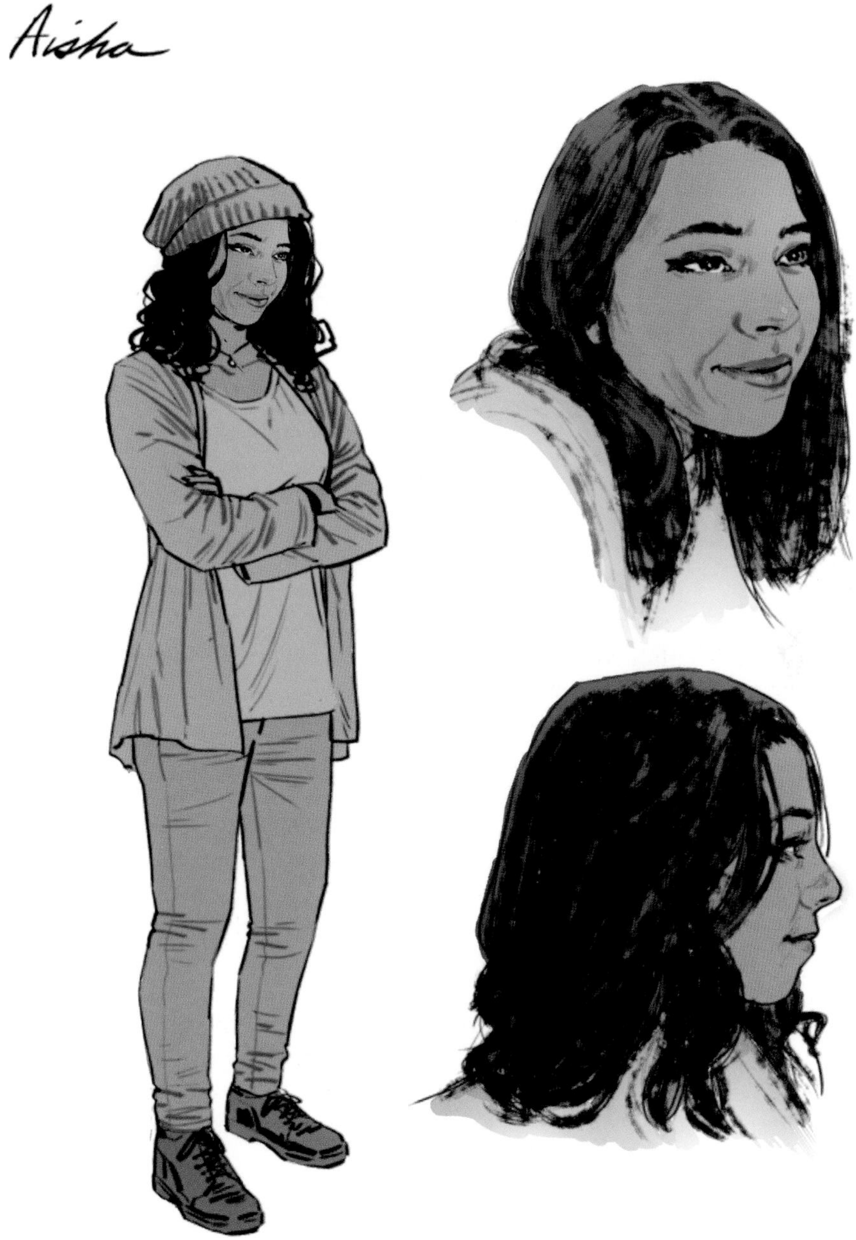
Aisha

Pakistani-American **AISHA HASAN** grew up a geek in suburban New Jersey. Although raised Muslim, as she grew older, her interpretations of Islam clashed with her devout mother's. Aisha's engagement to her agnostic boyfriend **TOM** ultimately led to her mother cutting off all ties with her.

MAIN CHARACTERS

Medina

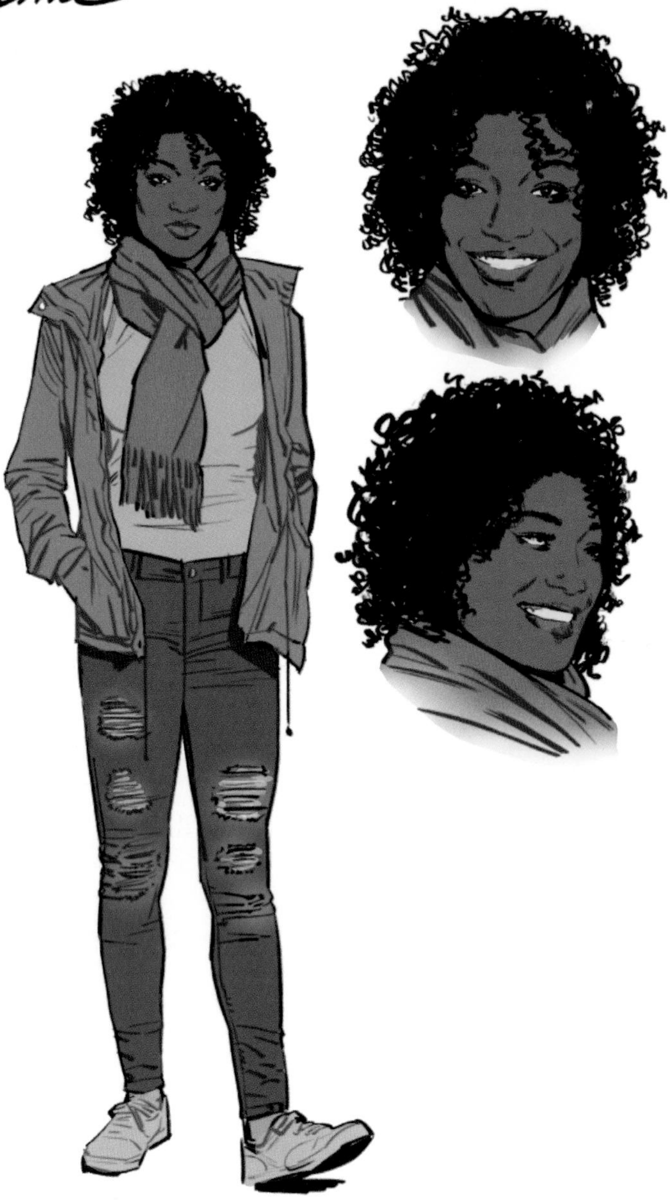

Since the days when their mothers would take the two girls to mosque, **MEDINA JACKSON** has been Aisha's best friend. Although Medina grew up to become an atheist, her loyalty to Aisha has never wavered. She'd follow her anywhere.

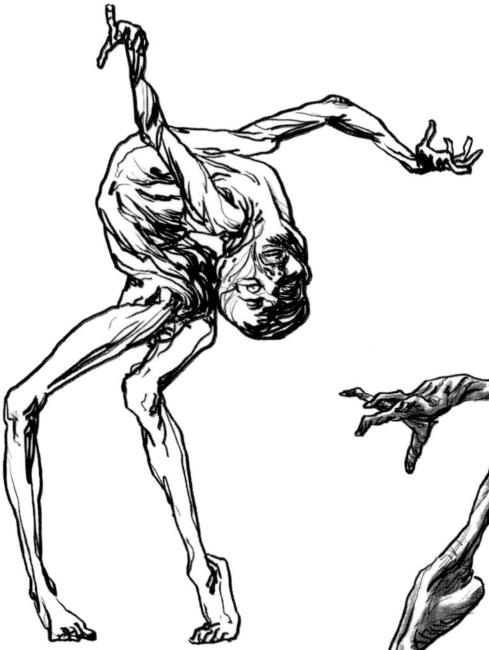

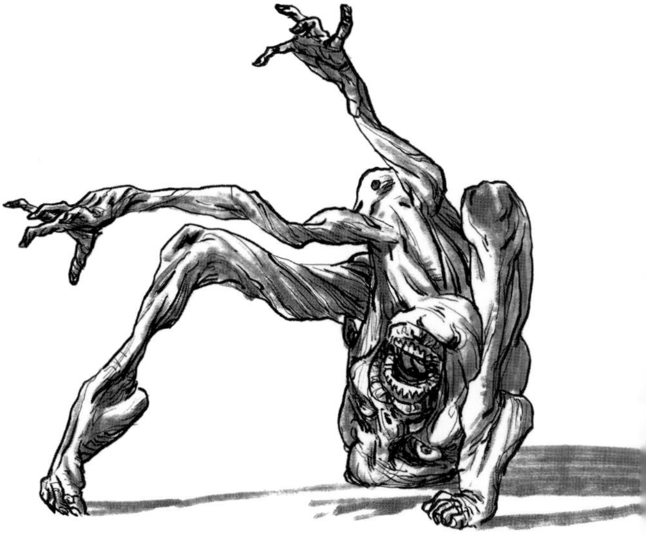

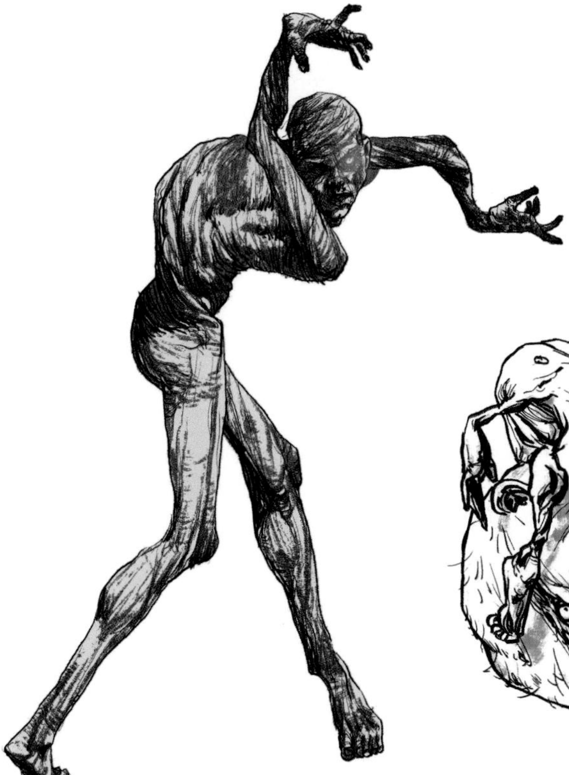

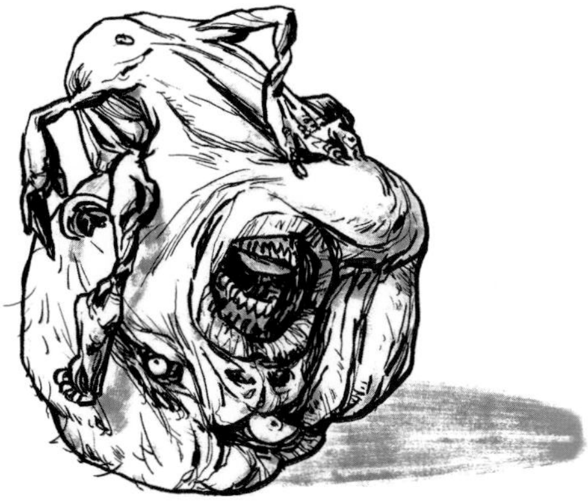

infidel

5-ISSUE SYNOPSIS

AISHA had been trying to keep the peace in **THE HARPER FAMILY**.

While **TOM**'s always resented his mother **LESLIE**, he cut ties with her completely after she began preaching Islamophobia to his young daughter KRIS. Months ago, homemade bombs went off in Leslie's building, killing a floor full of tenants. While the Arab bomber's motive was uncertain, his ethnicity alone was enough for both the news and politicians to label it terrorism. Worried about a traumatized Leslie, Aisha persuaded Tom into moving the family in with her to provide emotional support.

But Aisha has recently been haunted by disturbing nightmares. She attributes them to living in a building recently branded by tragedy. Worried Tom will use them as an excuse to desert Leslie, Aisha hides her dreams from both Tom and her best friend **MEDINA**, who's also moved into the newly vacant building. But as Aisha's dreams intensify, Tom reveals why he's been so angry at his mother: He discovered she had inquired about gaining custody of Kris, taking her away from them. Despite this, Aisha refuses to give up on Leslie. Aisha's own devout Muslim mother stopped talking to her after she got engaged to the agnostic Tom, and she refuses to lose any more family without a fight.

When Tom leaves town for business, Aisha's terrors escalate. They seem so real, and yet only Aisha can see them. Her reactions to those scares only stoke Leslie's prejudices. In a climactic confrontation when it becomes clear Aisha's faith in Leslie is justified – Leslie won't turn against her… the enraged spirits materialize and attack. In the meleé, Aisha accidentally slams against Leslie and Kris, knocking them down the building's steep stairs… to a fatal fall. A stunned Aisha can't protect herself as the spirits then viciously attack her…

A week later, Leslie is dead; Kris is in a coma; Aisha is catatonic; and Tom is near-hysterical with grief. The story's perspective shifts to follow Aisha's best friend Medina. Eyewitnesses believe they saw Aisha kill Leslie in cold blood, and Medina becomes obsessed with uncovering the truth.

But having witnessed two attempted mass murders, the building is now a powderkeg of paranoia. Looking to provoke answers, Medina reveals her Muslim background to some of her neighbors – and becomes the spirits' new target. They begin terrorizing her, and almost murdering Aisha has made them more distorted and deadly than before. Medina's search will fracture her new friendships with her fellow tenants, their differing ethnicities and backgrounds influencing their belief in Aisha's guilt – and Medina's judgement.

Medina uses the clues she unearths with their help alongside those Aisha discovered before the spirits dispatched her. Medina eventually uncovers the history of some of the building's deceased residents and their prejudices. Could some version of their hate be responsible for Aisha's and Medina's terrors?

The spirits then kill one of the tenants who have been helping Medina's search for answers. Realizing no one is safe, Medina retaliates, engineering a contained explosion in the basement that will render the building's structure intact but unlivable – an incredibly risky plan, but one Medina's sure will work. A distraught Tom returns, and delirious with grief, can now be directly controlled by the spirits. A bloody fight ensues, until Medina brings Tom back to his senses. The spirits are only angrier and deadlier now. With no other recourse, Medina and Tom sacrifice themselves to set off the explosion and save the rest of the tenants.

A year later, Aisha has awoken from her catatonia and wonders exactly what happened in the building. She now walks with a permanent limp. Psychiatrists have convinced her that trauma has skewed her memories. Despite the horrifying events, Aisha still wants to be an idealist. Because what's also true is a jury of her peers didn't find her guilty of Leslie's death. Her mother is now back in her life, helping her raise Kris, who has also awoken from her coma. Aisha's mother regrets their estranged time, adoring Kris.

And as Aisha anxiously opens an email that will reveal whether she's been granted adopted custody of Kris, we cut to a man surveying the haunted building — which he's recently bought. It's been deserted for a year, its furnace and electrical system decimated, but the structure remains intact. Man believes he can repair it without ripping down the whole facade. As he notices a trick of the light – one seemingly projecting a ghoulish face in the shadows – he reassures himself that in no time, this building will be up and running again, exactly how it was. He has faith.

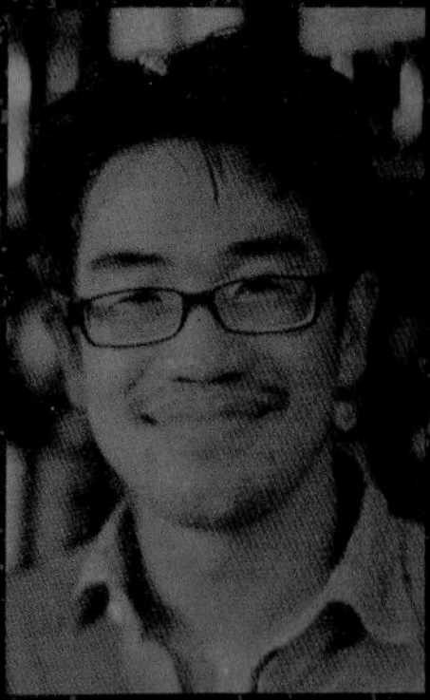

PORNSAK PICHETSHOTE was a Thai-American rising star editor at DC's Vertigo imprint where he worked on such comics perennials as *Sandman* and *Swamp Thing*. His books have been nominated for dozens of Eisner awards – be it the award-winning *Daytripper*, the *New York Times* bestseller *The Unwritten*, or critical darlings like *Sweet Tooth* and *Unknown Soldier*. He left Vertigo to become an executive in DC Entertainment's media team, where he started and oversaw DC TV's department. INFIDEL marks his first major comics work as writer.

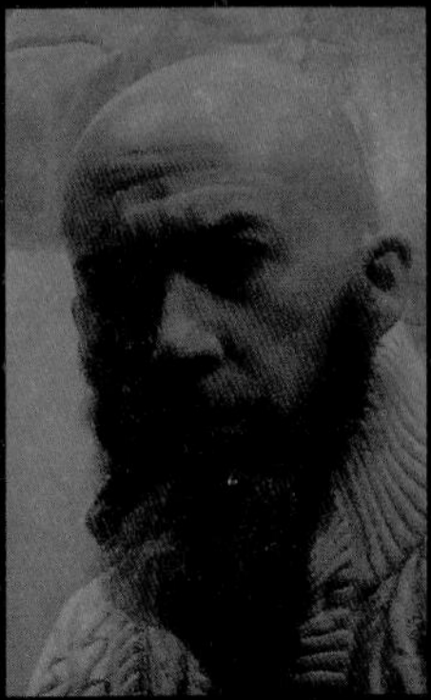

AARON CAMPBELL has been working as a comics artist for over a decade. In that time, he's illustrated the adventures of some of the world's most iconic characters, including *Batman, Harley Quinn, James Bond, Sherlock Holmes, The Shadow*, and *Green Hornet*, in the process working with such revered comics writers as Garth Ennis, Matt Wagner, James Robinson, and Andy Diggle. INFIDEL marks his first creator-owned book.

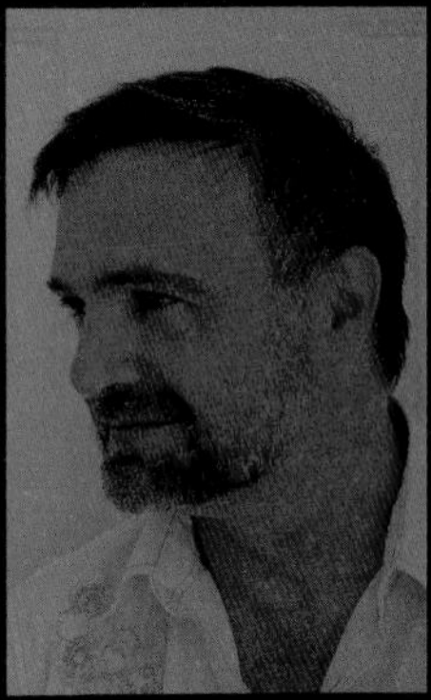

Harvey Award winner **JOSÉ VILLARRUBIA** is one of the most respected colorists in comics. In his prolific twenty-year career, he has often collaborated with artists Jeff Lemire (*Sweet Tooth*), Paul Pope (*Batman: Year 100*), Jae Lee (*Fantastic Four 1234*), and Richard Corben (*Cage*). As illustrator and photographer, he has worked with Alan Moore on *Voice of the Fire* and *The Mirror of Love*, and on the comics series *Promethea*. INFIDEL marks his first major comics work as editor.

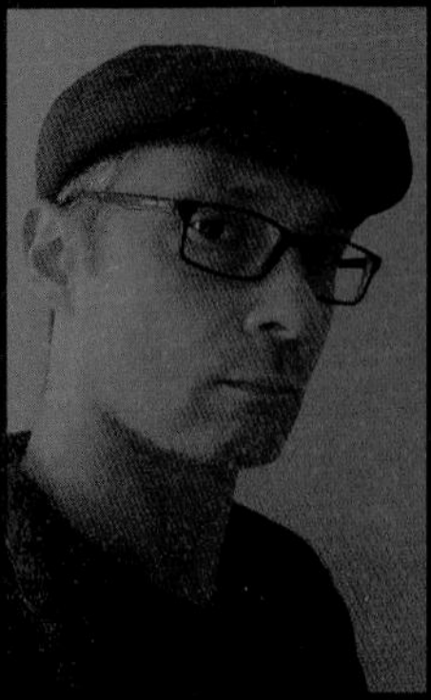

JEFF POWELL has worked on hundreds of comics in his over two decades in the industry. His work spans such beloved fan-favorite titles as DEADLY CLASS, *The Punisher, Deadpool, Teenage Mutant Ninja Turtles*, as well as currently lettering the Eisner-nominated *Atomic Robo*. He has designed books, logos, and trade dress for Marvel, Image, Archie, and more.